THE LORD

OF

HEAVEN AND MIDDLE-EARTH

A Commentary on Tolkien's Theological-Ethical Framework in The Lord of the Rings

THE LORD
OF
HEAVEN AND MIDDLE-EARTH

A Commentary on Tolkien's
Theological-Ethical Framework in
The Lord of the Rings

K. R. Harriman

GlossaHouse Media, Inc.
Wilmore, KY
www.glossahouse.com

The Lord of Heaven and Middle-Earth:
A Commentary on Tolkien's Theological-Ethical Framework in The Lord of the Rings

© GlossaHouse Media, 2025

All rights reserved. No part of this book may be reproduced or transmitted in any form or by any means, electronic or mechanical, including photocopying or recording, or by means of any information storage or retrieval system, except as may be expressly permitted by the 1976 Copyright Act or in writing from the publisher. Requests for permission should be addressed in writing to the following:

GlossaHouse Media
110 Callis Circle
Wilmore, KY 403409
www.glossahouse.com

The Lord of Heaven and Middle-Earth:
A Commentary on Tolkien's Theological-Ethical Framework in The Lord of the Rings
Harriman, K. R. 1989–

360 pp., Includes bibliographic references
ISBN: 978-1-63663-108-0

Quotations from *The Lord of the Rings* by J. R. R. Tolkien. Copyright © 1954, 1965, 1966 by J.R.R. Tolkien. Copyright © renewed 1982, 1983 by Christopher R. Tolkien, Michael H. R. Tolkien, John F. R. Tolkien and Priscilla M.A.R. Tolkien. Copyright © renewed 1993, 1994 by Christopher R. Tolkien, John F. R. Tolkien and Priscilla M.A.R. Tolkien. Used by permission of HarperCollins Publishers.

1. Tolkien, J. R. R. (John Ronald Reuel), 1892–1973—Religion. **2.** Tolkien, J. R. R. (John Ronald Reuel), 1892–1973—Ethics. **3.** Tolkien, J. R. R. (John Ronald Reuel), 1892–1973. *Lord of the Rings.* **4.** Good and evil in literature. **5.** Christianity and literature—England—History—20th century.

The fonts used to create this work are available from www.linguistsoftware.comlgku.htm

Cover design by Lisa E. Terris
Text layout and interior book design by Colton F. Moore and Andrew J. Coutras

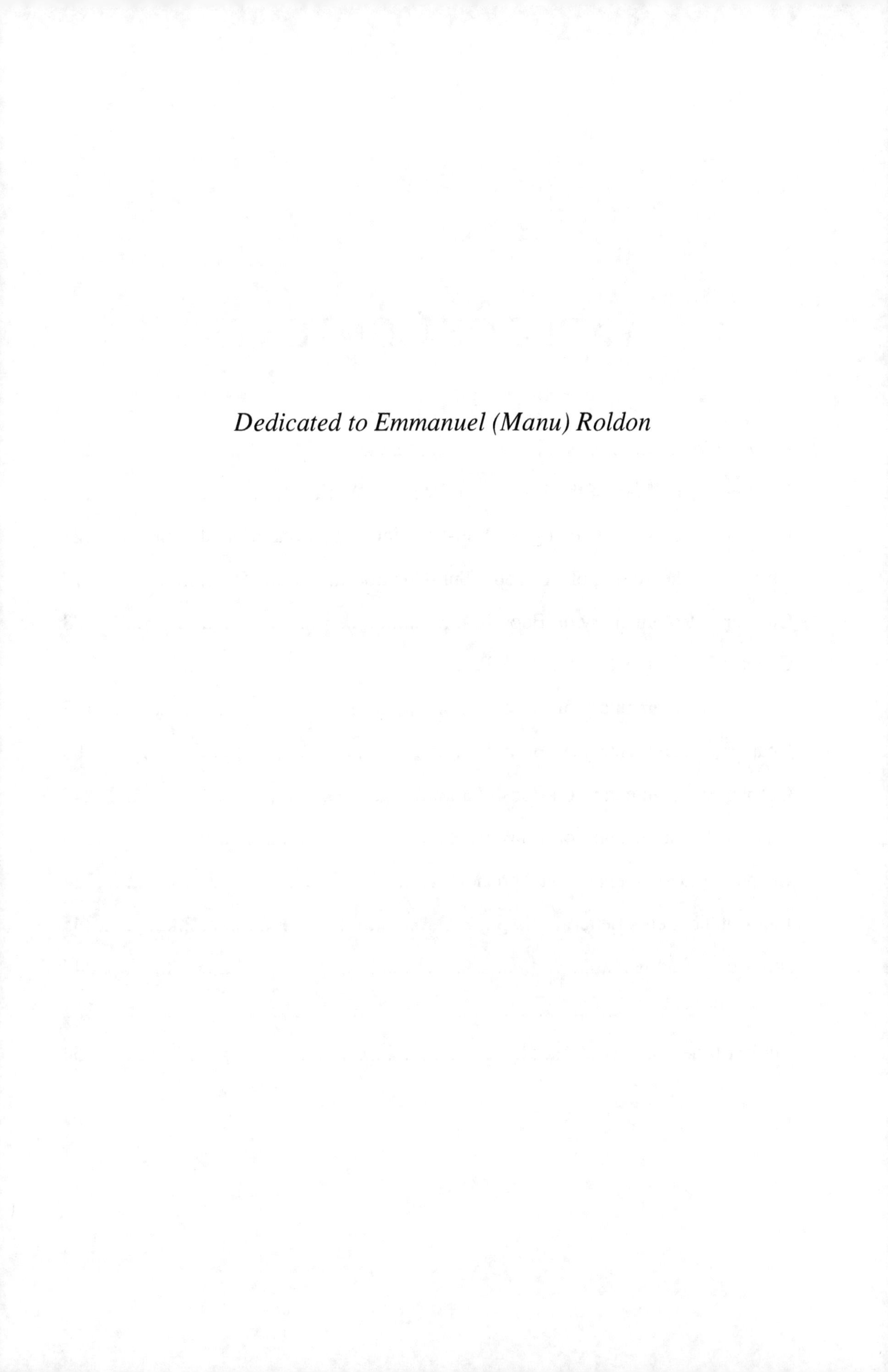

Dedicated to Emmanuel (Manu) Roldon

TABLE OF CONTENTS

ACKNOWLEDGMENTS

As I mentioned in my book on *The Hobbit*, my love for the works of J. R. R. Tolkien preceded my Christian conversion. In hindsight, I believe Tolkien's work prepared me for what was to come. My growth as a Christian has also deepened my appreciation for Tolkien's work and has given me a new way of reading it. I cannot pinpoint when exactly it happened, since I have had dreams of writing books for most of my life, but many years ago in the area of when I was starting college, an idea came to me for writing something of a commentary on Christian elements in Tolkien's fiction. That idea expanded and was refined many times over, and I kept notes starting back then, which grew each time I reread Tolkien's works. As time went on, and I became more aware of the demands of publishing and the pressures to specialize (or over-specialize), it seemed to me that it would not be feasible for me to write this book. At best, I thought I might as well keep the notes for my own interests and hold out hope that, if I ever became a well-published author with an established audience, I could potentially convince a publisher to publish a book I could write on this subject, or that I could potentially find myself connected to a group of authors that were writing an edited volume on Tolkien to which I could contribute. Whatever the case could be, and as increasingly far-fetched these scenarios appeared to be, it was clear that I had to put the work of actually writing this book on the back burner indefinitely. Additionally, my academic journey made it rather impractical to get around to writing a book of this scope if I was also going to be a responsible student and junior scholar. Then life kept happening and other projects and other concerns of life kept coming up. It seemed to me that this would be yet another unrealized idea.

As I also mentioned in my book on *The Hobbit*, last year, I experienced something providential, as my old professor Dr. Fredrick Long contacted me to let me know that GlossaHouse was beginning this Fiction and Fantasy series, which he wanted to include my work in. I then learned he would also be interested in a similar work on *The Lord of the Rings*. Dr. Long knows now but he could not have known then that he was giving me a chance to realize a dream I had well over a decade ago. And the fulfillment of the same proved to be the opposite of my expectations of when I could actually write it.

I am grateful to Dr. Long for giving me this opportunity to put to use the notes I have collected for most of my adult life as I have continued to revisit *The Lord of the Rings* over the years. Thank you for making a dream come true. And I am grateful to GlossaHouse for publishing what is now my third book with them. They are still the only publisher I have had experience with outside of academic journals, and it has been a good experience each time working with them.

I also want to acknowledge the man this book is dedicated to: Rev. Dr. Emmanuel Roldan, who I have habitually called "Manu" since our days in seminary (we are both fans of the San Antonio Spurs and lived through that team's glory days). He was the first person ever to hear some of the contents of this book thanks to his dedication to our reading group of two in 2016 and early 2017, which was a sort of in-between time that is similar to the one I am currently experiencing. As part of that reading group, we read *The Lord of the Rings* and even *The Silmarillion*, and I was able to share some observations from my notes. I am grateful to Manu for indulging me all those years ago and showing me that at least one person would be interested in my observations on *The Lord of the Rings*. I cannot adequately express how much your encouragement has meant to me.

Soli Deo Gloria

INTRODUCTION

The Lord of the Rings is the most renowned of works by John Ronald Reuel Tolkien (January 3, 1892–September 2, 1973). Because it has been sold in separate volumes, in boxed sets, and in single combined volumes, actual sales figures are difficult to come by, though estimates tend to be over 100 million, with some estimates being in the hundreds of millions since its publication in three volumes in 1954–1955. Another contributor to the difficulty is that there have been numerous translations, both authorized and unauthorized, of the book since the 1950s, including at least eighty-seven translations in at least fifty-seven languages. And this is despite all the complexities and difficulties that come with translating a work such as this.

Moreover, Tolkien meant for this sequel to *The Hobbit* to link that book with his larger mythos that he had been composing since World War I. While he never completed the composition of what he called *The Silmarillion* in his own lifetime, he left voluminous work for his son Christopher to sort through and publish after his death in *The Silmarillion, Unfinished Tales*, the twelve-volume *The History of Middle-earth*, and *The Great Tales* trilogy. Even after Christopher's death in 2020, more volumes of the work about the world before *The Lord of the Rings* have continued to be published, including *The Nature of Middle-earth* and *The Fall of Númenor*. The interest generated by *The Lord of the Rings* helped to ensure that these other books would have an engaged audience decades after the author's death.

The impact of *The Lord of the Rings* can be seen in many other ways as well. While Tolkien was not the first fantasy author or the first modern fantasy author (being preceded by those like George MacDonald, Lewis Carroll, and Robert E. Howard), his influence is apparent through the popularization and perpetuation of the fantasy genre to this day, especially as so many clearly draw inspiration from him. Online pages and bound volumes have arisen to help people learn languages that Tolkien invented for his fiction, languages with which most first became acquainted in *The Lord of the Rings*. There is now an entire genre of Tolkien scholarship dedicated to publishing and studying and his works—*The Lord of the Rings* most extensively—and multiple jour-nals have been particularly dedicated to publishing such studies, such as *Tolkien Stud-ies*, *Mallorn*, *Parma Eldalamberon*, *Vinyar Tengwar*, *Mythlore*, and *Lembas*, among others. Multiple massive fan sites, locales for fan fiction, and fan forums have popu-lated the Internet, including extensive wikis like *Tolkien Gateway*. Perhaps most obvi-ously, there have been many visual adaptations from fan films to the animated films of the 1970s and 1980s to the most critically and commercially successful of all: Peter Jackson's *The Lord of the Rings* adaptation.[1]

For all its popularity, it was not immediately striking as a "Christian" work in the obvious way that Tolkien's friend C. S. Lewis's work—whether his *Chronicles of Nar-nia* or his *The Space Trilogy*—has been. Part of that lack of a distinct "Christian" im-pression has to do with what one considers a "Christian" work. Is a work of art—whether narrative, visual, musical, or so on—to be considered "Christian" because of its explicit message(s), themes, and setting? Is it to be considered "Christian" simply because it is the work of a Christian? Or do other factors need to be taken into account to arrive at such a determination? Whatever one thinks on this subject, we do not all have the same assumptions about what is a "Christian" work. But as we will see in Chapter One, that is how Tolkien described his story.

Unsurprisingly, many have thus endeavored to explore *The Lord of the Rings* as a Christian work.[2] Some have been more devotional in character, where text from *The Lord of the Rings* has been used as a point of departure for meditation on something else related thereto (even where the connections are strained). Most have been some variation of thematic explorations or collections thereof focusing on its general Chris-tian characteristics, the specific Catholic characteristics, or some mix thereof (depend-ing on the author's disposition). Others have been quite detailed commentaries on spe-cific works or Tolkien's oeuvre as a whole, necessarily including his magnum opus. Many links with Christian theology and praxis have been identified, some quite clearly (with even Tolkien's own support), some with surprising illumination, and some only

---

[1] Quite apart from the fantastic box office returns (nearly $3 billion [over $5 billion when adjusted for inflation] on a cumulative $281 million budget) and DVD sales, the movies generated a massive new wave of interest in *The Lord of the Rings* and Tolkien's other works. I know, because I was one of the many caught in that wave. I have produced a book-length review series of Jackson's films on my Sub-stack beginning here: https://krharriman.substack.com/p/an-adaptational-review-of-the-lord.

[2] For overviews and responses to such readings, see Claudio A. Testi, *Pagan Saints in Middle-earth*, Cormarë 37 (Zollikofen, Switzerland: Walking Tree, 2018); idem, "Tolkien's Work: Is it Christian or Pagan? A Proposal for a 'Synthetic' Approach," *Tolkien Studies* 10 (2013): 1–47.

after the text has been subject to long sessions on the rack until it confesses what the author wants to hear.

In view of all that has come before, the reader may wonder what this book has to contribute, other than being an entry in a new series. First, most simply, each author has a peculiar perspective to offer, and mine is also shaped by my specialty. While philosophers (like Peter Kreeft), theologically informed historians (like Bradley J. Birzer), and theologians (like Austin Freeman, Fleming Rutledge, Ralph Wood, and others) have contributed to commentary both on *The Lord of the Rings* and on Tolkien's work more generally in their volumes, no other biblical scholar, as far as I am aware, has yet contributed a volume to the field. My development as a biblical scholar and as a reader of Tolkien have gone side by side, sometimes hand in hand where I found intersections. As I indicated in my Acknowledgments, this book has developed out of notes I have kept and expanded over the course of my adult life.

Second, as part of my ethos as a biblical scholar, I have sought to thoroughly ground my analysis, arguments, and commentary in the primary texts. Besides the multitudinous links with Scripture, this has meant that, where possible, I have sought to connect observations and reflections about the text with Tolkien's own words from his letters, as well as other pertinent works. Thus, this book contains hundreds of references to his letters, many of which help illuminate the consonance of his work with his Catholic worldview and the various links therewith. This commentary is most useful when the reader has at hand both *The Lord of the Rings* and Tolkien's letters.

Third, in illustrating the Christian and specifically Catholic character of Tolkien's story, I find it important not only to bring attention to his various statements on the matter, but also to expound his theology of sub-creation. Tolkien reflected deeply and often on the kind of work for which he has become known, and that included theological reflection. One reason he could refer to his work as "fundamentally" Catholic, as we will see later, is because of how it is shaped in its warp and woof by his theological reflection on fairy-stories, how they exemplify sub-creation, and how they can function as *evangelium*. These are points we will address in Chapter Two. Chapter Three will also show how the biblical and theological analysis of the commentary is pertinent to the setting of Tolkien's sub-creation.

Fourth, a crucial characteristic of the commentary is the fact that it is a running narrative commentary. Most works similar to this one tend to be thematic analyses, with a notable exception being Fleming Rutledge's *The Battle for Middle-earth*.[3] That is, they identify certain themes, find examples from the book, and discuss them accordingly. My commentary, like Rutledge's, follows the course of the narrative, like biblical commentaries of my native field most often follow the course of the text. This will lead to some inevitable repetition, which I have sought to reduce, but it will also mean tracking how certain ideas and character traits are developed in the course of the narrative.

Because of my focuses and interests here, it was necessary for me to limit the scope of what is already a book significantly longer than my dissertation. Although I am conversant to differing extents in the worlds of biblical scholarship, historical theology, systematic theology, and Tolkien scholarship, my focus is on primary texts. As such, I have attempted to avoid engaging with still broader debates in these worlds of scholarship beyond what I consider a minimal degree. This also means that, while focusing on the Christian and Catholic character of Tolkien's work is not *ipso facto* to deny other influences, I am only focusing on pertinent biblical, theological, and ethical/practical connections with *The Lord of the Rings*.[4]

In some ways, this book will repeat information that has been provided in my commentary on *The Hobbit*, especially in Chapter Three, which is an adapted and slightly expanded version of what I already wrote for that book. But one portion in particular that I will not be repeating is the biographical information I provided in that work that illustrates Tolkien's theological-ethical background. Since there are plenty more specific statements from Tolkien on the character of this work as opposed to *The Hobbit* (where it was more beneficial to reference his life story as illuminating the character of *The Hobbit* more generally), I will only be noting pertinent biographical information at various points. For more focused analysis and detail, I refer my readers to that book and to the cited biographies.[5]

---

[3] Fleming Rutledge, *The Battle for Middle-earth: Tolkien's Divine Design in The Lord of the Rings* (Grand Rapids: Eerdmans, 2004).

[4] Moreover, while I have entered into plenty of disputations about claimed links of Tolkien's work with this or that element of the Bible, Christian theology, or Christian praxis in the book reviews on my Substack, I do not wish to focus on engaging in such activity here. Although there are plenty of questionable connections made, I think it would be too much of a distraction to note and critique them at each point I could do so. Where I make note of questionable connections, they are only more common ones I have observed, rather than ones that are idiosyncratic to particular authors (although particular authors may exemplify them).

[5] K. R. Harriman, *God Has Chosen the Little Ones:* The Hobbit *and Tolkien's Theological Framework*, GlossaHouse Fiction and Fantasy (Wilmore, KY: GlossaHouse, 2024), 7–40. For a good, brief overview of Tolkien's Christian life, see Mark Horne, *J. R. R. Tolkien*, Christian Encounters (Nashville: Nelson, 2011). For a more detailed biography written from a Catholic perspective with plenty of helpful

What I aim to do is illuminate how *The Lord of the Rings* is a Christian and specifically Catholic work according to Tolkien's understanding by showing the connections with biblical and theological sources, as well as by citing and expounding his own words. In some cases, the ways in which his work is consonant with but not consciously conformed to Christianity are closer to the surface of the text. But the fact that we can speak of the text as "consonant with" but not "conformed to" Christianity is itself consistent with Tolkien's Christian theological-ethical framework (the phrasing used here is adapted from his Letter #269).[6] That is, his story fits his orthodox Christian worldview because of—not despite—its lack of direct Christian references or equivalencies. There are many links of consonance between his story and his theological-ethical framework, but they only appear in forms appropriate to the Secondary World setting.

To show this, I will proceed in the following steps. First, in Chapter One I examine how Tolkien himself declared the Christian character of his work, while also exploring what he meant by denying it was an allegory, whether of his Christian beliefs or anything else. Second, in Chapter Two I prosaically expound Tolkien's theology of sub-creation as he articulated it in his poem "Mythopoeia," his essay "On Fairy-Stories," and various letters he wrote over the years. This will show how Tolkien's ideas of sub-creation and his role as a sub-creator shaped how he presented what he would call "Primary World truths" in "Secondary World forms." Third, in Chapter Three I establish how Tolkien's understanding of the setting of his sub-creation shows how the fundamentally (generally) Christian and (specifically) Catholic character of his story is consistent with the lack of direct Christian references. Fourth, in Chapter Four through Chapter Ten I dive into the details of *The Lord of the Rings* to provide commentary on where we can perceive consonances of Primary World truths according to Tolkien's theological-ethical framework with their Secondary World forms as presented in Tolkien's story.[7] In describing Tolkien's "theological-ethical" framework—that is, his worldview as a context/frame for understanding his work—as informed by the Bible,

---

information for the reader, the best in show is Holly Ordway, *Tolkien's Faith: A Spiritual Biography* (Elk Grove Village, IL: Word on Fire Academic, 2023).

[6] All references and quotations of Tolkien's published letters are from J. R. R. Tolkien, *The Letters of J. R. R. Tolkien*, rev. and exp. ed., ed. Humphrey Carpenter and Christopher Tolkien (New York: Morrow, 2023). Letters drawn from other sources will be noted separately.

[7] Lest there be any confusion, I am not myself a Roman Catholic. I have my share of disagreements with Tolkien that are common between Protestants and Catholics, and I have others besides. But my aim is to present his beliefs about and his sources for Primary World truths accurately, not to use his work to promote my own beliefs.

Christian theology, and Christians praxis, I am expanding and correcting how I phrased my commentary on *The Hobbit*. There, I described Tolkien's framework as "theological," which could give the impression that I was only writing about beliefs, but I was, in fact, including ethical elements as well. It is proper to speak of "theological ethics" because the elements of ethics and proper practice in Tolkien's worldview are formed in relation to theological beliefs about God and humanity, so that, for example, ethical imperatives are grounded in theological indicatives and actions are to emerge with faith.

CHAPTER ONE

The Lord of the Rings as *a Christian Work*

In one respect, Tolkien could be fairly described as an indulgent author in the sense that he indulged his readers' questions and comments with responses to a large number of letters sent to him (although I am not sure what the proportion was of the letters to which he responded out of the letters he received). In another respect, Tolkien would not be properly described as an indulgent author in the sense that he was willing to entertain interpretations or connections his readers made from his story to things outside of the story. He was certainly not that kind of indulgent author. One of the last letters in the published collection (Letter #347a) states in no uncertain terms his distaste—even before such tendencies were turned on him—for "the dissection, source-hunting, interpretation, and biographical tunnelling and scavenging which are supposed (too often disingenuously) to assist in the dissection interpretation and 'understanding' of literary works."

Of course, his lack of indulgence in this respect did not end there. We will see later in this chapter how he rebuffed claims and questions of allegory on many occasions. One can also see less strident expressions of this attitude in how he responded to some attempted correlations of *The Lord of the Rings* (hereafter, *LOTR*) with biblical, theological, and ethical elements, a couple examples of which will be noted in the commentary proper. But it is notable that he did not reject all such links.

In fact, he noted on multiple occasions that his Catholic faith was relevant to understanding his work. He said in Letter #195 (to Amy Ronald):

> One point: Frodo's attitude to weapons was personal. He was not in modern terms a 'pacifist'. Of course, he was mainly horrified at the prospect of civil war among Hobbits; but he had (I suppose) also reached the conclusion that

physical fighting is actually less ultimately effective than most (good) men think it! Actually I am a Christian, and indeed a Roman Catholic, so that I do not expect 'history' to be anything but a 'long defeat' – though it contains (and in a legend may contain more clearly and movingly) some samples or glimpses of final victory.

We will have occasion to return to this comment in more detail later, but what is worth noting for now is that Tolkien can distance his own views from those of Frodo while still acknowledging that there is some sympathy between his beliefs as a Catholic and Frodo's attitude. He is giving at least limited warrant for a link here in seeing his Catholic faith as relevant for illuminating his story.

More significantly, in Letter #213, in response to Deborah Webster's request for biographical information, he was initially dismissive of literary critics who he thought excessively focused on authors' (and other artists') lives as opposed to their works in their attempts to make various psychological analyses. Despite this opposition to such a mindset, he described the fact that he is a Christian as not only a more important fact about himself than other biographical details he could give, but that it can be deduced from his work:

> Or more important, I am a Christian (which can be deduced from my stories), and in fact a Roman Catholic. The latter 'fact' perhaps cannot be deduced; though one critic (by letter) asserted that the invocations of Elbereth, and the character of Galadriel as directly described (or through the words of Gimli and Sam) were clearly related to Catholic devotion to Mary. Another saw in waybread (lembas)= viaticum and the reference to its feeding the *will* (vol. III, p. 213) and being more potent when fasting, a derivation from the Eucharist. (That is: far greater things may colour the mind in dealing with the lesser things of a fairy-story.) (emphasis original)

Beyond these biographical remarks connecting his faith with *LOTR*, he made several comments over the years explicitly characterizing it in Christian and Catholic terms. Likely the single most quoted remark to this effect comes from Letter #142 addressed to the Jesuit priest Robert Murray, who linked his involvement in the Roman Catholic Church with the influence of Tolkien specifically. Tolkien responded with the following remark when Murray had expressed his sense of the positive compatibility of Tolkien's book with the order of grace:

> *The Lord of the Rings* is of course a fundamentally religious and Catholic work; unconsciously so at first, but consciously in the revision. That is why I have not put in, or have cut out, practically all references to anything like

'religion', to cults or practices, in the imaginary world. For the religious element is absorbed into the story and the symbolism. However that is very clumsily put, and sounds more self-important than I felt. For as a matter of fact, I have consciously planned very little; and should chiefly be grateful for having been brought up (since I was eight) in a Faith that has nourished me and taught me all the little that I know; and that I owe to my mother, who clung to her conversion and died young, largely through the hardships of poverty resulting from it.

There is much of significance packed into this quote, and we will have occasion for revisiting it at multiple junctures throughout this book as one part or another becomes more pertinent. We will see as we go how much of "the religious element" is absorbed into the story in both the fundamental structure of his sub-creation and in many details. On other occasions, we will note by reference to the relevant portions of *The History of Middle-earth* where certain elements were in place from the start (when Tolkien was not conscious of them) and where other elements have been brought into sharper focus by Tolkien's revision. We also see here our first indication, which will only be clarified by other material and other letters, that he links the lack of explicit religious elements precisely to its religious and Catholic character. The fact that he "consciously planned very little" will prove to be a significant point he returns to in response to questions about *LOTR* being a supposed allegory. Finally, as with the aforementioned letters, he highlights the significance of his Catholic formation for the character of his work.

We also should comment on the matter of the order of grace and the sense of compatibility with it. Tolkien describes *LOTR* as a fundamentally religious and Catholic work because it is so at its foundation in that it is reflective of Primary Reality (truth in the actual world that we live in), particularly the transcendent qualities Tolkien knew in Catholicism, but it is so in that its Secondary Reality (the internal reality of the fantasy setting) reflects the truth in its own way. That is, Tolkien thus maintains the integrity of the order of nature (God's work of and in creation) through his Secondary World representation while also maintaining its continuity with Primary World truth that has benefited from God's order of grace (God's work of salvation). It is consistent with Tolkien's Catholic theology that what can be learned from general revelation and "natural theology," while necessarily incomplete, is, at its best, consistent with special revelation and revealed theology as articulated in Scripture; the order of nature is compatible with the order of grace. As Thomas Aquinas articulates throughout his works, the order of grace builds on, elevates, and completes or perfects the order of nature.[1] Hence, he reiterates in multiple works some version of the point that "grace perfects/completes nature," rather than that it destroys nature.[2] As the era of history that Tolkien presented in his work is a "monotheistic world of natural theology" (Letter #165 to Houghton Mifflin Co.), it was consistent with his Christian (specifically Catholic) beliefs to find ways of articulating ideas in continuity/compatibility with what God had revealed by the order of grace in special revelation to Israel and in Christ, while still remaining consistent with their being derived from the order of nature. We will return to these points in Chapter Three.

Tolkien also noted in an unpublished letter to L. M. Cutts (26 October 1958) what he would say more extensively in "On Fairy-Stories" (which we will examine later) that "no one of us can really invent or 'create' in a void, we can only reconstruct and perhaps impress a personal pattern on 'ancestral' material." He later puts a fine point on this by saying, "if I may say so, with humility, the Christian religion (which I profess) is far the most powerful ultimate source. On a lower plane: my linguistic interest is the more powerful force."[3] That is, the more pervasive immediate influential force on his work is his linguistic interest. That has been made clear from how the whole story of *The Hobbit* began with a sentence he wrote at random about "a hobbit," and it is what drives his sub-creative project and the shapes it takes in various places. After all, he had to figure out how various languages worked, in what contexts they worked, as well as how to name various entities, what those names meant, and how they worked in their contexts. And so on it went, since there are many, many such linguistic elements in his text to consider. And this is to say nothing about how the languages were conveyed in a story that is framed and presented as a translation project. But on a more overarching level, even if it shows up in some details as well, his own worldview as formed by the Christian religion—specifically, of the Roman Catholic tradition—is what he considers to be the most powerful influence. This will be borne out in this commentary. Even when Tolkien did not feel obligated to *conform* the text to his

---

[1] Thomas Aquinas, *Summa Theologiae* I,1.1.8.reply 2; I.1.2.2.reply 1; I,1.62.5; II,2.1.8; *De Malo* q. 2 a. 11 *In II Sententiarum* distinction 9 art. 8 ag 3; ibid., ad 3; *In III Sententiarum* distinction 24, q. 1, a. 3A; As specifically related to truth found in pagan sources that is compatible with God's revelation, the most obvious manifestation of this for Aquinas is how much of his thought was shaped through interaction with the writings of Aristotle and other Aristotelians.

[2] For more on this matter in Tolkien's context and his fiction, see Phillip Irving Mitchell, "'But Grace Is Not Infinite': Tolkien's Explorations of Nature and Grace in His Catholic Context," *Mythlore* 31.3/4 (Spring/Summer 2013): 61–81.

[3] Excerpts of this letter are available at https://tolkiengateway.net/wiki/Letter_to_L.M._Cutts.

Christian worldview per se, he sought to make it *compatible/consonant* (Letter #269), given its setting in a pre-Christian time (as we will explore in Chapter Three). Of course, as Tolkien stated in his letter on "The Name Coventry," which was published in the 23 February 1945 edition of *The Catholic Herald*, he saw his Catholic faith as being linked with his linguistic interest and philological work simply because he knew no way to do his work in keeping with Catholic tradition than by "seeking the truth without bias." This fits what he will say about maintaining the integrity of sub-creation and why his work is thus lacking in direct Christian references.

Although not as directly relevant to the Christian character of his work, Tolkien similarly reaffirmed this basic principle of the construction of his work in Letter #215 to Walter Allen by saying, "long narratives cannot be made out of nothing; and one cannot rearrange the primary matter in secondary patterns without indicating feelings and opinions about one's material." Likewise, in Letter #181 addressed to Michael Straight, a letter we will be revisiting on several other occasions, he stated that this fairy-story for adults inevitably needed to supply something worth considering because of its relevance to "the human situation," which entails that "something of the teller's own reflections and 'values' will inevitably get worked in." As such, the religious elements of Tolkien's own life have been absorbed implicitly in his fictional work because they were so absorbed by the writer.[4]

Furthermore, in Letter #211 to Rhona Beare, he made multiple theological comments in response to her questions. Yet, he ultimately said prior to wrapping up the letter, "since I have deliberately written a tale, which is built on or out of certain 'religious' ideas, but is *not* an allegory of them (or anything else), and does not mention them overtly, still less preach them, I will not now depart from that mode, and venture on theological disquisition for which I am not fitted" (emphasis original). Still, as he observed in an unpublished letter to G. S. Rigby Jr. (6 December 1965), in which he wrote all too briefly, "There is, in fact, quite a lot of theology included in <u>The Lord of the Rings</u> (I was surprised to find how much when the work was analysed some time ago in a theological periodical), though it is perhaps made more palatable by a sugar

---

[4] Relatedly, his daughter Priscilla noted that her father rarely spoke of his theology in an intellectual/abstract way, "In fact, I do not think it was ever in his heart to write or speak of religion didactically: his mode was to express religious themes and moral questions through the medium of storytelling." Priscilla Tolkien, quoted in Andrea Monda and Wu Ming 4, "Tolkien as Catholic Philosopher?," in *Tolkien and Philosophy*, ed. Roberto Arduini and Claudio A. Testi, Cormarë 32 (Zurich and Jena: Walking Tree, 2014), 86.

coating."[5] While Tolkien himself may not have been keen on writing a theological analysis or disquisition of his work as a whole, he affirmed that such links could be reasonably made between his story and his Catholic faith.

Beyond these general comments (and others outside of his letters), Tolkien himself even addressed links between his Primary World beliefs and both *LOTR* and his larger mythos as conveyed in *The Silmarillion* in Letters #109, #131, #148a, #153, #156, #163, #165, #181, #183, #186, #191, #192, #211, #212, #213, #246, #269, #297, and #320. We will have occasion to reference these letters (as well as various unpublished letters) as we go, so we will not review their contents here. But it should be clear enough that such theological reflection on the character of his work was important to him that he should return to it so many times.

Tolkien's Statements on Allegory

Another point Tolkien would return to many times in his letters was the matter of allegory and whether *LOTR* constituted allegory. Since its publication, *LOTR* has often been subjected to allegorical interpretation. Many readers wrote to him asking him if it was an allegory of something, usually related to the Second World War or its fallout,[6] given the time of its writing and publication. His comments on allegory have also often been noted in the context of discussions about the (generally) Christian/(specifically) Catholic character of his work, and so they will be relevant to explore here. His overall response to his readers prompted a kind of summary statement in his foreword to the second edition of *LOTR* in 1966. In his words:

> As for any inner meaning or 'message', it has in the intention of the author none. It is neither allegorical nor topical. But I cordially dislike allegory in all its manifestations, and always have done so since I grew old or wary enough to detect its presence. I much prefer history, true or feigned, with its varied applicability to the thought and experience of readers. I think that many confuse 'applicability' with 'allegory'; but the one resides in the freedom of the reader, and the other in the purposed domination of the author.[7]

---

[5] This letter is available online at https://tolkiengateway.net/wiki/Letter_to_G.S._Rigby_Jr. (emphasis original).

[6] Besides the letters referenced below, also see Letter #226.

[7] J. R. R. Tolkien, *The Lord of the Rings*, Illustrated Edition (Boston: Houghton Mifflin Harcourt, 2021), xix. All references hereafter to the text of *LOTR* will not use page numbers. Due to the variety of paginations in different published versions of *LOTR*, when I cite from it, I give the book number in

Readers who have sought to rebuke all attempts at any kind of correspondence between Tolkien's work and the Bible, Christian theology, or Christian praxis have been keen to note the sentence beginning with "But I cordially dislike allegory," and it has also been used more broadly to rebuke any claims to allegory. Unfortunately, this has also led to overstatement in various readers' circles that Tolkien *hated* allegory, which is obviously not what he said. Others have "cordially" disregarded this statement from Tolkien and have still sought to hold fast to this or that claim of allegory in Tolkien's story. Tolkien himself could be prone to overstatement in this fashion, as he could certainly use allegory as a rhetorical device in his famous essay "*Beowulf*: The Monsters and the Critics."[8] Scholars have also noted his short stories "Leaf by Niggle" and "Smith of Wootton Major" as allegories, but Tolkien himself did not regard these stories as allegories properly speaking.[9] Even so, he said in Letter #153 about "Leaf by Niggle" that "I tried to show allegorically how that [subcreation] might come to be taken up into Creation in some plane in my 'purgatorial' story *Leaf by Niggle*."

It is unsurprising that there has been confusion on this subject. Tolkien is not entirely clear or consistent in his use of "allegory" and "allegorical," and his statements can be ambiguous. What makes the matter all the more difficult is that those who respond to statements like the one in Tolkien's foreword do not necessarily have a clear idea of what they themselves mean when referring to allegory, so that the category becomes so broad as to mean anything and (thus) nothing. Even referencing dictionaries will not prove especially helpful. For example, the definitions that appear in the third edition of the *Oxford English Dictionary* use "allegory" in reference to both the use of symbols/symbolic representation and the subsequent interpretation of the same. It is easy for someone working with one definition to misunderstand someone using another.

While allegory is definitely a kind of representation, so that the thing signified is something other than the sign used, and the meaning is something other than what one says, the question remains of what one means by "representation." On the one hand, John Bunyan's *The Pilgrim's Progress* uses figures with rather apparent names to stand

---

Roman numerals, followed by a slash, which is then followed by an Arabic numeral giving the number of the chapter.

[8] J. R. R. Tolkien, "*Beowulf*: The Monsters and the Critics," in *The Monsters and the Critics*, ed. Christopher Tolkien (London: HarperCollins, 2006), 5–48.

[9] For the denial of allegory in the former, see Letter #241. On the latter, see Christina Scull and Wayne G. Hammond, *The J. R. R. Tolkien Companion and Guide*, rev. and exp. ed., vol. 2: Reader's Guide, Part 1: A–M (London: HarperCollins, 2017), 47.

in for characteristics of whatever they are named after, and it is among the clearest examples of allegory as a means of overarching storytelling that one can find. On the other hand, any character in any story can be said to exemplify certain characteristics and so, in that sense, could be taken to "represent" whatever they exemplify by sheer fact of embodying and enacting the characteristic in question. But does that mean it is proper to describe such a feature of a narrative as allegory?

Consideration of what constitutes allegory should also involve consideration of purpose. In that a story is an allegory, it should achieve some purpose that is in line with the author's purpose in making the story an allegory. Craig Blomberg notes, "Contemporary analysis largely agrees that there are at least three primary functions of allegory: (a) to illustrate a viewpoint in an artistic and educational way, (b) to keep its message from being immediately clear to all its hearers or readers without further reflection and (c) to win over its audience to accept a particular set of beliefs or act in a certain way."[10] These purposes could be applied to allegories like the parables of Jesus, but do they fit a narrative like Tolkien's?

Much, much more could be written on the matter of allegory, its usage, the history of difficulties surrounding it, and so on, but we need to narrow our focus. We must consider what Tolkien himself had to say on the matter that could possibly illuminate the relationship of his story with allegory. I will begin with his statement that is most helpful for giving us a theoretical framework to work with for how he understands allegory, and then I will proceed through his letters.

His most extensive comment on the matter of allegory comes in an introduction he composed for his translation of the poem *Pearl*. Tolkien noted that there was debate that had been going on for only a couple of decades at the time he wrote concerning whether this poem was an elegy on the death of the author's daughter, his "pearl," or if it was an allegory. He then explained why he wanted to distinguish between allegory and symbolism (in contrast to popular definitions that use them interchangeably).In his view, "it is proper, or at least useful, to limit allegory to narrative, to an account (however short) of events; and symbolism to the use of visible signs or things to represent other things or ideas."[11] To be a proper allegorical narrative, it should as a whole and in its significant details "cohere and work together" to the end of signifying in alternative terms some other "event or process."[12]

---

[10] Craig L. Blomberg, *Interpreting the Parables* (Downers Grove, IL: IVP Academic, 2012), 62.

[11] J. R. R. Tolkien, *Sir Gawain and the Green Knight, Pearl, Sir Orfeo* (New York: Del Rey, 1980), 10.

[12] Ibid., 11.

One can clearly see why Tolkien would deny that his work constituted allegory. He does not consistently describe by means of other terms "some event or process" other than what is stated, and no design of his was directed by the notion that the whole narrative and its details should cohere and cooperate to the end of referring to the other thing in question.

Moreover, as Tolkien's foreword indicates, he thinks that allegories are allegories by authorial purpose. If certain elements in the story happen to evoke something outside the scope of the story, show a resemblance thereto, or prove to be applicable to something outside of the story, he does not consider that allegory. This point of his foreword summarizes points he made in several of his letters.

One such example similar to his foreword is a letter he wrote to Charles Calleja the same year the second edition of *LOTR* was published, in which he said, "Being influenced by, or making use of, events or experience of one's life (which is inevitable) has nothing to do with allegory."[15] We have already seen how such internal resources like his faith shaped his work, according to his own declaration, but this does not indicate allegory. This is because, again, his story is not meant to "stand for" or be a sign for signifying those things other than what is in the story. He had stated in a letter he sent to G. E. Selby in 1955/1956, "There is, of course, no 'allegory' at all in [*The Lord of the Rings*]. But people are very confused about this word, and seem to mix it up with 'significance' or 'relevance',", which uses slightly different terminology from his foreword.[16] Around that same time, he wrote in a letter to Derrick Parnum that his story was simply meant to be a good tale for his own satisfaction of needing literature of its kind, "It is not an 'allegory', all the same. Though one soon discovers that the more you put into any story the more capable it becomes of being generally or particularly applied to other matters … It was imagined as a 'plot', and largely written before nuclear physics became political and mixed up with power."[17] Letter #205 features Tolkien's roundabout denial to a question of if the story was allegory, wherein he states a more specific version of the general idea of what his story was trying to accomplish, "Nobody believes me when I say that my long book is an attempt to create a world in which a form of language agreeable to my personal aesthetic might seem real. But it is true." He wrote similarly in 1963 in response to Baronne A. Baeyens's proper perception that the story is is "mythical-historical," rather than allegorical. He says that he

---

[15] Available online at https://tolkiengateway.net/wiki/Letter_to_Charles_Calleja.
[16] Scull and Hammond, *J. R. R. Tolkien Companion*, 2:46.
[17] Available at https://tolkiengateway.net/wiki/Letter_to_Derrick_Parnum.

simply tried to write a good story that would indulge his "personal pleasure in history, languages, and 'landscape'—and trees." But he laments how his book has been analyzed and how there are so many people who cannot just enjoy anything, "And still more who cannot distinguish between allegorical intention and 'applicability' (by the reader)."[18]

We see him continue to make use in his later writings of distinction between intentional/conscious allegory, on the one hand, and "applicability," on the other. He said in Letter #203 to Herbert Schiro, after denying that there was any conscious allegory in his story, "That there is no allegory does not, of course, say there is no applicability. There always is." After another denial that his story was allegory in Letter #215 to Walter Allen, he noted, "I do not like allegory (properly so called: most readers appear to confuse it with significance or applicability) but that is a matter too long to deal with here." In his statement that *Smith of Wootton Major* is not a proper allegory, he says, "Its primary purpose is itself, and any applications it or parts of it may have for individual hearers are incidental. I dislike real allegory in which the application is the author's own and is meant to dominate you. I prefer the freedom of the hearer or reader."[19]

Several other times, he simply denied his work was allegorical. Since he linked allegory with authorial design/purpose, he often found it sufficient to deny allegory by denying his intention of allegory (Letters #34, #165, #181, #183, #203, #215). Other times, he insisted that others were misusing the label of "allegory" (Letters #109, #181, #211). On one occasion, he mentioned how amused he was by various interpretations of this work, excepting those "in the mode of simple allegory: that is, the particular and topical" (Letter #163).

Similarly, Tolkien insisted in a letter to Maria Mroczkowska that he did not have an "analytical or allegorical mind." Therefore, he had to make sure that his Secondary World had deep historical roots in itself, rather than relying on some correspondence with an external object.[21] He said much the same thing to Naomi Mitchison in Letter #144 that his setting is mythical and not allegorical, since "my mind does not work allegorically." Relatedly, the aforementioned Letter #203 features Tolkien saying, "Allegory of the sort 'five wizards = five senses' is wholly foreign to my way of thinking."

---

[18] Letter to Baronne A. Baeyens (16 December 1963). A transcript and a photo copy of this unpublished letter is available online at https://www.manhattanrarebooks.com/pages/books/2144/j-r-r-tolkien/autograph-letter-signed-als-typed-letter-signed-tls?soldItem=true.

[19] Scull and Hammond, *J. R. R. Tolkien Companion*, 2:47.

[21] Available online at https://tolkiengateway.net/wiki/Letter_to_Maria_Mroczkowska.

He insisted in Letter #229 to Allen & Unwin that one allegorical reading linking Sauron and Stalin angered him and that "Such allegory is entirely foreign to my thought."

Also consistent with his foreword is how he would claim on multiple occasions to dislike allegory. He mentioned offhandedly to Christopher in Letter #60 that he did not care much for the concluding chapter of C. S. Lewis's moral allegory of lost souls visiting heaven (which eventually became *The Great Divorce*). He would mention the allegory again in Letter #69 without such a comment. Of course, this does not specifically ground his distaste in its allegorical quality. He said this more directly in Letter #131 to Milton Waldman, telling him, "I dislike Allegory – the conscious and intentional allegory – yet any attempt to explain the purport of myth or fairytale must use allegorical language." Presumably, the language is allegorical because it goes beyond the scope of the story and appeals to what Tolkien elsewhere called "universals" (Letter #181) in explaining the story in those other terms. We saw another such statement of his dislike for allegory in Letter #215. In a more roundabout fashion, he said in Letter #262, "I am not naturally attracted (in fact much the reverse) by allegory, mystical or moral." In an unpublished letter to Eileen Elgar in which he commented on Lewis's *The Chronicles of Narnia*, he said, "I do not like 'allegory', and least of all religious allegory of this kind."[22] However, in making this comment, Tolkien shows how he could be mistaken about what constitutes allegory. He is hardly alone in this error when it comes to *The Chronicles of Narnia*, or *The Lion, the Witch, and the Wardrobe* in particular, but those stories are not allegories by Tolkien's definition. Lewis considered the initial story—and, by extension to some degree, the others—to be "supposal," as in exploring what the gospel story would look like *supposing* it took place in another world with the features given.[23]

So far, this all seems straightforward, right? Well, as it turns out, Tolkien's strong denials did not entail that there were no elements in his story that he was not willing to describe as allegory. In fact, Tolkien described the story of Aragorn and Arwen in an unpublished letter to Rayner Unwin as, "an allegory of naked hope."[24] He also admitted allegory as a possible description of Frodo and Bilbo's fate in Letter #131 when he said that they had an Arthurian ending, "in which it is, of course, not made explicit whether this is an 'allegory' of death, or a mode of healing and restoration leading to a return."

---

[22] Available at https://tolkiengateway.net/wiki/Letter_to_Eileen_Elgar_(24_December_1971).

[23] For more on this subject and the letter, see Josh B. Long, "Disparaging Narnia: Reconsidering Tolkien's View of *The Lion, the Witch, and the Wardrobe*," *Mythlore* 31.3/4 (Spring/Summer 2013): 31–46.

[24] Available online at: https://tolkiengateway.net/wiki/Letter_to_Rayner_Unwin_(12_May_ 1955).

In these cases, "allegory" appears to be used in a way like "symbol," as in a footnote of his Letter #131 where he wrote on the "symbolical or allegorical significance" of the Light of Valinor. In the same way, he also wrote in Letter #153 of the desire of the Eregion Elves being, "an 'allegory' if you like of a love of machinery, and technical devices." Of course, the examples from Letters #131 and #153 present something of an ambiguity, since he puts "allegory" in quotes in such a way that he is suggesting that the aspects of his story could be applied this way, almost as if he is giving into the failure to distinguish between allegory and application, but only by putting "allegory" in quotes. It should also be noted that all the comments in this paragraph come from times before he was more frequently insistent on distinguishing the two in the late 1950s and the 1960s.

Moreover, there are yet other times when Tolkien used "allegory" in quite different ways from the examples that align more directly with his foreword. In Letter #71 he said to Christopher, "Yes, I think the orcs as real a creation as anything in 'realistic' fiction: your vigorous words well describe the tribe; only in real life they are on both sides, of course. For 'romance' has grown out of 'allegory', and its wars are still derived from the 'inner war' of allegory in which good is on one side and various modes of badness on the other." This is something closer to how the ancient and medieval Christians wrote of the allegorical sense of Scripture as that which was spiritual and mystical. Tolkien is here referring to larger, spiritual realities in which particular conflicts partake/participate as examples or instantiations. Similarly, he could speak of "the War" in Letter #101 (also addressed to Christopher), when he said, "the War is not over (and the one that is, or the part of it, has largely been lost). But it is of course wrong to fall into such a mood, for Wars are always lost, and The War always goes on; and it is no good growing faint."

Similarly, in Letter #109, which features one of Tolkien's denials that his story is an allegory, he noted:

> There is a 'moral', I suppose, in any tale worth telling. But that is not the same thing. Even the struggle between darkness and light (as he calls it, not me) is for me just a particular phase of history, one example of its pattern, perhaps, but not The Pattern; and the actors are individuals – they each, of course, contain universals, or they would not live at all, but they never represent them as such.

Notice how Tolkien distinguishes between the quality of an allegorical narrative in which individuals represent universals—that higher plane to which the allegory purposefully points—and the sheer fact that all individuals in any kind of story/history "contain" universals in that they embody and exemplify in varying ways the "Pattern" in which they participate by living.

He then commented later in Letter #109 on the relationship between Allegory and Story, the latter of which is what he aimed to write:

> Of course, Allegory and Story converge, meeting somewhere in Truth. So that the only perfectly consistent allegory is a real life; and the only fully intelligible story is an allegory. And one finds, even in imperfect human 'literature', that the better and more consistent an allegory is the more easily can it be read 'just as a story'; and the better and more closely woven a story is the more easily can those so minded find allegory in it. But the two start out from opposite ends. You can make the Ring into an allegory of our own time, if you like: an allegory of the inevitable fate that waits for all attempts to defeat evil power by power. But that is only because all power magical or mechanical does always so work. You cannot write a story about an apparently simple magic ring without that bursting in, if you really take the ring seriously, and make things happen that would happen, if such a thing existed.

He made a similar statement in Letter #131 that "the more 'life' a story has the more readily will it be susceptible of allegorical interpretations: while the better a deliberate allegory is made the more nearly will it be acceptable just as a story."[25] In another letter where he indicated his displeasure with allegorical interpretations of his work—namely, Letter #163—he nevertheless said, "In a larger sense, it is I suppose impossible to write any 'story' that is not allegorical in proportion as it 'comes to life'; since each of us is an allegory, embodying in a particular tale and clothed in the garments of time and place, universal truth and everlasting life."

We see varying senses drawn together as well in Letter #153 when Tolkien commented on Tom Bombadil. He insisted that he did not intend for him to be an allegory—that is, allegory in the proper narrative sense of the word for Tolkien—for he would not have given him such a name. But if one can put "allegory" in quotes, as in other

---

[25] This is the obverse of what he stated in his "On Fairy-Stories" when writing in opposition to the once dominant view that folk tales, fairy stories, and so on were derived from "nature-myths," wherein the Olympians were supposed to be personifications of aspects of nature and stories about them, which he said were better called "allegories" than "myths," were about processes and changes of nature (J. R. R. Tolkien, "On Fairy-Stories," in *The Monsters and the Critics*, ed. Christopher Tolkien [London: HarperCollins, 2006], 123). He thought that this theory was "the truth almost upside down. The nearer the so-called 'nature-myth', or allegory of the large processes of nature, is to its supposed archetype, the less interesting it is, and indeed the less is it of a myth capable of throwing any illumination whatever on the world" (ibid.).

instances seen previously, he says that this is the only way of "exhibiting certain functions," and that Tom can be described as, "an 'allegory' or an exemplar, a particular
embodying of pure (real) natural science: the spirit that desires knowledge of other
things, their history and nature, *because they are 'other'* and wholly independent of the
enquiring mind, a spirit coeval with the rational mind, and entirely unconcerned with
'doing' anything with the knowledge: Zoology and Botany not Cattle-breeding or Ag-
riculture" (emphasis original). While Tom is not an allegory in the narrative sense as
set out in his exposition on *Pearl*, Tom is an "allegory" in the sense that exemplars
"contain" universals and embody them particularly well. This sense of allegory as ex-
ample/exemplar seems to be behind how Tolkien describes "Leaf by Niggle" in this
letter: "I tried to show allegorically how that [subcreation] might come to be taken up
into Creation in some plane in my 'purgatorial' story *Leaf by Niggle*." If that is so, it
could explain how this statement squares with his denial of its character as allegory in
Letter #241, "It is not really or properly an 'allegory' so much as 'mythical'. For Niggle
is meant to be a real mixed-quality person and not an 'allegory' of any single vice or
virtue." In this case, he was referring to what he considered a proper allegorical narrative, as opposed to the earlier letter. That is, if he did not simply change his understanding of the story or revise his description to be more precise. Similarly, the aforementioned Letter #181 features Tolkien having one sense of allegory in mind when he denied that his story is that and he used the language of exemplification to distinguish
from allegorical representation, even though we have seen here how in other contexts
he used "allegory" in a fashion to refer to exemplification.

Letter #186 to Joanna de Bortadano has perhaps been the text most often considered
to give license to allegorical interpretation (and not simply application) because Tolkien opened the letter with, "Of course my story is not an allegory of Atomic power,
but of *Power* (exerted for Domination). Nuclear physics can be used for that purpose.
But they need not be. They need not be used at all. If there is any contemporary reference in my story at all it is to what seems to me the most widespread assumption of our
time: that if a thing can be done, it must be done" (emphasis original). The way he
wrote could easily be taken to mean that he did intend *LOTR* to be an allegory after all,
since the opening says that his story is not an allegory of Atomic power, but, by implication, *is an allegory* of Power. That is the most straightforward way to understand the
syntax. Of course, this is particularly linked with the One Ring, about which Tolkien
had already said elsewhere that one *could, if one liked*, make the Ring into an allegory.
But that is a matter of application in realizing the connections of the Ring with more
enduring matters outside of the scope of the story. One can obviously see from later

letters than this one in 1956 (and from the fact that his foreword was published ten years after this letter) that this was not Tolkien changing his tune on his story being an allegory the whole time. He was simply speaking more loosely here. It could also be that he was allowing the implication of allegory here because he is referring to the "universal," the larger spiritual theme in which his work participates by virtue of engaging the idea of Power. Moreover, he even went on to say in this same letter that Power is not a central matter in his story, but those concern Death and Immortality (he said much the same in Letter #211), as well as the themes of how the wheels of the world are turned by the hands of the unknown and weak (or, as he said in Letter #131, "without the high and noble the simple and vulgar is utterly mean; and without the simple and ordinary the noble and heroic is meaningless").

Tolkien regularly insisted that the story of *LOTR*, as well as others he wrote, was not an allegorical narrative. That is to say that he was not conscious of intentionally making connections between his story and matters outside of it. He did not consistently describe by means of other terms than what is stated "some event or process," and no design of his was directed by the notion that "its entire narrative and all its significant details should cohere and work together to this end" of referring to the other thing in question. On the one hand, he maintained that the story had much applicability for his readers to explore using their own imaginations, but he also maintained that this should not be confused with allegory. On the other hand, he acknowledged that there were connections between elements outside of his story, such as his Christian faith, so that they contributed to his sub-creative project, but that this also should not be construed as allegory so that elements of his story simply represented these things his story was connected to. However, there were other times that he used the terminology of allegory in different ways that could lead to confusion about his more direct statements. There were even times he could be as mistaken as anyone else about what does and does not constitute allegory, as in his view of Lewis's work in *Narnia*. But I have tried to show how it is possible for his views to be understood more coherently and consistently, even if his terminological usage is not always so, and even though he did make some overstatements. In any case, it appears that he was more consistent in his rejection of allegory as a description of *LOTR* in his later writings, which his foreword is consonant with as something he wrote in his 70s. And I think it is fair to say that the aforementioned purposes of conscious allegory do not apply to Tolkien's fiction.

In line with Tolkien's statements, my own work has not been one of suggesting allegory, in spite of what he said. That would be to adopt a different notion of what allegorical narrative is than what Tolkien said in his denials of his story being allegory.

Rather, I have sought to make connections with the resources of his faith out of which he drew to compose a narrative that was consonant with his faith but was not a designed allegory for its elements. He explicitly confirmed that his story was shaped by the former, and he explicitly denied that his story was properly characterized as the latter.

With these qualifications and this part of the framework established, we now must make a more precise inquiry into how Tolkien's faith shaped his fiction. That task will involve looking at the theology that is at the foundation of his fiction. That is, we must examine his theology of sub-creation.

CHAPTER TWO

Tolkien's Theology of Sub-creation as a Fictional Foundation

Human beings desire to make something. It is a broad statement to be sure, but it is demonstrable from broad experience. Some people make art—whether visual, auditory, olfactory, tactile, gustatory or what have you. Even if it is not art, others construct something. People make technology to address a need or want. They make gardens. They make clothes. They make games. They construct speeches and arguments. They write in personal journals/diaries, on the Internet, in letters/emails, on the walls of bathrooms, in graffiti, in stories, and in the forms of essays/articles, books, and so on. When children play with or without toys, they build scenarios and perform actions according to the resources of their imaginations. This desire is also global in scope as virtually every culture has its own variation of the aforementioned forms of making and other forms which have not received mention. This innate desire is naturally a subject of interest in terms of the reason(s) why this desire exists and, much more broadly, why its exercise takes the forms that it takes.

Tolkien's contributions to such considerations came mostly in addresses concerning language, storytelling, story-making (especially in terms of mythology), and world-making. He articulated his thoughts in the framework—and often the explicit terminology—of sub-creation. Tolkien referred to his work of fantasy and myth-making as "sub-creation" because any human artistry is not true creation (as in creation from nothing), but it is "sub-creation" in the sense of being derivative of God's creation and imitative of the same kind of activity.

The depth and significance of his thinking on this matter made a rather significant impression on one of his friends. Apart from his own books, perhaps the most wide-ranging impact Tolkien has had is indirectly through the fact that he was instrumental in the conversion of C. S. Lewis to Christianity. When they first met in 1926 while both were professors at Oxford, Lewis was an atheist. They became close friends and conversed on all fronts of their wide-ranging passions, and their conversations involved questions of faith as well. Both would later be involved in an informal literary society at Oxford that called themselves The Inklings, a group both authors would share their writings with as they developed over the years. By 1929, Lewis was a theist, but he was still skeptical of Christianity. The fateful change in his worldview came as a result of a conversation in September of 1931 that Lewis had with Tolkien and fellow Inkling Hugo Dyson.

The details of that conversation have only been indirectly preserved by Tolkien in poetic form in his poem "Mythopoeia" and by Lewis in his letters written in 1931.[1] Humphrey Carpenter has attempted reconstructions of that conversation that many now reference, and it has even been dramatized in the documentary *Tolkien's "The Lord of the Rings": A Catholic Worldview* (the relevant clip of which is available on YouTube).[2] Tolkien and Lewis shared a love for myths, but for Lewis this was ultimately about their artistry, as he also saw the value of myths as limited due to their character as lies, albeit lies breathed through a tongue of silver. And by virtue of apparent similarities he perceived between the gospel and the myths, he thought the gospel was simply another myth that could be dismissed as a silver-tongued lie with the rest of them.

For now, we will focus on but two points of Tolkien's response. One, he argued that myth is invention, but it is invention about truth, attesting in however fragmentary a form to the truth, even as language itself is invention meant to communicate about the world. People look at trees, call them such, and think nothing of it. Such people act similarly toward stars. They dimly apprehend the function of the objects of the world

---

[1] C. S. Lewis, letters to Arthur Greeves on 22 September 1931 and 18 October 1931, *Family Letters 1905–1931, vol. 1* of *The Collected Letters of C. S. Lewis*, ed. Walter Hooper (San Francisco: HarperSanFrancisco, 2007), 970, 976–77.

[2] Humphrey Carpenter, *J. R. R. Tolkien: A Biography* (New York: Houghton Mifflin, 1977) 150–52; Carpenter, *The Inklings: C. S. Lewis, J. R. R. Tolkien, Charles Williams, and Their Friends* (Boston: Houghton Mifflin, 1979), 42–45. One can see Lewis take to heart what he heard from Tolkien, as well as Owen Barfield (which he presented in his book *Poetic Diction*), in his essay "Myth Became Fact." C. S. Lewis, *God in the Dock: Essays on Theology and Ethics*, ed. Walter Hooper (Grand Rapids: Eerdmans, 1970), 63–67.

and think of them as "just so". Yet these names are not inherent to the objects themselves; they were discovered and given. The givers of those names were people participating in invention based on their judgment of what name is fitting for such an object (hence the discovery aspect). For the example of the tree, Tolkien cites its origin in the determination of a fitting title from those people responding to a stirring,

> by deep monition movements that were kin
> to life and death of trees, of beasts, of stars:
> free captives undermining shadowy bars,
> digging the foreknown from experience
> and panning the vein of spirit out of sense.[3]

Similarly, stars were not so named, except in the context of myth-woven songs articulating their beauty. These names originated from language that is invention about objects. But the purpose of this language is to determine an appropriate title for the object in question around which subsequent language could properly accrete. It is invention, but not deceitful concoction.

Two, as Tolkien would say in more detail in his essay "On Fairy-Stories," myths ultimately point to truth, in however fragmentary a fashion, that is embodied in the gospel story. The gospel takes basic structures of myth, most importantly the sudden, joyous turn to a happy ending, and fulfills them. Most importantly, it does this on the plane of history, so that the Creator himself has given this story actuality. The gospel is the truth to which the myths had been imperfectly pointing.[4] As Lewis would say later, in the gospel, "myth" became "fact."

To see how Tolkien articulated his ideas on this matter, we will proceed through the relevant works in a (mostly) chronological order. First, we will dive into the details of his aforementioned poem "Mythopoeia." Second, we will analyze his most extensive theoretical reflection on the subject in his essay "On Fairy-Stories." Finally, we will note instances where he treats the matter in his letters, although there we will be focusing on more general concerns and leaving specific applications to his fiction for the commentary proper.

---

[3] J. R. R. Tolkien, *Tree and Leaf* (including *Mythopoeia*), 3rd ed. (London: HarperCollins, 1988), 86.

[4] It should be noted that this appears to be modern argument. It is similar to what G. K. Chesterton wrote in *The Everlasting Man* (New York: Dodd, Mead, and Company, 1925), 307–11. But if one looks at how the ancient Christians argued, since they grew up in a world suffused with the myths in question, they either (explicitly or implicitly) accentuate the differences/discontinuities between the myths and the gospel, or they use them as examples for why pagans should not object to a belief in resurrection. For more detail on this, see here: https://krharriman.substack.com/p/early-christian-responses-to-purported.

"Mythopoeia"[5] (1931)

As noted above, this poem about myth-making originates from a conversation between Tolkien, Hugo Dyson, and C. S. Lewis. Lewis had previously asserted that myths are lies and have no worth but the aesthetic value, since they are after all lies "breathed through silver." A thirty-nine-year-old Tolkien, who was somewhere in the process of writing *The Hobbit*, had by this point been intermittently composing his own mythology for approximately a decade-and-a-half, and he had of course studied myths for even longer, coming to the opposite conclusion of Lewis. His belief in the inherent truth of myths in contrast to Lewis justified his use of the respective titles Philomythus ("myth-lover" or "word-lover") and Misomythus ("myth-hater" or "word-hater").

Tolkien's opening stanzas, reflecting the conversation on the night of September 19, draw from two resources as an introduction into the larger discussion of myth: language (especially nomenclature) and the surrounding world. Most people, including presumably Misomythus himself, look at trees, call them such, and think nothing of it. Such people act similarly toward stars. They dimly apprehend the function of the objects of the world and think of them as "just so" (notice the essential repetitiveness of the terms, "petreous rocks," "arboreal trees," "tellurian earth," "stellar stars," and possibly, "homuncular men"). As stated above, these names are not inherent to the objects themselves, they were discovered and given. These names originated from language that is invention about an object. But the purpose of this language is to determine an appropriate title for the object in question around which subsequent language could properly accrete. It is invention, but it is not deceitful concoction. The implication that becomes explicit in the next section is that myth is invention of the same manner, a way of telling the truth about the world. Indeed, the origins of language and myth belong closely together so that language is ultimately about communicating stories and meanings.

<u>Sub-creation and Human Vocation</u>

Tolkien uses this background to unpack his foundational points about mythopoeia and thus of sub-creation, which makes its first explicit appearance in the following lines:

> The heart of man is not compound of lies,
> but draws some wisdom from the only Wise,

---

[5] This is a portmanteau of two Greek terms, which could have the sense of "myth-making," "story-making," or "word-making."

> and still recalls him. Though now long estranged,
> man is not wholly lost nor wholly changed.
> Disgraced he may be, yet is not dethroned,
> and keeps the rags of lordship once he owned,
> his world-dominion by creative act:
> not his to worship the great Artefact,
> man, sub-creator, the refracted light
> through whom is splintered from a single White
> to many hues, and endlessly combined
> in living shapes that move from mind to mind.
> Though all the crannies of the world we filled
> with elves and goblins, though we dared to build
> gods and their houses out of dark and light,
> and sow the seed of dragons, 'twas our right
> (used or misused). The right has not decayed.
> We make still by the law in which we're made.[6]

There are several points to note in this excerpt. First, this defense of the heart of man indicates that Tolkien believed the heart to be the fount of mythopoeia. Myths can only be inherent lies if the heart is utterly compound of lies. If it is not, myths contain some truth or at least some grasping for truth. This truth or grasping thereof comes from the fact that humanity still draws wisdom from the only Wise (a reference to the God Tolkien worshiped).

Second, this connection between wisdom from God and mythopoeia potentially involves two foundations. The first inspires more confidence in its veracity as it is a belief Tolkien clearly demonstrates here and elsewhere that there is some divine truth to be found in pagan sources. According to this tradition, God revealed such truth to the pagans via general revelation (as opposed to special revelation like the direct encounters with God or the incarnation of the Son recorded in Scripture) in order to provide preparation for the gospel (or *praeparatio evangelica*), since God has not left himself without a witness to all nations (Acts 14:15–17; cf. 17:22–29; Rom 1:18–20). One can also find examples of this perspective in predecessors like Justin Martyr (*1 Apol.* 20–23; 44; 46; 59–60; *2 Apol.* 8; 10; 13), his disciple Tatian (*Or. Graec.* 21), Clement of Alexandria (*Strom.* 1.4–5, 13, 19–20), Eusebius of Caesarea (*Praeparatio evangelica/Preparation for the Gospel*), Basil the Great (*Address to Young Men*) Augustine of Hippo

---

[6] Tolkien, *Tree and Leaf*, 87.

(*Civ.* 8.1; *Doctr. chr.* 2.25), some medieval scribes who preserved the written legacy of pagan mythology and pagan philosophy, the *Beowulf*-poet, and many others.[7]

The second possible foundation is not as simple to demonstrate, but it does have some plausibility. That is, the link he makes between wisdom and sub-creation is a derivation of the link between wisdom and God's action of creation, hence the reference to God the Creator as "the only Wise." There is biblical precedent for such a belief in Ps 104:24 in the context of the psalm's celebration of God's creative work and in Prov 8:22–31 there is a personified image of Wisdom at work in creation (also see Prov 3:19). In Catholic Bibles, the Apocrypha is also included, featuring books such as Ecclesiasticus/Sirach and Wisdom of Solomon. These books further developed wisdom theology and connected the figure of Wisdom, among other divine works, with the creation and sustaining of the world (Sir 1:9–10; Wis 1:7; 7:22, 24, 27; 8:1, 5–6; 9:2, 9). (Also, Tolkien may not have known this much, but biblical scholars have often noted the Wisdom Christology of the New Testament identifying Jesus with Wisdom, as in John 1:1–18; Col 1:15–20; Heb 1:1–4.)[8] It is not possible to know for certain if Tolkien had such a theological background for the link between wisdom and creation in mind, especially since he never wrote about it. However, even if it was not part of Tolkien's thought, this background does provide theological depth to his beliefs via sources he would have accepted.[9]

Third, Tolkien's lens for understanding sub-creation and how humanity is capable of it is the divine-human relationship. Humans draw on the resources provided by God, whether realizing it or not. In the act of mythopoeia, humans recall God's creative activity by imitation. This stream of thought has an identifiable source in the Bible's picture of humans as the image-bearers of God who thus bear the capacity to represent God. One of the most basic ways of representing God is imitation of one of the most

---

[7] On the *Beowulf*-poet, see J. R. R. Tolkien, "Beowulf: The Monsters and the Critics," in *The Monsters and the Critics*, ed. Christopher Tolkien (London: HarperCollins, 2006), 19–24, 26. For how this belief functions in *LOTR*, see Tom A. Shippey, *J. R. R. Tolkien: Author of the Century* (New York: Houghton Mifflin, 2000), 174–87.

[8] I have addressed such links at various points on my Substack at the following links: https://krharriman.substack.com/p/appraising-the-case-for-wisdom-christology;   https://krharriman.substack.com/p/christology-and-eschatology-in-colossians;   https://krharriman.substack.com/p/a-mini-commentary-on-hebrews-part.

[9] Also note the wisdom theology, Christology, and pneumatology in Justin Martyr, *Dial.*, 126.1; Irenaeus, *Haer.*, 2.30.10; 3.24.2; 4.7.3; 4.20; 5.18; Origen, *Comm. John* 1.109–11, 289; Eusebius of Caesarea, *Hist. eccl.* 1.2.2–3; Cosmas of Maiuma, *Kanon for the Fifth Day of Great Week, Ninth Ode* ; Prudentius, *Hymns for Every Day* 11, *a Hymn for Christmas Day*; Athanasius, *Inc.* 16; 19; 31—32; 46; 48; Augustine, *Tract. Ev. John* 1.16–17; Augustine, *Doctr. chr.* 1.12.

basic modes in biblical theology of understanding God's identity: as Creator. In fact, in the opening chapter of Genesis what the audience first learns about this God is primarily that he is the sovereign Creator, that sovereignty and creatorship go hand in hand. Sovereignty is the explicit charge to humans as image-bearers, to reflect the divine rule into creation. Just as humans derive their sovereignty from God—and thus could be considered "sub-sovereign"—the implication would be that humans derive something of God's creativity, since it is essential to God's unique sovereignty, which he bequeaths in some measure to humanity. Because sub-creation, especially expressed in mythopoeia, is so basic to the capacities of humans as image-bearing creatures, it was not lost in the estrangement from God. Sin could corrupt but not dislodge this sub-creative capacity that is tied into the human identity of being bearers of the image and likeness of God. Hence, humans keep the rags of their lordship.

Of course, one could justly ask how this connection between the human purpose of being an image-bearer of God, the exercise of sovereignty, and sub-creation via mythopoeia works concretely. It seems fairly clear how it works in the process of world-making in the creation of such stories as the sub-creator becomes the originator, preserver, governor, and provider for that world (i.e., as God does for what Tolkien later calls the Primary World, according to the Bible). Perhaps most importantly, at least from a biblical perspective, mythopoeia and the consequent world-making entail the activity of assigning roles and functions for what populates that world.[10] This teleological assignment represents the crucial link between creativity and sovereignty so that the latter is contained within the former. Whatever innovation there may be, the sub-creator draws on elements from the world in which he/she lives and thus provides a story which makes some impact upon how one approaches those elements in the Primary World. Since myths are often metaphysical and explanatory in character, they provide the audience with tools for encountering the world according to the myth and the shape of that myth affects the shape of the tools. In Tolkien's view, myth is invention about truth and so its formation provides ways of grasping the truth of the world and figuring out how to live in it through understanding how other beings and objects function within the world. This narrative-produced wisdom enables humans to exercise the creativity and sovereignty appropriate to their position in creation.

Fourth, the reader can glimpse here a theme which will become more prominent in Tolkien's later works concerning the place of sub-creation in the post-Fall world.

---

[10] John H. Walton, *Genesis*, NIV Application Commentary (Grand Rapids: Zondervan, 2001), 71–72.

Although the capacity of sub-creation was a divine grant, it has of course been corrupted in this present time into idolatry. Humans have improperly worshiped the great Artefact rather than the true Artificer. Instead of using this capacity to the purpose of our existence as beings created in the image of God, it has been used to fill the world with gods sub-created after our own image and in whose images are found further corruption. It has become a divine right used to devilish purposes.

Yet, despite all of these problems created by the corruption of the right, the right itself still has good and important functions in this post-Fall world. The law by which we make and the law by which we were made remains and in that law humans still find the potential to be refractions of the original light. As such, sub-creation could be understood as a means of prevenient grace held out to all, in the sense that it is a gift of divine action that precedes human response. In light of Tolkien's Catholic theology, one might even suggest that sub-creation is near-sacramental. This underlying law of creation makes sub-creation a bearer of divine grace and thus a mode of transferring it. It is a sign pointing back to the law by which we were made, and it thus participates in that grace it signifies. Although its usage can be corrupted, sub-creation—as the name itself indicates—points back in some way or another to creation (and the vocation for humans instituted therein since sub-creation was to be an expression of derivative lordship/stewardship and being image-bearers). Furthermore, the reference to human sub-creators functioning as refracted light underscores one of Tolkien's ultimate points about myth in his conversation with Lewis. For all of its faults and the corruptions caused by the Fall, myth exists to tell truth, to refract the light from the original source of all truth in creative ways.

Fifth, the last half or so of the excerpt indicates that sub-creation is to be an endless combination of refracted colors, an explorative use of the right. While sub-creation is an act that—to varying extents in its character rather than its content—imitates God's creative action, it also involves exploring possibilities that are not actualized in the Primary World. Sometimes, those possibilities are things that could still be actualized—and perhaps in so doing one finds most clearly what it means to refract the original divine light most powerfully—and sometimes they are simply alternatives to the Primary World that can still have impacts on our perspective of the Primary World. It is in the nature of creativity, the sub-creative gift from God, to explore counterfactuals and possibilities as well as the previously unconsidered (or under-considered) aspects of creation. Of course, as will become even clearer later and as is hinted by the above focus on the truthfulness of myth, sub-creation is not free simply to lie and to deny the reality of the fundamental characteristics of the Primary World. All sub-creations and sub-creators are accountable to the Primary Creation and the Creator.[11] Properly, sub-creation is an exploration through the divinely granted right of our own imperfect reflections of God's infinite creative capacity, of things he could have done/made.

At this point, it is worth considering the bases Tolkien had for making such statements about sub-creation and storytelling. Tolkien was a philologist who was a true *Philomythus* as he believed in the power of language because it derived from the power of God. God created the world by word, as both Gen 1 and John 1 convey in their own ways.[12] While language cannot create *ex nihilo*—since that power belongs to God alone—it can, especially through sub-creational mythopoeia (both in the telling and in the receiving), form objects, peoples, and worlds in which they make the sense that they do. For Tolkien, myths—particularly the true myth of the Gospel—fulfill this highest function of language and, insofar as they convey truth creatively, they bring humans closer to living out the function for which God created them: to be image-bearers of the Creator. The first person who took on a sub-creative role in exercising some measure of creative sovereignty in assigning names and function—and as Tolkien himself already indicates, assigning names is a key work of mythopoesis and sub-creation—is *ha'adam* in Gen 2:19–20, who gives names to the animals, participating in God's own creative sovereign act of naming the creation.

The Transcendent Source of Mythopoeia

To return to the course of "Mythopoeia," Tolkien acknowledges another aspect of Misomythus's argument that myths are but beautiful lies. That is, myths often consist of vain dreams of wish fulfillment. They seem like a coping strategy for overlooking the pain caused by the evil of the world. After all, do not many people speak of fantasy, science fiction, or many kinds of movies in and outside of these genres as, "escapes from reality"? The evil that runs through reality disrupts the world, disorients us, destroys what we love, and our deepest wishes and the dreams we hold most dearly strike the wall of evil like a man hoping to push over a skyscraper with a running start. Faced with such obstacles, it can seem that myths and fairy-stories are our opportunities to see wishes come true, because we never see them become so in reality. But therein lies a question: where did such wishes and dreams come from? Could it be that they are

---

[11] On this, see Trevor Hart, "Tolkien, Creation, and Creativity," in *Tree of Tales: Tolkien, Literature, and Theology*, ed. Trevor Hart and Ivan Khovacs (Waco, TX: Baylor University Press, 2007), 43.

[12] On the frequent reading of John 1:1–14 in Catholic liturgy from *The Roman Missal* in Tolkien's time, see Ordway, *Tolkien's Faith*, 287–88, 386.

such brute facts about humans because they are of a similar character as the ultimate reality, the truth concerning which evil attempts to deceive? Can it be that they are actually signposts to the truths of myths, the means by which myths communicate truths, and the modes in which—and only in which—people learn the truths through participation in the story? Tolkien has already hinted at such conclusions with what has preceded in this poem, and they receive more extensive articulation elsewhere as well.

While the sub-creation of myth-making should not deny evil, it should defy it through proclaiming the truths of these dreams and the ways they point to the truth beyond the empirical. In these transcendent truth-telling stories, humans can, "build / their little arks,"[13] to provide some measure of deliverance from the oppression of evil, although full deliverance can come only from the true myth. But these arks can navigate toward, "a rumour of a harbour guessed by faith."[14] In a double allusion, Tolkien insists that the makers of legends do not necessarily call for a flight to lotus-isles or the neglect of life to gain a kiss from Circe. Rather, they have looked in the face of Death, "and yet they would not in despair retreat, / but oft to victory have turned the lyre / and kindled hearts with legendary fire, / illuminating Now and dark Hath-been / with light of suns as yet by no man seen."[15] As such, the sub-creator can, in some way like the Creator, be a revealer by sharing the light one has seen with others. And in revelation of the past and present, the sub-creator can, again like the Creator, provide a source of empowerment by which the participant of the myth can derive power from the paean and participate in the victory.

As Philomythus, Tolkien declares that he would rather share the company of such people in the work of sub-creation, whether minstrels, mariners, or those who would be called "fools," than the contemporaries who insist that they are the educated ones, the grown-up ones, the enlightened ones, the progressive ones. In such a world of "progress" there is given no place for the sub-creator as myth-maker. Precisely because the path—indeed, myth—of so-called "progress" is a deceptive one, it actually calls for humans—who have the universal call to be image-bearers, particularly through sub-creation—to lay down their divine rights, the gracious birthright bestowed on all image-bearers to be able to imitate their Creator in sub-creative action, and then to direct what vestiges of that capacity remain to the reductive ends of "progress" or

---

[13] Tolkien, *Tree and Leaf*, 88.

[14] Ibid.

[15] Ibid., 88–89.

"modernity" (or now, "postmodernity"). Such is the essence of selling a birthright for a mess of pottage.

Sub-Creation and Fulfillment in the Eschaton

For whoever follows the same road that Philomythus walks, there is an eschatological expectation that Tolkien expresses in the closing lines of the poem:

> In Paradise perchance the eye may stray
> from gazing upon everlasting Day
> to see the day-illumined, and renew
> from mirrored truth the likeness of the True.
> Then looking on the Blessed Land 'twill see
> that all is as it is, and yet made free:
> Salvation changes not, nor yet destroys,
> garden not gardener, children not their toys.
> Evil it will not see, for evil lies
> not in God's picture but in crooked eyes,
> not in the source but in the tuneless voice.
> In Paradise they look no more awry;
> and though they make anew, they make no lie.
> Be sure they still will make, not being dead,
>
> and poets shall have flames upon their head,
> and harps whereon their faultless fingers fall:
> there each shall choose for ever from the All.[16]

Several points are worth noting here, not least because they appear later in Tolkien's other expositions. First, in a seemingly retrospective sense, Tolkien claims that even in this eschatological scene one will find the myths and sub-creations of humanity to be revelatory. At least, it will be true of them insofar as they reflect the likeness of the actual character of Truth. Each are fragments of the true myth reflecting by angled vision what one glimpses in the whole. But the Truth does not dispose of all the fragments and reflections as no longer being of use (as is not the case in the present time either given the innumerable imperfections in our knowledge). Instead, it takes them up and makes them more fully what they are, renewing them as likenesses of the Truth to which they had been pointing all along. How this will happen remains a mystery after the fashion of the mystery of the resurrection. How will the body be identifiably

---

[16] Ibid., 90.

the person raised, yet also different in its transformed physicality and having the qualities of kingdom life? It is unclear how to articulate it, but Jesus has already carved out the path for how it will be (e.g., 1 John 3:2).

Second, this point leads into an observation of the divine hallowing of sub-creation. God upholds the sanctity of his human creation and of their sub-creations by making them part of his Primary one. Indeed, this hallowing is a way of making them complete through participation in what fulfills them, namely the Word through whom all things came into being. It is God's affirmation through sanctification that he created humans to bear his image in subordinate creation. Reciprocally, humans reflect their identity as image-bearers who worship (and facilitate the worship) of the Creator. Insofar as sub-creation is an outworking of this image-bearing identity, it becomes an act of worship dedicated to the Creator as an acknowledgment of his will. Tolkien's description of the poets having flames upon their heads is particularly noteworthy because of how it is derived from the Holy Spirit descending in what looked like tongues of fire on the apostles in Acts 2.

Third, the salvation brought by the new creation fulfills these sub-creational stories and thereby redeems them. Notice the interesting phrasing: "Salvation changes not, nor yet destroys." That sounds reminiscent of Aquinas's dictum of grace not destroying nature but perfecting/completing it. The combination of redemption and fulfillment that characterizes the new creation extends also to the capacity of sub-creation as well. In the present world, sub-creation is fraught with imperfections and even lies. But with the redemption of the capacity in which sub-creation finds its root, there is no more place for lies in sub-creation and myth-making, and the products of the image-bearers become as whole as the image-bearers themselves are made to be in the new creation. In this vision, the sub-creators are still at work in the new creation. They still make because they still live, and they express the life within them—the everlasting divine life that they partake of—through sub-creation. There is a sense here that myth-making is intrinsic to human life so that as long as there is the latter there will be the former. When that life becomes eternal upon the fullness of its redemption (Rom 8:18–23), so too will its sub-creational products that will undergo some similar process of redemption and perfection. These works will become more glorious because the makers will become more glorious, as Tolkien describes them as experiencing the fires of inspiration and empowerment (again, in imagery reminiscent of Pentecost) and as being able to play perfectly the instruments that accompany their lays. Like in Tolkien's own *Ainulindalë* in *The Silmarillion* (and its anticipation of the Last Song that will be greater still), each person is called to contribute to the music of the new creation. New creation is the renewal of creation and the full vivification of it to make it more fully itself. Thus, it only makes sense that this vivification would include the continuation and consummation of the sub-creation of world-making from the beings who are divine image-bearers and that they would fulfill the participatory vocation that is at the foundation of their identity.

Fourth, this participatory vocation emerges in the protean forms of participation in creation. Participatory creation is in some sense parallel to participatory grace and participatory victory. That is, that humans as sub-creators, when redeemed, will actually be called to participate in the action of creation, namely the new creation. They will, in fact, take part in fulfilling the beliefs, thoughts, dreams, and hopes present in their sub-creations. That work will become hallowed in a way unlike any we know now as it will receive the support of God's actual creative power. Texts such as 1 Cor 3:10–15; 15:42–49, and 58 indicate that the works of the present creation carry over in some mysterious and amplified way to the new creation,[17] but there is a more basic and wide-ranging truth that points to what Tolkien claims here. Is the notion that the works of the present creation—at least the ones that glorify God in their goodness—have some mysterious place in the new creation not part of the underlying logic of resurrection and final judgment? The works of the present have some role in the formation of the heirs of the new creation, and the resurrection body is the fitting climax for a life that bears the fruit of the kingdom by the presence and power of the Spirit. As such, they have some role in the final judgment as they stand in testimony to what the Spirit has done in the lives of believers. They stand as evidence and demonstration of the vindication of the justified. The works that have the character of participating in and anticipating the kingdom of God are vindicated in that God confirms that they are of that same character and thus belong in the everlasting divine kingdom. But they do not simply disappear afterwards; they become part of the renewed creation as creation itself undergoes a transformation similar to what happens to the righteous (whether resurrected or still living) as it remains God's good creation, has all evil removed from it, and becomes transformed to be eternal and a proper sacred space in which God is all in all. All of these things are the works of God, and God calls for humans to participate in them through bearing his image, including in how they function as sub-creators. Humans remain creatures, not creators in the sense that God is Creator. They remain

---

[17] See my dissertation, K. R. Harriman "Why Should God Raise the Dead? Worldview Foundations and Functions of Resurrection Belief in Dan 12, 1 Cor 15, and Q Al-Qiyamah 75" (PhD diss., Asbury Theological Seminary, 2022). Available on my website at: https://krharriman.substack.com/p/why-should-god-raise-the-dead.

subordinate and subservient to God; they are not creative sovereigns in the sense that the Creator God is Lord of all. But they are participants when they follow the creative purpose of God, and this function finds its fulfillment in the consummation of creation. These observations serve as a fitting climax to Tolkien's grand poem about a magnificent action and capacity that comes from the Creator.

"On Fairy-Stories"

Of all Tolkien's expressions of his theology of sub-creation, none is more extensive than this famous essay. This essay almost has the function of an apologia in that it is both a defense and an explanation of fairy-stories. Tolkien explains that much of the value and virtue of fairy-stories stems from the fact that they are the stories that most vividly exemplify the quality and act of sub-creation. It is this kind of story that uses words most effectively to create (or rather, sub-create) a world with Secondary Reality.

Language and Sub-creation

It is in the use of words as such that sub-creators come closest to their Creator who creates through Word. The root aspect of fairy-stories is the use of adjectives:

> But how powerful, how stimulating to the very faculty that produced it, was the invention of the adjective: no spell or incantation in Faërie is more potent. And that is not surprising: such incantations might indeed be said to be only another view of adjectives, a part of speech in a mythical grammar. The mind that thought of *light, heavy, grey, yellow, still, swift*, also conceived of magic that would make heavy things light and able to fly, turn grey lead into yellow gold, and the still rock into a swift water. If it could do the one, it could do the other; it inevitably did both. When we can take green from grass, blue from heaven, and red from blood, we have already an enchanter's power—upon one plane; and the desire to wield that power in the world external to our minds awakes.[19]

Indeed, it is fairy-story that takes the adjective to its fullest significance with its ability to combine such words vividly in a Secondary World through which one can look at the Primary World to make more sense of it and come to a greater love of it. In this vision, one might say that myths and adjectives, which make up their grammar, are ultimately indicators of transcendence. Adjectives are more evocative than the

---

[19] Tolkien, "On Fairy-Stories," 122 (emphases original).

empirical realities they may describe. In the act of naming something about reality, the describer takes on a role approximating the human action in Gen 2:19–20 and thereby the derivative sovereignty that comes with such naming and description of things in the world. And it is saying something more than describing a scientifically observable phenomenon. To say that grass is green, for example, is not simply an observation that one can describe in the language of biological taxonomy, chemical composition, photosynthesis, or the way light reflects off this plant that corresponds to a certain wavelength in the visible light spectrum. Nothing about such properties and processes logically leads to using the words "green" or "grass," but humans gave such names long before the scientific language developed in order to designate the characters of the objects so that the adjectival process is, from one perspective, an act of making and, from another perspective, an act of discovery. Mythopoeia, as the quintessence of sub-creation, consists of extending this adjectival logic to the level of story and world-setting.

Sub-creation can, of course, be subject to corruption and abuse of its elements—as the text after this excerpt shows—but it is properly an action that arises from love of the Primary World, the respect and love for creation because of who its Creator is. Tolkien's own sub-creation has its foundational reality in language, whether it is Eru Ilúvatar speaking the Ainur into existence, the Ainur participating in the music of Eru Ilúvatar with their own words from him, or Tolkien developing the story of the Third Age of Middle-earth from combining his earlier mythology with the question of what kind of world would exist in which the word "hobbit" makes the sense that it does. In a similar way, sub-creators can take the adjectival language and other parts of speech that fit in the Primary World (such as "green" and "grass") and make a Secondary World that explores their depth and richness more vividly. In such ways, they imitate the manner of God's creative action in how he forms, sustains, and designates functions/purposes for the objects and beings of his creation through the speech of his Word and Spirit. Once more, fairy-stories do not properly provide a flight from reality per se, but rather a passage to deeper engagement with the world through the enchantment of language. They can do so because they are naturally explorative, searching out the possibilities of creation and discovering new dimensions to reality by presenting them to us as alien things.

His first use of the term "sub-creator" here appears in the context of describing what Faërie is as a product of the imagination, a fantasy that makes new things. In brief, "An essential power of Faërie is thus the power of making immediately effective by the will the visions of 'fantasy.'"[20] The combination of imagination, will, and word (or as Tolkien says earlier, mind, tongue, and tale) gives rise to another world and, as such, provides an analogy to God's own creative activity. Of course, it is only an analogy because humans cannot be true creators like their own Creator and because humans suffer the effects of their fallenness (and thus have some further distance from fulfilling the identity of being image-bearers). Of course, one such effect—with multiple forms—of that fallenness on sub-creation in terms of mythology is that it often becomes a servant to the cause of idolatry.

In Tolkien's own sub-creation, the Marring of Arda and the Fall in general stems—in near-Miltonian fashion—from the prideful idolatry of Melkor, the mightiest of the Ainur. He too seeks to be Creator and to be worshiped as such. To this end, he seeks to claim Eru Ilúvatar's Flame Imperishable, to disrupt the *Ainulindalë* in each of its three themes (and thereby gaining some followers who conform to his cacophony, most notably the one later known as Sauron), to tear down whatever his fellow Valar build up, to rule over all of the world, and to make his own creatures by corrupting existing ones (most famously: the Orcs). Unlike the fourteen Valar and their servant Maiar who accept their places as subordinates and sub-creators, Melkor desires more and thus corrupts the gift of sub-creation that Ilúvatar gave him in order to rebel and to attempt usurpation. Such is the danger humans face in using the gift of sub-creation for reasons other than the love and respect of the creation and the Creator. And because of how corruptive sin has been for humans, no one has purely unmixed motives, and this danger of following through on the course of the Fall, including with the sub-creative capacity, is a potential danger for all.

Even so, mythology and fairy-story (Tolkien sees both as being on the same ground and born from the same stock) as sub-creation have provided revelatory glimpses of something higher; namely the sense of divinity and the One (though often not limited to one in historical expression) who is worthy of worship. Mythology and religion have a long history of close connection, both being at the service of each other. In Tolkien's view, such is as it should be—even if the exact actual character of that relationship has been problematic and idolatrous—because of the function of sub-creation in exercising the identity of being an image-bearer of God, the proper function of which is worship directed toward God. Fairy-story and mythology share this connection with religion because, while remaining critical of the human realm that they encounter, they illustrate the world with its transcendent dimension, which Tolkien considers the three faces of

---

[20] Ibid.

fairy-stories: the mystical towards the supernatural, the magical towards nature (what Tolkien calls the essential face), and the mirror of scorn and pity towards humanity.[21]

Because of this sense of transcendence, myth shares in another sphere alongside religion: history. In Tolkien's words, referencing the Anglo-Saxon and Norse myth of Ingeld and Freawaru, "History often resembles 'Myth,' because they are both ultimately of the same stuff. If indeed Ingeld and Freawaru never lived, or at least never loved, then it is ultimately from nameless man and woman that they get their tale, or rather into whose tale they have entered."[22] One of the ways of expressing the transcendent dimension of history that mythology has often taken is to analogize the lives of the gods with human lives, the divine history with human history, with proper amplifications, of course. Fundamental similarities between the stories of history and the stories of mythology are thus scarcely surprising. This connection and the transcendent dimension that mythology reveals gives mythology and fairy-story the "magical" power of enchantment. As Tolkien notes, "Small wonder that *spell* means both a story told, and a formula of power over living men."[23] In the true myth of the gospel (a word that derives from the Old English *godspell* [or *godspel*] or "good story"), this true transcendent power comes to its most powerful bearing on history while myth and history come together more deeply than they ever have before with the Incarnation of the Word who is the creative Lord of history.

<u>Sub-creation and Literary Belief</u>

The comportment of sub-creation with the Primary Reality of creation, in terms of both internal integrity (or inner consistency) and external correspondence, is essential to making sub-creation of proper quality as subordinate creation. In one of Tolkien's most defining passages, he explains the importance of the principle of sub-creation as being reflective of reality rather than a mere flight from it:

> Children are capable, of course, of literary belief, when the story-maker's art is good enough to produce it. That state of mind has been called 'willing suspension of disbelief.' But this does not seem to me a good description of what happens. What really happens is that the story-maker proves a successful 'sub-creator.' He makes a Secondary World which your mind can enter. Inside it, what he relates is 'true': it accords with the laws of that world. You therefore

---

[21] Ibid., 125.

[22] Ibid., 127.

[23] Ibid., 128 (emphasis original).

believe it, while you are, as it were, inside. The moment disbelief arises, the spell is broken; the magic, or rather art, has failed. You are then out in the Primary World again, looking at the little abortive Secondary World from outside. If you are obliged, by kindliness or circumstance, to stay, then disbelief must be suspended (or stifled), otherwise listening and looking would become intolerable. But this suspension of disbelief is a substitute for the genuine thing, a subterfuge we use when condescending to games or make-believe, or when trying (more or less willingly) to find what virtue we can in the work of an art that has for us failed.[24]

Ever since Samuel Taylor Coleridge coined the phrase "suspension of disbelief" in the early nineteenth century, it has entered popular parlance for audience approaches to fictional stories, especially ones of speculative fiction. But here Tolkien insists that this mindset is precisely backwards. Suspension of disbelief is, as he sees it, an acknowledgment of the failure of the sub-creative project for the audience. The audience thus resorts to a condescending "humoring" of the storyteller when, in fact, he/she has already lost them. It shows that the enchantment, the spell (with both senses that Tolkien has referenced) that attempts to give a Secondary World Secondary Reality, has failed. The experience of the story in this sub-creation becomes akin to watching a bad movie and trying to find something worthwhile (whether unintentional humor or actually good elements) to pass the time.

But the phrase *is* an attempt to capture a true effect of sub-creational enchantment. It seems intended to say that the audience is willing to overlook the facts that the story is not happening or did not happen, that it is not a definite foretelling of the future (when such a setting is applicable), or that there are elements of implausibility in it—according to the putative rules of reality—in order to enjoy an otherwise good story. Tolkien insists that the effect of fairy-stories in particular, as the quintessence of sub-creation, is to convince recipients of the plausibility of the story and the Secondary World in which it occurs because, in some way, that world is reflective of the Primary World. As much as its enchantment consists of its discontinuity with the world, it also comes from its continuity with it. A good Secondary World has grasped some profound and deep truth that people can recognize on reflection in the Primary World. Both of these broad dimensions of enchantment—along with the more particular features such as the unique features of the world, a sense of mythology within the mythology (i.e., a deep history), engaging characterization, vivid environments, an enthralling plot, and so on—help the mind enter this Secondary World and stay there for a while with the

---

[24] Ibid., 132 (emphasis original).

cornucopia for the senses and the imagination it offers. The spell (the formula of power) works through the power of the spell (the story told). That power comes from the greater reality featured and invoked in the process. The sub-creation is a larger world with a particular instantiation of a story that allows the audience a vision and journey into that world.

As I have sought to show in the equivalent of this chapter in my commentary on *The Hobbit*, and as we will see in this extended exploration, "the inner consistency of reality" is a particularly crucial concept of Tolkien's theology of sub-creation. Naturally, myth and fantasy do not have what Tolkien called "Primary Reality" because they are not actualized in the Primary World, which is to say the real/actual world. But the best works of sub-creation, the ones that are best imitative of God's creative work, make a Secondary World that has a convincing Secondary Reality. That is, it has a plausibility insofar as it reflects truths from the Primary World in this Secondary World setting with appropriate Secondary World modes.

Of course, the sub-creative project relies upon engaging the power of the faculty of imagination on the part of both the sub-creator and the audience. He describes this faculty in a traditional way as what makes the human mind, "capable of forming mental images of things not actually present."[25] Against some of his contemporaries, he refused the tendency to describe imagination as that which actually gives the inner consistency of reality to ideal creations. In his view, such is to confuse the beginning for the end. Imagination is the womb and birthplace of what could mature into sub-creation. He calls the link between the two—birth and maturation—art. For Tolkien's purposes, defining imagination in this way and making proper linguistic distinctions are essential to giving the proper respect to Fantasy and its laudable functions and purposes (contra its critics). While the contemporary definition of his interlocutors attempted to "salvage" imagination by exalting it above something so childish and preposterous as Fantasy, it does so by spurious means. If imagination forms mental images of things not present (by inspired mental action on the part of the author/artist/speaker/etc. or by excited mental action on the part of the audience), then it is the *sine qua non* of Fantasy, and Fantasy is the most nearly pure, most direct expression of that celebrated faculty through art, and therefore its potentially most potent exhibition (its potency being that of a sub-creative spell, as Tolkien has described heretofore). It is from imagination that Fantasy derives its alluring and wondrous strangeness, the character of discontinuity with the Primary World. Sub-creative Fantasy thus has the quality of being explorative

---

[25] Ibid., 138.

of this strangeness through the use of language. As befits Fantasy, the exploration resembles both a journey in a strange land and the practice by which one with power learns how to use it (e.g., in a spell).

Although Tolkien does not expound on the linguistic media of imagination, it is possible to discern at least a few of them from what this analysis has already noted from "Mythopoeia" and earlier in this essay. Some of the basic building blocks are nouns. Whatever else the sub-creator adds, nouns are the subjects and objects of action (verbs) and description (adjectives and adverbs), of thought and relation. They are the raw materials for the imagination of the sub-creator to use in forming and shaping the sub-creation and the imagistic impressions it can leave on the minds of the audience. They are the features of the world that will give it plausibility or implausibility and will provide all of the resultant characteristics that emerge from the choices of the sub-creator's will. Such choices include the selection of appropriate verbs befitting particular nominal subjects and nominal objects.

Adjectives and adverbs provide vividness, vigor, vitality, virtue, vice, variety, and various other qualities to the sub-creative work. If nouns are the raw materials that one could think of as being like dust in the hands of the Creator, then adjectives and adverbs are the breath breathed into the formed dust in order to give it life. They enliven and color the nouns (as well as the verbs describing their actions), thereby providing the spirit and character of the characters of the Secondary World. They are also what evoke images, inculcate the audience with interest in the sub-creation, and invite them to inhabit it for a while. Adjectives and adverbs have a function of a summons to explore.

Similarly, metaphors are the vigor of imagination. They are particularly effective at exciting the imagination and exploring the richness of imaginative treasures in the sub-creation. They function as such precisely because they are essential to imagination as imagination is essential to fantasy. After all, imagination is seeing/visualizing "as if" something is present, and metaphors are expressions and descriptions of things "as if" they are like other things. In this invigoration of the imagination, metaphors help guide one in exploring the continuity and discontinuity they perceive in the Secondary World, which Fantasy is especially capable of sub-creating.

Finally, the use of certain words to incite evocations through connotation/sense serves as a testimony to the power of the spell of language. Words have effects that go beyond their straightforward definitions that reflect typical usage. Connotations add depth to the spell of sub-creation in terms of storytelling and in terms of the formula of power as it aids the vividness of the story and invokes the multifarious and reverberating powers of particular words in order to introduce multitudinous effects into the sub-creation through the creative/sub-creative principles of words. Connotations are devices of reverberation, creating effects that emerge from an epicenter of a word and influence the setting of that word.

Revelation in Sub-creation and Its Challenges

But there was resistance to the "arresting strangeness"[26] in Tolkien's time (even as there is in the present time). As Tolkien says, "Many people dislike being 'arrested.' They dislike any meddling with the Primary World, or such small glimpses of it as are familiar to them. They, therefore, stupidly and even maliciously confound Fantasy with Dreaming, in which there is no Art; and with mental disorders, in which there is not even control: with delusion and hallucination."[27] In a footnote Tolkien qualifies his statement about dreams and art: "This is not true of all dreams. In some Fantasy seems to take a part. But this is exceptional. Fantasy is a rational, not an irrational, activity."[28] That which has power like Fantasy can be threatening, and there is danger in it (as Tolkien most vividly and succinctly portrayed, alongside the joys and wonders of Faërie, in "Smith of Wootton Major") and people have developed dismissive defenses against its power. The denigrators wrap their defenses in a veneer of rationality, yet the actual substance of their claims reveals the irrationality of them as they encounter a form of sub-creation but deny its power.

While Fantasy can be more truly sub-creative than other forms of art, the fact remains that it has an intrinsic deficit to overcome in the achievement of sub-creation, of that inner consistency of reality provided by giving a Secondary World Secondary Reality. This deficit comes from Fantasy's strangeness/discontinuity. The greater this strangeness, the more difficult it is for an inhabitant of the Primary World to provide it with that inner consistency that moves beyond superficial window dressing of the fanciful. Herein is an illustration of the essence of sub-creation as imitative of true (i.e., divine) creative action in not only sub-creating individual things, but also sub-creating a world with interrelationships, proper functions, and narrative logic that gives the individual things and features the context in which they make sense. The example Tolkien provides in this particular context is "the green sun":

> To make a Secondary World inside which the green sun will be credible, commanding Secondary Belief, will probably require labour and thought, and

---

[26] Ibid., 139.

[27] Ibid.

[28] Ibid.

will certainly demand a special skill, a kind of elvish craft. Few attempt such difficult tasks. But when they are attempted and in any degree accomplished then we have a rare achievement of Art: indeed narrative art, story-making in its primary and most potent mode.[29]

Paradoxically, then, Fantasy is the art form that provides the strongest inherent obstacles to the accomplishment of sub-creation, but, because it provides such obstacles to overcome, it is also the art form most capable of producing sub-creation in its fullness.

In the above quote, he identifies the prerequisite skill for accomplishing sub-creation as a kind of "elvish craft." But what is this elvish craft? After rejecting the names of Magic (being the operations of a Magician) and Art (being the process that can produce Secondary Belief, but which is not a sufficient condition of it), he settles on the name Enchantment. It is the sub-creative power that makes a Secondary World in which, by means of imagination exercised and incited through the spell of language, designer and spectator can enter and exercise Secondary Belief in that inner consistency of reality that Tolkien speaks of here. As such, it represents a will to art rather than a will to power, like Tolkien thinks of Magic. (Of course, the fact that there can be and is confusion between these wills is surely an effect of the Fall, in accordance with what was noted from "Mythopoeia"). Its power is something that the will to power can never attain even as the deceiver and destroyer can never be a true Creator, though desiring the worship as such. Sub-creation has a purity about it precisely because it stems from the vocation and capacity of image-bearing by which humans fulfill their creative purpose when they represent and imitate their Creator.[30] Sub-creation involves the imitation of the Creator's creative action in the Primary World.[31]

In response to people who question the legitimacy of Fantasy, he refers back to what he wrote several years prior in "Mythopoeia," which we need not reiterate in full here. Although Misomythus in that context may have been unusually appreciative of

---

[29] Ibid., 140.

[30] Ibid, 145.

[31] Tolkien's own mythology, particularly *The Silmarillion*, provides some examples of beings, generally Elves, who master this craft of Enchantment. Of course, the sub-creators *par excellence* are the Ainur, who each operate according to particular understandings of the *Ainulindalë*, the song which Eru Ilúvatar composed to form and shape the world he would bring into being, and the subsequent vision of history. In the way Lúthien sings the song of the travails of Elves and Men, she tells the story in such a way that she moves Mandos—ever stern and immovable—to pity and willingness to do a new thing for Lúthien and her lover Beren. Other descriptions can be cited from *LOTR*, but we will save commenting on those examples for later.

myths and fairy-stories for a modern person, he was typical of modern doubt and den-igration of these stories as legitimate stories that should be told and should demand the use of the sub-creative faculties. It is not only legitimate, but it also is a proper function of humanity, and even one that comes naturally. When it is done properly—contrary to popular criticism—it is actually rational and—as sub-creative activity—it brings about reflection of reality with an inner consistency that impresses itself upon the minds of spectators by means of Secondary Belief. Because Secondary Belief and the Secondary World are in some way derivative from Primary Belief and the Primary World (since the sub-creators are denizens of the Primary World), a stronger connection to reason is crucial to the formation of Secondary Belief, which is itself crucial to sub-creation.[32] The superstructure of Fantasy proper requires a substructure composed of reason, for, as Tolkien says, "If men really could not distinguish between frogs and men, fairy-stories about frog-kings would not have arisen."[33]

But *caveat emptor*, as Tolkien has noted elsewhere, including in "Mythopoeia," even Fantasy and its *telos* of sub-creation have not avoided the effects of the Fall. There is a kind of sanctity to it, just as humans are still beings made in the image of God. Thus, Tolkien can describe it as a good to be pursued. However, even as holy things can be corrupted and defiled, and even as that which is pure exists amidst a world of impurity, Fantasy does not remain untouched. It can go so far into the fantastic as to be world-denying, it can be poorly done (and thus poorly reflective of creativity/sub-creative capacity), and there could be other evil uses for it, such as deception and delusion (which are legitimate fears of some critics of Fantasy).

Yet, Tolkien is careful to note that a world of idolatry rather inevitably involves corruption of Fantasy. When the true God of the Primary World is denied, all else fol-lows. As such, Fantasy does have true risks for achieving evil ends, but it is mundane in that sense. Everything of the present world and time has suffered effects of the Fall. There is sense in recognizing the evils possibly associated with Fantasy, but there is no sense in singling it out even among literary/storytelling forms. Despite the risks, fantasy remains a good, a divinely granted right and gift. As with other corruptible goods and rights, in Tolkien's words, *abusus non tollit usum*.[34]

---

[32] Tolkien, "On Fairy-Stories," 144: "If men were ever in a state in which they did not want to know or could not perceive truth (facts or evidence), then Fantasy would languish until they were cured. If they ever get into that state (it would not seem at all impossible), Fantasy will perish, and become Morbid Delusion."

[33] Ibid.

[34] Ibid. Translation: "Misuse/abuse does not remove/exclude use."

As a matter of fact, Fantasy—by offering its fantastic perspective—indirectly un-veils the Primary World (due to being built with "materials" from the Primary World) and assists in the recovery of its truth by gaining some apparent distance. Fairy-stories do not properly provide a flight from reality per se, as in an avoidance of reality; rather, they supply a passage to deeper engagement with the world through the enchantment of language. As stated previously, they can do so because they are naturally explorative, searching out the possibilities or counterfactuals of creation and discovering new di-mensions to reality by presenting them to us as alien things. He describes the relation-ship of the sub-creator of fairy-stories (of which Fantasy is the core element) to the elements of the Primary World as being, "a good craftsman [who] loves his material, and has a knowledge and feeling for clay, stone and wood which only the art of making can give. By the forging of Gram cold iron was revealed; by the making of Pegasus horses were ennobled; in the Trees of the Sun and Moon root and stock, flower and fruit are manifested in glory."[35]

Because of the nature of craftsmanship that is Fantasy and sub-creation, the sub-creator also has a function akin to angels in many ancient apocalypses. These angels pulled back the veil between heaven and earth to show the transcendent dimensions of earthly features, events, and characters, as well as the characteristics of the heavenly realms. In Tolkien's view, when Fantasy is done right, sub-creators can similarly use Fantasy to reveal the true transcendent character of the Primary World by putting them in a seemingly strange and alien setting that is the matter of Fantasy. The story-maker (or "mythopoet") can perform this function because of a free relation of love with na-ture/creation over and against worldviews that promote having relations of corrupt power, whether as slaves locked in blinding bounds (as is the case in Tolkien's image here), or as would-be emperors attempting to bend and to dominate nature (the function Tolkien assigns to the Magician). And if—in reflection of the Creator—the sub-crea-tors' principles of making are words, they can reveal not only the character of the ref-erents, but of the words that bear symbolic relations to those referents.[36] Fantasy can accomplish this goal because it breaks the world free from the familiar, the triteness that comes from possessiveness:

> This triteness is really the penalty of 'appropriation': the things that are trite, or (in a bad sense) familiar, are the things that we have appropriated, legally or mentally. We say we know them. They have become like the things which once

---

[35] Ibid., 147.
[36] Ibid.

attracted us by their glitter, or their colour, or their shape, and we laid hands on them, and then locked them in our hoard, acquired them, and acquiring ceased to look at them.[37]

He borrows a word from G. K. Chesterton to describe this effect: *Mooreeffoc*, "the queerness of things that have become trite, when they are seen suddenly from a new angle."[38] Fantasy done right is, then, less about seeing the world "as it is," but about seeing the world as people are meant to see it, which can indeed have the potential for a redemptive liberation from a world imprisoned in fallenness (and thus it reflects the effect of the gospel, per Rom 8:18–27, though this is something we will need to return to later).

Sub-Creation, the Escapes of Fantasy, and Eucatastrophe

It is in such a context that Fantasy is properly escapist (and, as Tolkien describes the fitting concomitant, consolatory). Tolkien does not use this label with scorn like many of his contemporaries. Too often, more jaded or priggish critics have conflated escape with cowardly desertion and, intentionally or unintentionally, have become (or conspired with) the people who hate escapism more than anyone else: the jailers, "Why should a man be scorned if, finding himself in prison, he tries to get out and go home? Or if, when he cannot do so, he thinks and talks about other topics than jailers and prison-walls? The world outside has not become less real because the prisoner cannot see it."[39] As such, Fantasy can offer a true escape, not so much a flight *from* harsh reality as a flight *into* reality, the deeper reality that is above and beyond what Tolkien regarded as the scourges of modern life and its industrial/technological obsessions, as well as the more perpetual problems of the prison of transience (which technological advances have exacerbated to some extent even as they have provided some benefits), vicious cycles of sin and destruction that engulf the world (reinforcing its imprisonment), severance—even isolation—from the rest of creation, and, most of all, death. Fairy-stories have many ways of offering escape from some or all of these problems— such as the characteristic of talking animals to have some semblance of restorative reunion with other creatures—but one feature is more powerful and also more derided than all the others: the ending.

---

[37] Ibid., 146.

[38] Ibid.

[39] Ibid., 148.

It is in the ending that the fairy-story provides its greatest consolation and highest function. The "happy ending" is often regarded with scorn as dull, cliché, predictable, and unrealistic, but if the world is imprisoned with the aforementioned walls, bars, and chains, it is actually that which is most real, speaking redemptively to a world out of alignment with the will of God and therefore containing some measure of unreality. While tragedy often speaks to the world in its current state, fairy-stories have the opposite function, for which Tolkien coins the term *eucatastrophe*. He defines *eucatastrophe* as,

> The good catastrophe, the sudden joyous 'turn' (for there is no true end to any fairy-tale): this joy, which is one of the things which fairy-stories can produce supremely well, is not essentially 'escapist,' nor 'fugitive.' In its fairy-tale—or otherworld—setting, it is a sudden and miraculous grace: never to be counted on to recur. It does not deny the existence of *dyscatastrophe*, of sorrow and failure: the possibility of these is necessary to the joy of deliverance; it denies (in the face of much evidence if you will) universal final defeat and in so far is *evangelium*, giving a fleeting glimpse of Joy, Joy beyond the walls of the world, poignant as grief.[40]

This is a key quote for understanding Tolkien's theology of sub-creation because it describes an essential aspect of its *telos*, and there are at least five points worth noting before continuing to Tolkien's more extensive exposition on eucatastrophe. First, from the above analysis of "Mythopoeia," one should note that the terminology is different, but the points are fundamentally the same here as in Tolkien's response to Lewis's criticism of the wishful thinking of myths. There is, of course, deeper exposition here and below as this is an essay rather than a poem. It also seems that in the intervening years that Tolkien has finally devised a name for the highest function of fairy-stories—the highest form of sub-creation—and that he is in a better position to explore this function by using the word as a launching point.

Second, while Tolkien has defended the "escapist" label up to this point, so much as to rebrand it "fugitive" at certain points, he now thinks it better to leave it behind as describing the essence of eucatastrophe. Even in the setting of the fairy-story, the eucatastrophe is miraculous, not a typical feature of the sub-creative world as might be other features Tolkien would be more inclined to deem "escapist." Furthermore, it is more like a headlong flight into a deeper reality as it directly confronts dyscatastrophe and defeats it at the point of confrontation when the deeper reality found in deliverance

---

[40] Ibid, 153 (emphases original).

breaks through into the sub-created Secondary World as it does at times in the created Primary World. Though deliverance has an element of escape to it—as in the flight of Israel from Egypt through the Sea of Reeds—it is a larger event as it involves confrontation and victory.

Third, he describes eucatastrophe as being miraculous in character. In the immediate context, Tolkien refers to acts of special grace from the divine (in the context of the fairy-story) that are atypical divine action, and not repeatable, except by divine volition. Considering how unpredictable providence can be and how variegated its forms are, Tolkien insists that such miraculous grace cannot be counted on to recur simply because it is so irregular (e.g., even though Christian tradition and reports today have many cases of miraculous healing, there are many other similar cases in which it does not happen). Again, this is from the standpoint of the fairy-story and thus stands in contrast from denizens of the Primary World who may be inclined to complain about the "predictable" and "recurring" happy ending.

Beyond the immediate context, it might be helpful to consider what Tolkien means by "miraculous." In a letter written five years after this lecture, he describes miracles simply as seeming "intrusions" (though he thinks the term to be problematic) into real/ordinary life (Letter #89). In a draft of a letter written seventeen years later, he offers a more developed picture of the possible meaning of miracles being, "to produce realities which could not be deduced even from a complete knowledge of the previous past, but which being real become part of the effective past for all subsequent time" (Letter #181). Though these statements are later than his essay, they confirm the common sense of suddenness and turn/reversal, along with the sense of a providential initiative, that Tolkien sees in miracles and in eucatastrophes as a sub-category.

But there is still more to it. In the first aforementioned letter, he notes the most important quality of miracles and—as hinted here and explored later—eucatastrophes. In the Primary Miracle of the resurrection of Jesus, as well as the lesser Christian miracles, "you have not only the sudden glimpse of the truth behind the apparent Anankê[41] of our world, but a glimpse that is actually a ray of light through the very chinks of the universe about us" (Letter #89). Note how reminiscent this statement is of "a fleeting glimpse of Joy, Joy beyond the walls of the world, poignant as grief." Miracles and eucatastrophes are revelatory in that they unveil an enduring reality beyond the apparent bounds of the world, a reality that encounters the world of disorder, dysfunction, and death with order, proper function, and life. This briefly unveiled reality is that of

---

[41] A Greek term that has the sense of "necessity" or "constraint."

God's intention for the world, known in the Primary World as the kingdom of God and new creation.

As such, like miracles, eucatastrophes are perhaps best described as "transnatural." This term is similar to N. T. Wright's coined term "transphysical," which implies transformed physicality, so that it is no longer subject to obstacles, so that it becomes a *more* physical state.[42] In a similar manner, a "transnatural" action implies an action which produces, at least briefly, transformed nature, so that it is no longer restricted to its typical capacities, so that it becomes *more* natural (i.e., more aligned to the creative purposes of God, from which and whom creation came). Miracles—and by sub-creative extension, eucatastrophes—are brief transnatural acts of God which temporarily transform nature to bring it into accord with God's purposes, enabling it to become more authentically what it was created to be. Again, grace completes nature rather than destroys it. In other words, miracles are brief glimpses of new creation, creation that is in line with God's creative intention. Another term for such a state of affairs, which was more popular amongst the New Testament writers, is, "kingdom of God." The kingdom of God is creation's experience of God's kingship and reign in a new, more complete way than it currently knows. While the New Testament does not indicate that the kingdom had come fully yet, it shows that the dynamic power and transformative life which would be characteristic of the kingdom is present already through the work of the Holy Spirit (Matt 12:28//Luke 11:20; John 14:9–21; Acts 1:4–8; 2:14–39; 10:38; 1 Cor 4:20; 6:9–20; Gal 5:16–26; Eph 5:1–21; 2 Pet 1:3–11). In Rom 8:18–27 Paul describes creation as currently being in bondage to decay due to the wide-ranging effects of sin and that there are now groans of labor pains anticipating the bringing forth of the new creation, a birthing process that Paul here identifies with suffering and prayer, but could also apply to preview transnatural acts known as miracles or to eucatastrophes of Secondary Worlds that anticipate the consummate eucatastrophe of the Primary World.

Fourth, Tolkien notes the importance of the existence of dyscatastrophe to the occurrence of eucatastrophe. In painting, the juxtaposition of contrasting colors makes each one stand out even more. In characterization, stark contrasts between protagonist and antagonist (or between characters on either side of the distinction) enhance the vividness of both. The same principle is at work with the contrast between eucatastrophe and dyscatastrophe. The suddenness and joy that are characteristic of eucatastrophe

---

[42] N. T. Wright, *The Resurrection of the Son of God*, vol. 3 of *Christian Origins and the Question of God* (Minneapolis: Fortress, 2003), 477–78.

are results of that contrast. A world that never experienced death or its subordinates of sorrow and failure (along with other forms of suffering) would never know the joy of deliverance that overturns and overcomes that suffering. Confrontation is thus essential to deliverance and to eucatastrophe. An opiate that helps people ignore and avoid these problems of existence in the current world is not a eucatastrophe, nor is it deliverance, for it does not bring victory in any sense. The victory of deliverance clearly does not deny the existence of circumstances from which deliverance happens; it simply denies final victory to those circumstances. As Tolkien later notes, every deliverance in the present time—whether through eucatastrophe in sub-creation or otherwise—is a prelude to the consummate deliverance and victory to come.

Fifth, because of the peculiar joy that eucatastrophe produces, what Tolkien considers the true mark of a fairy-story, it is—in effect—a kind of *evangelium*. That is to say, it is a proclamation of the gospel, the good story with glad tidings. The joy of deliverance and the delivering joy found in eucatastrophe replicates, in fragmentary fashion, the joy of deliverance and delivering joy of the gospel. The way Tolkien describes it in the next paragraph is notable, for he says that the mark of a good fairy-story is that "however wild its events, however fantastic or terrible the adventures, it can give to child or man that hears it, when the 'turn' comes, a catch of the breath, a beat and lifting of the heart, near to (or indeed accompanied by) tears, as keen as that given by any form of literary art, and having a peculiar quality."[43]

The source of this joy produced is transcendent in that it comes from beyond the walls of the world. It is that same source as that of the gospel concerning the Word who came from beyond the world to the world to dwell among us and to give to the ones who receive him the power to become children of God (John 1:1–18). It is that joy which comes from some sense—even if only briefly perceived—of union with God (given the source of the joy). But there is also the poignant quality of grief to this joy, which adds to its unique character. Its character is that of resurrection, where sorrow and joy are reconciled in the new life of healing, for it emerges from confronting the cause of sorrow and coming out the other side with new vitality. Indeed, it is this joy that occupies Tolkien's epilogue in what is perhaps his most concentrated and extensive expression of the relationship between eucatastrophe and gospel, and thus of the eschatologies of sub-creation and creation (or Secondary World and Primary World).

---

[43] Tolkien "On Fairy-Stories," 153–54.

Sub-Creation, Eucatastrophe, the Gospel, and Eschatology

He returns to the importance of the inner consistency of reality, to the project of sub-creation and how its achievement fulfills the wish of writers of fantasy to be real makers. The Secondary Worlds they sub-create derive their reality from the Primary World and, if they are indeed to have Secondary Reality, there must be some form of participation/partaking in Primary Reality. If the true form, highest function, and purpose-fulfillment of fantasy and sub-creation comes through eucatastrophe, then the evangelical joy thereby produced is the sign of partaking of Primary Reality and Primary Truth:

> It is not only a 'consolation' for the sorrow of this world, but a satisfaction, and an answer to that question, 'Is it true?' The answer to this question that I gave at first was (quite rightly): 'If you have built your little world well, yes: it is true in that world.' That is enough for the artist (or the artist part of the artist). But in the 'eucatastrophe' we see in a brief vision that the answer may be greater—it may be a far-off gleam or echo of *evangelium* in the real world.[44]

Here, Tolkien expands on what he had said previously. While there is a sense in which internal consistency/coherence makes a eucatastrophe true in the secondary sense, Tolkien argues that there is a deeper truth that forges the true link between Secondary World and Primary World. The eucatastrophe derives its truth from the truth of the gospel, the story of the Primary Eucatastrophe. Conversely, without this truth, eucatastrophe could not speak truly to the Primary World as a reflection of the Eucatastrophe of this world.

If such is the case, Tolkien believes it is only fitting. Humans, who are making-creatures and storytellers by nature, created to bear the image of the Creator and Author of history, received redemption from God by story, the fulfilling story. They receive redemption by the way in which God made them: the Word, which became incarnate.[45] The stories they tell and the worlds they sub-create in exercise of their image-bearing capacities find their fulfillment (particularly if the stories involve eucatastrophe). Though humans are corrupt, sinful, and woefully incomplete, they can still reflect God in fragmentary form. But if humanity is created in the image of God for the purpose of

---

[44] Ibid., 155.

[45] This notion is the narrative-focused version of Justin Martyr's argument about the seeds of the Logos/Word of God spread among the teachings of the world in anticipation of the Incarnation, even if he accuses the devil and his demons of corrupting them (*1 Apol.* 20–23; 44; 46; 59–60; *2 Apol.* 8; 10; 13).

bearing that divine image, only God can provide the fulfillment of human identity and purpose when they are in proper relation to God.

By the same principle, human stories are, in their own ways, corrupt, flawed, and woefully incomplete, though they can still reflect the fulfillment of story in fragmentary form, particularly through eucatastrophe. But if story-making, world-making, and so on are functions of image-bearing, then stories would also find fulfillment in proper relation to the Author of authors, the one who has provided a eucatastrophe in the Primary World in anticipation of the consummate eucatastrophe of the eschaton to come at an unknown time. Eucatastrophes of fairy-stories anticipate the consummate fairy-story by which God redeems humans, and they thereby anticipate redemption. But the gospel is the consummate fairy-story because the features of fairy-story—including, most importantly, the ending—are raised from Secondary Reality when the Author of history writes them into Primary Reality, at which point, "the desire and aspiration of sub-creation has been raised to the fulfillment of Creation."[46] In the grand story of history, Tolkien describes the Birth of Christ as the eucatastrophe of history and the resurrection as the eucatastrophe of the story of the Incarnation, making it the eucatastrophe of a eucatastrophic story. It is thus a story with an *inclusio* of joy. And it achieves one of the primary goals of sub-creation in having the inner consistency of reality precisely because it has that quality by virtue of happening on the stage of creation/Primary Reality and bringing the art of God's action of creation to fulfillment in redemption.

The joy one would experience as a result of a fairy-story having Primary Reality is of the same kind and quality as the joy of eucatastrophe in a fairy-story with Secondary Reality. Of course, its degree would certainly be greater. For though the joy of the eucatastrophe has a taste of Primary Truth—the joy experienced is in fact an experience in Primary Reality—the joy of knowing eucatastrophe is actual in the Primary World is purer, more concentrated, and more potent because it is in closer proximity and union with the events that produce it. Truly, it is closer to the (final) cause, culmination, crystallization, and climax of eucatastrophe, towards which all other imitations draw, point, and (in some ways) testify. After all, it is here where Tolkien describes Legend (i.e., the Secondary World and the hidden dimensions of the Primary World glimpsed therein) and History (i.e., the story of the Primary World) meeting and fusing in a way that is not possible for any other fairy-story, and thus only this one can be the denouement of all other fairy-stories. It is also where the Author and the authors created in the Author's image know union impossible through any other means. Indeed, it is a

---

[46] Ibid., 156.

marriage of sorts between creation and sub-creation so that they become one and the joy experienced within the sub-creation and its eucatastrophe is multiplied by the joy of matrimonial union (itself an anticipation of the holiest of unions between heaven and earth as related in Rev 21). It is, in fact, where the Author upholds the verity of sub-creation, including its most important aspect, and makes it part of creation (so that, as he indicates, God is not only the God of humans and angels, but also of elves). And since the ending of eucatastrophe is the most exalted of aspects, the Author uses it as a way to show the true eschatological climax of the Primary World being one of eternal eucatastrophic outflow.

Although it is tempting to think of fairy-stories and their eucatastrophes as mere—though lovely—signs and thus fit to discard when all have reached the destination and reality to which the signs were pointing, Tolkien has a different view, as one would gather from "Mythopoeia." Rather, since fairy-stories are proper expressions of divine image-bearing, he suggests that God incorporates them into the kingdom—inaugurated and later consummated via eucatastrophe—and thereby hallows them, redeems them, and makes them participatory in new creation.[47]

Just as Christ's presence in the kingdom of God does not render the presence of people superfluous, neither should one expect that the fact of the gospel happening in the Primary World of creation should render the Secondary Worlds of sub-creation superfluous. Particularly noteworthy is his statement that "The Evangelium has not abrogated legends; it has hallowed them."[48] Grace does not destroy nature; it perfects it. The kingdom and the gospel story that brings it to fruition make sub-creations hallowed (or sanctified) by virtue of their union with the same, as well as by virtue of the divine vindication of their storylines insofar as they align with the divine will. If story-making, world-making, fantasy, and other such activities are part of being an image-bearer of God, then they would not wither away in the kingdom, but flourish in ways not possible before due to the lack of such union with the Creator.[49]

---

[47] Ibid., 156–57.

[48] Ibid., 156.

[49] Of course, there is potential for thinking that one of Tolkien's implications is that it is a logical consequence that the ones thus united to the Creator necessarily sub-create better or make better art. There could be a sense in which this idea is possibly true if the Christian aims to glorify God, but it is only possibly so. There are many qualities in these actions that need cultivation and the humility to learn from any source. Believers are not the only ones who bear the divine image, and even if many have glorified false gods or have otherwise devoted their gifts to the decay of the fallen creation, God has still gifted them with good capacities that they may still use well.

The logic here also seems to be an extension of—or at least related to—Gregory of Nazianzus's paradigmatic statement about the Incarnation of Jesus: that which is not assumed is not healed/saved.[50] While Tolkien would most likely agree with a specific application of this statement to the sub-creative faculties Jesus assumed (and it would further buttress his theology about the importance of sub-creation to being human), such a claim is not his interest here. His extension comes in that he uses the positive variation on this formulation—that which is assumed is saved—and broadens it to include God's assumption of both the sub-creative faculties and the sub-creative results/artifacts. Through the story of the gospel, God brings the sub-creative hopes to bear on the Primary World and thereby assumes the exercises of these faculties—imperfect though they are in conveying that human sub-creators bear the image of the Creator—and redeems them by that assumption. And their redemption means that humans are to continue contributing to the eschatological reality of the kingdom in this way because it is part of their vocation as image-bearers to be reflective of God and to contribute to the flourishing—or, in his words, "effoliation" and "enrichment"—of creation.[51]

It seems that Tolkien here goes even further than before in the eschatological impact of sub-creation as he sees humans participating in creation by divine enablement. He does not violate one of his fundamental assumptions that only God truly creates; but in God's assumption and use of human sub-creation—which they are only able to make because of God's gift—God graciously and willingly allows and features human works as part of the new creation, and Tolkien posits that this includes sub-creation. Participation in the life of the kingdom of God in anticipation of when the kingdom comes consummately undergirds New Testament ethics because it is of a piece with the logic of final judgment in which God vindicates and confirms the works for the kingdom of God, which are themselves divinely sourced by means of the Holy Spirit (Acts 2:14–39; Rom 8:9–27; Gal 5:16–25).

All of these points are further enveloped in the logic of eschatological resurrection (and new creation), which has elements of both continuity and discontinuity in that the one resurrected is identified as the person who died, but the resurrected person is also transformed and takes on a new kind of life (i.e., the everlasting divine life of the kingdom). What the discontinuous state of the resurrection body will be is not easily

---

[50] Gregory of Nazianzus, *Ep.* 101 (NPNF[2] 7:440–441).

[51] Though he does not explicitly relate it to the gospel, Tolkien provides an imaginative vision of sub-creation being taken up into creation in "Leaf by Niggle."

discernible and only a few hints about it appear in scattered texts (1 Cor 15:35–49 describes the glory of resurrection bodies and 1 John 3:2 states that believers will be made like him, but both of these texts only provide faint hints). To affirm belief in God's power to resurrect the dead is not the same as knowing precisely what resurrected people will look like or otherwise be like (even the comparison to Jesus in 1 John presents the challenge that the qualities of Jesus's body post-resurrection are mysterious in the resurrection appearances). In the same way, to say that sub-creation is redeemed is not to say what consummate redemption will look like for it as the logic of resurrection entails that there will be transformation that none of us can truly anticipate, except to say that what God redeems consummately will have identifiable continuity with what God redeems now.[53]

"On Fairy-Stories" is certainly the richest source of Tolkien's theology of sub-creation and it represents a continuation and development of "Mythopoeia" that would further solidify many of his convictions in this regard. While not as extensive or focused, over a dozen of his letters feature relevant material that draws from the well-spring of "On Fairy-Stories" or adds another element to it. These letters also contribute to the picture of Tolkien's theology of sub-creation in that the reader sees how he applies thoughts he developed elsewhere in relation to the general subjects of fairy-stories and myths to his own fantasy since most of these letters concern either *The Hobbit*, *LOTR*, or *The Silmarillion*. Any pertinent references to particular text will be saved for the commentary proper, so here we will focus on his more general comments, with one exception.

Letter #17 (15 October 1937 to Stanley Unwin)

Stanley Unwin had noted the complaint of Richard Hughes that as much as *The Hobbit* is aimed at children, there are certain parts of it that are too dark for children. In response, Tolkien reiterates—with the even-more strengthened conviction of a sub-creator whose work has gone through the scrutiny of others—a theme that he continues to emphasize particularly throughout this period in which he writes *LOTR*. He insists that Hughes's complaint is a common problem, "though actually the presence … of the terrible is, I believe, what gives this imagined world its verisimilitude. A safe fairy-land is untrue to all worlds." As much time as Tolkien famously devoted to maintaining

---

[53] See my articles: K. R. Harriman, "Expectations and the Interpretation of Resurrection as 'Bodily,'" *JETS* 65 (2022): 753–71; Harriman, "On the Terminological Issue of Describing Resurrection as 'Physical,'" *EvQ* 93 (2022): 149–70.

the internal consistency and integrity of his sub-creation, he also wanted to ensure that his sub-creation was realistic in terms of reflecting accurately the character of the Primary World. Sub-creation in its truest form comes from a desire to be creatively truthful. To lie as part of sub-creation is to corrupt the result and to deny the reality of the image-bearing identity of humanity. As long as terrible evil is part of the Primary World, it is only honest for the Secondary Worlds to reflect that fact in whatever way they can.

Letter #87 (25 October 1944 to Christopher Tolkien)

This particular letter offers a singular point of interest. Tolkien relates to his son that a twelve-year-old from Pennsylvania named John Barrow had written him with praise for *The Hobbit*. He had read the book eleven times and thought of it as being beyond description. He then asks Tolkien to tell him if he had written any other books. Tolkien found such a response amusing and saddening. That his own fantasy could have such an effect on someone was, to Tolkien, also a demonstration of the dearth in fantasy, myth, and the exercise of imagination that this boy had otherwise known in his life. And the boy was but one example of dearth in the impoverished field of modern humanity that made Tolkien say, "What thousands of grains of good human corn must fall on barren stony ground, if such a very small drop of water should be so intoxicating! But I suppose one should be grateful for the grace and fortune that have allowed me to provide even the drop." As we will see later, "fortune" is one of the ways Tolkien writes of divine providence, and "grace" already has clear theological overtones in light of what we have covered so far. Tolkien has made it clear that he regards fantasy, story-telling, and world-making as human necessities, and in situations of necessity-deprivation even the slightest provision gives a refreshment that has the quality of deliverance. Hence, Tolkien sees his role as a fantasy writer in his time as being a recipient of divine grace in order to become a participant in the outpouring of divine grace for others. This is an example of carrying out the vocation of image-bearing so that one becomes a divine instrument through which God exercises grace.

Letter #89 (7–8 November 1944 to Christopher Tolkien)

This letter describes a Sunday (the 5th of November) when Tolkien went to mass at St. Gregory's with his daughter Priscilla. The sermon concerned the stories of the healing of Jairus's daughter and of the woman with an issue of blood. The priest also mentioned three healings in more recent times, one of which especially drew Tolkien's attention. This story was of a little boy (in 1927) with "tubercular [tuberculous] perito-nitis" who was mortally ill and taken on a train by his parents, supposedly to go die in peace. But as the train passed by a Marian grotto—apparently the one at Lourdes, judg-ing by the context—he was suddenly well and went to play with a little girl on the train.

The suddenness of this turn produced an emotion he has associated peculiarly with eucatastrophe. It was a particular experience of what he had tried to describe analyti-cally, "For it I coined the word 'eucatastrophe': the sudden happy turn in a story which pierces you with a joy that brings tears (which I argued it is the highest function of the fairy-stories to produce)." This effect comes from the sudden glimpse of Truth, the truth that transcends typical perceptions of life bound in the chains of decay and death (which later in the letter he refers to as, "the apparent Ananké of our world"), and the turn shows humans the truth of Primary Reality and their nature with a relief that is as if, "a major limb out of joint had suddenly snapped back." No other eucatastrophe pro-vides the relief and distinctive effect like the eucatastrophe of the fairy story that hap-pened in the Primary World; namely, the resurrection of Jesus. In his description of the emotional effect the resurrection produces for those with Primary Belief, he gives his most poetic description of Christian joy, which "produces tears because it is qualita-tively like sorrow, because it comes from those places where Joy and Sorrow are at one, reconciled, as selfishness and altruism are lost in Love." This is the same quality of resurrection life that we noted previously in his exposition in "On Fairy-Stories." The memory of sorrow, as such, is not wiped out, but it is taken up into a new life of healing.

Tolkien echoes this description of eucatastrophe in the celebration of the eucatas-trophe of *LOTR* on the Field of Cormallen (VI/4), as we will observe later. Tolkien's language there exemplifies what he thought eucatastrophe ought to accomplish both in storytelling and for the people within the story. Insofar as it accomplishes such effects, it points to the eucatastrophic story of the gospel of which it is a fragmentary reflection.

Similarly, in *The Silmarillion* he describes the proper Third Theme of the *Ainulindalë*—the music that intentionally followed Eru Ilúvatar's direction rather than Melkor's and which concerned the history of the Children of Ilúvatar—as follows: "The one was deep and wide and beautiful, but slow and blended with an immeasurable sorrow, from which its beauty chiefly came." [54] Such is what happens when

---

[54] J. R. R. Tolkien, *The Silmarillion*, 2nd ed., ed. Christopher Tolkien (Boston: Houghton Mifflin, 2001), "Ainulindalë". As with *The Lord of the Rings* and *The Hobbit*, there have been various editions with different paginations used. My imperfect solution to addressing this problem is to reference the chapter title that is consistent across all editions.

eucatastrophe meets dyscatastrophe, the true light of the world meets its characteristic deceptive darkness, and the delivering love of God meets a rebellious world. When the response to eucatastrophe is the joy of deliverance that comes from beyond the walls of the world and Primary Belief, the result is a holistic redemption for the believer. The condition becomes a lasting part of who the believer is, and thus the mix of joy and sorrow characterizes the believer's existence as they await the consummation of hope.

He also reiterates his point about the gospel redeeming humans in a manner consonant with human nature by giving them a story that affects them in a way that fulfills the fairy-story. It is fitting that God should do such for beings created to be divine image-bearers, that secondary authors who express hope for redemption in fairy-stories experience redemption through the story from the Primary Author. By God's action of having the story of the Primary World climax with eucatastrophe, God reveals the truth about the world that transcends empirical observation, a revelation God had anticipated by using fairy-stories (among other means) as instruments to reveal the salvation that comes from beyond the circles of the world. Grace does not destroy nature (including fairy-stories); grace completes nature.

Letter #109 (31 July 1947 to Sir Stanley Unwin)

In this letter Tolkien responds to Rayner Unwin's comments on Book I of *LOTR* via a letter to his father the publisher. Rayner Unwin had noted that the number of events happening all at once was almost overpowering and that the struggle of darkness and light had become much more intense relative to *The Hobbit*. Of course, Book I was also the most comical of the six—as one would expect from a narrative spending so much time in the Shire and featuring Tom Bombadil prominently—and it provided some levity while Tolkien was still trying to figure out the character of this story.[55] At the same time, Tolkien saw it as his task to balance the comedy with the growing sense of darkness, especially in the chapters "The Shadow of the Past," "Fog on the Barrow-Downs," "A Knife in the Dark," and "Flight to the Ford" (not to mention the several other scattered intimations of danger and near-encounters). Again, just as contrasting colors make each more vivid, comedy and darkness (against which comedy arises) complement each other in storytelling. Tolkien saw this contrast as reflective of real life. As Tolkien has stated several times, having this inner consistency of reality is essential to the project of true sub-creation. And while he has made what is horrible in

---

[55] Shippey, *J. R. R. Tolkien*, 65–68.

the circumstances the Hobbits face to be "really horrible," he has also taken care to show how the Hobbits could surmount their obstacles, including "by grace (here appearing in mythological forms)." We will return to this fascinating comment later.

The elements of inner consistency lead him to his typical eschewal of classifying his work as allegory, which we have already noted in Chapter One. There is a moral point—or multiple such points—to it in that it is a worthwhile story. There are universals in the particular characters—because all people/characters instantiate universals to varying degrees—but they do not simply represent those universals (such as darkness and light). Characteristics of allegory—like other stories—derive from reality because they are ways of presenting truth. By extension, the stories that have an inner consistency of reality will have some perceived or intended allegory to them. Any allegorical impressions or connections of applicability arise only because Tolkien's story has that inner consistency of reality that would lead to certain definite consequences if something like the One Ring existed in a world populated by the wise and simple, the powerful and the weak, the exalted and the humble (though the story focuses on particular characters that have varying measures of these characteristics and others, not to mention that these characters include products of fantasy such as the Istari, Elves, Dwarves, Hobbits, and so on).

Letter #113 (Septuagesima [25 January] 1948 to C. S. Lewis)

This letter of apology and repentance concerns some situation of Tolkien's criticism of a work of Lewis during a meeting of the Inklings, but it also gives one ray of insight into how he thought of sub-creation. Tolkien had caused some sort of offense, and he writes hoping for Lewis's forgiveness. At one point he writes that this situation reminds him about a correspondence between G. M. Hopkins (an English poet and Jesuit priest) and Canon (Richard Watson) Dixon, the latter of whom wrote a *History of the Church of England* that the former expressed appreciation for (much to Dixon's surprise). The exchange had brought to Hopkins's mind the words of Edward Burne-Jones (an English artist) that, "one works really for the one man who may rise to understand one." But Tolkien agrees with Hopkins's response that, "Burne-Jones' hope can also in this world be frustrated, as easily as general fame: a painter (like Niggle) may work for what the burning of his picture, or an accident of death to the admirer, may wholly destroy. He summed up: The only just literary critic is Christ, who admires more than does any man the gifts He Himself has bestowed." Niggle's story—written almost a decade and published a few years prior to this letter—represents Tolkien's own experience with sub-creation with its interminable labor, his obsessive attention to detail, the endless duties and distractions that take him away from the work, and the looming "trip" (death) for which he has not prepared. Tolkien thus knows in a personal way—which has become more and more apparent as he had already spent around thirty years working on *The Silmarillion* off-and-on to this point while working on *LOTR* for around a decade—what it means to have such a dream constantly deferred. Instead, he quotes Hopkins to see the value in what is higher than any human evaluation. While people make many criticisms about art that are right and wrong, just and unjust (as well as criticisms that are neither here nor there), the only critic that can fully appreciate works of literary art—particularly sub-creative art—is the one from whom the gifts for it come. At once, Tolkien describes sub-creation as the exercise of a divine gift and thus as a gift for which Christ has a unique appreciation, since Christ is the one through whom the world and its ages came to be (John 1:3; 1 Cor 8:6; Col 1:16–17; Heb 1:2). The Word through whom the Father speaks all things into existence, orders, sustains, purposes, reveals, redeems, and renews has the greatest appreciation for the gift of language, its sub-creative power, and its many uses.

Letter #131 (late 1951 to Milton Waldman)

One of the letters richest in theology is this one written to Milton Waldman, an editor of Collins. Tolkien wrote this letter at a time when he had broken off a professional relationship with Allen & Unwin—as of April 1950—because they were hesitant to publish *The Silmarillion* along with *LOTR* (despite their long-standing interest in the latter). Waldman had expressed interest in publishing both works, especially since he had read part of the unfinished *Silmarillion*. However, negotiations on the actual publishing process thereafter became stagnant and confusing. Late in 1951, Tolkien wrote a letter around ten thousand words in length to Waldman outlining the story of his sub-creation including *The Silmarillion*, *The Hobbit*, and *LOTR* in order to show the interdependence of the first and third works in particular. It was one long demonstration that they belong together in conception, writing, and publication. In the process, he also gave insight into the nature of his sub-creative work and how he thought about it, though we will only address some of the material here and leave the rest for the commentary proper.[56]

---

[56] For more on the story of the conflicts Tolkien had with Allen & Unwin and then with Collins, see Carpenter, *Tolkien*, 211–16.

One of his passions in myth-making and fairy-story-making (initially) was to give to the English what they lacked but the Greeks, Celts, Romans, Germans, Scandinavians, and Finnish already had: high-quality myths of their own concerning their own lands in their own languages with their own heroes. The closest equivalent the English had beforehand was the Arthurian stories. But Tolkien thought of them as not being of a high enough quality, belonging to the land of Britain, but not quite English enough. Its elements of "faerie" actually work against the goal of the inner consistency of reality, as does the explicit presence of Christian religion on the level of the Secondary World. In his evaluation, "For reasons which I will not elaborate, that seems to me fatal. Myth and fairy-story must, as all art, reflect and contain in solution elements of moral and religious truth (or error), but not explicit, not in the known form of the primary 'real' world." In other words, the appearance of these elements in the Arthurian legends makes them something of an amorphous hybrid which attempts to have its Secondary World cake and eat it in the Primary World. The hybrid is not truly part of either creation or sub-creation, and therefore it has the inner consistency of neither. While all sub-creation is by nature derivative in some fashion, Tolkien seems to think that the Arthurian stories are both too derivative—in drawing too much on the explicit forms of the Primary World—and not derivative enough—in not pursuing far enough the inner logic of sub-creation by framing Primary World matters in appropriate Secondary World forms. He believes these unnamed moral and religious truths (or errors) to be true (or false) across Primary and Secondary Worlds, but a proper Secondary World does not have them appear explicitly in the same forms as they do in the Primary World if that world has the inner consistency of reality, in accordance with which there are proper forms for these truths (or errors) to appear. Tolkien even stated that these forms and their stories that make up his Secondary World in *LOTR* and the larger mythos had a curious relationship to his mind. For he said, "yet always I had the sense of recording what was already 'there', somewhere: not of 'inventing'."

As noted before, Tolkien stated his dislike of intentional allegory, but he recognized that the use of its language is indispensable when addressing the purpose of myth or fairy-story. Thus, he explains that his mythology fundamentally conveyed and addressed the problem of the relationship between Art (and sub-creation) and Primary Reality. He divides this fundamental concern into three categories of problems: Fall, Mortality, and Machine. As we will have occasion to go through his explanation of these terms later, we will pass over it for now.

Letter #142 (2 December 1953 to Robert Murray, S.J.)

This letter has already proven significant for our interests, and we need not reiterate Tolkien's comments on the Catholic character of his work. But what we can say in light of what we have addressed in this chapter so far is that it makes sense for the inner consistency of Secondary Reality if the explicit forms of religion in Primary Reality do not appear as such. While there are more clearly religious elements of ritual and practice appearing in manuscripts documented in *The History of Middle-earth*, as well as a few trace elements in *The Silmarillion* and *LOTR* (which we will note in the latter case), explicit religion is generally absent. Indeed, he sees the religious element absorbed into the structure, characters, and other elements of the story, as well as the symbolism contained therein. The elements were not apparent to Tolkien at first because he was not conscious in inscribing them. The transcendent nature of Primary Reality comes through in Tolkien's Secondary Reality because he had lived by the Catholic faith for decades at this point in his life. As such, the religious elements have been absorbed implicitly in the sub-creation because they were so absorbed by the sub-creator. It is a fundamentally religious and Catholic work at its foundation because it is reflective of Primary Reality, particularly the transcendent qualities Tolkien knew in Catholicism, but it is so in that its Secondary Reality reflects the truth in its own way, so that there is a continuity of nature and grace that characterizes Catholic theology.

Letter #153 (draft: September 1954 to Peter Hastings)

This unsent draft to Peter Hastings provides among the most extensive epistolary expositions of his thoughts on sub-creation. Hastings was a manager of the Newman Bookshop in Oxford and while he was enthusiastic about *LOTR*, he expressed several metaphysical concerns to Tolkien. Among the problems he found inconsistent with a Catholic worldview were the apparent notion—which he took from Treebeard—that the Dark Lord could create beings (or that there could be any tendency to good in such creatures), the metaphysical character of Tom Bombadil (which Hastings thought amounted to treating him as God), and (especially) the reincarnation of Elves. To Hastings, all of these elements detracted from—though he does not use the phrase—the inner consistency of reality because Tolkien had been, "over-stepping the bounds of a writer's job." Tolkien never sent this response because, "It seemed to be taking myself too importantly."[57] Even so, no other correspondence to a reader does more to clarify Tolkien's concern for reflecting Primary Reality and having an inner consistency of Secondary Reality in his theology of sub-creation and how it works in his own sub-creation. As with Letter #131, the value of this letter for our analysis will come mostly in specific details of the commentary, but we can focus on general matters for now.

It seems that in the case of readers like Hastings, Tolkien's spell of sub-creation has worked. They treat it seriously to the point that Tolkien wonders if they have treated it too seriously. Each reader who had corresponded with Tolkien had treated it particularly seriously according to their different interests, and thus at times they have criticized for being unrealistic or vague, "Its economics, science, artefacts, religion, and philosophy are defective, or at least sketchy." But the fact that readers have examined these aspects of Tolkien's world—and continue to do so in essays, books, online articles, lectures, and so on—is a testament to Tolkien's success in casting a spell of historical depth and three-dimensionality.

He reiterated what he had written in Letter #131 that the whole mythology fundamentally concerns the relation of creation to sub-creation (though he explicitly notes this time that a subsidiary matter is that of mortality). It is entirely possible for aspects of the sub-creation to be wrong in relation to the Primary World of creation (they could be conveying something that is, in actuality, false), but as such it is incoherent to say they are wrong in relation to the Secondary World. Even when properly understood—and Hastings has made errors in interpretation—these aspects simply are part of the sub-creation and how it is made.

The divergence between Hastings' concerns and Tolkien's beliefs about his sub-creation stems from the fundamental difference in how they view the relationship between sub-creation and creation. While Hastings seems—from this limited evidence—to resemble something close to the Arthurian perspective that leads to an incoherent sub-creation (by imitating the logic of creation in sub-creation but without the appropriate Secondary World form), Tolkien insists that,

> liberation "from the channels the creator is known to have used already" is the fundamental function of 'sub-creation', a tribute to the infinity of His potential variety, one of the ways in which indeed it is exhibited, as indeed I said in the Essay. I am not a metaphysician; but I should have thought it a curious metaphysic—there is not one but many, indeed potentially innumerable ones—

---

[57] A recurrent theme in Ordway's biography is Tolkien's connection with St. Philip Neri and how it helped to inform his tendency to avoid taking himself too seriously.

that declared the channels known (in such a finite corner as we have any inkling of) to have been used, are the only possible ones, or efficacious, or possibly acceptable to and by Him!

This statement is reminiscent of what Tolkien wrote around twenty years prior in "Mythopoeia," as we have already addressed. It is the duty of the sub-creator to be explorative, which can include drawing out the possibilities of what could have been if the Creator had created differently and how it could have been. It is a way of bearing the finite image of the infinitely creative One. Given a particular disposition, such exploration could be a form of worship (which, if humans are image-bearers of God, would be the fulfillment of the sub-creative faculty). It declares that God was not limited to the actual (Primary) channels of creativity, but he actively chose those channels to serve particular purposes that other channels, for one reason or another, did not serve. The Creator upholds this variety by endowing humans with the gift of imagination and by hallowing the sub-creation (in anticipation, in Tolkien's view, of the eschatological kingdom in which Secondary Worlds will have an ontological character that it is not possible for them to have now). But if the Creator does such, it is not proper to reject a sub-creation's logic out-of-hand before trying to understand it (though there is of course place for naming incoherence through criticism).[58] Indeed, for Tolkien it has taken on such a life of its own that some parts seemed revealed *through* him rather than *by* him. Even then, just as the God who creates and reveals has left many things a mystery, Tolkien leaves mysteries about his sub-creation when he knows the answers (such as, in *LOTR*, what the wizards are and where they came from). Of course, unlike the Creator, there are mysteries to his sub-creation that even he does not know the proper explanation for (like Tom Bombadil).

Tolkien admits that his world is not entirely explained coherently, as, for example, he struggles to explain how "counterfeit" creatures like Trolls can have the power of speech. But even Primary Reality does not appear to be wholly coherent (indeed, certainly not entirely explicable) and he wonders if, "though in every world on every plane all must ultimately be under the Will of God, even in ours there are not some 'tolerated' sub-creational counterfeits!" It is unclear what Tolkien has in mind here—if anything

---

[58] Tolkien notes here that he regarded perhaps his heaviest problem in terms of the inner consistency of reality as the biological one of having Elves be immortal yet still able, rarely, to produce offspring with Men. Of course, another problem that caused him significant trouble was his cosmological mythology in terms of the shaping of the earth, as well as the creation of the sun and moon with their courses. For more on this, see J. R. R. Tolkien, *Morgoth's Ring*, The History of Middle-earth 10, ed. Christopher Tolkien (New York: Houghton Mifflin, 1993).

in particular at all—but it is an attempt to illustrate a further dimension of realism to Tolkien's project if Eru Ilúvatar allows on the level of Secondary Reality what God allows on the level of Primary Reality. What is also noteworthy about this quote is how Tolkien perceives some measure of ontological reality and significance for his own Secondary World and others that they should be under the sovereign will of God. If one believes that God is Sustainer and that all things exist simply because God creates and sustains them by power according to God's will, then Tolkien's statement implies that there is something that God does to hallow and to sustain the existence of these Secondary Worlds.

In response to Hastings's overarching concern of Tolkien overstepping his bounds, he questions if there are any bounds except the bounds of reality itself in the laws of contradiction and bounds of the writer in mere finitude. Even so, there is need for writers to be self-limiting in humility before the power God endows humanity with through the capacities of sub-creation. With the divinely granted freedom of sub-creation, there is clear potential and precedent for use of freedom for the sake of harm and other wickedness. Similarly, sub-creations may be imperfect reflections and extensions of reality, but therein lies a risk of proclaiming and explaining "truths" that are not true and providing guidance in morality by what is not moral. Given that Tolkien agrees that good stories (myths in particular) can be well suited for teaching religious and moral truths—though in some lesser light than the divine radiance of the gospel—it is not surprising that this proper end is corruptible. But Tolkien also insists that he needs convincing that he has run afoul here and written something truly harmful before he is willing to recant or rewrite anything.

Letter #163 (7 June 1955 to W. H. Auden)

This letter addresses W. H. Auden, one of the most favorable literary critics to Tolkien at the time of *LOTR*'s release. He had been asked to give a talk on the BBC Third Programme in October of 1955 about *LOTR*. He wrote to Tolkien to get his input on what he should talk about and about the genesis of the story. Tolkien's response is filled with how he thinks his life has influenced the story and the need to write it. As a philologist, Tolkien naturally gave much attention to linguistic interests and how they gave rise to his interest in writing such stories as he has. In the process, he provided insight into how he thought of his sub-creative project, some of which will be addressed in the commentary proper.

What is significant to note here is how his love of language ultimately gave birth to his own stories. As is often noted, the origin of *The Hobbit*—and *LOTR* by extension, though it was more substantially mixed with the earlier elements of his mythology— was from the sentence he wrote on a blank sheet of a student's exam paper: "In a hole in the ground there lived a hobbit." As Tolkien related to Auden after summarizing his extensive philological background, "All this only as a background to the stories. They are and were so to speak an attempt to give a background or a world in which my expressions of linguistic taste could have a function." Even as words are the source of this Secondary World's existence and purpose—as, in a related fashion, it is through the Word that the Primary World exists and has its purpose—it is the Secondary World and the story of it that give the words their sense and significance.

It is also noteworthy that we see here yet another hint of Tolkien seeing something else at work besides his own mind. He mentions in a footnote how he proceeded in writing at multiple junctures. Although he is specifically referring to the Ents, he suggests that it is applicable to his project more generally, "daresay something had been going on in the 'unconscious' for some time, and that accounts for my feeling throughout, especially when stuck, that I was not inventing but reporting (imperfectly) and had at times to wait till 'what really happened' came through." There is obviously invention involved in sub-creation, as Tolkien himself said, but a proper work of sub-creation also involves some mysterious aspect of revelation, wherein the author experiences a hint of the Secondary Reality of the Secondary World.

Letter #165 (30 June 1955 to the Houghton Mifflin Co.)

Tolkien penned this letter to his American publisher in response to how a columnist named Harvey Breit—writing for the *New York Times Book Review*—had handled his correspondence in reply to questions about him and his work. It serves as a clarification and expansion on the answers he had given. It also serves to give some implicit hints on how Tolkien thinks of his sub-creation.

As in the last cited letter, Tolkien insists that his entire work is, "*fundamentally linguistic* in inspiration" (emphasis original). It is an expansion on what he wrote in the previous letter that "I am a philologist, and all my work is philological." On the one hand, this fact befits a work produced by a professor of philology. On the other hand, because of those professional interests, others could easily think of Tolkien's work in storytelling as a creative outlet, a diverting hobby taken up when professional responsibilities are not of concern. But Tolkien insists that—because he is a philologist with interests in the relation of philology and myth who has written stories as an extension of his professional work—his stories are not results of hobby, even if they are part of his private amusement (amusement that he takes in his professional work, meaning that he does not consider himself a man of hobbies at all). The fact that there is deep continuity between his professional work and his stories shows itself in his reiteration, "The invention of languages is the foundation. The 'stories' were made rather to provide a world for the languages than the reverse." As a grand linguistic construction, Tolkien claims that it, "is not 'about' anything but itself."

Furthermore, he gives clarification on the religious nature of his sub-creation against the claim that it contains no religion. He has already indicated in other letters that he does not regard it as proper for a Secondary World to contain the explicit forms of Primary World religion. The world's seeming lack of religion, at least insofar as the world is disclosed through *LOTR*, is simply due to Tolkien's attempt at being realistic about the character of this world. We will have more to say about the setting of this Secondary World in the next chapter, but what can be said for now is that Tolkien is clear that it would be historically incoherent for such forms of religion to appear in a time when revealed theology and its attendant religion have yet to arrive.

Letter #212 (unsent draft of a continuation of Letter #211 to Rhona Beare)

The letter prior to this one was Tolkien's reply to some questions Rhona Beare, a student at Exeter at the time, asked in anticipation of a meeting with other devotees (though it seems Tolkien was late in responding due to prior commitments). We will have multiple occasions for referring to that letter in the commentary proper, but what is of interest for our purposes now is this unsent continuation. Here, Tolkien mentions how, unsurprisingly, his sub-creation prominently features sub-creation from the beginning of its story. The difference here is that the Ainur are sub-creators working according to a different pattern than sub-creators in the Primary World: "They interpreted according to their powers, and completed in detail, the Design propounded to them by the One. This was propounded first in musical or abstract form, and then in an 'historical vision'." While there is a sense in which Tolkien has described sub-creators being imitative—with varying degrees of intention—of God's creative activity, there is a definite pattern and instruction to follow here in the sub-creation that the Ainur engage in at the formation of the world. Furthermore, the work of the sub-creators is of such a scale that they can already see their contributions being taken up into the grand primary design (whereas for sub-creators of the Primary World such a vision is eschatological).

Even at the point of the historical vision the One showed to the Ainur, Tolkien states that it had only the ontological quality (or "validity" in his words) like a story. Simply put, "it 'exists' *in* the mind of the teller, and derivatively in the minds of hearers, but not on the same plane as teller or hearers. When the One (the Teller) said *Let it Be*, then the Tale became History, on the same plane as the hearers; and these could, if they desired, *enter into it*" (emphases original). Such is ultimately what separates creation from sub-creation: the fiat of the Creator (as well as the Flame Imperishable sent to dwell at the heart of creation and to vivify it). While words have sub-creative power too, only the Creator has the power and authority to speak things into "primary exist-ence" (the phrase "Let it Be" closely resembles the words of God in Gen 1). Only the Creator has the ability to hallow sub-creations and to take them up into the Primary Creation by fiat. At this point, sub-creations are no longer engaged with by imagination (such as the historical vision), but by every faculty.

Letter #269 (12 May 1965 to W. H. Auden)

The occasion for this short letter is that W. H. Auden had written Tolkien asking him if he thought that his views about the Orcs were heretical, since they seemed to be a completely evil and irredeemable race. Naturally, that means it will be pertinent to address this letter in the commentary proper. Here, we may note that Tolkien does de-fend himself against this charge, rather than simply being dismissive of it. At the same time, as in Letter #153, he asserts a sub-creator's right to be free in his relation to the actual reality of the Primary World. He sees no obligation to *conform* (or "make … fit") his sub-creation to established Christian theology, though, as a faithful Catholic, he aimed to be *compatible/consonant* with it. There is a strong emphasis on freedom here and the explorative character of sub-creational activity. Even as the sub-creator surely believes in the importance of reflecting and conveying their "primary" beliefs and thereby maintaining consonance with the Primary World, he/she understands that the Secondary World must have its own inner consistency of reality. Therefore, the Secondary World need not utterly conform to the Primary World per se.

Letter #328 (draft: Autumn 1971 to Carole Batten-Phelps)

The last relevant letter to this analysis is another draft, though this time he focused on sub-creation and sub-creator as divine instruments. Carole Batten-Phelps had given to Tolkien only his most recent example—if only he could imagine how many more there would be—of people expressing profound appreciation and love for what he had done in *LOTR*. This outpouring had led him to believe that his work had become a vessel of light that had proven redemptive in the deprived, dark world of modernity. Although he had described this effect of fairy-stories in his essay many years prior to this letter, he had only reluctantly, and with goading from others, thought of his own work in this way on occasion (cf. Letter #87). What helped him "turn a corner" in this regard was a man who showed him pictures and asked if he had seen them prior to writing *LOTR* given the similarities. Tolkien said that he had not seen them before and the man—in Gandalfian fashion—asked him, "Of course you don't suppose, do you, that you wrote all that book yourself?"

He had since no longer been able to suppose otherwise, but the thought of providential use of him and his work as a divine instrument was not an instigation for pride. He was one learned in the stories of Scripture, the stories of the saints (including that of St. Philip Neri, who taught much about not taking oneself too seriously), and the stories from many other sources, which had led him to realize, "the imperfections of 'chosen instruments', and indeed what sometimes seems their lamentable unfitness for the purpose." As with the letter he received in 1944 (Letter #87), his response is one of being deferential and grateful that he has been used in this way. It is perhaps another sense of the "sub" in "sub-creator" that one must remember one's subordination to the Creator and that one is thus subject to the Creator's providential use for creative purposes. He reflects this Primary World belief also in his Secondary World, particularly in that quintessential story of the relationship of creation and sub-creation in the *Ainulindalë*.[59]

Whatever beams of transcendent light there may be in his story, Tolkien attributes them to that transcendent source. It is a light that shines through him, not from him. At the same time, he notes that people such as the woman who wrote this letter would not be able to observe the sense of "sanity and sanctity" in it unless they also had it. Hence, there is a sense of God preparing at least some to receive the divine work through human sub-creations.

---

[59] That chapter of *The Silmarillion* contains the following declaration from Eru Ilúvatar: "Behold your Music! This is your minstrelsy; and each of you shall find contained herein, amid the design that I set before you, all those things which it may seem that he himself devised or added. And thou, Melkor, wilt discover all the secret thoughts of thy mind, and wilt perceive that they are but a part of the whole and tributary to its glory."

CHAPTER THREE

The Setting of Tolkien's Sub-creation[1]

With such emphases on the importance of truths being manifested in their properly Secondary World forms in successful sub-creation, one must ask: what kind of setting is Tolkien's Secondary World? Is it like the world from the novel that *Planet of the Apes* is based on in that it is completely disconnected from our own Primary World? Or is it one that is more closely related than we might think, like the movie world of *Planet of the Apes*? As a matter of fact, Tolkien's Middle-earth, and the world of Arda it is part of, is nothing other than a setting from our world in an imaginary time of history. This is a point he explains several times in his letters.

In Letter #165 Tolkien made note of this when giving clarification on the religious nature of his sub-creation against the claim that it "contained no religion." For reasons we have gone over, he did not regard it as proper for a Secondary World to contain the explicit forms of Primary World religion. Rather, "It is a monotheistic world of 'natural theology'. The odd fact that there are no churches, temples, or religious rites and ceremonies, is simply part of the historical climate depicted.... I am in any case myself a Christian; but the 'Third Age' was not a Christian world." That is, the races of Middle-earth operate according to what they can determine from general revelation of creation, what they can discern with reason, and what wisdom has been passed down through the ages. There is general belief that there is one God above all, but the means of having a more direct connection with this God have not yet been revealed for those in Middle-earth. This is the best that can be hoped for in the absence of special revelation, which

---

[1] Readers of my book on *The Hobbit* will note that this is a slightly expanded form of a section of Chapter Two in that book.

has not even come to Israel yet in this setting. As Tolkien noted in another letter (Letter #153):

> There are thus no temples or 'churches' or fanes in this 'world' among 'good' peoples. They had little or no 'religion' in the sense of worship. For help they may call on a Vala (as Elbereth), as a Catholic might on a Saint, though no doubt knowing in theory as well as he that the power of the Vala was limited and derivative. But this is a 'primitive age': and these folk may be said to view the Valar as children view their parents or immediate adult superiors, and though they know they are subjects of the King he does not live in their country nor have there any dwelling. I do not think Hobbits practised any form of worship or prayer (unless through exceptional contact with Elves). The Númenóreans (and others of that branch of Humanity, that fought against Morgoth, even if they elected to remain in Middle-earth and did not go to Númenor: such as the Rohirrim) were pure monotheists. But there was no temple in Númenor (until Sauron introduced the cult of Morgoth). The top of the Mountain, the Meneltarma or Pillar of Heaven, was dedicated to Eru, the One, and there at any time privately, and at certain times publicly, God was invoked, praised, and adored: an imitation of the Valar and the Mountain of Aman. But Númenor fell and was destroyed and the Mountain engulfed, and there was no substitute. Among the exiles, remnants of the Faithful who had not adopted the false religion nor taken part in the rebellion, religion as divine worship (though perhaps not as philosophy and metaphysics) seems to have played a small part; though a glimpse of it is caught in Faramir's remark on 'grace at meat'.

Because this is a setting before the revelation of Christ Incarnate, Tolkien saw no need to insert analogs of his own religious practice. But it would likely not sit well with him to portray upright characters as explicitly pursuing other gods either. After all, Tolkien does not imagine the One he refers to as "God" (called Eru Ilúvatar) is anyone other than the One he worships as the One God in the Primary World. He actually spoke directly to this point in an interview published in 1968 (though the original interview was held in late 1966). When the interviewer asked who the One God of Middle-earth is, he responded, "*The* one, of course! The book is about the world that God created—the actual world of this planet."[2]

Of course, a further complication is that there are other expressions of religion in this setting that are idolatrous, as Sauron (and his lord, Melkor/Morgoth) sought to be worshiped. This fits the characterization of the conflict in *LOTR* and Tolkien's larger

---

[2] Charlotte and Denis Plimmer, "The Man Who Understands Hobbits," *Daily Telegraph Magazine* (22 March, 1968), 35 (emphasis original).

mythos as being about, "God, and His sole right to divine honour" (Letter #183). Thus, religious practices prior to special revelation could have negative associations for many who have resided too close to the physically manifest Dark Lords.

Tolkien further stated in Letter #165 that his setting is not a fantasy setting of another planet:

> 'Middle-earth', by the way, is not a name of a never-never land without relation to the world we live in … It is just a use of Middle English *middel-erde* (or *erthe*), altered from Old English *Middangeard*: the name for the inhabited lands of Men 'between the seas'.[3] And though I have not attempted to relate the shape of the mountains and land-masses to what geologists may say or surmise about the nearer past, imaginatively this 'history' is supposed to take place in a period of the actual Old World of this planet.

Even more clearly, he says in Letter #183, "Middle-earth is not an imaginary world. The name is the modern form (appearing in the 13th century and still in use) of *midden-erd > middel-erd*, an ancient name for the *oikoumenē* [the Greek equivalent found in the NT], the abiding place of Men, the objectively real world, in use specifically opposed to imaginary worlds (as Fairyland) or unseen worlds (as Heaven or Hell). The theatre of my tale is this earth, the one in which we now live, but the historical period is imaginary."[4]

Although the historical period is imaginary, Tolkien has still sought to maintain "literary credibility," as he says in Letter #211, by positing a long gap in time between the climax of *The Lord of the Rings* and the present day. In a footnote in that same letter, he says more specifically, "I imagine the gap to be about 6000 years: that is we are now at the end of the Fifth Age, if the Ages were of about the same length as S.A. [Second Age] and T.A. [Third Age, during which *The Hobbit* and *The Lord of the Rings* take place] But they have, I think, quickened; and I imagine we are actually at the end of the Sixth Age, or in the Seventh."[5] He said more directly in a draft of "The Awakening of the Quendi [Elves]" preserved in *The Nature of Middle-earth* that we are "in

---

[3] As one example, the Old English poem *Exodus*, which Tolkien translated and commented on, refers in its opening to "middle-earth" as where Moses declared his ordinances. Moreover, as Tolkien notes in Letter #211, it is also described as "middle" in Old English and related languages because of a concept of the inhabited lands of humans being between ice to the north and fire to the south.

[4] He also referred in Letter #156 to the "supposed ancient history of this actual world of ours" as the implicit description of his setting.

[5] Thus, he wrote in one of his latest letters—Letter #347a (to 'Miss T. R. C.')—that he wrote in *The Hobbit* and *The Lord of the Rings* "about the imaginary history of the Third Age (*of this world*)" (emphasis original).

1960 of the 7th Age," which he wrote in 1960.[6] This may be connected to the Roman Martyrology, used in the Proclamation of the Birth of Christ before the Christmas Vigil Mass, saying that Christ was born "in the sixth age of the world."[7]

Since the time is imaginary, and since Tolkien's mode of storytelling is mythical, he is not in any way attempting to write history as it happened 6,000+ years ago to the best of his knowledge. It is rather like how Robert E. Howard thought of his own work, as his stories of Conan and others were set in an imagined ancient age. Tom Shippey compares it to Tolkien's own native field of philology, specifically in the area of etymology, by saying Middle-earth as Tolkien portrays it is an "asterisk-reality," in that "it had not been recorded, like the *-forms of early words, but again like the *-forms it could be inferred, or reconstructed, with high plausibility if not complete certainty. The guarantee of Middle-earth, as of the verbal reconstructions of philologists, was inner consistency."[8] In any case, for our purposes, what is important to note here is that Tolkien imagined the story of *The Lord of the Rings* to be set in a time well before the time of Israel. Even the events of God forming a covenant with Abraham are thousands of years after when this story is supposed to be set.

Other letters also make this point rather clearly. In Letter #297 Tolkien confirmed what he had said in these other letters: "The Fall of Man is in the past and off stage; the Redemption of Man in the far future. We are in a time when the One God, Eru, is known to exist by the wise, but is not approachable save by or through the *Valar*, though He is still remembered in (unspoken) prayer by those of Númenórean descent" (emphasis original). Moreover, he said in an unpublished letter to Baronne A. Baeyens, "It would, of course, have been destructive of the 'historicity' of an imaginary period in the remote past, if alignment with religion or religious organizations now existing were clearly perceptible. But I am in fact a Roman Catholic—not by inheritance from my German protestant ancestors in Saxony."[9] Clearly, such a setting is crucial to understanding how Tolkien's Catholic Christian worldview is compatible with the apparent lack of religion in Middle-earth and the absence of explicit links with Catholic Christianity as such. But we need not pursue that argument again here, given what we have shown to this point.

---

[6] J. R. R. Tolkien, *The Nature of Middle-earth*, ed. Carl F. Hostetter (Boston: Houghton Mifflin Harcourt, 2021), 39.

[7] Carl F. Hostetter, "Metaphysical and Theological Themes," in *The Nature of Middle-earth*, 402–3.

[8] Shippey, *J. R. R. Tolkien*, 84.

[9] A transcript and a photo copy of this unpublished letter is available online at https://www.manhattanrarebooks.com/pages/books/2144/j-r-r-tolkien/autograph-letter-signed-als-typed-letter-signed-tls?soldItem=true

Tolkien also indicates this setting in *LOTR* itself. This is more apparent early in the Prologue and late in the Appendices (especially Appendix F). But another comment near the middle of the story also attests to this intended setting. In a note from the narrator describing the Mûmak that Sam saw (which he thought of as an Oliphaunt he heard tales of as a child): "Fear and wonder, maybe, enlarged him in the hobbit's eyes, but the Mûmak of Harad was indeed a beast of vast bulk, and the like of him does not walk now in Middle-earth; his kin that live still in latter days are but memories of his girth and majesty" (IV/4). This is in reference to elephants of the present world, showing that the "latter days" are our own days in the present world.

Indeed, this was Tolkien's vision from the beginning of his attempts to construct his Secondary World. If one reads the earliest draft of his earliest story connected to this world—the Fall of Gondolin—that he initially wrote in 1916/1917 (and completed revisions for by 1920), he compares the city of Gondolin and its fall with those of Bablon (Babylon), Ninwi (Nineveh), Trui (Troy), and Rûm (Rome). More interesting for our purposes is the short story "Athrabeth Finrod Ah Andreth" that is now featured in the volume *Morgoth's Ring*. This piece of fiction is arguably the theologically densest one that Tolkien ever wrote, and included in the conversation between the Elf lord Finrod and the wise woman Andreth is speculation from Finrod of how Eru himself would need to enter into the world to redeem it. Thousands of years later in the setting of *LOTR*, such an event is still thousands of years in the future. And this speculation is not the result of Eru's special revelation to Finrod or anyone else; it is simply a case of an exceptionally wise Elf taking what he has learned from the world around him and, by natural theology (from his perspective, at least), arriving at the conclusion of what must happen.

As we have seen throughout these first three chapters, all of this matter on setting is consonant with his Catholic theology. Tolkien is dealing with the "order of nature" in a "monotheistic world of natural theology," where the One God is none other than *the* One God who by grace completes nature instead of destroying it. Tolkien thus needed to find ways of expressing the work of the Lord of Heaven and Middle-earth that fit the order of nature of this imaginary period of history while remaining consonant with what would later be revealed in the order of grace.

We now have a framework by which to understand the (generally) Christian and (specifically) Catholic character of Tolkien's work from his own statements and clarifications of how his work relates to his theology without being an allegory of them, as well as from his theology of sub-creation. We have also established that the setting of Tolkien's Secondary World itself facilitates an imaginative consonance with his

Primary World beliefs because it is set in an imaginary period of the same world in which the gospel story would come to pass. At the same time, that distance in history and other elements of the alien setting, including various statements we have seen from Tolkien about how he approached his own fiction, allow for him to creatively re-present Primary World truths in Secondary World forms without strictly and precisely conforming himself to a formalized Christian theology and praxis that belongs to an era of history thousands of years after which this story is set. We have already seen some of his more general comments on how he approached his fiction and how that activity related to his Primary World beliefs, and we will have occasion to see others as they relate to specific issues that arise in his sprawling sub-creative project. And so with all of these points in place, and with guidance from his comments where applicable, we will examine the biblical and theological-ethical links to the Primary World that appear in proper Secondary World forms in *LOTR*. As noted in the Introduction, this commentary will be done in narrative order. Chapters Four through Nine will focus on the respective books that make up the main story of *LOTR*, while Chapter Ten will wrap up this commentary with analysis of Tolkien's Appendices.

CHAPTER FOUR

Commentary on Book I

On the Matter of "Christ-Figures" in LOTR

One preliminary matter to address is the question of whether or not there are "Christ-figures" in *LOTR*. I am inclined to agree with Austin Freeman that we should recognize "a difference in finding a 'Christ-figure'—that is, a fictional stand-in for the Redeemer such as Aslan—and finding christological types, or partial echoes that point forward to a full realization."[1] We have no examples of the former in *LOTR*,[2] but there do appear to be examples of the latter.

To explain further, a "type" is an imprint or impression bearing analogous correspondence to what it is patterned after.[3] The method of interpretation known as "typology," which has often been used in biblical interpretation, looks for a person/people, event, or institution that helps to understand another such entity or action via their analogous correspondences. The description of Christ as the Passover lamb is but one early example of this (1 Cor 5:7; compare Exod 12:46 and John 19:36). Christ is the corresponding anti-type, the fuller reality to which the type that was the Passover lamb of the old covenant pointed towards in its pattern.

---

[1] Austin M. Freeman, *Tolkien Dogmatics: Theology Through Mythology with the Maker of Middle-earth* (Bellingham, WA: Lexham, 2022), 240.

[2] For my extensive response to a recent argument to the contrary, see https://krharriman.substack .com/p/review-of-the-good-news-of-the-return.

[3] The language of "type" comes from the Greek term τύπος referring to something left via stamp, imprint, or impression by the shape of what left it. The language could also be used more extensively for a model, sketch, example, image, or pattern.

I cannot presume to give a full theoretical exposition on the history of reference to types and of the varieties of typology here.[4] But for the purposes of this analysis, a christological "type" is a lesser analogy of Christ partially corresponding in significant ways to him. However, this correspondence is not so extensive as to make them simply a Christ in other guise or with "another name" as Aslan says in *The Voyage of the Dawn Treader*. These types are also not allegories of Christ, since they are not means for Tolkien to refer to Christ in other terms, and he did not mean for them to be so. The correspondences simply arise from Christ's formative influence on Tolkien's imagination.

While Tolkien still lived, Barry Gordon argued in his unpublished paper "Kingship, Priesthood, and Prophecy in *The Lord of the Rings*" that the schema of the threefold redemptive offices of Christ, which are represented by him being Prophet, King, and Priest, are embodied in the story of those who bring about Middle-earth's redemption. Namely, he identifies Gandalf with what is signified by the shorthand of the prophetic office, Aragorn with the royal office, and Frodo with the priestly office. He also argues that these characters go on to take on more qualities of the other offices as they progress in sanctification as a result of accepting the responsibilities of their respective offices. Tolkien sent the paper to Clyde Kilby and wrote to him, "Much of this is true enough—except, of course, the general impression given (almost irresistibly in articles having that analytical approach, whether by Christians or not) that I had any such 'schema' in my conscious mind before or during the writing."[5]

As we go, we will have occasion to note how each character supplies echoes or embodies christological types. But one should be cautious about putting too much weight on any of these correlations of redemptive office with the respective characters. Each of these characters are exalted in different ways that do not correspond to how we ought to think of the relations or relative importance of Christ's work as Prophet, King, and Priest. Gandalf's correlation with "Prophet" is the weakest of the correlations, and he seems to be placed here because the correlations needed to be rounded out.

Gandalf's correlations with Christ are more significant outside of the attempt to force him into this categorization. As much as Tolkien himself will identify significant biblical and theological echoes in Frodo's Quest and the perfection/fulfillment of the same in the gospel story, the crucial moments of the eucatastrophe and what leads up

---

[4] For more on this subject, see Frances M. Young, *Biblical Exegesis and the Formation of Christian Culture* (Grand Rapids: Baker Academic, 1997), 148–57, 192–201, 209–13.

[5] Clyde S. Kilby, *Tolkien &* The Silmarillion, (Wheaton, IL: Shaw, 1976), 56.

to them in the gospel story and this story are remarkably different. Particularly, they are markedly different in that Frodo is ultimately overcome by the power of the Ring, and he himself does not destroy it. Aragorn presents the strongest "office" correlation, but he is not the one to achieve ultimate victory, and indeed ultimate victory is not possible in his time, given that his reign is set in an imaginary time thousands of years before Christ. Nor are the circumstances in which he takes up his kingship comparable to the gospel story, even if there are various correlations of character that we will observe as we go.

Indeed, not least because of when and where Tolkien has set his story, there can be no "Christ-figure" as such.[6] Gandalf is analogous to Christ in that he is a transcendent being who became incarnate, but he is properly among those (like Saruman and Radagast) who are "the near equivalent in the mode of these tales of Angels, guardian Angels" (Letter #131). Tolkien similarly said in a later letter (Letter #156 to Robert Murray) that Gandalf was an incarnate "angel" (or ἄγγελος), being "an emissary of the Lords of the West."[7] He further clarified in that letter, "By 'incarnate' I mean they were embodied in physical bodies capable of pain, and weariness, and of afflicting the spirit with physical fear, and of being 'killed', though supported by the angelic spirit they might endure long, and only show slowly the wearing of care and labour." He reiterated these same points in Letter #181, which then led him to make a contrast with the Incarnation, "But though one may be in this reminded of the Gospels, it is not really the same thing at all. The Incarnation of God is an *infinitely* greater thing than anything I would dare to write. Here I am only concerned with Death as part of the nature, physical and spiritual, of Man, and with Hope without guarantees" (emphasis original). He stressed here that "there is no embodiment" of the One/the Creator/God in the setting of his stories, although the aforementioned text of the "Athrabeth Finrod ah Andreth" in *Morgoth's Ring* hints at this happening in the future.

---

[6] This is another way in which his approach contrasts with C. S. Lewis's *Chronicles of Narnia* series or his *Space* trilogy, which were set in roughly contemporary times to when he wrote, years which were referred to as "the year of our Lord (*anno Domini*) X."

[7] This was not always how Tolkien conceived of Gandalf or of the order of Wizards. On when this comparison of Wizards and angels first appeared, see J. R. R. Tolkien, *The Treason of Isengard: The History of the Lord of the Rings Part Two*, The History of Middle-earth 7, ed. Christopher Tolkien (Boston: Houghton Mifflin, 1989), 422.

Concerning Hobbits

The Prologue serves the functions of telling the reader more about Hobbits and of recapitulating the story of *The Hobbit* that was the prequel to *LOTR*. In both respects, it provides the framework for the proceeding story. Early in the first section of this prologue we have this poignant summary statement:

> Yet it is clear that Hobbits had, in fact, lived quietly in Middle-earth for many long years before other folk became even aware of them. And the world being after all full of strange creatures beyond count, these little people seemed of very little importance. But in the days of Bilbo, and of Frodo his heir, they suddenly became, by no wish of their own, both important and renowned and troubled the counsels of the Wise and the Great.

The Hobbits are a branch of the race of Men characterized by remarkably small stature. Tolkien said in Letter #131 that from his Primary World perspective as author of this story, "They are made *small* (little more than half human stature, but dwindling as the years pass) partly to exhibit the pettiness of man, plain unimaginative parochial man – though not with either the smallness or the savageness of Swift, and mostly to show up, in creatures of very small physical power, the amazing and unexpected heroism of ordinary men 'at a pinch'" (emphasis original). As he said elsewhere in the letter, the Hobbits "exemplify most clearly a recurrent them: the place in 'world politics' of the unforeseen and unforeseeable acts of will, and deeds of virtue of the apparently small, ungreat, forgotten in the place of the Wise and Great (good as well as evil)." Most of the story juxtaposes these Hobbits with the great people of their time. In the process, it presents the moral point that "without the high and noble the simple and vulgar is utterly mean; and without the simple and ordinary the noble and heroic is meaningless."

In Letter #165 he wrote of this aspect of the story being especially moving to him: "There are of course certain things and themes that move me specially. The inter-relations between the 'noble' and the 'simple' (or common, vulgar) for instance. The ennoblement of the ignoble I find specially moving." Likewise, when he wrote of the development of his sub-creation in Letter #180, he stated, "The hobbits had been welcomed. I loved them myself, since I love the vulgar and simple as dearly as the noble, and nothing moves my heart (beyond all the passions and heartbreaks of the world) so much as 'ennoblement' (from the Ugly Duckling to Frodo). I would build on the hobbits." It was actually for this reason that, for as much importance as Tolkien attached to the story of Aragorn and Arwen, he placed it in an appendix "because it could not be worked into the main narrative without destroying its structure: which is planned to be 'hobbito-centric', that is, primarily a study of the ennoblement (or sanctification) of the humble" (Letter #181). The theological tinge of the language is especially notable in this last example, as it is in his remark in Letter #281 concerning his response to a blurb:

> Hobbits were a breed of which the chief physical mark was their stature; and the chief characteristic of their temper was the almost total eradication of any dormant 'spark', only about one per mil had any trace of it. Bilbo was specially selected by the authority and insight of Gandalf as *abnormal*: he had a good share of hobbit virtues: shrewd sense, generosity, patience and fortitude, and also a strong 'spark' yet unkindled. The story and its sequel are not about 'types' or the cure of bourgeois smugness by wider experience, but about the achievements of specially graced and gifted individuals. I would say, if saying such things did not spoil what it tries to make explicit, 'by ordained individuals, inspired and guided by an Emissary to ends beyond their individual education and enlargement'. (emphasis original)

We will address some of the particular manifestations of this grace later as the occasions arise. The Emissary is, of course, Gandalf. He is an emissary from the Valar, the Lords of the West, sent to help Middle-earth in the struggle against Sauron. But he is also ultimately an emissary from the One, the All-Father, Eru Ilúvatar. Eru/God is the one who can properly be described as the agent who "specially graced and gifted" or "ordained" the individuals in question. That is also why in the quote from *LOTR* we are focusing on that it is said they became important and renowned "by no wish of their own." For indeed, it was the wish of another will, another power who will be mentioned again and again, albeit not by name. Furthermore, the fact that this happened through no wish of their own illustrates why the Hobbit heroes are proper heroes. As Tolkien said in Letter #163:

> Anyway I myself saw the value of Hobbits, in putting earth under the feet of 'romance', and in providing subjects for 'ennoblement' and heroes more praiseworthy than the professionals: *nolo heroizari* [I do not wish to be a hero] is of course as good a start for a hero, as *nolo episcopari* [I do not wish to be a bishop] for a bishop. Not that I am a 'democrat' in any of its current uses; except that I suppose, to speak in literary terms, we are all equal before the Great Author, *qui deposuit potentes de sede et exaltavit humiles.*

While Bilbo, Sam, and Frodo each had an interest in adventure beyond the Shire, it is only there deep down, a "spark" that is fanned into flame by Gandalf and the sense of necessity each of them, along with their companions, must face, and this is what excites both the interest in actually going on the adventure and the heroism needed. That heroism otherwise might have remained buried beneath their lifelong conditioning of denial of the spark. And it is precisely because they are not "professional" heroes—like Gandalf, Aragorn, or any other non-Hobbit heroes involved in the story—and do not even see themselves as the hero types that they are best suited to be the heroes of Tolkien's story. The Latin quote is from Mary's *Magnificat* (specifically, Luke 1:52), which Tolkien had heard in Mass for most of his life, and it puts a fine point on the character of Tolkien's story as one of ennoblement. It is a story that imitates God's action as Creator, Judge, King, and Redeemer in humbling the exalted and exalting the humble (besides the rest of the Christmas story, see 1 Sam 2:1–10; Ps 9:11–20; Phil 2:1–11).

In part, this is why they trouble the counsels of the Wise and the Great. We will see other expressions of this idea later in story, and it is noteworthy how much biblical resonance this theme has. As noted already, it is a key theme of Mary's *Magnificat*, reflecting her own situation as a humble virgin exalted to be the mother of the Messiah and God Incarnate, as well as reflecting the expectations of the coming eschatological future (Luke 1:46–55), which has made this text so fitting for Advent. Beyond the many, many cases of the Bible declaring God's vindication and exaltation of the humble and humbling of the exalted, there are some other texts worth noting. For example, one is reminded of Jesus's praise of the Father that he has hidden the things of the kingdom from the wise and learned, instead revealing them to little children (Matt 11:25–26 // Luke 10:21), the opposite of what many might have expected, and all the more remarkable because of how lowly children were held in this regard. Likewise, Paul reminds the Corinthians that the message of the cross is considered utter foolishness to those who ignore it, and yet through this message and through those who have accepted it, God has chosen the foolish things of the world to shame the wise and the weak things of the world to shame the strong (1 Cor 1:18–31).

The Common Grace for the Hobbits

While certain Hobbits are chosen and equipped for special purposes, they also participate in the common grace the Creator has given the people as a whole. One such expression of grace that is particularly outstanding in this story is how, despite seemingly being such soft creatures because of how easy their lives would be, "ease and peace had left these people still curiously tough." Tolkien continues,

> They were, if it came to it, difficult to daunt or to kill; and they were, perhaps, so unwearyingly fond of good things not least because they could, when put to it, do without them, and could survive rough handling by grief, foe, or weather in a way that astonished those who did not know them well and looked no further than their bellies and their well-fed faces. (Prologue)

Such is the first piece of build-up that Tolkien gives for how curiously tough Hobbits could be. In response to Rayner Unwin's feedback in 1947 about how in *LOTR* the "struggle between darkness and light (sometimes one suspects leaving the story proper to become pure allegory) is macabre and intensified beyond that in 'Hobbit,'" he acknowledged the apparent success he had in making the horror elements really horrible, "But I have failed if it does not seem possible that mere mundane hobbits could cope with such things. I think that there is no horror conceivable that such creatures cannot surmount, by grace (here appearing in mythological forms) combined with a refusal of their nature and reason at the last pinch to compromise or submit" (Letter #109).

The last part of the second sentence is reminiscent of the comment from *LOTR* that is our focus here. But it also signifies grace. It is not the special grace/gift given to some for specific tasks like Tolkien refers to with the specific use of the term "grace" here; it is the common grace given to a people. It is the same principle in a different form of the spirit of courage Tolkien observed in the Norse and Old English stories he loved.

The expressions of this spirit most compelling to Tolkien are found in *Beowulf* and the incomplete Old English poem *The Battle of Maldon* (a story he even wrote a continuation of, which he called *The Homecoming of Beorhtnoth Beorthelm's Son*).[8] Tolkien is critical of certain expressions of this spirit of courage when heroes use it to pursue their own glory, but he finds it best exemplified by servants who express this spirit in the form of unflinching fidelity in service. The northern spirit was one defined by indomitable will chafing against inevitable defeat. As such, although the direction of logical causation is less clear, related to this spirit are elements of Norse theology, such as Valhalla being for those who die in battle (expressing indomitable will in the

---

[8] Beyond his famous essay, see J. R. R. Tolkien, *Beowulf: A Translation and Commentary*, ed. Christopher Tolkien (Boston: Mariner, 2015); Tolkien, *The Battle of Maldon Together with The Homecoming of Beorhtnoth Beorhthelm's Son and "The Tradition of Versification in Old English*, ed. Peter Grybauskas (New York: HarperCollins, 2023).

face of death) and their eschatology being expressed in the battle of Ragnarök, wherein almost all of the gods die in battle against the forces of chaos. In this theology, right and wrong had nothing to do with victory or defeat. Even the greatest warrior, like a Beowulf, can fall to the forces of chaos as exemplified by the monsters, but their greatness in Norse estimation was not measured by "competence" or ability to finally overcome all obstacles, for final defeat is inevitable. Rather, their greatness is measured by absolute resolution to not be cowed by such final defeat, to exert one's will to the bitter end, never wavering amidst the waves of chaos, even if one must ultimately be drowned by them.

Norse mythology and Norse theology, resonating as they did in Old English tales like *Beowulf*, are defined by tragedy, for human existence itself is a tragedy in the face of this final defeat, as Tolkien observes in his famous essay.[9] But *Beowulf* is, of course, not an undiluted presentation of Norse paganism, for it comes from the Christian era reflecting on the era of Beowulf as the darkened past. It is thus "a fusion that has occurred *at a given point* of contact between old and new, a product of thought and deep emotion."[10] In the distant past of Tolkien's England, "this imagination was brought into touch with Christendom, and with the Scriptures. The process of 'conversion' was a long one, but some of its effects were doubtless immediate: an alchemy of change (producing ultimately the mediaeval) was at once at work."[11] For the *Beowulf*-poet, one of the most significant contributions the Norse make to this fusion of horizons is "the theory of courage," "the creed of unyielding will" that defines the valued character of the Norse.[12]

Christian eschatology, shaped as it is not only by the eschatological visions of the OT (a shaping seen most poignantly in Revelation), but also by the remembrance of Jesus's resurrection, presents a hope of final, everlasting victory. The Messiah who was crucified was ultimately vindicated by the God who raises the dead, and he took up the everlasting life that utterly conquers death. Those who are in him will likewise receive this vindicative and ultimately vivifying victory, which in turn promotes living as he has called us to live.[13] The tragedy of human life is given its great eucatastrophe by the

---

[9] Tolkien, "*Beowulf*," 18.

[10] Ibid., 20 (emphasis original).

[11] Ibid., 21.

[12] Ibid., 20, 21.

[13] Similarly, Tolkien summarizes the fusion well in an unpublished letter to Bruce Mitchell, "I think we fail to grasp imaginatively the pagan 'heroic' temper, the almost animal pride and ferocity of 'nobles' and champions on the one hand; or on the other hand the immense relief and hope of Christian ethical

Author. The condemnation of final defeat is overturned by the great Arbiter with his verdict of victory, the same verdict he gave to the Christ he raised from the dead (and whom he unites others to by the Holy Spirit). The monsters persist for now, but there is hope for a time when they will be no more, when God will be all in all (1 Cor 15:20–28).[14] The ending humans and their enemies receive in the Christian story is starkly different from the one they receive in the Norse story of Ragnarök.

Hobbits, bearing the resemblances that they do to the English while being set in an imaginary time long before the Anglo-Saxons were known as such, partake of that "northern spirit of courage" exemplified in *Beowulf*, but in ways more apropos to common English country folk than ancient warrior heroes.[15] Thus, their valor, their courage, their strength is often hidden, even from themselves, as Tolkien says in both *LOTR* and *The Hobbit*. That "northern spirit of courage" is nevertheless something of a preparation for the gospel in the view of the *Beowulf*-poet and Tolkien. That indomitable will that represented the highest ideals of the North was a gift of empowerment, courage, and even integrity from God, preparing people for the life of perseverance that characterizes the faithful, although it was incomplete in itself until the gospel came (even as the indomitable human could not hope to attain final victory outside of this Christian story). As the poet looks back on this past in writing this elegy, he presents his fusion of horizons as what Tolkien describes as "essentially a balance, an opposition of ends and beginnings. In its simplest terms it is a contrasted description of two moments in a great life, rising and setting; an elaboration of the ancient and intensely moving contrast between youth and age, first achievement and final death."[16] Beowulf thus becomes the paradigmatic figure for this pagan past in his own progression through this opposition, but he is now given a new frame. And this new frame, as we have noted earlier, is presented by Tolkien through making the little, lowly Hobbits central heroes of *The Hobbit* and *LOTR*, wherein Eru Ilúvatar exalts the humble as instruments of his providence and brings to fruition the seed of courage he himself planted in them at their creation.

As for the special grace that Tolkien references, he says it appears here in "mythological forms." This is something else to pay attention to as we proceed through this

---

teaching amidst a world with savage values." Bruce Mitchell, *On Old English: Selected Papers* (Oxford: Blackwell, 1988), 53–54.

[14] On this text, see Harriman, "Why Should God Raise the Dead," 172–202.

[15] Wayne G. Hammond and Christina Scull, *The Lord of the Rings: A Reader's Companion* (London: HarperCollins, 2008), 27.

[16] Tolkien, "*Beowulf*," 28.

commentary, for the mythological forms are many. Some of them are seemingly internal, and others are external, as noted in my *Hobbit* commentary. Key words to watch for include uses of "fate," "fortune," "luck," "chance," and so on, which function as references to divine providence by other names. In general, for whatever differences they have in precise nuance, these various terms share the sense of referring to what is beyond one's control that can have positive or negative effects on one's capability to achieve an end.[17] This is not to say that every use of such terms can be substituted with "providence" without remainder. But the more suggestive a certain use of this language is of something more than randomness—i.e., being suggestive of a benefactor, of agency, and of a larger purpose, including implications of something being more than "mere" X—the more likely it is that one can find in such texts references to divine providence in appropriate Secondary World (or "mythological") forms. Indeed, Tolkien even refers to Frodo in Letter #246 as "an instrument of Providence."

Providence by Many Names

By "providence" I mean actions of divine agency in both senses of the word in theological tradition: preservation and governance. In terms of preservation, God's providence means God's action in taking care of creation by sustaining it, providing for it, giving gifts to it, and planning for the same in order to preserve it; the most remarkable cases of this come in instances of timely provision. Miracles, as such, have often been described as acts of *providentia extraordinaria* (whether as the category itself or a subset of that larger category of extraordinary acts of providence), in distinction from acts of *providentia ordinaria*.[18] In terms of governance, God's providence refers to his ultimate authority over and action taken in directing the course of history, for preservation and other such purposes according to his will, though the account one gives for this will be complicated by the influence of evil in the world. Still, in various ways God guides history to his ultimate/eschatological purposes, and this is seen in foreshadowing and fragmentary fashion in some events in the course of history,

---

[17] Helpful in this regard is Kathleen E. Dubs's outline, following the influential theologian Boethius in distinguishing, "providence, which orders the universe; fate, the temporal manifestation of that order; chance, that 'fate' which occurs not according to our expectations, and for causes of which we are unaware; and, of course, freedom of will, which operates as part of this providential order." Kathleen E. Dubs, "Providence, Fate and Chance: Boethian Philosophy in *The Lord of the Rings*," in *Tolkien and the Invention of Myth: A Reader*, ed. Jane Chance (Lexington: University Press of Kentucky, 2004), 141. See Boethius, *Consolation of Philosophy*, Books 4 and 5.

[18] In our exploration of "On Fairy-Stories," we have already noted Tolkien's descriptions of miracles from Letters #89 and #181.

especially when various forces and/or wills come together in instances of remarkable timing that achieve some great end, or in cases where something seemingly insignificant has its significance exponentially multiplied by the context of subsequent events.

As the ultimate Author, God is constantly at work both to sustain his creation to keep it going toward its goals and to guide all the storylines contained therein towards the authorial purposes to weave the grand Story. God, named "Eru Ilúvatar" in Tolkien's sub-creation, works similarly in this story and Tolkien's other stories. Of course, the extent to which he exercises direct control varies, and the forces and agents he uses to bring about his purposes are many. Nor in the Primary World does God always act in the ways we have deemed miraculous (though that term has admittedly been used ambiguously), but he often works on more subtle—and often seemingly ordinary—levels. Yet all of these levels and kinds of action are contained within the parameters of what is called "providence."

As we go, we will see how pervasive the work of Providence is in the story itself, but we should note its larger significance for Tolkien as well. I have already noted in my other volume at multiple points how the theme of divine providence appears in *The Hobbit*. It is present to a greater and more explicit degree in *The Silmarillion*, not least because it is more likely in that story for Tolkien to name the instruments of Providence. As already noted, he wrote in Letter #246 that Frodo is "an instrument of Providence." In cases in his letters when he might otherwise be inclined to despair about the course of history, he resorts to his trust in God's providence, referring to history being in God's hands (Letters #61 and #102). He also wishes for God's guidance of Christopher's ways (Letter #81). And, of course, he saw in retrospect God's providence in guiding his own writing (Letters #142, #163, and #328).

As Tolkien himself will declare more clearly in the opening chapter of *The Silmarillion*, providence entails that all things, every force and every being, even those in opposition to God, are within God's realm of preservation and governance, and all of them will ultimately redound to the accomplishment of God's purposes. It is often difficult to see this providence while in the process of events, but sometimes in hindsight we can see God's orchestrating hand. The supreme example of this is, of course, the three-stage narrative of major gospel events of the cross, the resurrection, and the ascension or exaltation of Jesus. The cross, by any measure of the time in which it took place, certainly seemed to signify an utter failure and disaster for Jesus and the purported purposes of God in him if the story had simply ended there. But the resurrection and exaltation that followed thereafter showed that the cross was a supreme mode of divine providence working even in the circumstances of humans working together with the demonic forces of sin and death to thwart the purposes of God by seeking to destroy God Incarnate.

The notion of "providence" is also often invoked in contexts where seemingly small actions and events can have results in kinds and scales that we cannot comprehend. A well-known biblical example of this is in Genesis with the story of Joseph and his brothers that occupies the last major section of that book. Out of jealousy and bitterness, Joseph's brothers decided to sell him into slavery, yet we see by the end of the narrative that God worked through this event—and even Joseph's imprisonment—to accomplish the salvation of many lives and, ultimately, the slavery in Egypt followed by God's long-promised exodus, and all that pertained thereto. All of this came as consequences of Joseph's brothers selling him into slavery.

One can see such providence as well in the story of Esther, a book that famously never mentions God by name (that is, before the Greek additions that sought to correct that omission) and features several seemingly small actions and placements of people moving the story to its resolution. As in much of Tolkien's stories, God is not named, per se, but he is certainly not absent. And indeed, we see this providential work all the time in our lives and in broader history in how seemingly small or insignificant happenings turn everything around for someone or for a group of people. One conversation can change someone's life. One act of prudence or imprudence, wisdom or foolishness, kindness or apathy can profoundly affect a person's life. God can use any such small openings for the work of his purposes, so that they become instruments of his governance.

Tolkien's particular choices in terminology were influenced not only by parlance (since one of the conceits of *LOTR* is that it is a translated work, per Appendices E and F), but also by the medieval stories he knew well. Perhaps the most remarkable is *Sir Gawain and the Green Knight*, a text about a supposedly pre-Christian time which is nevertheless suffused with explicit Christianity, wherein we see a direct parallel between referring to "luck" and referring to God's action. In stanza 38, when Gawain arrives at a castle, the narrator says that the lord of the castle learns "whom luck had brought him," but the lord says more specifically a little later, "God has given us of His goodness His grace now indeed, / who such a guest as Gawain has granted us to have" (38).[19] Likewise, in *Beowulf*, a text Tolkien knew thoroughly and which impacted him deeply, the Christian poet telling a story from a pre-Christian time refers to God's providence as "fate," "fortune," and even by the name of Metod (Ordainer/Arbiter/Maker;

---

[19] Tolkien, *Sir Gawain and the Green Knight*, 58.

cf. also the Old English *Exodus* poem that Tolkien translated).[20] These authors were not reluctant to refer to God, nor were they imagining that some other benefactor was acting besides God, but uses of such terms highlight how they incorporated parlance in their theological expressions. They exemplify declarations like that found in Prov 16:33: "The lot is cast into the lap, but its every decision is from the LORD" (NASB).

This notion has already been introduced subtly with the comment that the Hobbits became important and renowned "by no wish of their own," but it is also present in the description of the story of *The Hobbit* in this prologue. First, the narrator tells us, "Yet, though before all was won the Battle of Five Armies was fought, and Thorin was slain, and many deeds of renown were done, the matter would scarcely have concerned later history, or earned more than a note in the long annals of the Third Age, but for an 'accident' by the way." Tolkien has already added the scare quotes here to indicate at this early point in the text that the "accident," while it certainly seemed to be so, was, in fact, no accident. This will be unpacked in later dialogue, but there were multiple wills at work, including one above all, to make this "accident" happen. Like so many other acts of providence, it could only be perceived as something more in retrospect. A similar statement appears not much later to this effect: "In the end Bilbo won the game, more by luck (as it seemed) than by wits." There will be other such suggestive comments like this that have the same effect as the scare quotes. What seemed like luck was another will at work giving him what he needed to win the riddle game and to be able to escape with the Ring.

Thin and Stretched

In *LOTR* from the beginning of chapter 1, we are told of one of the effects of the Ring on Bilbo: his prolonged vigor. He found the Ring when he was fifty, and he is now turning 111 looking no worse for wear. Between this and the wealth he possessed (largely as a result of his quest with the Dwarves to Erebor), Bilbo seemed to have far too much going for him. Other Hobbits said, "It will have to be paid for … It isn't natural, and trouble will come of it" (I/1). On both accounts, they were right.

Bilbo's being so "well-preserved" was a result of his possession of the Ring. But it came at a cost. In his words, "'I am old Gandalf. I don't look it, but I am beginning to feel it in my heart of hearts. *Well-preserved* indeed!' he snorted, 'Why, I feel all thin,

---

[20] J. R. R. Tolkien, trans., *The Old English Exodus*, ed. Joan Turville-Petre (Oxford: Clarendon, 1981). Since, as far as I am aware, the latter text has not been reprinted, it is available at: https://archive.org/details/document_20230827.

sort of *stretched*, if you know what I mean: like butter that has been scraped over too much bread. That can't be right. I need a change or something'" (I/1; emphases original). Bilbo realizes that his life is not as others perceive it to be and that he requires a change, but when he knows what needs to be done and the time comes to make his decision, he finds that he cannot bring himself to do it. It is only after a prolonged struggle with Gandalf that he is able to do what must be done.

While the Ring is a symbol—for in the story this is the nature of its origin—of "the will to mere power, seeking to make itself objective by physical force and mechanism, and so also inevitably by lies" (Letter #131), the power presents itself as an overwhelming force by which to work one's will. That is what it was to be for Sauron to use as a way to dominate the wills of others, to make the world ordered as he thought it should be ordered, and ultimately to be worshiped as this world's Creator. In fact, Tolkien said that the conflict in *LOTR* "is not basically about 'freedom', though that is naturally involved." Tolkien continues,

> It is about God, and His sole right to divine honour. The Eldar and the Númenóreans believed in The One, the true God, and held worship of any other person an abomination. Sauron desired to be a God-King, and was held to be this by his servants; if he had been victorious he would have demanded divine honour from all rational creatures and absolute temporal power over the whole world. (Letter #183; cf. Letter #131)[21]

To make the Ring powerful enough to potentially achieve his goals, Sauron needed to put much of himself into it to concentrate such power. As Tolkien says in Letter #211, "I should say it [the Ring] was a mythical way of representing the truth that *potency* (or perhaps rather *potentiality*) if it is to be exercised, and produce results, has to be externalized and so as it were passes, to a greater or lesser degree, out of one's direct control. A man who wishes to exert 'power' must have subjects, who are not himself. But he then depends on them" (emphases original).

This is a point also exemplified by Sauron's master Melkor. While one will need to read *The Silmarillion* and *The History of Middle-earth* for more details, Melkor had achieved a wider scope of domination than Sauron did, not only because he had been

---

[21] Christopher Tolkien likewise describes a coincidence of Frodo originally being named "Bingo" and how the toy koalas named "the Bingos" he and his siblings played with had a demonic character "composed of monomaniac religious despotism and a lust for destruction through high explosive" (J. R. R. Tolkien, *The Return of the Shadow: The History of the Lord of the Rings Part One*, The History of Middle-earth 6, ed. Christopher Tolkien [Boston: Houghton Mifflin, 1988], 34).

at work in marring the world of Arda from its conception, but also because, "Sauron's, relatively smaller, power was *concentrated*; Morgoth's vast power was *disseminated*. The whole of 'Middle-earth' was Morgoth's Ring, though temporarily his attention was mainly upon the North-west."[22] Melkor had been the most powerful of Eru Ilúvatar's creatures, but over time he expended so much of his power in dominating the wills of others and corrupting them into being servants, even worshipers, of his, as well as in making other abominable corruptions of creation. It was because he had introduced a corruptive element of his own power into the substance of gold that Sauron could use it for his perverse magical ends in the first place.[23] But in expending so much of himself, he made himself weaker and more dependent on those he had dominated. Sauron appears to have sought to achieve a dominion like his master's while concentrating his power chiefly in one object.

And so with this power he expended and concentrated came the amplification of his character as a tempter and deceiver in the image of his master Melkor. As we will return to later, he hastened the fall of Númenor, the greatest kingdom of Men the world had ever seen, by deceiving them, including about their ability to claim immortality for themselves. Here and elsewhere, he had sought to confuse Men about the nature of true immortality, making them think it consists of "clinging to Time" rather than "freedom from Time" (Letter #208).

This is ultimately where the temptation of the Ring comes from, even if it is not something the bearer is conscious of. After all, the tale is "mainly concerned with Death, and Immortality; and the 'escapes': serial longevity, and hoarding memory" (#211).[24] While the Ring is not the only way this is manifest in the story, it is rather clearly the most potent source of temptation to surpass creaturely limitations (Letter #131). One like Bilbo may not necessarily wish to use the power of the Ring to press others to be worshipers of oneself, as one more potent and more arrogant like Sauron would wish to do, but it would still present temptation in its apparent power to ward off death and the natural deterioration of mortality. As Tolkien says in a footnote in Letter #131: "each 'Kind' has a natural span, integral to its biological and spiritual nature. This cannot really be *increased* qualitatively or quantitatively; so that prolongation in time is like stretching a wire out ever tauter, or 'spreading butter ever thinner' – it becomes an intolerable torment."

---

[22] Tolkien, *Morgoth's Ring*, 400 (emphases original).

[23] Ibid.

[24] In an unpublished letter to a Mrs. Munby, he says that his story "is really about Death and pity and Self-sacrifice." For more on this letter, see https://tolkiengateway.net/wiki/Letter_to_Mrs_Munby.

By the will of Eru Ilúvatar, there is more beyond death for Men, and thus for Hobbits, but it is beyond the bounds of this world and time, and what exactly it is remains unclear at this time. Only those most acquainted with the Elves or most knowledgeable of history and tradition might be aware of what has been said of the Second Music that will come with the new creation. But much trust and acceptance of creaturely limitations ordained by the Creator are necessary. As a messenger to the Númenóreans says in a draft of Tolkien's preserved in *Sauron Defeated* concerning the fate of Men,

> [O]f you is required the greater trust, knowing not what lies before you in a little while. But whereas we know nothing of the mind of Eru in this … we say to you that that trust, if you give it, will not be despised; and though it take many ages of Men … that Iluvatar the Father will not let those perish for ever who love him and who love the world that He has made.[25]

Yet the love for the world by those who will ultimately leave it means that life within this world can become the only life imaginable to them, and so one may seek the prolongation of the same in place of a greater, yet currently inscrutable, immortality. Thus, Tolkien says in Letter #212, "To attempt by device or 'magic' to recover longevity is thus a supreme folly and wickedness of 'mortals'. Longevity or counterfeit 'immortality' (true immortality is beyond Eä) is the chief bait of Sauron – it leads the small to a Gollum, and the great to a Ringwraith." The power to confer this counterfeit immortality also seemingly implies the power to do what one wants with that life.

The Ring is even beneficial to Bilbo in *The Hobbit*, as it enables him and his fellows to complete their quest. But the longer he possessed it, the more *it* possessed *him*. This becomes clear in the conversation he has in this book with Gandalf as he reaches a point of no longer acting like himself, even sounding like Gollum in referring to the Ring as his "Precious."

Bilbo had already become more like Gollum than he ever intended because the Ring's corrupting effects, masked as they are by its more apparent benefits, are subtler than he knew. While Sauron's will to power and domination poured into the Ring was designed to give him the means of making others into his worshipers, those who came into possession of it could still be shaped into those who were made into the likeness of Sauron. As we will explore later, this would be more literally the case for the Wise and Great in Middle-earth, as they would functionally be new Saurons, assuming they could vanquish him in the first place. For those like Bilbo and Gollum, their shaping in

---

[25] J. R. R. Tolkien, *Sauron Defeated: The End of the Third Age; The History of the Lord of the Rings Part Four*, The History of Middle-earth 9, ed. Christopher Tolkien (London: HarperCollins, 1992), 346.

Sauron's likeness would not necessarily manifests in the wish to dominate—though in the wrong circumstances, this could happen as well—but it would manifest in the underlying will to transgress their creaturely limitations. Even though they might not become worshipers of Sauron per se without the Ring in his possession, they would nevertheless become like him because of becoming like what they worshiped according to their own wills. That is a still a form of idolatry in that something else is being put in place of God and the will of one other than God Is being treated as supreme.

Although the Ring is not a mere stand-in for sin, the dynamics of temptation and the deterioration brought by giving oneself over to temptation are well exemplified. The more one gives into temptation, the weaker the will becomes until one's will becomes a tool for whatever controls it, even when one wishes to do otherwise and knows it ought to be done. The Ring and its tempting power had such an effect on Gollum that it resulted in a split in personalities and wills with one being typically obsequious to the other so that they work towards satisfying a common desire. As the rest of the story will show, he is the most vivid example of the will dominated by sin that Paul describes in Rom 7:14–25. The other example that Tolkien gives in the aforementioned Letter #212 of a Ringwraith is even deeper in this state because of how long his will has been enthralled to Sauron's. Bilbo is nowhere near as far along as either Gollum or the Ringwraiths, but he has possessed the Ring long enough, and it has had enough of an impact on his will that he can no longer do what is right in giving the Ring up without the work of divine providence. In this case, that work of divine providence is embodied in a literally angelic interventionist named Gandalf.

Gandalf, being faithful to his mission, does not attempt to overwhelm Bilbo's mind and will by his sheer power in an attempt to dominate him, so that he could thereby make him do "what's best for him." As Tolkien said in Letter #156, Gandalf's mission and the mission of his fellows was to "train, advise, instruct, arouse the hearts and minds of those threatened by Sauron to a resistance with their own strengths; and not just to do the job for them." But in this case, Gandalf must be more forceful because of the power he is contending with. At this point in the conversation, he has had to stand up and speak sternly, saying, "You will be a fool if you do, Bilbo … You make that clearer with every word you say. It has got far too much hold on you. Let it go! And then you can go yourself and be free" (I/1). As sin entraps and enthralls by offering a seeming good if one will but transgress, only to bring ultimate decay and death—which was the case all the way back in Gen 3 with how the serpent talked Eve (and ultimately Adam) into violating God's will—salvation from the same is presented as liberation. As Jesus says in John 8:34–36, "Truly, truly I say to you, everyone who commits sin is a slave of sin. Now the slave does not remain in the house forever; the son does remain forever. So if the Son sets you free, you really will be free" (NASB). Gandalf's work here is not one of proclaiming the gospel that has yet to be announced, but it is ultimately about Bilbo accepting the Creator's will, whether or not Bilbo knows of the Creator at this point (though it seems probable), and accepting the way out he provides through relinquishing the Ring (and all the seeming benefits and the actual costs pertaining thereto) and, thus, staying true to his own word. In a way, it is a natural theological preparation that is fundamentally consonant with the gospel.[26]

Bilbo not only continues to resist Gandalf's exhortation, but he even threatens to pull his small sword on him. Only here does Gandalf flash his power to illustrate how foolish Bilbo would be to fight him: "He took a step towards the hobbit, and he seemed to grow tall and menacing; his shadow filled the little room" (I/1). This is the first of several "transfiguration" scenes, wherein someone gains sight of the hidden power and/or glory of someone else, like Peter, James, and John saw of Jesus in his Transfiguration. But this is not Gandalf's gambit to compel Bilbo's will, for the struggle continues after this. It is merely to bring him to his senses with a dramatic, though still understated, display. Indeed, Bilbo initially asks Gandalf what has come over him, not at first recognizing that it was Bilbo who had something come over him, which in turn causes him to reflect on his attachment to the Ring:

> But I felt so queer. And yet it would be a relief in a way not to be bothered with it anymore. It has been growing on my mind lately. Sometimes I felt it was like an eye looking at me. And I am always wanting to put it on and disappear, don't you know; or wondering if it is safe, and pulling it out to make sure. I tried locking it up, but I found I couldn't rest without it in my pocket. I don't know why. And I don't seem to be able to make up my mind. (I/1)

This is reminiscent of obsessive attachments to particular ways of sin (e.g., Ps 106:43; Isa 59:7). And even with the realization of his problem, Bilbo still finds it exceedingly difficult to relinquish the Ring. The resolution is worth noting: "Bilbo took out the envelope, just as he was about to set it by the clock, his hand jerked back, and the packet fell on the floor. Before he could pick it up, the wizard stooped and seized it and set it in its place. A spasm of anger passed swiftly over the hobbit's face again. Suddenly it gave way to a look of relief and a laugh" (I/1). We see Bilbo resist giving up the source of his temptation until the last possible moment. He is only able to do so

---

[26] As Tolkien said, this is a monotheistic world of natural theology (Letter #165; see also Letters #153, #156, #181).

when Gandalf takes the matter out of his hands and does what the better side of Bilbo promised to do. And Bilbo was still on the verge of rage when this happened. Ultimately, though, he feels relief and laughs. Laughter is a motif of resolution to track in *LOTR*. It often signifies delivering joy (or the joy of deliverance), but there will be other times when it has a decidedly different significance for characters given over to despair. For Bilbo, the delivering joy accompanies his temporary victory over the source of his temptation. But we will see later that this victory is not final. It will need to be sustained by other decisions.

The Road Goes Ever On

As Bilbo leaves Bag End for Rivendell with his Dwarf companions, he sings a song that he composed:

> The Road goes ever on and on
> Down from the door where it began.
> Now far ahead the Road has gone,
> And I must follow, if I can,
> Pursuing it with eager feet,
> Until it joins some larger way
> Where many paths and errands meet.
> And whither then? I cannot say. (I/1)

This song is then reprised by Frodo two chapters later, of which he says, "He [Bilbo] used often to say there was only one Road; that it was like a great river; its springs were at every doorstep, and every path was its tributary" (I/3). The resonance of this song for our purpose may not be obvious, but it is important to recognize the relation of this song to the last comment of Gandalf from *The Hobbit*:

> 'Then the prophecies of the old songs have turned out to be true after a fashion!' said Bilbo.
>
> 'Of course!' said Gandalf. 'And why should not they prove true? Surely you don't disbelieve the prophecies, because you had a hand in bringing them about yourself? You don't really suppose, do you, that all your adventures and escapes were managed by mere luck, just for your sole benefit? You are a very fine

person, Mr Baggins, and I am very fond of you; but you are only quite a little fellow in a wide world after all!' (ch. 19)[27]

Gandalf was thus conveying to Bilbo that he had been an instrument of Providence whose entire journey had participated in larger purposes than he could conceive at the time. The song thus represents his acknowledgment of his place within and connection with the larger world as well as the providential purpose that guides it. He must follow the way, even when he does not know where it is going, because he has already been guided by larger purposes on that Road before, and this is his expression of faith—both in terms of trust and in terms of fidelity—that he ought to follow it wherever that One leads him on it.

The Shadow of the Past

The succeeding chapter, "The Shadow of the Past," includes some reiteration of points already made. In the interest of largely maintaining narrative order in this commentary, I have decided to allow the degree of repetition to see how the various points observed reappear in the narrative rather than, say, addressing each manifestation of a theme the first time it appears. As an example, there is this comment from Gandalf early in his explanation to Frodo about the Rings of Power and their history:

> A mortal, Frodo, who keeps one of the Great Rings, does not die, but he does not grow or obtain more life, he merely continues, until at last every minute is a weariness. And if he often uses the ring to make himself invisible, he *fades*: he becomes in the end invisible permanently, and walks in the twilight under the eye of the dark power that rules the Rings. Yes, sooner or later—later, if he is strong or well-meaning to begin with, but neither strength nor good purpose will last—sooner or later the dark power will devour him. (I/2)

This shows the power that the Ring wields through (most of) the Great Rings and how they affect mortals. The condition described is the state of the Ringwraiths, who have become invisible to the Seen world, save by their raiment, because they have long since faded and been consumed by the Dark Lord whose will is their life. Gollum,

---

[27] As in my book on *The Hobbit*, I have only used chapter references. There have been many editions of *The Hobbit* with many differences in pagination. No solution to the problem created by this for citation purposes is perfect for readers who will have a variety of editions. My own imperfect solution is to reference what is consistent across all the editions: the chapter numbers. The edition I recommend for reference is J. R. R. Tolkien, *The Annotated Hobbit*, rev. and exp. ed., annotated by Douglas A. Anderson (Boston: Houghton Mifflin, 2002).

particularly because he was not exposed to the direct influence of the Dark Lord while he possessed the Ring, is not yet so far down this road as to have faded altogether, but the Ring has obviously left an indelible mark on him. Bilbo was not even so far as Gollum, and he is representative of the surprising strength of Hobbits, "Soft as butter they can be, and yet sometimes as tough as old tree-roots. I think it likely that some would resist the Rings far longer than most of the Wise would believe" (I/2). But the fading of his will had begun, and the counterfeit immortality took a toll on his spirit, which further demonstrates Gandalf's point that "neither strength nor good purpose will last." This is another way in which Hobbits trouble the counsels of the Wise and Great, for we will see some among the Wise and Great who will not resist Sauron's influence (even minus the Ring) like Bilbo could or Frodo and Sam will. Such is the combination of common and special grace given to the Hobbits who would need it for the One's ultimate purpose for the Ring. But we will have more to say about that later.

Sauron's Vindictive Viciousness

As indicated earlier, Sauron had entirely overlooked Hobbits. There had been no reason for him to take notice of them. By the time he had returned to Mordor, they lived on the opposite side of the continent from his realm. Before that, they were even more obscure, and so he had no reason to seek them out. They had no power, prowess, or special skill for him to exploit. They were of no utility to him, being as insignificant to his designs as an ant in Arnor. But as soon as he knows them, he hates them, for Gandalf warns, "your safety has passed. He does not need you—he has many more useful servants—but he won't forget you again. And hobbits as miserable slaves would please him far more than hobbits happy and free. There is such a thing as malice and revenge" (I/2).

Sauron is not absolute evil, but he is the chief embodiment of the powers of evil at the time of this story, and so it is appropriate that he embodies such naked malice and the desire to enslave for the sake of enslavement. We have already noted that it is a major function of sin to enslave those under its power for the sheer sake of domination (cf. Rom 6:15–23). As Sauron, like Satan and his demons, cannot be the Creator and giver of life, he settles for the counterfeit of the worship due to the Creator that he enforces by domination, destruction, and corruption of what is good (cf. Letter #183). Tolkien said of Sauron in comments preserved in *Morgoth's Ring*, "He did not object to the existence of the world, so long as he could do what he liked with it. He still had the relics of positive purposes, that descended from the good of the nature in which he began: it had been his virtue (and therefore also the cause of his fall, and of his relapse) that he loved order and coordination, and disliked all confusion and wasteful friction."[28]

The Hobbits thus doubly enraged him. On the one hand, they were unworthy of his notice for all his years in the world, and so being made aware of them—and their lack of usefulness to him—would upset his sense of proper order in the world. If the situation had been otherwise, he probably would have enslaved them just to satisfy his own sense of where they fit. On the other hand, precisely because he was among the Wise who overlooked them, he could not have fathomed that the object of his desire should have come into the possession of such an insignificant creature. But now these people he had overlooked were his obstacle to possessing the Ring. Now he would enslave them for sheer malice and petty revenge.

Time and Responsibility

After Gandalf explains more about what the Ring is to Frodo, about Sauron's desire for it, and how he has arisen again to seize it, we have one of the most well-known exchanges from *LOTR*:

> 'Always after a defeat and a respite, the Shadow takes another shape and grows again.'
> 'I wish it need not have happened in my time,' said Frodo.
> 'So do I,' said Gandalf, 'and so do all who live to see such times. But that is not for them to decide. All we have to decide is what to do with the time that is given to us.' (I/2)

All of this well exemplifies Tolkien's philosophy of history, which I will address in more detail in the next chapter. In the normal course of history, there is no final victory. All of that waits for the eschaton, and Tolkien's hope is eschatologically informed by the Christian expectation of the Lord's coming again and all the other events that will follow thereafter. There are hints of eschatology in Tolkien's work, and he struggled with how to balance articulating such expectation with the setting of this work in an imaginary time before the coming of Christ and even before Israel. But until that final victory, every person of every time has the same responsibility of deciding what to do with the time given to them.

A similar principle is behind the commands to be vigilant in the NT (Matt 24:42–43; 25:13; Mark 13:34–35, 37; Luke 12:37–39; 21:34–36; 1 Thess 5:2–6; 1 Pet 5:8).

---

[28] Tolkien, *Morgoth's Ring*, 396.

As I have argued elsewhere,[29] the point of such instructions is not about looking for signs to see if the time is near. After all, Jesus himself said to his disciples before his ascension, "It is not for you to know times or seasons that the Father has fixed by his own authority. But you will receive power when the Holy Spirit has come upon you, and you will be my witnesses in Jerusalem and in all Judea and Samaria, and to the end of the earth" (Acts 1:7–8, ESV). Vigilance has to do with being vigilant about one's conduct in doing what needs to be done regardless of the time one finds oneself in. Final victory is not in our hands, but what is in our hands is the same responsibility to decide what to do with the time that is given to us and to be vigilant in doing what is right. And as with the heroes of this story, we may participate in "samples or glimpses of final victory" (Letter #195) by this vigilance.

The Tragedy of Sméagol

Gandalf then tells Frodo more about the history of the Ring and how it has come to be in Frodo's possession, which requires him to tell the story of Sméagol (and Déagol). After Frodo hears the story of Sméagol, he calls him loathsome. Gandalf is not so hasty: "I think it is a sad story … and it might have happened to others, even to some hobbits that I have known" (I/2). Gandalf is of one mind with Bilbo concerning when the time came that he had a chance to kill Gollum to protect himself in *The Hobbit*:

> He must get away, out of this horrible darkness, while he had any strength left. He must fight. He must stab the foul thing, put its eyes out, kill it. It meant to kill him. No, not a fair fight. He was invisible now. Gollum had no sword. Gollum had not actually threatened to kill him, or tried to yet. And he was miserable, alone, lost. A sudden understanding, a pity mixed with horror, welled up in Bilbo's heart: a glimpse of endless unmarked days without light or hope of betterment, hard stone, cold fish, sneaking and whispering. (ch. 5)

This pity, motivated by the compassionate thought of what Gollum's life must have been like for years beyond Bilbo's reckoning, is something of the natural theological equivalent of "there, but for the grace of God, go I." And that is what Gandalf similarly conveys to Frodo, as he knows better than Frodo that other Hobbits could well have become a Gollum.

This pity is grounded in Tolkien's own formation by Scripture and observance of the Mass. In the case of the former, despite its frequent misuse for rebuking any

---

[29] See my post at: https://krharriman.substack.com/p/watch-therefore.

negative statement not affirmed by the person using the text, one text that likely reso-nates here is Matt 7:1–2: "Do not judge, so that you will not be judged. For by what judgment you judge, you will judged, and by what measure you measure out, it will be measured out to you" (LEB). Similarly, Rom 3:9–18 (as well as the more famous 3:23) speaks to the common lot of sin that enslave all of humanity, so that neither Jews nor gentiles are immune. Paul also reminds us of how we will all appear before the judg-ment seat of God in Rom 14:10. Whatever judgments we make in the present time should be tempered with discernment in accordance with right thinking rather than su-perficial appearance (John 7:24).

For this matter, Tolkien's Letter #250 to Michael Tolkien is particularly apropos. His son had written to him to express the struggles he was having with his faith and with the Church. One ought to read the letter as a whole for the insight it gives into Tolkien's faith and his specifically Roman Catholic devotion. One can see in it how Tolkien was, at least in this way, like his written character. First, he compares the Church to the academy, which should no doubt still resonate today for how much peo-ple continue (both rightly and wrongly) to bemoan the states of both institutions, even suggesting they should be done away with. Both the Church and the academy are also degraded by the fact that they must be occupied by humans marred by imperfection and sin. Failings in the Church inevitably give the sense of being worse because the aim of the Church's mission is higher than the academy or any other institution filled with humans. But in the end, Tolkien insisted you cannot maintain a tradition of learn-ing without institutions of learning,

> And you cannot maintain a religion without a church and ministers; and that means professionals: priests and bishops — and also monks. The precious wine must (in this world) have a bottle, or some less worthy substitute. For myself, I find I become less cynical rather than more – remembering my own sins and follies; and realize that men's hearts are not often as bad as their acts, and very seldom as bad as their words. (Especially in our age, which is one of sneer and cynicism. We are freer from hypocrisy, since it does not 'do' to profess holiness or utter high sentiments; but it is one of inverted hypocrisy like the widely cur-rent inverted snobbery: men profess to be worse than they are.)

The fact that the Church is composed of humans makes problems inevitable, for the Christian faith entails a communion not only between us and God, but also between us and others who were made in God's image, though they are also fallen like we are. This is nothing new to Church history for anyone who has even a passing knowledge of it. Indeed, problems appear all across the NT, and problems are often the occasions for writing the various letters. Cynicism is easy to develop with an awareness of such history, but cultivating an awareness of one's own sins—for which the practice of confession is helpful (Jas 5:16; 1 John 1:9)—goes a long way in curtailing this mindset and attitude towards the Church. In light of teachings on judgment like Matt 7:1–5 and teachings on forgiving as we have been forgiven (Matt 6:12, 14–15; 18:21–35), one ought to become less cynical, not more, towards the Church and more cognizant of how the Holy Spirit has been at work in surprising ways in this community of broken people.

Second, Tolkien noted in the same letter that scandals caused by others are problems, of course, but he reminded his son that they are occasions of temptation, which can become convenient excuses for us to eschew the cultivation of awareness of our own sinfulness and need for mercy, because at least we are not like those truly awful hypocrites. Before we know it, we become Pharisees all the same (Luke 18:9–14). He then told his son that the only cure for "sagging or fainting faith" is the Communion/Eucharist. He even told him to take it in circumstances that affront his taste, including with priests he does not like, people who annoy him, and others who might make him ask "what are they doing here?" All of this helps to remind us who we worship, who we are (as someone our Lord came to bring into his kingdom), who others are (as those our Lord came to bring into his kingdom), and to participate in that same grace by how we interact with others with fitting mercy and pity.

As Gandalf reminds us, we are not so beyond the potential for falling as we might think, and others are not so far gone as we might think, "Even Gollum was not wholly ruined. He had proved tougher than even one of the Wise would have guessed—as a hobbit might" (I/2). This is another reminder of how the Hobbits can trouble the Wise and the Great, for they not only defy their expectations, but they exceed how they would have done in similar situations. Given the wrong situation, it is their very wisdom and power that can make them more susceptible to the influence of the Ring than those who are not among the Wise and Great. And because Gollum was not wholly ruined, he still had one of his wills and one part of his mind that was not so entirely consumed by the Precious that he could not recall his past. That was what Bilbo, as a fellow Hobbit, brought to him in their conversation, as he heard for the first time in centuries a kindly voice, "bringing up memories of wind, and trees, and sun on the grass, and such forgotten things" (I/2). Light was able to enter his mind from outside, even if only "as through a chink in the dark" (I/2).[30]

---

[30] Fleming Rutledge compares this description to the situation of the Gerasene demoniac (*Battle*, 60–61).

After all, the darkness and isolation that Gollum drove himself into, in part out of exploratory interest, had only promoted his hatred when he found so much emptiness beneath the mountains he inhabited. As Gandalf says, "he hated the dark, and he hated light more: he hated everything, and the Ring most of all" (I/2). Indeed, "He hated it and loved it, as he hated and loved himself. He could not get rid of it. He had no will left in the matter" (I/2). The last sentence in particular shows how Bilbo was at risk of reaching that same despairing end. He had a hard enough time giving up the Ring after he possessed it for a much shorter time than Sméagol, and he could not have brought himself to do as he did without the insistent help of Gandalf. Gollum had reached a point of having split his personality and will, but one was largely obsequious to the other, and in the matter of his Precious it was completely so. As with the man dominated by sin that Paul portrays in Rom 7:14–25, part of him knows what he ought to do, but he cannot do it. That is at least part of what motivated him to hate himself, as he was too weak to be rid of the Ring and to change his life for the better. In turn, he hated the Ring because he knew it did this to him by that power it had over him that he never had the knowledge of lore to define. But at the same time, he is where he is because he loved the Ring that he hated most of all, so that he called it his Precious, even loving it as he loved himself, for the Ring allowed him to prolong his existence. The longer he possessed it, the more it came to possess him, so that an internal voice and will was implanted in him, and the Ring became part of him, so to speak.

The Strangest Event in the History of the Ring

At this point, Gandalf must speak about the transferal of the Ring in what he calls "the strangest event in the whole history of the Ring so far: Bilbo's arrival just at that time, and putting his hand on it, blindly, in the dark" (I/2). It seemed to have happened "by accident," but it was not so. The power of the Ring was at work in this. As it had betrayed Isildur and Déagol, it now abandoned Gollum in the hopes of being brought back to its master who was bending his thought to it. But it could not have intended for a Hobbit, a race its master had completely overlooked, to pick it up.

Since Bilbo did not intend to find it, and he came upon it at just the right time without realizing it, Gandalf declares, "Behind that there was something else at work, beyond any design of the Ring-maker. I can put it no plainer than by saying Bilbo was *meant* to find the Ring, and *not* by its maker. In which case you were also *meant* to have it. And that may be an encouraging thought" (I/2). Tolkien's own italicized words are an example of a kind of formally agentless construction using a passive verb that nevertheless implies agency, specifically of the agency that God is exercising in the action of the verb. This construction formally focuses on the action itself, though in its own fashion it brings to the hearer's/reader's mind the matter of who could be the agent.

Since Gandalf is speaking of "another will," he is obviously referring to a person. This other will is powerful enough to envelop Sauron's designs into his own and thereby thwart them. And this other will has a plan for the Ring that spanned so many years so that not only was Gollum in the right place at the right time for Bilbo to find the Ring on his way to somewhere far away, but so that Bilbo should possess it for long thereafter in order for Frodo, ultimately, to have it (even though Frodo would not be born for twenty-seven more years after Bilbo found the Ring). And this is an encouraging thought because this will is of One who is good. What other will could this be but the will of the One (Eru), the All-Father (Ilúvatar)? And thus, what else could we be talking about here but the work of divine providence? Tolkien used this very text as an example in Letter #156 when he said,

> I have purposely kept all allusions to the highest matters down to mere hints, perceptible only by the most attentive, or kept them under unexplained symbolic forms. So God and the 'angelic' gods, the Lords or Powers of the West, only peep through in such places as Gandalf's conversation with Frodo: 'behind that there was something else at work, beyond any design of the Ring-maker's'; or in Faramir's Númenórean grace at dinner.

Eru Ilúvatar himself had said in the account of the *Ainulindalë*—the music he composed for the angelic spirits of the Ainur by which he created the world—to Melkor, Sauron's master, when he set forth the vision of what music had wrought, "And thou, Melkor, shalt see that no theme may be played that hath not its uttermost source in me, nor can any alter the music in my despite. For he that attempteth shall prove but mine instrument in the devising of things more wonderful, which he himself hath not imagined."[31] This encompassing statement about the history of the world propounded in the Music—known in its entirety only to the One—sets the framework for understanding this set of events in the history of the Ring as the providential work of the One. This is yet another instance in which we can see why Tolkien wanted *The Silmarillion*

---

[31] Tolkien, *Silmarillion*, "Ainulindalë." In an earlier draft of this part of the chapter of *LOTR*, Tolkien added further elaboration after the statement about Bilbo and Frodo being meant to have the Ring, "But the evil they [the Rings] work according to their maker's design turns often to good that he did not intend, and even to his loss and defeat." Tolkien, *Return of the Shadow*, 262. This part was removed because it does not fit as well with Frodo's subsequent dialogue to not see how this can be comforting.

published alongside *LOTR*, not only for the hundreds of links between them,[32] but also for how it provides the framework for *LOTR* (albeit imperfectly, since Tolkien never finished his revisions of what his son would publish as *The Silmarillion*).

Pity

In any case, Frodo ultimately does not find encouragement in what Gandalf says, since he does not have Gandalf's broader and higher perspective on these events. He cannot yet imagine what good could come of this; he is mostly just baffled that he should have such a thing in his possession and that it should put him in such danger. After Gandalf then explains to Frodo how Sauron has been made aware of the name "Baggins" via Gollum, Frodo at first only thinks of it as a pity that Bilbo did not kill Gollum when he had the chance, as that would mean he would not be in the predicament he is in now with Sauron knowing the name. Gandalf once again attempts to give Frodo a different perspective: "Pity? It was Pity that stayed his hand. Pity, and Mercy: not to strike without need. And he has been well rewarded, Frodo. Be sure that he took so little hurt from the evil, and escaped in the end, because he began his ownership of the Ring so. With Pity" (I/2).

The capitalization is noteworthy. It appears to signify that it is the result of an external power described as a proper person. The way the event is described in *The Hobbit* likewise signifies providential action. God's providence comes by internal influence as well, where something can come upon a character as if from within. Yet the description of that influence maintains the impression that its ultimate source is from something or someone other than the character. We have seen one example of this in how Bilbo was saved by "luck" in having the right answer come to him at the right time in the riddle game. And from the same part of the story, when Bilbo considered killing Gollum, there is this description: "A sudden understanding, a pity mixed with horror, welled up in Bilbo's heart: a glimpse of endless unmarked days without light or hope of betterment, hard stone, cold fish, sneaking and whispering. All these thoughts passed in a flash of a second" (ch. 5). Rutledge has analyzed this latter text especially well:

> Note the phrasing: "A sudden understanding … welled up in Bilbo's heart" and "as if lifted by a new strength and resolve." These are early examples of a syntactical technique that Tolkien will use repeatedly throughout his epic. He does not write "Bilbo suddenly understood," or "Bilbo acquired a new strength." Bilbo is not the acting subject. Understanding and pity *well up*; a new

---

[32] See https://krharriman.substack.com/p/links-between-the-silmarillion-and.

strength and resolve *lift him*; they are active agents. Grammatically, Bilbo is the passive recipient of understanding and pity, strength and resolve. They come to him from outside himself. We will see this sort of thing happening over and over again throughout the Ring saga, and it is of the greatest importance. Bilbo is *enabled* to put his new gifts to work, so that we admire what he does; but he is not the author either of the gifts or of the consequent actions. The actions flow out of the gifts.[33]

Indeed, this fits more broadly with what we have seen of divine grace (both common and special) at work in gifts including courage, strength, and, now, pity. Tolkien saw "pity" as a word of "moral and imaginative worth" (Letter #153). Properly speaking, "Pity must restrain one from doing something immediately desirable and seemingly advantageous" (Letter #153). Elsewhere, he said pity "is also an absolute requirement in moral judgement (since it is present in the Divine nature)" (Letter #246). In that same letter he said in a footnote that pity "to be a true virtue must be directed to the good of its object. It is empty if it is exercised *only* to keep oneself 'clean', free from hate or the actual doing of injustice, though this is also a good motive" (emphasis original).

Such is the virtue that supplied a sort of inoculation for Bilbo. Bilbo could not escape the effects of the Ring for as long as he possessed it. But the fact that he began his ownership of it with pity—a virtue beyond the ken of the Ring or its master and completely inimical to both, a virtue which welled up within him from the influence of the other will at work here—is why the effects on him were not as severe as they could have been.

Moreover, when Frodo insists that Gollum deserves death for what he has done (as he has been made aware only now of the story of how Gollum came to possess the Ring), Gandalf acknowledges that he does, but with a caveat:

> Many that live deserve death. And some that die deserve life. Can you give it to them? Then do not be too eager to deal out death in judgement. For even the very wise cannot see all ends. I have not much hope that Gollum can be cured before he dies, but there is a chance of it. And he is bound up with the fate of the Ring. My heart tells me that he has some part to play yet, for good or ill, before the end; and when that comes, the pity of Bilbo may rule the fate of many—yours not least.[34] (I/2)

---

[33] Rutledge, *Battle*, 27 (emphases original).

[34] By contrast, an earlier draft featured Gandalf saying, "Yes, he deserved to die ... but we did not kill him. He is very old, and very wretched. The Wood-elves have him in prison, and treat [him] with

In case it was not obvious how important this and the larger exchange of Frodo and Gandalf is, some portion is repeated in *The Two Towers* (IV/1) and *The Return of the King* (VI/3). When Frodo's own chance comes when he has the advantage over Gollum and it would seem in his best interest—as he thought it was in Bilbo's best interest—to kill Gollum to prevent him from causing further trouble, he will instead make the harder and (to Sam, as to Frodo himself when considering Bilbo's decision) seemingly ill-advised decision to let him live. Frodo could not have imagined at the time how true Gandalf's words would be, which he could only appreciate in retrospect, that "the pity of Bilbo may rule the fate of many—yours not least." Because Bilbo, and then Frodo, exercised the divine virtue of pity, divine providence then took up their actions to bring this story to its divinely planned end. In such ways, one can become a participant in the same grace by which God brings salvation.

The rest of the story will also bear out the complexities of the workings of Providence, morality, and choice. Not a few times, actions that are evil in themselves or that appear to be foolish will still be taken up by Providence to accomplish an unanticipated good end. Tragically, especially in one of the scenes by which Tolkien was most moved, heroic and generally upright characters can make poor decisions that can frustrate a good end. Even in the latter cases, Providence can bring about something extraordinary. Even the wisest often cannot discern how such complexities will resolve or should be resolved. This serves as a reminder that final judgment is not the province of any creature. It is the province only of the Creator who alone knows all. What is not the sole province of the Creator is the call to temper any inclination to judgment—particularly since we cannot execute final judgment—with fitting mercy and pity. Indeed, the Creator himself calls upon us to embody such divine virtues.

The Choices of Frodo

Despite all that Gandalf has said, Frodo remains convinced that matters are less complicated than he presents them. He wonders why the Ring has not been destroyed. In fact, he is sure that he would have destroyed it if Gandalf had simply warned him to this point. But when Gandalf challenges Frodo's certainty, Frodo attempts the simple

---

such kindness as they can find in their wise hearts. They feed him on clean food. But I do not think much can be done to cure him: yet even Gollum might prove useful for good before the end." Tolkien, *Return of the Shadow*, 264–65. This is an example of Tolkien revising the story in a way that better fit the theological-ethical framing/context he would give Gollum's part in the story, which will be outlined more extensively later. This is one of those areas where he was more conscious of the religious and Catholic character of his work in the revision, as he referenced in Letter #142.

matter of throwing it away. When he takes it out of his pocket, he begins examining it and admiring its beauty. He had intended to throw it into the same fire that had revealed the inscription on the Ring, "But he found now that he could not do so, not without a great struggle. He weighed the Ring in his hand, hesitating, forcing himself to remember all that Gandalf had told him; and then with an effort of will he made a movement, as if to cast it away—but he found that he had put it back in his pocket" (I/2). Frodo had never even used the Ring to this point, yet despite having a better understanding of what the Ring was than Bilbo did when he first possessed it, his will has already been compromised by the Ring. That which seems so easy when the responsibility is put on others is suddenly shown for the difficulty it is for one whose judgment has not yet been tempered with pity and mercy.

When Frodo puts himself to this initial test, he finds to his astonishment that he cannot pass it. He thus asks why the Ring should come to him—i.e., why this other will should mean for him to have it—and why he was chosen. While Frodo does not know the agent behind the passive verb "chosen" like Gandalf does, he now puts the question back to Gandalf, albeit in more succinct and indirect terms, of, if [God] indeed chose him, why [God] would choose him to have the Ring. Gandalf responds, "Such questions cannot be answered ... You may be sure that it was not for any merit that others do not possess: not for power or wisdom, at any rate. But you have been chosen, and you must therefore use such strength and heart and wits as you have" (I/2).

As people have reflected on biblical stories over the years, the same questions have been asked. Why, of all people in the world, were childless Abram/Abraham and Sarai/Sarah chosen? Why was Moses chosen? Why were Deborah, Gideon, and Manoah and his wife chosen? Why was David chosen? Why was Jeremiah chosen? Why was Mary chosen? Why were the apostles chosen, especially when one of them was to betray Jesus? Such questions could be multiplied indefinitely for anyone God chose for certain tasks, for delivering certain messages, for having certain ministries, and so on. Sometimes speculations have been offered to attempt to make various people appear "worthy" of their callings. But in the end, Gandalf's answer is the wisest. We cannot know, there is no reason to think it has anything to do with one's inherent or acquired qualities, and it is not important (besides, if we knew the reasons, would we arrogate ourselves a basis for disputing them?). What is important is the simple fact that one has been chosen for the purpose and one must respond accordingly. That includes using what one has—which is itself already a gift from God, as we have seen already—and trusting that if anything else is needed, it will be provided. That is the ultimate decision everyone listed above had to make.

Attempted Shifting

Naturally, Frodo struggles with the idea that he should have such a responsibility, since he has little of the qualities Gandalf has just listed. He thus offers the Ring to Gandalf, thinking him to be more worthy of being chosen for this task than him. Gandalf must set him straight:

> 'No!' cried Gandalf, springing to his feet. 'With that power I should have power too great and terrible. And over me the Ring would gain a power still greater and more deadly.' His eyes flashed and his face was lit as by a fire within. 'Do not tempt me! For I do not wish to become like the Dark Lord himself. Yet the way of the Ring to my heart is by pity, pity for weakness and the desire of strength to do good. Do not tempt me! I dare not take it, not even to keep it safe, unused. The wish to wield it would be too great for my strength. I shall have such need of it. Great perils lie before me.' (I/2)

Ralph Wood insightfully notes that "Tolkien understands the odd danger posed by virtue cut off from the Good. Over and again, he demonstrates his fundamental conviction that evil preys upon our virtues far more than our vices.".[36] As Gandalf's virtue is pity, the Ring's temptation of overwhelming power would have divorced that pity from justice and his will to do good from his humility of service to the One. Similarly, in Letter #246, after pursuing a hypothetical in which one of the powerful among the Free Peoples had come to possess the Ring and met Sauron in direct confrontation and assuming the conclusion that Gandalf defeated Sauron with his own Ring, Tolkien stated, "Gandalf as Ring-Lord would have been far worse than Sauron. He would have remained 'righteous', but self-righteous. He would have continued to rule and order things for 'good', and the benefit of his subjects according to his wisdom (which was and would have remained great)." He also adds in the margin, "Thus while Sauron multiplied [illegible word] evil, he left 'good' clearly distinguishable from it. Gandalf would have made good detestable and seem evil."

An earlier draft of "The Last Debate" (V/9) had also featured a similar declaration from Gandalf to a different audience. He said that if one of power were to become the new Ringlord, he would not only grow more powerful and desirous of power, but, moreover, he would subdue all minds under his will to make them follow his will:

---

[36] Ralph Wood, *The Gospel According to Tolkien: Visions of the Kingdom in Middle-earth* (Louisville: Westminster John Knox, 2003), 62.

And he could not be slain. More: the deepest secrets of the mind and heart of Sauron would become plain to him, so that the Dark Lord could do nothing unforeseen. The Ringlord would suck the very power and thought from him, so that all would forsake his allegiance and follow the Ringlord, and they would serve him and worship him as a God. And so Sauron would be overthrown utterly and fade into oblivion; but behold, there would be Sauron still.[37]

In light of these various comments, it is little wonder that Tolkien described the conflict in *LOTR* as one about "God, and His sole right to divine honour" (Letter #183). All who are tempted by the power of the Ring are tempted to transgress creaturely limitations. The benevolent with power are tempted to act as Sauron has in trying to put himself in the place of God. As upright as Gandalf is, he knows he cannot utterly resist this temptation if the Ring were given to his possession. There can be no shifting of this burden of bearing the Ring to him.

Frodo's Decision

At this point, it is finally apparent to Frodo that either he must bear the Ring for a while longer and take it away from the Shire, or everyone and everything he knows and loves will be destroyed when the Enemy reclaims his Ring. He is the only one who can do it for now, and so he makes his sacrificial resolve:

> I should like to save the Shire if I could—though there have been times when I thought the inhabitants to be too stupid and dull, and have felt that an earthquake or an invasion of dragons might be good for them. But I don't feel like that now. I feel that as long as the Shire lies behind, safe and comfortable, I shall find wandering more bearable: I shall know that somewhere there is a firm foothold, even if my feet cannot stand there again.
>
> Of course, I have sometimes thought of going away, but I imagined that as a kind of holiday, a series of adventures like Bilbo's or better, ending in peace. But this would mean exile, flight from danger into danger, drawing it after me. And I suppose I must go alone, if I am to do that to save the Shire. But I feel very small, and very uprooted, and well—desperate. The Enemy is so strong and terrible. (I/2)

I will save more extensive commentary on this for later when it comes to fruition, but I wanted to note it here for my readers as the moment at which the seed of the narrative and character resolution is planted. As Tolkien said in Letter #148a to

---

[37] J. R. R. Tolkien, *The War of the Ring: The History of the Lord of the Rings Part Three*, The History of Middle-earth 8, ed. Christopher Tolkien (Boston: Houghton Mifflin, 1990), 401.

Katharine Farrer, "In fact I was delighted that you stressed the 'morality'. I think actually it is that which gives the story its 'realness' and coherence – which my critics seem to feel – rather than any pictorial vividness. It was not 'planned', of course, but arose naturally in the attempt to treat the matter seriously; but it is now the foundation." That is, Tolkien did not necessarily plan the moral picture that he will present through Frodo's actions and character arc, but it flowed naturally from the author who was formed as a Christian that one of his heroes, the hero who bears the Ring for most of the story, should need to make such a sacrificial resolve. We will revisit this later at the resolution of the plot and the resolution of the story.

Traveling Providence

After this discussion with Gandalf, and accompanied by the eavesdropping Sam, as well as Pippin, Frodo sets out on his journey, which he tells others is to Crickhollow (which is true, but necessarily incomplete). Even early in this journey, he gets a sense of the danger ahead with the Black Riders searching for him. In one particular case, we see a marker of Providence. When the company hears a horse on the road, Frodo at first wonders if it is Gandalf, "but even as he said it, he had a feeling that it was not so, and a sudden desire to hide from the view of the rider came over him" (I/3). It is like an external feeling he received from another source. This is an interesting way of describing one of the subtler works of Providence, but it is, of course, quite crucial. Who knows how the situation would have gone if the Hobbits stayed in place and waited, thinking it was Gandalf? Instead, this sudden feeling saved his life and their lives.

Another marker of Providence early in this journey is the comment from Gildor, whose company of Elves had encountered the Hobbits on the road. He says, "Our paths cross theirs [Hobbits'] seldom, by chance or purpose. In this meeting there may be more than chance; but the purpose is not clear to me, and I fear to say too much" (I/3). This comment shows how the work of Providence can resemble chance but constitutes something "more than chance." He himself does not try to claim too much, but he clearly has the sense that something significant is happening here.[38] But without a clear notion of the purpose, he stops short of saying what he thinks would be too much. That

---

[38] This is a case where the final draft has seemingly sharpened the providential sense, as it was once written: "Our paths cross those ways seldom, and mostly by accident. In our meeting there is perhaps something more than accident, yet I do not feel sure that I ought to interfere." Tolkien, *Return of the Shadow*, 64.

is what differentiates him from Gandalf, who has a better—but still hardly complete—understanding of the purpose and agent at work here.

Elbereth

Besides the preceding hymn,[39] the conversation with Gildor also features the first of what will be several invocations of Elbereth: "May Elbereth protect you" (I/3). Elbereth or Varda is, besides being the Queen of the Valar, one of Tolkien's Marian figures. As we noted in a quote of his Letter #213 in Chapter One, one of potential hints to his Catholicism in his story that he pointed to, as identified by one critic, was the invocations of Elbereth as being connected to Catholic devotion to Mary. This is not to say that Elbereth is a one-to-one correspondence for Mary, as that does not make sense in Tolkien's mythology. But in some ways, she is reminiscent of Mary, particularly in how she is invoked. He also said in a footnote of Letter #153:

> For help they may call on a *Vala* (as *Elbereth*), as a Catholic might on a Saint, though no doubt knowing in theory as well as he that the power of the Vala was limited and derivative. But this is a 'primitive age': and these folk may be said to view the Valar as children view their parents or immediate adult superiors, and though they know they are subjects of the King he does not live in their country nor have there any dwelling.

Elbereth is the Vala most frequently invoked in this way, and it will be worth observing other times when she is called upon, for her invocation is something Frodo learns from the Elves.

Providential Companions

As the journey has taken a pause at this point, it is worth pausing to consider the matter of Providence in the formation of Frodo's present fellowship (which foreshadows titular Fellowship of the Ring). Divine providence takes many forms, as we have established. Sometimes God's providential work manifests in who is placed in relation to oneself. Frodo would not be here if Bilbo, who had earlier found the Ring, had not returned to the Shire and adopted Frodo after his parents died. He would not have been Bilbo's heir, and thus he would not have had the Ring. And he would also not be able to complete his Quest without those he was related to as friends and family.

---

[39] For comparison of this hymn to Elbereth, see the hymn "Hail, Queen of Heaven, the Ocean Star."

Consider Sam. While it is possible that they may have ended up being friends otherwise, they would not have grown together in their particular situation where Sam was a gardener to him as his Gaffer was to Bilbo. If not for that situation in life, he would not have been in a position to eavesdrop under the thin guise of trimming the grass. If he had not thus been eavesdropping, he would not have been volunteered by Gandalf to accompany Frodo. If he had not been in this position, neither would his other Hobbit companions have been able to join him as they did. And the Quest would have ultimately failed without Sam, the chief hero (Letter #131).

As a result of the meeting with the Elves, something Sam dreamed of doing for a long time, Sam's resolve is reinforced. It is here where he first says he was told by the Elves, "Don't you leave him!" and he responds, "I never mean to." Sam does not yet comprehend, since Frodo does not, that the Quest will end up taking them all the way to Mount Doom, but neither his current ignorance nor what he learns later perturb Sam or upset his will. In his own words, "I know we are going to take a very long road, into darkness; but I know I can't turn back. It isn't to see Elves now, nor dragons, nor mountains, that I want—I don't rightly know what I want: but I have something to do before the end, and it lies ahead and not in the Shire. I must see it through, sir, if you understand me" (I/4). Sam, too, was chosen for his task. He himself does not put it in quite those terms, but everything about his story to this point signals it.

The next chapter reveals that he was a conspirator with other Hobbits as well who Frodo grew up with and knew well, including Merry, Pippin, and Fatty Bolger (the one who would stay behind). When Frodo arrives at Crickhollow and converses with these friends and relatives, he learns that they knew a surprising amount of his secret business. They are not nearly as insightful, knowledgeable, or powerful as Gandalf, but they know enough to know that Frodo needs help, and they refuse to be daunted:

> 'You do not understand!' said Pippin. 'You must go—and therefore we must, too. Merry and I are coming with you. Sam is an excellent fellow, and would jump down a dragon's throat to save you, if he did not trip over his own feet' but you will need more than one companion in your dangerous adventure.'
>
> 'My dear and most beloved hobbits!' said Frodo deeply moved. 'But I could not allow it. I decided that long ago, too. You speak of danger, but you do not understand. This is no treasure-hunt, no there-and-back journey. I am flying from deadly peril into deadly peril.'
>
> 'Of course we understand,' said Merry firmly. 'That is why we have decided to come. We know the Ring is no laughing matter; but we are going to do our best to help you against the Enemy.' (I/5)

> [From Merry:] You can trust us to stick to you through thick and thin—to the bitter end. And you can trust us to keep any secret of yours—closer than you keep it yourself. But you cannot trust us to let you face trouble alone, and go off without a word. We are your friends, Frodo. Anyway: there it is. We know most of what Gandalf has told you. We know a good deal about the Ring. We are horribly afraid—but we are coming with you; or following you like hounds. (I/5)

"Greater love has no one than this, that a person will lay down his life for his friends" (John 15:13, NASB). Not only is this principle exemplified here, but we are reminded again how Providence has long been at work here in forming these family and friends together. And now more recently this work has come to bear fruit in having the right people in the right places at the right times for this conspiracy to be formed and for Frodo to be compelled to bring these most valuable companions with him on his Quest to his relief.[40]

In the case of this story, furthermore, not only is Providence at work in how these people should be related to Frodo and have known him for so long, as well as their forming a conspiracy; the work is also seen in another case of being in the right place at the right time. In the midst of this chapter, Merry tells of how he was in a spot to see Bilbo use the Ring to escape the Sackville-Bagginses, though he kept it a secret. And that was his cue to start keeping an eye out and his ears open for anything related to the business of this Ring, only acting on it when he needed to with Gandalf's visit in the spring, for which he had intel from Sam. And it is Merry who attempts to take the lead of the group through the Old Forest on to Bree, though that stage in the Quest met plenty of hiccups, which leads us to our next subject.

Tom Bombadil

Old Tom Bombadil is a merry fellow, and an odd one at that. Although various theories have been and will continue to be proffered about who and what he is, by Tolkien's own account, he is an intentional enigma (Letters #144; #153). Tolkien describes what Tom represents in Letter #144:

---

[40] One could similarly consider the work of Providence in Ruth. The story as a whole is all about the providentially orchestrated relations between Naomi, Ruth, and Boaz, which provide for the good of each one after much suffering. Moreover, the work of Providence before, during, and after this short biblical story means that these providential relations will lead to the birth of King David and, eventually, the Messiah.

The story is cast in terms of a good side, and a bad side, beauty against ruthless ugliness, tyranny against kingship, moderated freedom with consent against compulsion that has long lost any object save mere power, and so on; but both sides in some degree, conservative or destructive, want a measure of control. But if you have, as it were taken 'a vow of poverty', renounced control, and take your delight in things for themselves without reference to yourself, watching, observing, and to some extent knowing, then the question of the rights and wrongs of power and control might become utterly meaningless to you, and the means of power quite valueless. It is a natural pacifist view, which always arises in the mind when there is a war. But the view of Rivendell seems to be that it is an excellent thing to have represented, but that there are in fact things with which it cannot cope; and upon which its existence nonetheless depends. Ultimately only the victory of the West will allow Bombadil to continue, or even to survive. Nothing would be left for him in the world of Sauron. (Cf. Letter #153)

We can see, then, how Tolkien puts a particular spin on the presentation of monastic pursuits and their value through the narrative incorporation of Tom Bombadil, a character he had written about quite independently in his poems, some of which compose *The Adventures of Tom Bombadil* (which was published much later). There is a purity and simplicity about him that makes him uniquely immune to the influence of the Ring (I/7). But that is also what would make him a bad keeper or bearer of the Ring, as he would be neglectful of it and would not venture far from the Old Forest where he is master (II/2).

Frodo first encounters him when he desperately cries for help in the Old Forest after Old Man Willow captures and threatens to kill Merry and Pippin. The efforts Frodo and Sam make to free them prove vain, but in this final counsel of desperation, they find one who can subdue Old Man Willow with a song. He then invites them to stay a while with him and his wife, Goldberry. When Frodo inquires whether Tom came in response to his call or if it was mere chance that they met when and where they did, Tom says, "Did I hear you calling? Nay, I did not hear: I was busy singing. Just chance brought me then, if chance you call it. It was no plan of mine, though I was waiting for you" (I/7). Thus, this meeting is another arrangement of Providence. As with other suggestive texts we have seen to this point that qualified references to accident, luck, and chance, so too does Tom here say, "if chance you call it," clearly implying that he is merely using the established parlance here, though one could just as well say that it was not chance. The event simply resembled chance. He was waiting for the Hobbits, but it was not by any plan of his that he should just happen to be where he was when he was there to be able to help the Hobbits. Another will was at work to arrange this meeting that saved the Hobbits.

Courage in the Barrow-downs

After a respite, the Hobbits leave Tom's house with warnings about the Barrow-downs. Unfortunately, despite his warnings, the Hobbits are trapped there by the Barrow-wights. Frodo awakes while the others are kept in a deep sleep. Although Frodo has shown courage to this point, this is the first time since he set out that he must show it more actively by attempting to free his friends. The narrator tells us that it is such final and desperate dangers that cause "a seed of courage" that is hidden in the heart of every Hobbit to grow in him (I/8). This is reminiscent of what we have already observed about the "spirit of courage" Tolkien saw among his forebears and how it is embodied in the Hobbits. This is part of the common grace Eru Ilúvatar has given to the Hobbits that such jovial and soft creatures can, when put to it, show remarkable bravery to do what must be done.

Even so, there is a point at which he wavers when he sees a fiendish arm reaching for his friends to enact a demonic ritual. It appears as if he is dealing with a power here beyond his comprehension, and he already has one of those, plus his chief servants, threatening him. But the immediacy of the threat means that he can only do what he can with what strength he has, as Gandalf told him at the outset that he would need to do, and so, "resolve hardened in him," and he hews the hands off the creeping arm while the sword he used was entirely splintered (I/8).

This is a reminder of the nature of courage. Peacefulness does not consist in simply being nonviolent, as one can merely be harmless. But one who is capable of great violence and chooses the way of peace is the one who is truly peaceful. In the same way, courage does not consist of the absence of fear; that is simply fearlessness, and that can be dangerous for oneself and others who depend on one, just as cowardice is similarly dangerous. Rather, courage works in the face of fear and what inspires it (danger, the unknown, and so on), overcoming fear with resolute acts of will, not allowing what is feared to control oneself. Courage is a virtue that upholds other virtues in supplying the resolution to do what must be done in the face of obstacles. And in its fullest exercise, it is a virtue that is itself upheld by others like the theological virtues of faith, love, and hope. This is part of that fusion of horizons Tolkien has described elsewhere when the gospel came to the northern Europeans. Thus, various expressions for courage in the Bible involve being strong/strengthened (Num 13:20; Deut 1:38; 3:28; 31:6–7, 23; Josh

1:6–9, 18; 10:25; Judg 7:11; Ruth 1:18; 2 Sam 10:12 // 1 Kgs 2:2 // 1 Chr 19:13; 22:13; 28:20; 2 Chr 32:7; Ezra 10:4; Dan 11:32; Mic 3:8; Zec 8:9, 13), resolution in heart (Pss 27:14; 31:24; Isa 35:4; Jer 51:46; Hag 2:4; John 14:27) being comforted in the face of trial (1 Sam 23:16; John 16:33), and speaking/acting with freedom (Acts 4:13, 29, 31; 9:27–28; 13:46; 14:3; 18:26; 19:8; 26:26; 28:31; 2 Cor 3:12).

Tom Bombadil's Anticipatory Note of Final Victory

Of course, while Frodo has been given strength to do what he needs to do to face the immediate problem, he cannot ultimately solve the larger problem on his own. At this point, he remembers the song Tom gave the Hobbits to sing if they needed to call on him for help. This shows one of the links between faith and courage, as he must trust that this will work. And indeed, it does. Tom not only saves the Hobbits; he also banishes the Barrow-wights from these lands once and for all. And he does it, of course, with a song:

> Get out old Wight! Vanish in the sunlight!
> Shrivel like the cold mist, like the winds go wailing,
> Out into the barren lands far beyond the mountains!
> Come never here again! Leave your barrow empty!
> Lost and forgotten be, darker than the darkness,
> Where gates stand for ever shut, till the world is mended. (I/8)

On the one hand, the description of where Tom banishes the wight to is reminiscent of where the rebellious are held for judgment in 2 Pet 2:4 and Jude 6 (cf. Rev 20:1–3). On the other hand, the last line is especially interesting. The banishment to this place until the world is mended implies that there will be a final reckoning, a final judgment. And this will be tied in with the world being restored, mended, and healed. That is the expectation that has been declared since the narration of the *Ainulindalë*, as the Music of the Ainur by which Eru Ilúvatar created Eä will be surpassed by the Second Music that will also involve the Children of Ilúvatar. This refers to the hope of new creation, or the healing of creation, which is also the biblical hope. The hope is for the world to be made complete, not for its abandonment. As we have seen many times at this point, grace completes nature rather than destroys it.

The Will of Bondage Strikes Back

While Frodo was in Tom Bombadil's house, the Ring appeared less threatening. After all, Tom put it on with no effect, and he could see Frodo plain as day even after he put it on to become invisible. As long as the Ring stayed in the domain where Tom was master, it did not seem to be so perilous as early indications would have it. But when Frodo makes it to Bree and he can no longer rely on the security of Tom, the threat becomes reestablished. The Ring has a will of its own, after all. And so just as divine providence can manifest as an external force, as something "coming over" the recipient of the action, and even as something coming from within the recipient, the counterfeit—whether the Ring or the powers of sin and death—can work in ways that are superficially similar. We saw already in Bilbo's finding of the Ring how two opposing wills were at work in that event, one of which was the Ring's.

And so it is when Frodo comes to Bree. When he feels uncomfortable speaking in front of the crowd at the Prancing Pony, "quite unaccountably the desire came over him to slip it on and vanish out of the silly situation. It seemed to him, somehow, as if the suggestion came to him from outside, from someone or something in the room." (I/9).[41] Frodo is initially able to resist the temptation and redirect his mind to his remarkable song and dance performance. But as he loses himself in that performance, drawing attention to himself when secrecy was supposed to be the name of his game, he slips and finds that the Ring is on his finger, which alerts the agents of the Enemy and eventually brings the Ringwraiths. Frodo wonders if the Ring played a trick on him to get him to this point.

For as much as Frodo's struggle is against a physical object and an embodied Enemy, it is nevertheless also a spiritual struggle. And for as strong as Frodo is, and for as much heroic courage as he has already demonstrated that he has, this event makes clear that he cannot carry on this Quest alone left to his own devices. As with our spiritual struggles, he is not to confront his all alone. Companions and community are crucial for each individual's struggles. The counsel is never to do it all oneself.

---

[41] This is one of several cases in which Tolkien heightened the sinister character of the Ring beyond what he had written in his initial drafts: "Bingo suddenly felt very nervous, and found himself, as was his habit when making a speech, fingering the things in his pocket. Vaguely he felt the chain and the Ring there, and jingled it against a few copper coins; but this did not help him much" (Tolkien, *Return of the Shadow*, 138–39).

Aragorn

It is also at Bree that we first meet the last of the major characters who will provide christological echoes and be a christological type: Strider, later revealed to be Aragorn son of Arathorn. One way in which Aragorn echoes and anticipates Jesus is in that he is part of a long line of kings that has long since lost the throne. Aragorn is of the line of Isildur who was supposed to rule over all the Dúnedain, although his line was ultimately reduced to reigning over the lesser northern kingdom of Arnor until it fell. Jesus was of the line of David, who did rule over the united kingdom of Israel, although his line was ultimately reduced to reigning over the smaller southern kingdom of Judah until that kingdom fell. In both cases, the line did not fail, but the heirs of the respective thrones must operate incognito until their time comes. Of course, it is important to remember that Aragorn is an echo of Christ and not a Christ-figure himself. His reign has a climactic role in the story of *LOTR*, but it is not the everlasting kingdom/reign of God. Nor is Aragorn's kingdom inaugurated by the equivalent of the major gospel events, for there is no true equivalent of the major gospel events in Tolkien's story (except in the sense that there is a eucatastrophe), since there is no incarnation of the One as yet, even if there are more distant echoes reverberating in anticipation of his coming and a eucatastrophe precipitating Aragorn's reign.

Part of what aids Aragorn being incognito in the present time is that, like the Servant spoken of in Isa 53:2, he is lacking in any sort of majestic form or appearance, not least because of his many years in the wilderness and traveling across the continent awaiting his time, not unlike Jesus waiting until he is around thirty years old to begin his ministry. Frodo even remarks that he felt that Aragorn was not an agent of the Enemy because he thought they would look fair and feel foul, though he is polite enough not to say outright the obverse of that statement and what it says about Aragorn (I/10). Of course, the verse that goes with Aragorn's name illustrates much the same:

> All that is gold does not glitter,
> Not all those who wander are lost;
> The old that is strong does not wither,
> Deep roots are not reached by the frost.
> From the ashes a fire shall be woken,
> A light from the shadows shall spring;
> Renewed shall be blade that was broken,
> The crownless again shall be king. (I/10)

We later learn that Bilbo composed these lines for Aragorn (II/2). It reflects the hope he has for Aragorn and that Aragorn has for himself, that after generations of disinheritance he will be the one to inherit the throne of his ancestor, as will be true also of Christ, his anti-type who fulfills the type.[42]

Similarly, when Strider reveals his identity as Aragorn, something of a transfiguration takes place before he declares his name and promises to do what he can to save Frodo by life or death. It is not so phenomenal as the Transfiguration that in each of the Synoptic Gospels follows Peter's affirmation of Jesus's identity, but it is similar in concept and only foreshadows others to come. For the narrator tells us, "He stood up, and seemed suddenly to grow taller. In his eyes gleamed a light, keen and commanding" (I/10). This is similar to what we saw earlier with Gandalf in Bag End. And it is another example of the dynamic of transfiguration whereby something of the greater glory of a person is revealed.

Surprising Courage

Even as Frodo and the Hobbits are surprised to learn who Strider is, Strider has his own turn to be surprised by the Hobbits. Merry had been out during the conversation of this chapter, and he came close to a Nazgûl without being detected. Thus, the two characters have this exchange:

> Strider looked at Merry with wonder. 'You have a stout heart,' he said; 'but it was foolish.'
> 'I don't know,' said Merry. 'Neither brave nor silly, I think. I could hardly help myself. I seemed to be drawn somehow.' (I/10)

This is another case of the subject being rendered passive by the action of another in a way that suggests divine providence. Merry "seemed to be drawn" because another will was at work to bring this about. And it is a significant event, as this prevents the Nazgûl from getting the drop on Strider and the Hobbits.

---

[42] In the phrasing of typology, the "anti-" in "anti-type" should be understood as something like "corresponding" rather than "opposing" or "against." Additionally, in terms of historically considered typology, it has the sense of what will come "in place of" the type and fulfill it by its correspondence to and amplification of the type.

A Knife in the Dark

The story then follows the expanded group with Strider in the lead to Weathertop. While there, they are detected by the Ringwraiths. There is no avoiding them this time. Strider simply tries to prepare a defense as best he can, but he cannot stop the Lord of the Nazgûl (otherwise known as the Witch-King of Angmar) from facing down Frodo. Frodo once again feels a sudden temptation to put on the Ring:

> The desire to do this laid hold of him, and he could think of nothing else. He did not forget the Barrow, nor the message of Gandalf; but something seemed to be compelling him to disregard all warnings, and he longed to yield. Not with the hope of escape, or of doing anything, either good or bad: he simply felt that he must take the Ring and put it on his finger…. He shut his eyes and struggled for a while; but resistance became unbearable, and at last he slowly drew out the chain, and slipped the Ring on the forefinger of his left hand.[43] (I/11)

Besides the words of Gandalf and his cited example of Bilbo, this experience may be the most significant influence on Frodo eventually acting graciously towards Gollum. We have seen already that he initially regarded Gollum as loathsome, condemned him, and spurned Gandalf's attempts to warn him that other Hobbits he knew could well have become Gollum. He even thought it would be a simple matter to get rid of the Ring and destroy it. He had experienced some strong temptations to put on the Ring and was able to overcome them when they came, save a seemingly accidental lapse. But despite his courage, despite the warnings of Gandalf that he could not forget, in the end the will and power of the Ring, amplified by the presence of the Ringwraiths, was simply too much for him. This is some tragic foreshadowing, for Frodo does not fail morally here. He simply is not capable of resisting such a force. In turn, this will give him a more compassionate and generous perspective on those who have borne it longer and also found themselves being cowed into submission to the will of the Ring. In a hard way, he is learning the wisdom demonstrated in Jesus's teaching in Matt 7:1–5, so that his judgment will now be tempered with pity and mercy.

---

[43] Interestingly, despite the differences in tone between the earlier drafts of Book I and what became Book I, this text is remarkably similar between the drafts, even with the presentation of the Ring's power. See Tolkien, *Return of the Shadow*, 185.

Invoking Elbereth

Of course, when Frodo puts on the Ring, it does not hide him from the Ringwraiths. In fact, they can see him more clearly, even as he can see them more clearly. One of them, who is later said to be the Lord of the Nazgûl, bears down on him with a sword in one hand and a knife in the other. Having no other recourse, Frodo summons his courage and throws himself forward while crying *"O Elbereth! Gilthoniel!"* and strikes at the Nazgûl's foot with his Arnorian blade (I/11). As will be said (indirectly) later, this courage proves providential not only because it was a grace given to Frodo, but also because if Frodo had not taken action, the wound would have been more severe from the Nazgûl's aim at his heart. Instead, he has stabbed him in his shoulder. It is still a horrible wound, but not nearly as bad as it could have been with them still so far from Rivendell.

This is also another case in which Elbereth is invoked like Mary. This is something Frodo learned from the Elves. Strider also says that the name of Elbereth was more deadly to the Nazgûl than the sword stroke (I/12). He says this in a context of noting that the stroke did not do much damage to the Nazgûl, but the fact that he says it was "more deadly" indicates that the invocation does have some measure of power. The one who is the Enkindler was, after all, the Vala that Melkor, Sauron's master, hated and feared the most. She saw through his darkness, and her beauty was an effect of her face radiating the light of Eru Ilúvatar himself.

Made of Sterner Stuff

The rest of my comments for Book I will be on rather brief texts. First, Strider echoes what Gandalf said earlier about the strength and durability of Hobbits that would surprise the Wise. In his words, "Your Frodo is made of sterner stuff than I had guessed, though Gandalf hinted that it might prove so. He is not slain, and I think he will resist the evil power of the wound longer than his enemies expect" (I/12). This speaks to the common grace given to the Hobbits that surprises those who do not know them better, as Gandalf had established earlier. But it also speaks to the special grace the One has given Frodo, for we have been told elsewhere, "indeed, though he did not know it, Bilbo (and Gandalf) had thought him the best hobbit in the Shire" (I/8). We will discuss later some important comments from Tolkien on the grace given to Frodo for his Quest.

Estel

Strider also has some interesting bits of dialogue in this chapter that demonstrate his virtue of hope. As we will see again later, one of Strider's names is *Estel*, one of the Elvish words that can be translated as "hope" (the other being *amdir*). But this particular variety is a deeper, more significant one that has the sense of "trust." It is not some vague optimism trusting that things will go well in the end. Rather, it is trust in Eru Ilúvatar and that his designs will be for the good of his Children, whom he loves.[44] This is a paraphrase of how Finrod explains the concept in "Athrabeth Finrod ah Andreth,"[45] The aforementioned paraphrase and the quote it comes from are similar to Rom 8:28: "And we know that for those who love God all things work together for good, for those who are called according to his purpose" (ESV). Early in his life, Strider was named *Estel* to signify that he is an instrument of such hope, the instrument of Eru Ilúvatar in bringing his designs for his Children (including both Men and Elves) to fruition, at least up to a point, as the coming of the Messiah he is a type of is still far in the future.

Aragorn, including in the very name he bears of *Estel*, thus also exemplifies one of Tolkien's Primary World beliefs. The point from Elvish tradition anticipates more developed Christian belief. This brings us to one of the most fascinating letters from Tolkien for theological interests. It is one he wrote to Camilla Unwin, the daughter of Rayner Unwin, the frequent reader of his work for Allen & Unwin (Letter #310). Here, Tolkien provided a summary of his ideas about the purpose of life, as this was from a question Camilla asked him. After a relatively brief framing of the question of life's purpose, he summarized his thoughts, which should be familiar to any Christian who has engaged with Christian tradition:

> So it may be said that the chief purpose of life, for any one of us, is to increase according to our capacity our knowledge of God by all the means we have, and to be moved by it to praise and thanks. To do as we say in the *Gloria in Excelsis*: *Laudamus te, benedicamus te, adoramus te, glorificamus te, gratias agimus tibi propter magnam gloriam tuam.* We praise you, we call you holy,

---

[44] See also Tolkien, *Sauron Defeated*, 346.

[45] "*Estel* we call it, that is 'trust'. It is not defeated by the ways of the world, for it does not come from experience, but from our nature and first being. If we are indeed the *Eruhini*, the Children of the One, then He will not suffer Himself to be deprived of His own, not by any Enemy, not even by ourselves. This is the last foundation of *Estel*, which we keep even when we contemplate the End: of all His designs the issue must be for His Children's joy" (Tolkien, *Morgoth's Ring*, 320).

we worship you, we proclaim your glory, we thank you for the greatness of your splendour. (Letter #310).

Probably the most well-known similar statement—though not from a Catholic source—comes from the Westminster Shorter Catechism, which defines the chief end of humans: "Man's chief end is to glorify God, and to enjoy him forever." But more fittingly exemplifying Tolkien's Catholic tradition is the Penny Catechism that was popular at the time, which responded to the question, "Why did God make you?" with the answer, "God made me to know him, to love him and to serve him in this world, and to be happy with him forever in the next." The reader should consult Letter #310 for more of Tolkien's exposition on the subject. While such notions are obviously more developed than what Tolkien describes as this "primitive age" (Letter #153), the continuity of the need for what he describes as *estel* remains.

In Strider's case, with the awareness that he is an instrument of hope, he can say confidently that though his heart is in Rivendell (since Arwen is there), "it is not my fate to sit in peace, even in the fair house of Elrond" (I/12). For he knows that he has a much different purpose, a place in a story much bigger than his own, which has been composed by an Author far higher than him. And he has already decided to submit to that purpose, though the timing and circumstance of when his fate will be fulfilled remain mysterious to him.

Later, as Frodo's condition worsens, Strider informs Sam that the poison of the Morgul blade is beyond his skill to heal, yet he says, "But do not give up hope, Sam" (I/12). This is something Strider will continue to do throughout this story: he enkindles hope where he can. He trusts that the One's designs for Frodo—and Strider is one who is definitely aware of the One—will not end here, perhaps not least because of the signs of God's grace he has already seen in Frodo and his mission. And his words do not prove empty either. Not long after this, the group meets Glorfindel, who, quite beyond the designs of Strider himself, was out looking for the group. And not only does Glorfindel supply the horse Frodo needs to outrun the Black Riders, but he also proves crucial in driving these enemies away. Glorfindel himself is an instrument of Providence, considering how he was sent back to Middle-earth for such purposes as this. But that is something we will have to address in the next chapter.

Finally, there are two more points to observe from the end of Book I. One, after Frodo crosses the Ford of Bruinen, he keeps telling the Ringwraiths to go back. His voice weakens as they beckon him to surrender. While his strength is failing, he says, "By Elbereth and Lúthien the Fair … you shall have neither the Ring nor me" (I/12).

This is similar to the almost Marian invocation we have seen previously. But now with the addition of Lúthien, it further resembles invocations of the saints. Such an invocation gives him the strength he needs for one last effort.

Two, as Frodo is on the verge of fainting, he sees across the river "a shining figure of white light; and behind it ran small shadowy forms waving flames, that flared red in the grey mist that was falling over the world" (I/12). This shining figure is Glorfindel transfigured in Frodo's sight. To explain why this is so, we must turn to the next chapter.

CHAPTER FIVE

Commentary on Book II

Indications of Providence

At the start of Book II, the setting is Rivendell. Frodo has arrived safely and has been on the mend since being treated by Elrond. He awakens to find Gandalf in his room, and while he is obviously relieved to see him, he is naturally curious about where he has been and why he did not meet him. Gandalf will provide explanation later, but he only says for now, "I was delayed … and that nearly proved our ruin. And yet I am not sure: it may have been better so" (II/1). This appears to be a subtle indicator that Gandalf sees the work of Providence even incorporating negative action like Gandalf's delay (due to imprisonment). He does not have a full view of all events to yet say definitively that it was better for him to be delayed, and so he speaks with qualification. But it does seem that his intuition is right. The Hobbits were made to become more reliant on each other because of Gandalf's delay, and that, in turn, drives their development as heroes, especially Frodo's. They also met Tom Bombadil, who they otherwise might not have met, whose cleansing of the Barrow-downs could prove beneficial for others in the future who find its treasures, and from whom they receive the Arnorian daggers, one of which will prove to be crucial in a battle that is to come. The journey from Bree has also encouraged the bond between Strider/Aragorn and the Hobbits, which will have lasting effects for many years to come, including even to the extent of shaping what Aragorn will call his house after a translation of "Strider" (Telcontar; V/8), the name the Hobbits first knew him by.

Another indicator of Providence is the element of common grace given to the Hobbits. Gandalf has already noted this, and he reaffirms it here now that he has not only seen the Hobbits' durability in relation to the Ring, but he has now known of it in reaction to a Morgul blade: "And it seems that Hobbits fade very reluctantly, I have known strong warriors of the Big People who would quickly have been overcome by that splinter, which you bore for seventeen days" (II/1). Yet again, the Hobbits thus challenge and thus trouble the counsels of the Wise and the Great. For the One has chosen these Little People for his purposes.

In further recognition of this, Gandalf tells Frodo, "Yes, fortune or fate have helped you … not to mention courage. For your heart was not touched, and only your shoulder was pierced; and that was because you resisted to the last. But it was a terribly narrow shave, so to speak" (II/1). The terms "fate" and "fortune," being related but different in nuance, are, in this context, still indicative of the work of Providence, of the will of the One to appoint ends and bring them about by what can appear to be something like luck. And as we have seen already, courage is itself a gift, a grace from the All-Father planted within his creatures, which circumstances like Frodo has seen on his Quest help to cultivate into fruition. The understanding of divine providence on display here is that the process does not simply work by carrying its recipients along while they are entirely passive, but they are often incorporated as active participants in achieving the purpose. In the process, the recipients are gifted and empowered, whether more immediately or by what has been built up long before the event in question. While courage is useful for being able to deal with circumstances within one's immediate purview to one's best capability, "fate" and "fortune" refer to what is beyond the control or capability of oneself, including the involvement of others beyond oneself.

Seeing the Unseen

There is also an element of transcendence here as Gandalf explains to Frodo what he saw on Weathertop when he put on the Ring and when he saw Glorfindel appear more glorious. He initially says that when Frodo put on the Ring he was "half in the wraith-world" so that he could see them and they could see him (II/1). As for his vision of Glorfindel prior to fainting, that was once again an indication that Frodo was fading and starting to cross over into the other world, as he saw Glorfindel's hidden glory as one who has dwelt in the Blessed Realm of Aman where the Valar and Maiar live. As Gandalf says of the High Elves like Glorfindel, "They do not fear the Ringwraiths, for those who have dwelt in the Blessed Realm live at once in both worlds, and against both the Seen and the Unseen they have great power" (II/1).[1]

---

[1] Interestingly, an older draft of this text featured another note of theological significance here: "The Elves of Rivendell are indeed descendants of his chief foes: the Gnomes, the Elvenwise ones, that came

This clarifies what we have seen already. It is not so much that the Ring grants a cloak of invisibility (though it does essentially have that effect), but that it enables the wearer to enter the Unseen world (the spiritual realm that supervenes on the Seen world) and to make that which is invisible (because it is in the Unseen world) visible. This is why Frodo sees the true forms of the Ringwraiths, who have long since slipped into the Unseen world after possessing their own Rings of Power under the corruption of Sauron with his Ring. It would not necessarily have this effect on the great Elf leaders who bore the Great Rings because these individuals already exist in both the Seen and Unseen worlds and can see in both. Indeed, in the case of Maiar like Gandalf and Sauron, the physical form is typically like raiment that they put on (even though Gandalf has gone further than other Maiar and Valar in becoming properly incarnate, and Sauron has tied his presence in Middle-earth to a physical object), as their natural form is to be invisible to the Seen world. Thus, Sauron was not invisible when he wore the Ring, and Gandalf would not be either. On the other hand, because a bearer of the Ring would cross over into the Unseen world, the use of the Ring would make the bearer more conspicuous to Sauron and to his servants who also exist in the Unseen world, the Nazgûl (who otherwise cannot see as clearly by themselves in the Seen world in the daytime, as they operate by other senses).

This is akin to the vision provided by apocalyptic texts, most notably Revelation, as well as portions of Daniel, Ezekiel, Zechariah, and others. Such revelations showed what was happening beyond the curtain of empirical reality, thereby helping the audience to remember that more was going on in heaven and on earth than what they could see. This is also shown in the exorcisms done by Jesus and his disciples, as well as the apostles and evangelists in Acts. And we see the awareness of the operations of angels and demons throughout the NT, most extensively in Eph 6:10–20. Thus, we are also to have this transcendent vision of the unseen, neither reducing what is important only to the material, nor imagining that the drama of our world involves only us or only us and God.

Glorfindel

At this point, we should also say something about Glorfindel because of the issues he presents. This is Glorfindel's second time in Middle-earth. He was among the High

---

out of the Far West, and whom Elbereth Gilthoniel still protects." Tolkien, *Return of the Shadow*, 212. While Elbereth is certainly invoked, there is no clear sense that the Elves are specially under her protection in the rest of Tolkien's final draft.

Elves/Calaquendi who came to Aman and dwelt in the light of the Two Trees. Later, he was among the vast majority of the Noldor (one of the Three Kindreds of the High Elves) who joined the journey to Middle-earth aiming to reclaim the Silmarils and establish Elven kingdoms. He died after the Fall of Gondolin as he cast a Balrog and himself down a mountainside.[2] Though he was among the Exiles who was condemned for his part in the Kinslaying the Noldor carried out while leaving Aman, he was pardoned for his sacrificial action, which proved crucial to Tuor and Idril's escape, and thus to Eärendil's voyage, which was, in turn, crucial to the salvation of Middle-earth by the Host of Valinor. After a time of purgatory, he was allowed to reincarnate in Aman and there his spiritual power was greatly increased by virtue of his self-sacrifice, and he became a follower and friend of Olórin (which was the name Gandalf was known by in Aman). He must have returned to Middle-earth before the Change of the World, and his return must have been for the purpose of strengthening Gil-galad and Elrond in their resistance of Sauron. He is thus an instrument of Providence like Gandalf, being empowered by his time with Gandalf/Olórin and others for the work Ilúvatar still willed for him to do.[3]

Unsurprisingly, some have taken issue with such a presentation of reincarnation in Tolkien's fiction. Peter Hastings even wrote to him that he thought it was bad metaphysics and theologically problematic: "God has not used that device in any of the creations of which we have knowledge, and it seems to me to be stepping beyond the position of a sub-creator to produce it as an actual working thing, because a sub-creator, when dealing with the relations between creator and created, should use those channels which he knows the creator to have used already" (preface to Letter #153). We have already noted how Tolkien wrote in reply in Letter #153 that he categorically disagreed, since a sub-creator should, as part of the fundamental function of the work, be able to pay tribute to the infinity of God's creativity by exploring counterfactuals and "channels" he did not use. Specifically concerning the reincarnation of the Elves, he said,

> 'Reincarnation' may be bad *theology* (that surely, rather than metaphysics) as applied to Humanity; and my *legendarium,* especially the 'Downfall of

---

[2] Christopher Tolkien notes that Tolkien once thought of the use of Glorfindel in *LOTR* as "one of the cases of the somewhat random use of the names found in the older legends, now referred to as *The Silmarillion,* which escaped reconsideration in the final published form of *The Lord of the Rings.*" Tolkien, *Return of the Shadow,* 214. But he still came to the conclusion early in the process that the Glorfindels of both stories were the same person (*Return of the Shadow,* 214–15).

[3] For all of this, see J. R. R. Tolkien, *The Peoples of Middle-earth,* The History of Middle-earth 12, ed. Christopher Tolkien (New York: Houghton Mifflin, 1996), 379–82.

Númenor' which lies immediately behind *The Lord of the Rings, is* based on my view: that Men are essentially mortal and must not try to become 'immortal' in the flesh. But I do not see how even in the Primary World any theologian or philosopher, unless very much better informed about the relation of spirit and body than I believe anyone to be, could deny the *possibility* of re-incarnation as a mode of existence, prescribed for certain kinds of rational incarnate creatures [i.e., not humans]. (Letter #153; emphases original)

The framework for reincarnation in Tolkien's work is also fundamentally different than what is shared by the various Indian religions (Hinduism, Buddhism, Jainism, and Sikhism) and their offshoots, as well as the theories of metempsychosis professed by Pythagoras, Plato, and their followers. For all the differences between these different philosophies, the cycle of reincarnation (called *samsara* in Hindu religions and other beliefs) is a problem for which the solution is liberation (called *moksha*). Again, all of these belief systems vary in how they conceive of reincarnation, what causes the cycle and the particular forms it can take, and how liberation is achieved, yet none of those elements apply to Tolkien's presentation of the Elves. In contrast to Men, who are part of the created world for a relatively brief time and then after death pass beyond it to the Timeless Halls of Eru Ilúvatar, Elves are immortal in the sense that their lives are bound to the created world of Eä. They live, whether embodied or not, for as long as it lives. Thus, an Elf could live in perpetuity without ever once experiencing death. But if they do die, they are sent to the Halls of Mandos, which was once in Arda and is still in the scope of the created world, where after a time of purgatory their spirits are allowed to reincarnate if they choose (although they rarely do so more than once).[4]

Reincarnation is thus Eru Ilúvatar's grace given to the Elves as a result of their life being tied to the life of creation. It is not something to be liberated from, at least within the scope of history. Of course, the ultimate hope of the Elves is for the new creation where they trust/hope that the All-Father will have a place for them in the Second Music (the Valar do not know that they will or will not, but this is the hope of the Elves), and that all the Children of Ilúvatar will thus be brought together in and have their lives tied to a world where death is no more

Frodo's Sanctification

Near the end of this conversation between Frodo and Gandalf, the latter takes notice of a change in Frodo, "a faint change, just a hint as it were of transparency, about him,

---

[4] For more on this matter, see Tolkien, *Morgoth's Ring*, 217–46.

and especially about the left hand that lay outside upon the coverlet" (II/1). Gandalf says to himself that this must be expected, "He is not half through yet, and to what he will come in the end not even Elrond can foretell. Not to evil, I think. He may become like a glass filled with a clear light for eyes to see that can" (II/1). This vision from Gandalf signifies Frodo's *sanctification*. That is even the alternative term Tolkien himself uses to refer to Frodo's "ennoblement" in Letter #181. Frodo has not only been chosen for this purpose, but he is being transformed in accordance with that purpose, and he is progressively made more like what God intends for him to be. This reflects our own sanctification process in Christ of being transformed "from glory to glory" (2 Cor 3:18), being conformed to the image of Christ (Rom 8:29), which is a result of knowing Christ and "the fellowship of his sufferings" (Phil 3:10, NASB) in order that we may be conformed to his glory (Phil 3:11, 21). As we have noted already, Frodo is a type of Christ through whom we hear distant christological echoes, even though he is not himself a Christ-figure.

The last part of Gandalf's statement implies a special insight. This is akin to what we have already noted in "seeing the unseen." But it is also comparable to the refrain from Jesus calling the one who has an ear to hear what is being said (Matt 11:15; 13:9, 43; Mark 4:23; Luke 14:35; Rev 2:7, 11, 17, 29; 3:6, 13, 22; cf. Rev 13:9).

Disfiguration

Since we have been tracking transfigurations in this story, it is only appropriate to note a subversion of the same. To this point, we have seen good transfigurations that show a hint of the glory of someone. Yet in this same chapter we see a case not so much of showing the true evil of someone, but rather a case which nevertheless shows the true damage evil has wrought on someone. At a party Elrond has put on for his guests, Frodo has many meetings (as the chapter is called). One of those is with Bilbo. In the course of their conversation, which is otherwise pleasant, the tone takes a bad turn as Bilbo asks to see his old Ring. When Frodo shows it to him, Bilbo puts out his hand, and Frodo draws the Ring back. What Frodo sees as a result of this action is noteworthy:

> To his distress and amazement he found that he was no longer looking at Bilbo; a shadow seemed to have fallen between them, and through it he found himself eyeing a little wrinkled creature with a hungry face and bony groping hands. He felt a desire to strike him.
>
> The music and singing around them seemed to falter, and a silence fell. Bilbo looked quickly at Frodo's face and passed his hand across his eyes. 'I

understand now,' he said. 'Put it away! I am sorry: sorry you have come in for this burden: sorry about everything. Don't adventures ever have an end? I suppose not. Someone else always has to carry on the story. Well, it can't be helped.' (II/1)

Everything returns to normal after this, but the impact of the scene is undeniable. In a flash, Frodo sees a Gollum-like disfiguration come over Bilbo, a darkness put upon him by the enduring influence of the Ring, even after he has been without it for seventeen years. Even one as cheerful and wholesome as Bilbo can be turned without warning into an unsightly creature when the influence overcomes him, even if only for a moment. Likewise, if we could really see how sin disfigures, we might treat it more seriously than we tend to do. At the same time, as with Frodo, such an event can give us more compassion for those who have been under its power for too long, and who can be capable, via the Spirit's sanctification, of much better. No one should be written off too soon, but at the same time no one is too strong to not rely on the power of God made available by his grace to us (2 Cor 12:7–10). While Frodo cannot learn this lesson in full, given his position in history, he receives such light as he can from his entire Quest, especially from his showing pity to Gollum, as well as from how his Quest will end

Sub-creation

There is one other element from this chapter to note for our purposes. We have explored elsewhere Tolkien's theology of sub-creation, so we need not enter a full exposition on the matter here. But I ought to mention that Tolkien provides a vivid example of its enchantment not only by his story as a whole, but also within a particular instance in the story from his Elves. As Frodo sits in the hall and hears the music of the Elves combined with the song of Bilbo and Aragorn about Eärendil, which itself extends from one of the roots of Tolkien's own sub-creation, this is how the narrator describes the enchantment:

> At first the beauty of the melodies and of the interwoven words in elventongues, even though he understood them little, held him in a spell, as soon as he began to attend to them. Almost it seemed that the words took shape, and visions of far lands and bright things that he had never yet imagined opened out before him; and the firelit hall became like a golden mist above seas of foam that sighed upon the margins of the world. Then the enchantment became more and more dreamlike, until he felt that an endless river of swelling gold and silver was flowing over him, too multitudinous for its pattern to be comprehended; it

became part of the throbbing air about him, and it drenched and drowned him.
Swiftly he sank under its shining weight into a deep realm of sleep.

There he wandered long in a dream of music that turned into running water,
and then suddenly into a voice. (II/1)

This is how Tolkien shows the power of music and story meeting the imagination
that lies at the foundation of his work. It represents his theoretical foundation insofar
as it articulates his explanation of the enchantment of sub-creation. It represents the
emotional/sensual foundation insofar as it articulates the power of sub-creation to draw
one in. It represents the theological foundation insofar as it articulates the successful
sub-creation that is imitative and derivative of the creative power of God's Word. And
it possibly represents the "historical" foundation in that one of the roots of Tolkien's
whole sub-creative work is the poem *The Voyage of Éarendel the Evening Star*, which
he wrote in September 1914 (as recounted in *The Book of Lost Tales, Part Two*). It was
inspired by lines from the *Crist A* (or *Christ I*) poem once thought to be by Cynewulf,
which originally referred to John the Baptist as the star that preceded the Sun/Son (as
Christ was often referred to in Advent/Christmas contexts as the Sun of Righteousness
from Mal 4:2). Tolkien attests to this inspiration in Letter #297.

The Council of Elrond

The heaviest chapter of exposition in the book naturally also has much that is of
interest for this commentary. The account of the Council, which according to the narrator is not complete, begins with Glóin recounting a messenger of Sauron coming to
request news of the Ring (though the messenger diminished its significance in his
speech). The messenger and the implicit threat of the whole encounter (for Bilbo and
for the Dwarves) has troubled the Dwarves, and Elrond informs him that it is connected
with the problems of all those at the Council. His initial counsel even before all else is
heard is simply, "There is naught that you can do, other than to resist, with hope or
without it. But you do not stand alone" (II/2). This is a reminder of the theory of courage
that undergirds this whole story, as we have seen previously. Regardless of the chance
of victory, resistance to evil is still necessary, and to do what one must do regardless
of outcome is an exercise of the crucial virtue of perseverance. This virtue is, in turn, a
key aspect of the Christian life, and it is not until the Christian framework meets this
spirit of courage that the latter is given its proper *telos* as it provides the final victory
that completes it. At this time, those like the Dwarves can resist without hope, by which
is meant in this case *amdir*, "An expectation of good, which though uncertain has some

foundation in what is known."[5] But they can still resist with the hope of *estel*, as we have seen earlier. Such a notion is supported by what Elrond says next.

He tells Glóin and all who attend the Council that they must decide what to do with the Ring: "That is the purpose for which you are called hither. Called, I say, though I have not called you to me, strangers from distant lands. You have come and here met, in this very nick of time, by chance as it may seem. Yet it is not so. Believe rather that it is so ordered that we, who sit here, and none others, must now find counsel for the peril of the world" (II/2).[6] In fact, representatives had come from as far north and east as Erebor, as far west as Lindon, and as far south as Gondor, each with different matters to address, having the common purpose of seeking Elrond's counsel while not yet realizing the common purpose of having to deal with the Ring, and they all came together at the right time without any of them being summoned by Elrond himself. What could be a clearer indication of a singular will besides Elrond and others attending the Council being the one ordering all of these events? What could be a clearer indication that this is the work of divine providence? Even as Bilbo finding the Ring was a strange but crucial step in the divine plan for the Ring, so too is this collection of seeming coincidences a strange but crucial step in the divine plan for the Ring and the formation of the Fellowship. Just as there is a common malevolent will affecting them all, there is a singular, greater, benevolent will bringing the Free Peoples together.

A further suggestion of Providence may be in Aragorn's response to Frodo. Frodo learned that Aragorn was descended by many generations from Isildur, and so Frodo thought surely the Ring belongs to Aragorn and not to him. Of course, Aragorn reminds him that it does not belong to either of them, since Isildur ought not to have kept it anyway. But he also says, "it has been ordained that you should hold it for a while" (II/2).[7] This naturally raises the question, "Ordained by whom?" Aragorn appears to

---

[5] Tolkien, *Morgoth's Ring*, 320.

[6] As Christopher Tolkien demonstrates in *The Return of the Shadow* and *The Treason of Isengard*, the Council of Elrond went through many iterations and revisions. But this crucial bit of framing for this meeting and, indeed, for the formation of the Fellowship was a late addition, since as late as the fifth version Elrond was saying that he called the members of the Council together, yet now he is attributing the assemblage to another will. Truly, this appears to be one of those places where Tolkien was more conscious "in the revision" (per Letter #142) of such matters characterizing his work as religious and Catholic.

[7] An exchange closely resembling this one, including the reference to it being "ordained" for Frodo to hold the Ring, had appeared in an earlier draft in Frodo's meeting with Trotter (as he was named then instead of Strider) when the former had received Gandalf's letter from Butterbur, and Trotter was identified not only as Aragorn, but as being of the line of Elendil through Isildur (Tolkien, *Treason of*

once again be acknowledging, as he has before, the higher will that has ordained his fate as well. He has recognized the same hand at work in Frodo, although he does not yet know that Frodo will continue to bear the Ring.

Courage in Defense of Others

Another point demonstrated around this time in the Council is how both Boromir and Aragorn embody the spirit of courage. Boromir declares how his people of Gondor still preserve the blood, pride, and dignity of Númenor. They have been a bulwark against the Enemy and his forces east of the Anduin. But Boromir also shows that while he has undeniable courage and valor in battle, he still lacks wisdom that comes from knowing better the lands of others: "But still we fight one, holding all the west shores of the Anduin; and those who shelter behind us give us praise, if ever they hear our name: much praise but little help" (II/2).

The problem Is that Boromir has been solely focused on the issues Gondor faces and its efforts to keep the enemies of the Free Peoples at bay, so that he has both underestimated the reach of Sauron and overestimated the reach of Gondor in their defense. He knows nothing of the trouble in the North, where Aragorn has lived his life and fought since before Boromir was born. Without the vigilance of the Rangers, the North would know nothing of the peace and freedom Boromir claims that Gondor alone maintains. They are the chief guardians of lands Gondor has long forgotten, being sundered from what was once the Northern Kingdom, "And yet less thanks have we than you. Travellers scowl at us, and countrymen give us scornful names. 'Strider' I am to one fat man who lives within a day's march of foes that would freeze his heart, or lay his little town in ruin, if he were not guarded ceaselessly. Yet we would not have it otherwise" (II/2). In both cases, Boromir and Aragorn do what is right because it is right and not because of what it earns them from others, but Boromir's is a more limited vision due to being younger and less worldly wise.

The rest of the chapter, and indeed other portions of this book, will show that the difference in their perspectives comes from their difference in trust in the strength of arms. Boromir thinks that there is a chance of defeating Sauron if the right alliances can be forged, and if the right weapons and assets can be gathered. He is a warrior through and through, and that fact unfortunately limits his vision. Aragorn agrees about the protective value of strength of arms, but his experience, as well as his deeper and

---

Isengard, 50). This further shows that someone unnamed had already "ordained" Frodo to bear the Ring, at least to that point.

broader wisdom, inform him that decisive victory in this war will not be achieved this way. A solution beyond the battlefield will be required. He knows that courage, valor, and their tools are valuable and even necessary in the struggle that they face, but they are not sufficient.

Treason and Providence in Spite of It

Gandalf is then able to fill in his part of the account of the Ring. Here, Gandalf notes how Saruman dissuaded the White Council from taking any open action against Sauron, but that he at last yielded to the Council's will to drive Sauron from Dol Guldur, which happened in the year of the finding of the Ring. He observes that this coincidence was, "a strange chance, if chance it was" (II/2). Again, there is a suggestion of something more at work here. Sauron did not know the Ring was found at that time, and so Saruman also could not have known of it. As yet, Gandalf had not voiced any suspicions about Bilbo's Ring to the Council, and Saruman did not know where it was either. But in spite of Saruman's intentions regarding the Ring, his consent to drive Sauron from Dol Guldur was ultimately helpful to Bilbo and the ultimate safekeeping of the Ring until all things were in place for the One's designs to be completed. Thus, Gandalf speaks in qualified fashion about whether or not there was simple chance involved.

We have already seen how the One incorporates evil intent into his contrary plans, and so it is also with Saruman's treason. As Gandalf says, in the wars against Sauron (and even before that), "treason has ever been our greatest foe" (II/2). The worse opposition to faith is not simple unbelief; it is what can be described as "treason," among other things. The terms for "faith" in the NT primarily signify "trust," "loyalty," "fidelity," "faithfulness," "allegiance," and so on.[8] One who acts treasonously is one who once enacted these qualities and then despised them. Theirs is a worse action than one who never had these qualities in the first place. Judgment Day is said to be worse for those who actively rejected Jesus and the gospel than for those the supposed faithful condemned on other grounds (Matt 10:15; 11:22, 24; Luke 10:12, 14), and Jesus says the one who handed him over to Pilate is guilty of a greater sin (John 19:11). And yet, such treason was worked into the plan of God by which Jesus was crucified, resurrected, and ascended into heaven.

---

[8] See also Tolkien, *Sauron Defeated*, 341, 358, where the faithful relationship with Eru is defined as "allegiance."

Another element of divine providence appears in Gandalf's story when Aragorn narrates how, at Gandalf's behest, he sought Gollum. For a long time, Gandalf and Aragorn could spot no trace of him, until, Aragorn says, "by fortune, I came suddenly on what I sought: the marks of soft feet beside a muddy pool" (II/2). We have seen already that "fortune" is providence by another name in many cases, as it is here, given the event's connection with the larger purposes for the Ring.

If not for Aragorn finding Gollum and keeping him for Gandalf to interrogate, Gandalf would not have learned of his story, and that obviously would have had significant effects (or, perhaps more properly speaking, lack thereof) for Frodo in his Quest. He also would not have been left in the care of the Elves of the Woodland Realm. And thus, Legolas would have had no reason to come to Rivendell when he did to report that Gollum had escaped after they attempted to follow Gandalf's counsel to treat him with gentleness in hope for his cure. And if he had not come to Rivendell when he did, he would not have been able to join the Fellowship of the Ring. And both he and the rest of the Fellowship would have been the worse for that absence.

Indeed, even in Gollum's escape, Gandalf reaffirms his trust in Providence. He concedes, "We have no time to seek for him again. He must do what he will. But he may play a part yet that neither he nor Sauron have foreseen" (II/2). This reiterates what he had foretold to Frodo earlier, and it will prove prescient.

Treason Is as Treason Does

As Gandalf continues with his story, he comes to the report of Saruman's betrayal. Despite his foreboding and acknowledged mistakes in judgment, he answers Saruman's summons to meet him at Orthanc if he wants his help. There he instead learns how Saruman has fallen, rejecting his responsibility as the White Wizard to instead become one of his own making as Saruman the Many-Colored. And this is a result of having allied himself with Sauron. But despite playing the part of one obedient to Sauron, Saruman remains prideful enough to plot as if he can outsmart Sauron. His allegiance to Sauron began with treason, so it is not surprising that he still thinks as a traitor.

He attempts to sugarcoat the matter for Gandalf, saying that they can take advantage of the sheer power Sauron can provide for his allies, but they can take that power for themselves and redirect it to their own ends:

> We can bide our time, we can keep our thoughts in our hearts, deploring maybe evils done by the way, but approving the high and ultimate purpose: Knowledge, Rule, Order; all the things that we have so far striven in vain to

accomplish, hindered rather than helped by our weak or idle friends. There need not be, there would not be, any real change in our designs, only in our means. (II/2)

This statement from Saruman represents a stark rejection of his mission in two ways. On the one hand, the scorn with which he speaks of those who were supposed to be the friends of the Wizards shows how he has rejected the nature of the Wizards' mission that we have already seen. They were not to use the Free Peoples as means to their own ends for whatever they thought best for everyone involved. And yet Saruman despises all those weaker than him for how they have made it more difficult for him to accomplish his designs while maintaining his opposition to Sauron. He was not to use his own power to compel, and now he thinks to use another's power to fulfill that end. Instead of being the chief servant in the cause of resisting the Enemy, he has sought to become the ultimate ruler to replace the Dark Lord himself.

On the other hand, his talk of means and ends shows his rejection of Providence. In his pride he had failed to learn an important lesson about how we really have less control over the accomplishment of our ends, however good they may be, than we think we do. Unintended consequences abound. So much depends on matters outside of our control, which is one of the reasons why *estel* is so crucial. To have *estel* is to trust that following means that are truly righteous, just, good, loving, and so on will be taken up by the One who will accomplish the ends befitting those means. Our responsibility is ultimately not in the accomplishment of the ends but in being faithful with the means we use. The goal ought to shape the means accordingly. Saruman has instead deceived himself into thinking that the means are not really important, and we may not really have control over them, which means he has gotten the logic exactly backwards. He no longer trusts the plan or care of Eru Ilúvatar, and he seeks to impose a divergent will on a creation that is not his.

Gandalf, ever the faithful minister of the One's will, rejects this parallel to Satan offering the kingdoms of the world to Jesus if he would but abandon his mission and worship him. For this, Saruman keeps Gandalf locked at the top of the Tower of Orthanc. But Providence would supply a means of escape.

The Eagles as Instruments of Providence

Among the most concrete manifestations of the work of Providence is the involvement of the Eagles. In Tolkien's larger mythos, the Great Eagles are one of the most remarkable tools of divine providence, being incarnate spiritual beings serving the will of Manwë, the King of Arda and chief servant of Eru Ilúvatar. As Gandalf himself is an emissary of the Valar (including Manwë) and the One whom they all serve, he is himself an instrument of Providence, and he knows whence the Eagles come and what significance they have.

Beyond this more general significance, Gwaihir the Windlord is specifically present at this right time because Gandalf had asked Radagast to call upon the Eagles and others of his friends to bring any news pertaining to servants of the Enemy to Orthanc, where he would be with Saruman. Saruman neither knew of this request from Gandalf nor did he take Radagast seriously as a potential threat. As such, Gwaihir did as Radagast asked and came to deliver news to Orthanc, but instead he found the situation was other than he expected and came to Gandalf's rescue. Thereafter, Gwaihir bore him to Edoras, where Gandalf was able to take Shadowfax as his steed and come to Rivendell in timely fashion.

What Is to Be Done?

Once Gandalf's account is complete, the Council shifts to deciding what must be done with the Ring. By the narrator's own telling, this is not a complete account, but the various options discussed—including, as noted before, giving it to Tom Bombadil—have a common thread of bringing up issues of responsibility and control. For example, to send it to Tom would be irresponsible because he would neglect it, and the shirking of responsibility for the Ring would ultimately mean his end as well, since he does not have the power to resist Sauron himself and all his forces when all others have been conquered. Similarly, dropping it into the sea would be irresponsible because it takes the Ring out of the Free Peoples' hands, they do not know that Sauron could not reclaim it from the sea with whatever means he may use, and it would do nothing to address the problem of Sauron, as he would eventually conquer them all anyway.

This is also part of the reason why the issue of taking the Eagle taxis to Mordor was not broached at the Council. Not only was it beyond the scope, as the Council concluded with the decision to destroy the Ring and who would be responsible for taking it, not addressing how they would get to the destination, but such a route would be against everything else that had been established about the other options at the Council. While it would take us too far afield to address the various layers of this issue, I want to note here an overarching point that is not brought up enough in discussions. Besides the other risks that would be involved with including the Eagles in the planned Quest to Mount Doom, the simple fact is that taking to the air allows for less control when you need to adapt to the situation, and no one knew what exactly they would find in Mordor in terms of what Sauron had prepared. They would be more compromised flying from a height where one wrong move could mean the Fellowship plummeting to their deaths. This option would be irresponsible in the risks it posed and how little control it allowed the bearer to take.

For similar reasons to these other rejected options, the idea of sending it into the West to the Powers in Valinor is also rejected. This would be the ultimate abdication of responsibility in asking those who do not dwell in Middle-earth to fix all their problems. They would not receive it, "for good or ill it belongs to Middle-earth; it is for us who still dwell here to deal with it" (II/2). Indeed, as Gandalf says, "it is not our part here to take thought only of a season, or for a few lives of Men, or for a passing age of the world. We should seek a final end of this menace, even if we do not hope to make one" (II/2).

That is, the Council is to discern what is right to do here and not what is the most comfortable or seemingly easiest. They must have the wisdom and the courage to do what is right regardless of the chance of success. All other roads lead to destruction.

In the Beginning, All Is Good

Boromir, ever the martial thinker, believes everyone is missing the point and wonders why they cannot use the Ring against Sauron. This thinking is akin to Saruman's, in which there are only good and evil ends, not good and evil means, so that seemingly good means are optional to a seemingly good end. Like Saruman, he does not imagine that the means will ultimately corrupt the fair-seeming end. Gandalf has already told Frodo why he cannot take the Ring, and now Elrond reiterates it for Boromir and tells him why none can take the Ring to use it against Sauron:

> The very desire of it corrupts the heart. Consider Saruman. If any of the Wise should with this Ring overthrow the Lord of Mordor, using his own arts, he would then set himself on Sauron's throne, and yet another Dark Lord would appear. And that is another reason why the Ring should be destroyed: as long as it is in the world it will be a danger even to the Wise. For nothing is evil in the beginning. Even Sauron was not so. I fear to take the Ring to hide it. I will not take the Ring to wield it. (II/2)[9]

---

[9] See also this line from Imrahil in an earlier draft of "The Last Debate": "Victory is in itself worthless. Unless Gondor stand for some good, then let it not stand at all; and if Mordor doth not stand for

This is also a keen reminder that there is no such thing as Absolute Evil in Tolkien's mythology. He himself says in Letter #183, "In my story I do not deal in Absolute Evil. I do not think there is such a thing, since that is Zero. I do not think that at any rate any 'rational being' is wholly evil." After all, Tolkien is steadfastly committed to orthodox Christian ontology, particularly as it was influenced by the articulations of Augustine. As Augustine argues in his *Enchiridion* 11–15 (and other places), evil is parasitic of good and there can be no absolute evil or absolute dark in the way that there is the One who is Absolute Good and Absolute Light (Jas 1:17; 1 John 1:5). All things that exist are good for that reason if nothing else simply because they partake in the good of existence by God's will (note how God calls what he created "good" in Gen 1), although that which is not the Absolute Good has the potential to be corrupted.

Beyond other points of *LOTR* that we will observe in due course, Tolkien's dedication to this belief is clear in multiple letters. Besides what we have seen from Letter #183, he had also rejected the idea that his conception of the Orcs was heretical because he did not regard them as an inherently evil or unredeemable race, as he sought to write consonantly with the orthodox Christian theology he held to (Letters #153 and #269; cf. #71 and #78). Also interesting in this regard is Letter #291, where he criticizes C. S. Lewis for positing a kind of dualism of a Miserific Vision corresponding to the Beatific Vision that Tolkien said was "rationally nonsense, not to say theologically blasphemous."

This aspect of orthodox Christian doctrine also underscores our own weakness. Great villains like Sauron and Saruman were once good, as were less powerful creatures like Gollum. But they, like us, were susceptible to corruption. The line between good and evil runs through all of us. None of us are immune to evil, and no one is truly beyond saving before the end if they do not reject every last opportunity. And neither the awful villains nor the exemplary heroes get where they are by accident. A series of (often incremental) conscious decisions are made, habits are formed, characteristics are cultivated, and so on. Discipleship and sanctification are important, as we can too easily fall to evil if we become too passive, and before we know it, we become a Gollum, a Saruman, a Ringwraith, or a Sauron. God's warning to Cain that sin is crouching at the door and that it seeks mastery (Gen 4:7) has not ceased to be applicable. But thanks be to God, who gives us the victory through our Lord Jesus Christ (1 Cor 15:57).

---

some evil that we will not brook in Mordor or out of it, then let it triumph." Tolkien, *War of the Ring*, 401.

The Tragedy of the Elves

Glóin then asks whether the other Rings of Power could be used in a united fight against Sauron. The Nine are spoken for, of course. The Seven are lost or taken by Sauron. That leaves the Three, the greatest besides the One Ring. But Elrond informs Glóin that they were not made for war. Their power lies in how they were made for "understanding, making, and healing, to preserve all things unstained" (II/2). This exemplifies what Tolkien sees as a central theme of his story above the themes of power or domination others have perceived: "The real theme for me is about something much more permanent and difficult: Death and Immortality: the mystery of the love of the world in the hearts of a race 'doomed' to leave and seemingly lose it; the anguish in the hearts of a race 'doomed' not to leave it, until its whole evil-aroused story is complete" (Letter #186). Understandably, Men have often envied the Elves' immortality. Even one of our earliest tales, *The Epic of Gilgamesh*, concerns how Gilgamesh sought immortality and could not keep it, and so many stories since then have shown the wish for immortality. Men must ultimately depend on faith/trust/hope that God has something beyond death for them.

But eventually the Elves and even the Valar come to envy mortality, known as the Gift of Ilúvatar to Men (a point we will address later). Their being bound to the circles of the world means that they must endure change in ways their mortal counterparts can scarcely imagine. If they befriend mortals, they will live to see many generations of them live and die, enduring the pain of loss again and again and again. Their immortality binds them to the life of the world, and this world is marred, broken, corrupt, and decaying. This, too, the Elves must endure. Their attachment to the world brings them greater love and appreciation for the loveliness of creation, but inevitably they also must endure loss in this as the things they love change—not always for the better—and die. They were thus tempted to become embalmers (Letters #131 and #154), attempting to slow change and decay for as long as possible. And this became the way of temptation for Sauron to reveal to the Elves how to make the Rings of Power to accomplish their ends (though his secret end was to enslave their wills through these Rings). While he did not participate in making any of the Three, their crafting nevertheless partook of the arts that Sauron taught, and their fate is ultimately tied with the fate of Sauron's Ring. In the end, then, the Elves' wish to embalm is in vain. Their place is ultimately either to journey to the Uttermost West (if permitted) or to fade and give way to the Dominion of Men until the eschaton, although their wisdom passed on to Men was to help in their sanctification,[11] and that is the best-case scenario. The worst-case scenario is, of course, that Sauron would gain mastery and subjugate them anyway, forcing them to watch as he destroyed all that they loved, even if only out of spite.

In the end, both Men and Elves must live by *estel* that the One has designs for their good beyond the regular course of history. Only from the One will they receive the everlasting life that fulfills both of them, as that life will be tied to the new creation that is not subject to marring and decay like this one is. And so it is with *estel* that they must decide what to do at this Council. As Glorfindel says, the Elves are willing to endure the chance that the Three will fail and what they love will pass away, "if by it the power of Sauron may be broken, and the fear of his dominion be taken away for ever" (II/2). Given Glorfindel's past and character, it is fitting that he should voice such a self-sacrificial will.

Despair or Folly

Erestor, a counsellor of Elrond, says that the path to destroying the Ring at Mount Doom is the path of despair. He would dare say it was the path of folly, but he is hesitant to question Elrond's wisdom. Gandalf replies that it may seem to be folly, but it is certainly not despair: "It is not despair, for despair is only for those who see the end beyond all doubt. We do not. It is wisdom to recognize necessity, when all other courses have been weighed, though as folly it may appear to those who cling to false hope" (II/2).

. We see that Gandalf's mindset is one for which as long as there is any trace of hope, there is no room for despair. And no one knows enough about the future to be reasonable in their despair. This is why he hoped for Gollum's cure, even if he did not think it likely. The course of action the Free Peoples take may not be ideal, but it is necessary, and it is wisdom to recognize necessity. And there is wisdom that resembles folly, but it is divine wisdom that is higher than the wisdom of the world. We have noted this in the previous chapter, and it is especially emphasized in the opening chapters of 1 Corinthians in reference to the gospel, which was a stumbling block for the Jews and folly to the Greeks. Just as Gandalf had regard for the little ones the other Wise overlooked and who troubled their counsel, he sees again the divine wisdom in this that only looks like folly to the world and to the evil powers. The ultimate hope for

---

[11] J. R. R. Tolkien, "The Qenya Lexicon," *Parma Eldalamberon* 12 (1998): 35. See also Letter #246, which we will review in Chapter Nine.

the Free Peoples is effectively cloaked the same way as the ultimate hope for the Primary World.

Elrond also acknowledges this higher wisdom: "This quest may be attempted by the weak with as much hope as the strong. Yet such is oft the course of deeds that move the wheels of the world: small hands do them because they must, while the eyes of the great are elsewhere" (II/2). This is a text Tolkien points to as exemplifying one of the main points of the story (Letter #186). It is a point that fits with Tolkien's philosophy of history as articulated in Letter #69 to his son Christopher during WW2. While he had some sense of the enormity of human iniquity in the course of history, he could still say, "at the same time one knows that there is always good: much more hidden, much less clearly discerned, seldom breaking out into recognizable, visible, beauties of word or deed or face – not even when in fact sanctity, far greater than the visible advertised wickedness, is really there" (Letter #69). And the significance of Elrond's statement is also highlighted for how it resonates with the first quote we attended to in this commentary that sets the framework for Tolkien's story. After all, this is how Elrond frames the decision that will lead to the ultimate series of events by which the Hobbits arose to trouble the counsels of the Wise and Great.

At first, Bilbo attempts to accept the Quest. Interestingly, Boromir is the only one at this Council who has only now become familiar with Bilbo's story, and so he is the only one who is even tempted to laugh at the gesture, that is until he realizes that no one else was laughing. Bilbo already has an established record of heroism, and he thinks it is his responsibility, even in his extremely old age, to finish what he thinks he started. But Gandalf reminds him that he has not, in fact, started this whole affair. Its roots go back thousands of years before him. He also reminds him, "only a small part is played in great deeds by any hero" (II/2). This is consonant with what we have noted already about the level of control one has over means and the accomplishment of ends. This applies just as well to heroes like Bilbo. In any case, Bilbo no longer has the strength needed for such a quest. Bilbo even acknowledges that he lacks the strength and the luck to do what needs to be done (II/2). This signifies that the providential support has passed to someone else, though he does not yet know who.

The one now supported by Providence is the one who speaks up after a long silence. It is none other than Frodo. And the fact that he is being guided by another will is made apparent by the narration:

> At last with an effort he spoke, and wondered to hear his own words, as if some other will was using his small voice.

'I will take the Ring,' he said, 'though I do not know the way.'

Elrond raised his eyes and looked at him, and Frodo felt his heart pierced by the sudden keenness of the glance. 'If I understand aright all that I have heard,' he said, 'I think that this task is appointed for you, Frodo; and that if you do not find a way, no one will. This is the hour of the Shire-folk, when they arise from their quiet fields to shake the towers and counsels of the Great. Who of all the Wise could have foreseen it? Or, if they are wise, why should they expect to know it, until the hour has struck?

'But it is a heavy burden. So heavy that none could lay it on another. I do not lay it on you. But if you take it freely, I will say that your choice is right; and though all the mighty Elf-friends of old, Hador, and Húrin, and Túrin, and Beren himself were assembled together, your seat should be among them.' (II/2)

This other will is the same One who meant for Bilbo and then Frodo to have the Ring, and he is speaking through Frodo's voice to call upon him for this task. And now Frodo humbly and freely submits himself to this will. It comes from within him, stoking his internal fire in recognition of the necessity of the situation until it bursts forth in a way that surprised even him. In the same way, Paul calls on his audience in Philippi, "just as you have always obeyed, not as in my presence only but now much more in my absence, work out your own salvation with fear and trembling; for it is God who is at work in you, both to desire and to work for his good pleasure" (Phil 2:12–13, NASB). As an instrument of Providence, Frodo is not entirely passive in this process. He must also actively accept the work of the will of the One and participate in it by his submission, as Paul similarly instructs. Others may be incorporated into the work of Providence despite their contrary wishes, but Frodo as a hero and humble servant is thus defined as one who works in concert with Providence. Tolkien himself in a footnote of Letter #246 even referred to this as an instance of Frodo being given "grace" so that he could answer the call to this Quest.

Elrond affirms that Frodo is an instrument of Providence in saying that the task is appointed for him. He also echoes the words that frame this whole story that we commented on in the previous chapter. This is divine wisdom at work, not something any of the Wise themselves could have foreseen (though he is perhaps excepting Gandalf since Gandalf knew Frodo best). Each of the Elf-friend heroes he lists not only have in common their remarkable deeds, but they were also instruments of Providence in various ways.

Of course, Frodo is not the only one appointed for this task. As will become clearer later, Sam has also been appointed, as his stubborn refusal to leave Frodo is also his

way of working in concert with the will of the One for him.[12] After the Council con-
cludes, the other Hobbits who accompanied him will join as well and go to take up the
tasks appointed for them (II/3), although for now they only know that they want to
accompany Frodo, no matter what danger lies ahead. In their own ways, they will cultivate the seeds of courage the One has planted within them. Frodo will also reaffirm
his commitment to his word in submission to the will of the One who spoke through
his voice when he is given the opportunity (II/3).

The Forming of the Fellowship

The final formation of the Fellowship does not come until Frodo makes this reaf-
firmation. Elrond sees it as appropriate that the Fellowship should be Nine Walkers to
oppose the Nine Riders. But he does not insist that they all must go the entire way with
him, as he says they will go "as far as they will or fortune allows" (II/3). In the end, the
hand of Providence must be acknowledged in the direction of the Fellowship, and the
One will ultimately determine who goes the entire way. It is not on Elrond to lay that
responsibility on anyone.

In the process of selecting companions, Elrond tries to select Elves of his house.
But Merry and Pippin insist on going with Frodo. And in this they have the support of
Gandalf. The strength of their fidelity born from long friendship is more valuable than
the power of even a great Elf lord like Glorfindel. While Glorfindel would be able to
do things these Hobbits could not, other events are directed by Providence with longer-
reaching consequences that were set in motion by Providence bringing them to
Rivendell and their joining the Fellowship. Events related to Rohan, Fangorn Forest,
Faramir, and the Battle of the Pelennor Fields might not have happened or would have
gone otherwise.

As the Fellowship prepares to set out, Elrond reiterates that it is not for him or
anyone else to lay the burden on anyone for Frodo's companions to go the entire way
with him. He says they are free to depart from the Quest "as chance allows" (II/3). His
wisdom throughout this statement is akin to Jesus's teaching that those who wish to be
his disciples ought to count the costs (Luke 14:27–31). That is, both forms of counsel

---

[12] An earlier version of a scene in which Gandalf and Elrond discussed the members of the Fellowship (who were to be limited to seven rather than nine, leaving out the other two Hobbits) included
comments from Elrond that "my heart tells me that their [Frodo and Sam's] fates are woven together."
Likewise, Gandalf says that he must go, "and indeed *my* fate seems much entangled with hobbits." Tolkien, *Treason of Isengard*, 114 (emphasis original). While the words were removed, the notions remained.

advise not to commit oneself too hastily, lest one becomes all the worse for breaking their word.

However, Gimli counters with notions characteristic of a stubbornly loyal Dwarf:

> 'Faithless is he that says farewell when the road darkens,' said Gimli.
> 'Maybe,' said Elrond, 'but let him not vow to walk in the dark who has not seen the nightfall.'
> 'Yet sworn word may strengthen quaking heart,' said Gimli.
> 'Or break it,' said Elrond. 'Look not too far ahead! But go now with good hearts!' (II/3)

There is truth in what each character says. As we have already noted, Elrond's teaching is consonant with Jesus's on the matter of counting costs. But it is also wise to avoid oaths and vows just to make one's words seem stronger. As Jesus taught (and James echoed), let your "Yes" be "Yes" and your "No" be "No" (Matt 5:34–37; Jas 5:12). Elrond may have in the back of his mind the notorious Oath of Fëanor, which was spoken all too haughtily and hastily, and which brought ruin beyond reckoning because Fëanor and his sons could not turn back on such an oath as they made.

Yet what Gimli says is also true. One would be faithless to turn back just because matters became more difficult than when they initially committed themselves. (This is also a keen reminder of what "faith" properly is, not being merely reducible to belief.) Fair weather friends may be acquaintances for a time, but they are "friends" in name only, not "friends" in the truest sense, as in Jesus's famous quote about laying down his life for his friends (John 15:13). And marriage vows and pledges of covenant can reinforce one's commitment to one's word as something one obligates oneself to when times get hard, though it is obviously not always so.

Of course, Gimli is just the kind of person who never had any intention of turning back once he set his mind to his goal. Despite his declaration about sworn words, he never needed to swear anything to establish his own commitment. He would have gone with Frodo to the end, if Frodo had not taken it upon himself to split from the Fellowship and Gimli and others had not been put in the position they were in. That also illustrates the wisdom in Elrond's words that the element of "chance" factors into how far one may go, and what one commits oneself to may take turns beyond one's anticipation.

Recognizing Necessity

The Fellowship then departs from Rivendell heading south. They find that the southern path around the Misty Mountains is watched, so they attempt to cross Caradhras. That path also fails. As the frustrated Fellowship discusses what to do next, Gandalf says the path remaining is the path through Moria.[13] He reiterates what he said earlier about how it is wisdom to recognize necessity: "However it may prove, one must tread the path that need chooses" (II/4). After all, Gandalf knows that necessity is an indication of Providence at work. By such means, Providence guides the course of events, and so it will be here. Many things would not have happened but for the journey through Moria, particularly concerning Gandalf. For Aragorn's words will ring true in ways he could not have imagined at the time: "He has led us in here against our fears, but he will lead us out again, at whatever cost to himself" (II/4).

Till Durin Wakes Again

As the Fellowship journeys through Moria, they come to what was once the great city of the Dwarrowdelf. This prompts Gimli to sing the Song of Durin in memory of the days of the founding of Khazad-dûm. What is most interesting about this song for our purposes is the last few lines:

> The shadow lies upon his tomb
> In Moria, in Khazad-dûm.
> But still the sunken stars appear
> In dark and windless Mirrormere;
> There lies his crown in water deep,
> Till Durin wakes again from sleep. (II/4)[14]

Dwarves believe that Durin and the rest of the Seven Fathers of the Dwarf kindreds are reborn at various times. The recognition of this rebirth for Durin would be a Dwarf taking on the name of Durin. By the time of this story, Durin VI had been dead for over a thousand years, and Durin VII would not be born until long afterwards. But it is not

---

[13] It should be noted that one biblical correlation that Tolkien explicitly rejected was from a reader who wondered if there was some link between this name and the Moriah mentioned in Abraham's story in Gen 22. As he says in Letter #297: "that has no connexion (even 'externally') whatsoever. Internally there is no conceivable connexion between the mining of Dwarves, and the story of Abraham. I utterly repudiate any such significances and symbolisms. My mind does not work that way; and (in my view) you are led astray by a purely fortuitous similarity, more obvious in spelling than speech, which cannot be justified from the real intended significance of my story."

[14] See also II/6: "There lies the Crown of Durin till he wakes."

said that the crown emerges or is reclaimed whenever Durin is thought to be reborn. Rather, the indication is that Durin waking again from sleep signifies resurrection.[15] This is an eschatological hope.

Likewise, Thorin had told Bilbo what he expected for himself, "I go now to the halls of waiting to sit beside my fathers, until the world is renewed" (ch. 18). Of course, such a remark makes sense in the Secondary World setting, as Tolkien establishes in *The Silmarillion* the expectation for a Second Music/Last Music of new creation and of the renewing of the world, which includes the participation of the Children of Ilúvatar. This presumably includes Ilúvatar's adopted children, the Dwarves, who were initially made by Aulë (the Craftsman of the Valar), though they were hallowed and given sentience by Ilúvatar after his initial rebuke of his servant. We are told in *The Silmarillion* that the Elves do not know what to expect for the Dwarves in that time to come, as they seem to think that the Dwarves will return to stone. But the Dwarves expect that they will have a part in the renewed world alongside Aulë. No one, not even the Valar, knows when that time of renewal will come, except for Eru Ilúvatar himself. Until such a time, the dead wait. When the time does arrive, the implicit expectation is for resurrection in order to partake of the renewed world.[16]

Gandalf's Profession and Sacrifice

The Fellowship continues their journey through Khazad-dûm, eventually encountering Orcs. But the greatest threat of all is unveiled as they approach the Bridge of Khazad-dûm (or Durin's Bridge) that leads to the eastern exit: a Balrog of Morgoth. If Gandalf is an angelic emissary, the Balrog is a fallen angel, a servant of Morgoth from long ago who found refuge in the depths of the earth after the destruction of his master's domain and (almost) all of Beleriand with it in the War of Wrath. While Aragorn and Boromir valiantly try to join the struggle, Gandalf protects the Fellowship by facing this threat alone.

---

[15] On the linguistic connections of sleep/waking up with death/resurrection, see Harriman, "Expectations and the Interpretation of Resurrection as 'Bodily,'" 759–61.

[16] Tolkien was never entirely settled on the fate of the Dwarves, and *The Hobbit* is the only writing where a Dwarven perspective is not recorded "secondhand" but is spoken directly by a Dwarf. But it would be especially curious if, as the Dwarves believe (but is never confirmed otherwise), their seven foremost forefathers reemerge bodily every so often to rule again, but that the new creation would not involve them all reemerging bodily to partake of the new creation and the work in shaping it.

In this confrontation, Gandalf reveals more of who he is and what the Balrog is. The Balrog has already been established by his description as a creature of shadow and flame. He is one wreathed in dark fire, being a flame of Udûn (also known as Utumno) of old. This was Melkor's original abode in Arda and the name "Udûn" could be translated as "underworld" or "hell." It was not only where Melkor, the equivalent of Satan, dwelt with those among the Maiar that he corrupted: the fallen angels who became known as Sauron, the Balrogs, and others. It was also where Melkor took the creatures of the world and corrupted them into his own perversions of Ilúvatar's creation. As Udûn was a place of darkness and flames, the Balrogs took on the form of demons of dark fire. This is what characterizes this Balrog to the very day of the story, so many millennia after he fell for Melkor's lies.

But Gandalf says this dark fire will not avail the Balrog. For Gandalf is "a servant of the Secret Fire, wielder of the flame of Anor" (II/5). This is another name of the Flame Imperishable mentioned in the chapter "Ainulindalë" of *The Silmarillion*—as shown in the "Valaquenta" of the same volume—as Eru Ilúvatar's power of creation and animation, being the equivalent of the Holy Spirit in Tolkien's mythology (though not as clearly described as a person like the Holy Spirit).[17] Two, he describes himself as, "wielder of the flame of Anor."[18] This phrase ("flame of Anor") is not used anywhere else, but "Anor," being the Sindarin equivalent of "Sun" (as in Minas Anor, "Tower of the Sun"), is a suitable contrast to the Balrog coming from "the Shadow." It may refer as well to the power he has from Eru Ilúvatar by the Flame Imperishable or to "Sun" as a metonym of light and in reference to the Powers of the West—given how,

---

[17] Kilby, *Tolkien and The Silmarillion*, 59. See also Tolkien, "Qenya Lexicon," 81; Tolkien, *Morgoth's Ring*, 345. For more on the Holy Spirit in Tolkien's work, see Freeman, *Tolkien Dogmatics*, 32–36. Curiously, an early draft of what would become "The Shadow of the Past" has Gandalf saying this about how to destroy the Ring, "I fancy you would have to find one of the Cracks of Earth in the depths of the Fiery Mountain, and drop it down into the Secret Fire, if you really wanted to destroy it." Tolkien, *Return of the Shadow*, 82. It is not entirely clear in this initial conception that this is the same Secret Fire that is referenced in this different place in the finished text or if there was only shared terminology and not a shared idea between these two texts. But if there was a shared idea, it is notable that the creation story includes Eru Ilúvatar animating Arda by sending the Flame Imperishable to burn at its heart. Personally, I would think it is the same Secret Fire, given that Tolkien referred to "the Secret Fire" as early as "The Music of the Ainur," which Tolkien initially drafted sometime between 1918 and 1920. See J. R. R. Tolkien, *The Book of Lost Tales 1*, The History of Middle-earth 1, ed. Christopher Tolkien (New York: Del Rey, 1983), 51, 53.

[18] An earlier version of this text made no reference to Gandalf being a servant of the Secret Fire, but he did say, "I am the master of the White Fire. The red flame cannot come this way." Tolkien, *Treason of Isengard*, 198 (also see 203). This appears to be another case of Tolkien being more conscious in his revision of the religious and Catholic character of his story, and so he subtly sharpened the reference to accentuate its theological implications.

for example, Anorien and Minas Anor referred to westward regions of Gondor—which would still ultimately be linked with allegiance to and empowerment by Eru Ilúvatar.[19] The dark fire will not avail the Balrog because Gandalf is a servant of the Fire that was before all fires, which is the Fire of the light that enlivens. Gandalf is reminding him that he serves the One who is above all, the One the Balrog scorned long ago, the One who is served by the Powers who destroyed his kin and cast his master into the Void.

Gandalf's confrontation with the Balrog must ultimately mean his self-sacrifice. He exemplifies the foundational morality we have noted earlier in laying down his life for his friends, not knowing if he can take it up again in Middle-earth, and doing what he can to bring Middle-earth's salvation, even if it means the loss of his own life (cf. Letter #148a). For all he knew, his death would ultimately mean the failure of the Wizards' mission in Middle-earth, but he did what was right here regardless of the apparent chance of success. And in the end, he needed to have *estel* by putting his trust in Eru Ilúvatar that by his providence he would accomplish his will whether or not Gandalf remained involved in Middle-earth. And for all the Fellowship knows, this would be the end of Gandalf's story, but we must return to this matter next chapter.

The Quest Continues

Despite the loss of Gandalf, there is little time now for mourning. Aragorn himself wonders what hope the Fellowship has without Gandalf, but what he says to the Fellowship is: "We must do without hope … At least we may yet be avenged. Let us gird ourselves and weep no more! Come! We have a long road, and much to do" (II/6). The tone has changed from Aragorn's earlier reassurance for Sam to have hope. But it should be observed that the difference is that Aragorn was then speaking about the hope in the One who is beyond the present situation and may yet work things to good ends by means that they do not foresee (that is, *estel*), but here he is referring to the hope that is *amdir*, which was explained earlier as being based more on what is already known. This is what the Fellowship must continue without for now because their capabilities are significantly diminished, and they do not know what all awaits them on the remainder of the Quest. The only course is to persevere in what was already decided as the right course of action. Until unforeseen special grace is given to them again, they must rely on the common grace given in what strength, courage, and wisdom they have. It will only be in retrospect that what is deemed at the present time as fortune being

---

[19] See also Tolkien, *Morgoth's Ring*, 380. There, in an alternate version Tolkien conceived for the origin of the sun, it is said that its light is a portion of the gift of Ilúvatar that Varda/Elbereth received.

less kind (II/6) will eventually be seen to have borne greater fruit than could be imagined at the time

Perilous Good

When Aragorn states his intention to lead the Fellowship into Lothlórien, Boromir objects. It was against his judgment that they entered Moria, and he thinks this path would also be perilous in light of what he has heard in Gondor that the few who leave the land do not do so unscathed. Aragorn, being a Man who has gone in and come out of the Golden Wood, corrects him that it would be more correct to say "unchanged" rather than "unscathed." That this is the framing for how Gondorians speak of Lothlórien shows that something has gone wrong in the tradition of what was once wisdom in that land. But in any case, he does affirm that it is perilous, "fair and perilous; but only evil need fear it, or those who bring some evil with them" (II/6).

This is a fine reminder that good truly can be dangerous to that which is evil. This notion appears in various forms throughout the Bible from Genesis to Revelation, whether in God's action of judgment, the many pictures of cosmic conflict between God and evil, or the need for sanctification lest one be subject to wrath. By extension, this idea undergirds how Paul speaks about our participation in spiritual warfare (2 Cor 10:3–6; Eph 6:10–20) and how Jesus speaks of the gates (defensive structures) of Hades not prevailing against the Church's offensive (Matt 16:18).

Perils of Other Kinds

Of course, the motif of peril recurs in this chapter once the Fellowship has entered Lothlórien and met with the Galadhrim led by Haldir. They are protective of their realm and are thus leery of strangers. This is most clearly demonstrated by how they treat Gimli. They insist that he must walk to their city blindfolded. Given what the reader will have known of Gimli to this point, he is unsurprisingly resentful of those who are so automatically distrustful of one as stout-hearted, faithful, and trustworthy as he. The situation threatens to take a turn for the lethal, but Aragorn deescalates tensions by suggesting Haldir blindfold the whole company so that Gimli is thus not singled out. Eventually, this suggestion is accepted. As with Paul's counsel regarding "weaker" brothers and sisters (Rom 14; 1 Cor 8 and 10), giving up privileges one can rightly use (as with Aragorn being able to walk freely in these lands) can be crucial for maintaining fellowship with those who, for one reason or another, may be caused to stumble by the use of such privileges. Even when Gimli said he would be satisfied if Legolas shared his blindness, Aragorn insists that all will share in the same condition. This reaffirms the value of Gimli to the Fellowship, of his character (particularly his trustworthiness), and of the bonds of the Fellowship when they were at risk of dissolving so soon after their first major crisis.

The Galadhrim are keeping to the policies of their realm, but it is because of the peril they find outside their realm that they observe those policies. So too it was with the Woodland Realm in *The Hobbit*. When Legolas decries the folly of these days that all those who share a common enemy cannot be more trusting of each other, Haldir acknowledges that this policy is unfortunately the result of the work of the Enemy: "Indeed in nothing is the power of the Dark Lord more clearly shown than in the estrangement that divides all those who still oppose him" (II/6).

This is a truth with which Tolkien was all too familiar in the Primary World as a Catholic living in a context where Catholicism was often denigrated and that largely by other Christians.[20] He had once planned to write a history of the Church in England, and if his work had extended into the era of the Reformation and beyond, this denigration would have been a recurrent theme.[21] He had even had the personal experience of his widowed mother being cut off by her family when she became Catholic. Of course, many of his friends over the course of his life were Protestants, and he did support ecumenical efforts to some degree (Letter #306), but he knew all too well how even some of his friends harbored strong anti-Catholic biases. Even as he saw God's saving grace extending to the Protestants, he saw the devil and his minions at work in the enmity between them and the Catholic Church.[22] Indeed, the ecumenical efforts of his day were overlooking the harm that had been done to the Catholics by the Protestants, but in the end he said, "But charity must cover a multitude of sins! There are dangers (of course), but a Church militant cannot afford to shut up all its soldiers in a fortress. It had as bad effects on the Maginot Line" (Letter #306). This principle comes from 1 Pet 4:8, and its context further suggests what is necessary for Christian unity in being hospitable to one another (4:9), serving one another with the gifts God has given each person (4:10), and glorifying God in all things by speaking as one who speaks the words of God and serving as one who serves with the strength God supplies (4:11). And this

---

[20] For more on this, see Ordway, *Tolkien's Faith*, 17–30.

[21] The incomplete manuscript of the work titled *Church in Ancient England* is in the special collections of the Bodleian Library.

[22] For more on the subject of Tolkien and Christians of other traditions, see Ordway, *Tolkien's Faith*, 267–74.

corresponds with what will ultimately become true of the relationship between Gimli and these Elves.

When Haldir asks the Hobbits about the Elves who live west of them, they too remark on how the Hobbits have similarly kept to themselves and have not ventured far beyond their realm. Indeed, if Merry had known how perilous the world was, he would have been content to stay home. Haldir acknowledges that this is a fallen world, but there is more to see in it: "The world is indeed full of peril, and in it there are many dark places; but still there is much that is fair, and though in all lands love is now mingled with grief, it grows perhaps the greater" (II/6). This is something Merry will certainly learn more about as his part in the story continues. So too can biblical texts declare the glories of God's creation in the face of their authors' keen awareness of the fallen state of the world (among others, see Job 38–41; Pss 8; 104; Prov 8). It is also consonant with Tolkien's theology of sub-creation in how he notes that humans are fallen, and that their capacity for image-bearing is marred, but they still bear the image of God and still have the capabilities of sub-creation. Likewise, in his "On Fairy-Stories" he notes how the eucatastrophe of a fairy story allows for a glimpse beyond fallenness, providing the joy of deliverance, which is poignant as grief (see Chapter Two).

An Island of Beauty

In the end, the company is guided ever so slowly deeper into their realm. When they are able to walk free of their blindfolds, they are struck by the beauty of this land. This is how the experience is told from Frodo's point of view:

> It seemed to him that he had stepped through a high window that looked on a vanished world. A light was upon it for which his language had no name. All that he saw was shapely, but the shapes seemed at once clear cut, as if they had been first conceived and drawn at the uncovering of his eyes, and ancient as if they had endured for ever. He saw no colour but those he knew, gold and white and blue and green, but they were fresh and poignant, as if he had at that moment first perceived them and made for them names new and wonderful. In winter here no heart could mourn for summer or for spring. No blemish or sickness or deformity could be seen in anything that grew upon the earth. On the land of Lórien there was no stain. (II/6)

Here, we thus see another kind of vision beyond fallenness in this world. It cannot last, of course, as the Elves must eventually depart into the Uttermost West or dwindle, but this supplies a glimpse of beauty that transcends the fallen state of things. It is a vision of Arda Unmarred, but even it will pale in comparison to Arda Healed (or Arda Remade). There, the artistry of Elves, Men, Dwarves, Maiar, and Valar will be taken up together and enhanced by the creative power, wisdom, and will of Ilúvatar. But for now, visions like this one provide islands of beauty amidst the marred world to point beyond its bounds to a yet greater glory.

Arrival at Caras Galadhon

When the Fellowship arrives in Caras Galadhon and meets Celeborn and Galadriel, Celeborn at first greets them all warmly, even Gimli, thereby extending a sign of reconciliation to him in hopes of extending the same to other Dwarves. However, after Celeborn and Galadriel hear the account of the Fellowship's journey, Celeborn questions allowing them within their borders after having stirred the Balrog, and he questions if Gandalf did not ultimately fall into folly by going needlessly into Moria. But Galadriel corrects him, "Needless were none of the deeds of Gandalf in life. Those that followed him knew not his mind and cannot report his full purpose" (II/7). This statement reflects how Galadriel had perhaps the deepest appreciation of Gandalf's wisdom. It also reflects her cultivated *estel*, as she had to trust the Powers who sent him and the One who empowered and guided him for his task, whatever its scope was.

But she also tells her husband not to renege on his welcome of Gimli. She sympathizes with him and his situation of exile, and she knows well if any of them were in a similar situation, they also would have wished to turn aside and look upon their realm, no matter what evil had taken it over. The direct interaction she has with Gimli after this is worth quoting in full:

> 'Dark is the water of Kheled-zâram, and cold are the springs of Kibil-nâla, and fair were the many-pillared halls of Khazad-dûm in Elder Days before the fall of might kings beneath the stone.' She looked upon Gimli, who sat glowering and sad, and she smiled. And the Dwarf, hearing the names given in his own ancient tongue, looked up and met her eyes; and it seemed to him that he looked suddenly into the heart of an enemy and saw there love and understanding. (II/7)

Celeborn's gesture of reconciliation was sincere, but this is something deeper. Galadriel had put herself in his boots and even spoke his language. There is nothing necessarily wrong with benevolent expressions, but true reconciliation requires what is mentioned above: love and understanding. And this, in turn, causes Celeborn to ask Gimli to forget what he had said, for he did not understand how evil his plight was. This interaction is the root of what will bind Gimli in fellowship with the Elves for the rest of his life. Because she made that first step, a new relationship can form here across lines of traditional enmity, the relationship of Gimli with Legolas will become deeper, and throughout this story Gimli will speak in praise and defense of Galadriel, an event no one could have guessed would have happened before this Quest began.

The Long Defeat and Tolkien's Philosophy of History

Galadriel makes another remark in this meeting that is worth commenting on. She says something of her and Celeborn's history together, ending with, "and together through ages of the world we have fought the long defeat" (II/7). The reference to a "long defeat" is a fascinating and evocative phrase, but people have read too much into it. Particularly, people think because of this statement and some others that his philosophy of history is pessimistic because they cannot imagine a philosophy of history that is not squeezed into the contrast of optimism/pessimism.[23] It is but one example of Tolkien being forced into a side of a debate he does not really fit in, simply because he pushed against the popular myth of progress in his day.

One can see an example of his more complicated philosophy of history in Letter #64 to his son Christopher. He is appalled at the inconceivable scale of human misery in the world, but he keeps a few things in mind to prevent being swallowed by the abyss of despair. The first is the reality of our limited judgment based on our limited knowledge of what is really happening from the perspective of eternity. The second is a lesson we can nevertheless glean from experience: "All we do know, and that to a large extent by direct experience, is that evil labours with vast power and perpetual success – in vain: preparing only the soil for unexpected good to sprout in." The third is the need for both courage and faith to face the evil that befalls us between now and the reception of our hope from God (see also Letter #101). Hope motivates perseverance as the goal of the same (Rom 5:1–5; 8:18–25; Heb 10:23–25).

---

[23] One more often encounters this idea in online discussions. A popular example of someone making the argument for this claim more extensively is Wisecrack's YouTube video "The Philosophy of J. R. R. Tolkien: Why Things Keep Getting Worse" (available at: https://www.youtube.com/watch?v=_-sTbaH-aA0). Also see Judy Ann Ford and Robin Anne Reid, "Into the West: Far Green Country or Shadow on the Waters?," in *Picturing Tolkien: Essays on Peter Jackson's* The Lord of the Rings *Film Trilogy*, ed. Janice M. Bogstad and Philip E. Kaveny (Jefferson, NC; London: McFarland, 2011), 171–72.

Tolkien obviously does not think that history progressively builds to its eschatological crescendo. Yet, he does think that events in history, including the experience of God's mercy on the temporal plane and the gift of familial love, provide glimpses that offer foretastes of that crescendo in which the defeat of evil will be final and permanent. His eschatological view of history gives him comfort that the sprawling labors of evil are all in vain.

Likewise, in Letter #69 (also to Christopher), he wrote the following:

> A small knowledge of history depresses one with the sense of the everlasting mass and weight of human iniquity: old, dreary, endless repetitive unchanging incurable wickedness. All town, all villages, all habitations of men – sinks! And at the same time one knows that there is always good: much more hidden, much less clearly discerned, seldom breaking out into recognizable, visible, beauties of word or deed or face – not even when in fact sanctity, far greater than the visible advertised wickedness, is really there. But I fear that in the individual lives of all but a few, the balance is debit – we do so little that is positive good, even if we negatively avoid what is actively evil. It must be terrible to be a priest!

In both of these letters, Tolkien shows that it is too simplistic to call his view of history "pessimistic." It is a rather complicated and thoroughly Christian view of history, one which is all too aware of the intransigent problems of history at the individual, collective, and systemic levels, but which is all too hopeful of a delivering eschatological conclusion. This is further supported by the underlying conviction demonstrated in subtle ways throughout his fictional work that God is providentially guiding history to its ultimate end, even when such action is often not obvious.

Of course, Tolkien himself did use the phrase from Galadriel in Letter #195 to say that he does not expect history to be anything but a "long defeat." But it does no good to quote that comment by itself. Here it is in context:

> One point: Frodo's attitude to weapons was personal. He was not in modern terms a 'pacifist'. Of course, he was mainly horrified at the prospect of civil war among Hobbits; but he had (I suppose) also reached the conclusion that physical fighting is actually less ultimately effective than most (good) men think it! Actually I am a Christian, and indeed a Roman Catholic, so that I do not expect 'history' to be anything but a 'long defeat' – though it contains (and in a legend may contain more clearly and movingly) some samples or glimpses of final victory.

As with the other letters noted here, Tolkien's philosophy of history is shaped by his Christian eschatology. It is precisely because Tolkien is Catholic that he does not believe that any human processes will lead to final victory. But it is also precisely because Tolkien is Catholic that he always accompanies such statements about the power of evil in human history with statements about final victory guaranteed by his Lord Jesus Christ. And because of his beliefs about divine providence, he can believe that there are, in fact, glimpses of this final victory through God's work in the present time.

The description of the "long defeat" thus resonates with both his Secondary World storytelling and his Primary World beliefs in two general ways. First, the "long defeat" more broadly refers to how the Elves, especially the leaders who bore the Rings of Power—of whom Galadriel is one—have sought in vain to resist change and decay in perpetuity in their attempts to preserve (or even "embalm," to use Tolkien's description) what they love. Although we have seen the description of Lothlórien as being of unstained, unblemished beauty, the fact is that the preservation efforts cannot last forever. This realm also must change and diminish. Thus it is with any similar attempts in the Primary World to act as embalmers. Everlasting preservation, like everlasting life, is not possible in the normal course of history. It can only happen after the eschaton with the new/renewed creation in which death and decay have no place.

Second, the "long defeat" also includes the struggle with the forces of evil, mostly Sauron. Because of how recurrent the powers of evil are, the different shapes they take over the years, and the influence they wield in the very fallenness of the world, no conventional victory will be everlasting. Galadriel has seen this especially in how her people have waxed and then waned, never to wax again, but the powers of evil rise and fall and rise again. The Elves have seen enough of history unfold to know that the final solution to the problems of history must transcend the regular course of history, hence the speculation we see in "Athrabeth Finrod ah Andreth" that Eru Ilúvatar himself would need to become incarnate. But though the victories over evil are temporary, that does not mean they are insignificant. They may, in an anticipatory fashion, partake of the final victory by providing samples or glimpses of the same. Tolkien clearly does believe there will be final victory, and he has noted this as a solution that Christian eschatology provided to Northern culture where Norse theology was previously pervasive, wherein such a notion of final victory was lacking. Both Tolkien and Galadriel exemplify *estel* in acknowledging that the final, eschatological victory must come from God and not be accomplished by any other fashion available in the regular course of history.

Magic

As the Fellowship rests afterwards, there is an interesting exchange between Frodo and Sam. Sam is reflecting on the wonder of this realm of Lothlórien when he says:

> 'If there's any magic about, it's right down deep, where I can't lay my hands on it, in a manner of speaking.'
>
> 'You can see and feel it everywhere,' said Frodo.
>
> 'Well,' said Sam, 'you can't see nobody working it.' (II/7)

This resembles language that Tolkien would read in a letter sent to him in 1971 that he references in Letter #328 concerning what the reader called "a sanity and sanctity" in Tolkien's work that has its own power, which another reader described as "some sort of faith [that] seems to be everywhere without a visible source, like light from an invisible lamp."

> You speak of 'a sanity and sanctity' in *the L.R.* 'which is a power in itself. I was deeply moved'. Nothing of the kind had been said to me before. But by a strange chance, just as I was beginning this letter, I had one from a man, who classified himself as 'an unbeliever, or at best a man of belatedly and dimly dawning religious feeling ... but you', he said, 'create a world in which some sort of faith seems to be everywhere without a visible source, like light from an invisible lamp'. I can only answer: 'Of his own sanity no man can securely judge. If sanctity inhabits his work or as a pervading light illumines it then it does not come from him but through him. And neither of you would perceive it in these terms unless it was with you also. Otherwise you would see and feel nothing, or (if some other spirit was present) you would be filled with contempt, nausea, hatred.

In Tolkien's insistence that he is not the source of this sanctity, he acknowledges providence both in how God has used his story (which is something he acknowledges elsewhere in the letter, as I have quoted previously) and in how God has preveniently enabled people to perceive this aspect of his story that comes from another source. And so it is with the "magic" that is at work here, for though we have been acquainted with the ones who have beautified this realm, the ultimate source of the work and power, and the One who sustains it for a time (especially as it will help in the sanctification of others), is beyond sight.

But we must say something about the use of the term "magic." Magic has naturally set off alarms for some Christian readers. The curiousness of the term's usage is something one of Tolkien's characters acknowledges. When Frodo and Sam come to see

Galadriel at her Mirror, she offers them the chance to look into the Mirror: "'And you?' she said, turning to Sam. 'For this is what your folk would call magic, I believe; though I do not understand clearly what they mean; and they seem to use the same word of the deceits of the Enemy. But this, if you will, is the magic of Galadriel. Did you not say that you wished to see Elf-magic'" (II/7). By Tolkien's own admission (esp. Letters #131 and #155), he has not used the term "magic" consistently. This inevitably means that there is no distinct terminology used for the devices of Melkor, Sauron, and others as opposed to the works of Gandalf, Elrond, Galadriel, and others. There is also no different terminology used for when the work is the result of inherent power (such as angelic beings like Gandalf have) or when the work is the result of invocation of another power by spells or some other kind of manipulation. Thus, in Tolkien's fictional work, the term can have a positive connotation or a negative connotation, depending on such factors as the action's motivation, purpose, or whether it comes from a capacity of the being or something they are using some illicit manipulation to achieve. It is really a combination of these factors, since those like Melkor and Sauron can use inherent capacities for evil ends, and others can use magical manipulation for at least seemingly good or initially good ends.

In the Bible the matter is more straightforward simply because all things associated with "magic," "sorcery," "witchcraft," and so on are attempts to go outside of the covenantally established means of appealing to God (which would generally be by prayer and/or casting lots, or even using the Urim and Thummim in certain situations), usually as a shortcut or workaround to achieving one's own ends and in one's own sense of the proper time, rather than waiting upon the Lord, seeking his will, and waiting for his timing, all of which are essential exercises of faith, as we see throughout the Bible. Magic, in this condemned sense, operates on the notion that one is not only appealing to a supernormal power other than God (or occasionally attempting to manipulate God by such formulas of power), but that that power is to render service to oneself for some purpose of transgressing creaturely limitations. This is in stark contrast to the expectation that those who are faithful to God are to humble themselves before him. There is much more that could be said here on the subject of "magic" in the ancient world and today, its varieties, and the motivations, but this basically indicates what is at issue. And it is not what is at issue here or in other cases in Tolkien's story when he refers to "magic" that has a potentially beneficent sense.

One also must consider the various contexts in which the term "magic" is used. In *LOTR* as a whole the conceit of the story is that it is based on the Red Book of Westmarch, a work of Hobbits, and thus it is told primarily from a Hobbit perspective. What they call "magic" would not necessarily be called the same by others who know more than they do, as we see in the statement from Galadriel quoted earlier. For Hobbits, anything that may seem to be operating "out of the normal" or was seemingly "summoned to be" as if out of nothing would appear to be what they call "magic." Of course, in the opening of *The Hobbit* the narrator tells us of Hobbits having an ordinary everyday sort of magic. This simply refers to the inherent capacity of Hobbits for stealth and being able to hide quickly, which would seem strange, incomprehensible, and thus "magical" to us, as the narrator is speaking from the perspective of a person living in the modern world. "Magic" also has the connotation in this context of something wondrous, as also fits with how the Hobbits think of "magic," even though they would not think of their own capacity to do what they do as "magical," even as Galadriel does not quite understand what the Hobbits mean by "magic."

We can explore further in comments Tolkien made in his letters on the matter of magic. When he explained to Milton Waldman in Letter #131 how his mythology fundamentally conveys and addresses the problem of the relationship between Art (and sub-creation) and Primary Reality, he divided this fundamental concern into three categories of problems: Fall, Mortality, and Machine:

> With Fall inevitably, and that motive occurs in several modes. With Mortality, especially as it affects art and the creative (or as I should say, sub-creative) desire which seems to have no biological function, and to be apart from the satisfactions of plain ordinary biological life, with which, in our world, it is indeed usually at strife. This desire is at once wedded to a passionate love of the real primary world, and hence filled with the sense of mortality, and yet unsatisfied by it. It has various opportunities of 'Fall'. It may become possessive, clinging to the things made as its own, the sub-creator wishes to be the Lord and God of his private creation. He will rebel against the laws of the Creator – especially against mortality. Both of these (alone or together) will lead to the desire for Power, for making the will more quickly effective, – and so the Machine (or Magic). By the last I intend all use of external plans or devices (apparatus) instead of developments of the inherent inner powers or talents – or even the use of these talents with the corrupted motive of dominating: bulldozing the real world, or coercing other wills. The Machine is our more obvious modern form though more closely related to Magic than is usually recognised.

In this context, it is clear that Magic in this specific sense concerns the same matter as the One Ring of transgressing creaturely limitation, as we explored in Chapter Four. "Magic" in this negative sense certainly does intersect with biblical condemnations of magic and practitioners thereof.

Despite what he wrote of Magic and Machine, he did not use the former consistently, even in his mythology. He noted that there is a regular confusion in human stories in terminology for what the Enemy does and for what the Elves do, but what he could say was:

> But the Elves are there (in my tales) to demonstrate the difference. Their 'magic' is Art, delivered from many of its human limitations: more effortless, more quick, more complete (product, and vision in unflawed correspondence). And its object is Art not Power, sub-creation not domination and tyrannous re-forming of Creation. The 'Elves' are 'immortal', at least as far as this world goes: and hence are concerned rather with the griefs and burdens of deathlessness in time and change, than with death. The Enemy in successive forms is always 'naturally' concerned with sheer Domination, and so the Lord of magic and machines; but the problem: that this frightful evil can and does arise from an apparently good root, the desire to benefit the world and others – speedily and according to the benefactor's own plans – is a recurrent motive. (Letter #131)

He also focused on the specific problem with the terminology of magic in the unsent Letter #155, which is an expansion of Letter #154 addressed to Naomi Mitchison. He noted the old distinction between *magia* (which was more often regarded positively) and *goeteia* (which was more often regarded negatively) as an analogous one to the distinctions between kinds of magic in his story. Ultimately, the distinction of good and bad in the case of magic in his world does not have to do so much with the power itself as with the motive, purpose, or use thereof. Furthermore, the distinction between the two kinds of magic, as he continued to use the terms, is that *magia* is some inherent power, such as both Gandalf and Sauron have by virtue of their being Maiar, while *goeteia* is not inherent and usually involves external manipulation, often on the level of creating visions or illusions.

Magic in this framework, where it does not concern inherent powers of superhuman creatures, is a two-faced form of idolatry and pride. On the one hand, one generally seeks a power apart from God to accomplish a given purpose, either because they know it is improper to ask this of God or because they expect better, quicker results by going to another power than the one God they are supposed to worship. On the other hand, even as it involves appeal to another god as the supposedly more dependable power, magic also works on the presumed ability to manipulate the deity to one's own ends. Sometimes this presumption even involves YHWH, as there are magical texts that include this name. As such, magic operates on the conceit that one is not only appealing to a supernormal power, but that that power is to render service to oneself, and this is for some purpose of transgressing creaturely limitation.

Although Tolkien did not deal with the relationship to the biblical text as such, he made some important notes about the framework of this discussion in his closing paragraph:

> Anyway, a difference in the use of 'magic' in this story is that it is not to be come by 'lore' or spells; but is in an inherent power not possessed or attainable by Men as such. Aragorn's 'healing' might be regarded as 'magical', or at least a blend of magic with pharmacy and 'hypnotic' processes. But it is (in theory) reported by hobbits who have very little notions of philosophy and science; while A. is not a pure 'Man', but at long remove one of the 'children of Lúthien'.

We will have occasion to comment on Aragorn's healing capabilities in the commentary on Book V.

Tests of the Will

The whole scene of the Mirror of Galadriel involves multiple tests of resolve. Galadriel warns the Hobbits that the Mirror "is dangerous as a guide of deeds" (II/7) as she does not control it and it provides a mixture of visions of things that were, are, may be, and may never be. Sam sees visions of the Shire's destruction and is thus tempted to forsake the Quest and return home, but in the end his faithfulness and courage are resolute: "No, I'll go home by the long road with Mr. Frodo, or not at all" (II/7). Frodo is also given visions, some of which will be foreshadowing, but without context that will come with a proper experience of the future, they cause doubts about the viability of his Quest, especially with the sense he has of the power of the Enemy. But in the end, he will resolve to continue his Quest, even if he thinks (wrongly) that he must do it alone.

Galadriel, too, has her will tested. She acknowledges that Frodo's Quest ultimately spells doom for her and her people: "For if you fail, then we are laid bare to the Enemy. Yet if you succeed, then our power is diminished, and Lothlórien will fade, and the tides of Time will sweep it away" (II/7). When Frodo asks her what she wishes, she simply says, "That what should be shall be ... The love of the Elves for their land and their works is deeper than the deeps of the Sea, and their regret is undying and cannot ever wholly be assuaged. Yet they will cast all away rather than submit to Sauron: for they know him now" (II/7). This reaffirms what Glorfindel had said earlier. It exemplifies again the virtue of *estel* and the will to sacrifice oneself that comes with it should it be necessary. But Frodo's offer of the Ring puts her commitment to *estel* to the test. At first, she laughs, and here laughter has more of a foreboding sense, as she acknowledges that she has desired the power that the Ring offers, and she pondered what she would do if she had it for herself. What makes it all the more tempting for her is that she could excuse taking the Ring because it was freely offered to her, and it would be for the succor of her guest. And so she says, "And now at last it comes. You will give me the Ring freely! In place of the Dark Lord you will set up a Queen. And I shall not be dark, but beautiful and terrible as the Morning and the Night! Fair as the Sea and the Sun and the Snow upon the Mountain! Dreadful as the Storm and the Lightning! Stronger than the foundations of the earth. All shall love me and despair" (II/7).

With this speech comes a transfiguration as Frodo beholds her in her glory, "seeming now tall beyond measurement, and beautiful beyond enduring, terrible and worshipful" (II/7). Thus she would be, albeit twisted into a dark reflection of the same were she to possess the Ring. As Gandalf and Elrond have already highlighted, the Wise and the Great are particularly susceptible to the weaknesses the Ring can exploit. Those qualities that make her supremely lovely would be turned into an overwhelming desire to *make* others love her. After all, Sauron had meant to make others into his worshippers through the power of the One Ring (Letter #183). Even though he cared less about being *loved* per se, the Ring could naturally corrupt this characteristic of Galadriel to a similar evil end so as to lead others to despair. And as we have noted previously from other quotes, one who had the power to wield the Ring would ultimately use it to cow the wills of other people.

But instead of giving into this temptation that appeals to her strengths and desires, she laughs again, and this time the laughter signifies deliverance from that dark end. Wordlessly, she has resisted the temptation and passed the test. Instead of taking the power to have all things as she might wish (though, in fact, she would become ensnared and enslaved by a will to power and domination), she submits her will to the One in whom she has *estel* and resolves, "I will diminish, and go into the West, and remain Galadriel" (II/7). This echoes and anticipates the path Jesus chose to his exaltation, for it was the path that led to and through the cross and resurrection by his trust in God, rather than by having immediate dominion at the cost of worshiping Satan (Matt 4:1–11 // Luke 4:1–13).

Choice and Fate

The conclusion of this scene and another early part of the next chapter highlight something that we cannot fully explore here. Tolkien's thought on the relationship of fate and free will is complicated. Tolkien's most extensive articulations on the subject in his fiction came circa 1968, well after the publication of *LOTR*, and we will not be exploring it here, as what he wrote has been published in *The Nature of Middle-earth* (the chapter is titled "Fate and Free Will").[24] Since our focus is on *LOTR* here and not on his later developed thought, we will stick with the evocative comments here.

After the trials surrounding the Mirror of Galadriel are completed, Galadriel says to Frodo and Sam, "In the morning you must depart, for now we have chosen, and the tides of fate are flowing" (II/7). Likewise, at the end of the initial conversation in the next chapter when the Fellowship says they are not clear what path all of them will take (besides Boromir, who has been set on returning to Minas Tirith since the Quest began), Galadriel sends the Fellowship off to bed and comforting them saying, "Maybe the paths that you each shall tread are already laid before your feet, though you do not see them" (II/8).

Both of these quotes fit what we have seen already. Providence incorporates the choices of creatures into the divine design, here described in terms of "fate." But Providence is a higher will than any creature, is at work long before any choice a creature makes, and is working well ahead of them. Eru Ilúvatar is the only one who knows the entirety of the Music and the only one who knows for sure the end he is directing it to ahead of time, as well as how and when it will be brought to that goal, as well as the glimpses of the goal beforehand. That is why Galadriel can say their paths are already laid before them, even if they cannot see them. Eru meant for Frodo to have the Ring as he meant for Bilbo to have it, but Frodo also needed to willingly submit to the Quest. Similarly, as Paul says, we were created by God for good works that he prepared in advance for us to do, but we must be active in doing them (Eph 2:10). The instruments of Providence, when they are living creatures, are not presented as entirely passive in a process where they are whisked away to whatever end. Rather, they are active in participating in the work of which they and their choices are only a part.

---

[24] Tolkien, *Nature of Middle-earth*, 226–31.

Parting Gifts

As the Fellowship prepares to depart from Lothlórien, Celeborn and Galadriel meet them to give them supplies—most importantly, the *lembas*—and parting gifts for each member. It is not so much each of the individual gifts that are of interest for our purposes here. But there are some points to note. First, Aragorn has another sort of transfiguration here when Galadriel gives him the Elfstone, "Then Aragorn took the stone and pinned the brooch upon his breast, and those who saw him wondered; for they had not marked before how tall and kingly he stood, and it seemed to them that many years of toil had fallen from his shoulders" (II/8). This is yet another preview of what is to come for him.

Second, Gimli's only request for a gift is one strand of her hair, which he says he will set in imperishable crystal as an heirloom of his house and "a pledge of good will between the Mountain and the Wood until the end of days" (II/8). Galadriel not only obliges, but she gives him three of her hairs. And so the reconciliation deepens between their peoples, and she forever alters the course of Gimli's life. This impression that her loveliness and beauty make on him is reminiscent again of Mary, as Tolkien confirms about Robert Murray's comments in saying that it is with reference to Mary/Our Lady "upon which all my own small perception of beauty both in majesty and simplicity is founded" (Letter #142).[25]

Third, she gives to Frodo her Phial, which is filled with the waters of her fountain capturing the light of Eärendil's star. Such a gift shows the long-reaching work of Providence, as the light of Eärendil's star is a Silmaril, which he used to find his way to Aman to appeal for aid from the Valar, which, in turn, provided salvation for Middle-earth by the defeat of Melkor and his forces. And the fact that it was set in the heavens enabled its light to be captured by Galadriel, which in turn will prove to be a crucial help to Frodo (and Sam) in the darkest of places.[26]

---

[25] Although it is not a subject of extended comment in this commentary, I should note that Tolkien said the Elvish chant *Namárië* that Galadriel sings as the Fellowship departs at the end of this chapter is also influenced by his Catholic faith. He mentioned that the song "has in mind the tones used in the *Lamentatio* of Tenebrae." Stuart D. Lee, "A Milestone in BBC History? The 1955–56 Radio Dramatization of *The Lord of the Rings*," in *The Great Tales Never End: Essays in Memory of Christopher Tolkien*, ed. Richard Ovenden and Catherin McIlwaine (Oxford: Bodleian Library, 2022), 147.

[26] That same star is called "Gil-Estel" (Star of High Hope) by the Elves. It should be noted that this is another case where Tolkien rejects a direct Christian connection. While there is a definite line of inspiration from the reference to *éarendel* in *Christ I/Crist A*, the actual Christian usage is not in his story, especially since it is set well before John the Baptist, to whom the term referred (Letter #297).

Love and Loss

In further demonstration of how Gimli's life has been fundamentally altered by meeting Galadriel, he says in his conversation with Legolas as they row down the river out of her realm that this was the greatest peril of this entire Quest for him. If he were to go straightaway to the Dark Lord, be captured, and be tormented unto death, he would think his worst loss came from light and joy. The idea that he should be parted forever from this new love he has found—which for Tolkien resembles love for Mary rather than an infatuation for a potential romantic mate (cf. Letters #142 and #213)— is the more grievous thought than that he should die on this Quest having never known Galadriel. Legolas tells him that this is sadly the way of it, to find, to love, and to lose, "But I count you blessed, Gimli son of Glóin: for your loss you suffer of your own free will, and you might have chosen otherwise. But you have not forsaken your companions, and the least reward that you shall have is that the memory of Lothlórien shall remain ever clear and unstained in your heart, and shall neither fade nor grow stale" (II/8).

Rutledge has written well of this conversation:

> This important exchange identifies once again the pain and loss that must accompany the discovery of real love, real friendship, and real service in the cause of a greater good. Once again, we emphasize the melancholy that permeates the book. This mood has nothing in common with aesthetic languor or romantic vapors. It is combined with a steely resolve and a clear-sighted understanding that this is the nature of a life lived responsibly.[27]

Gimli embodies that same courage that was called upon for Joshua and the people of Israel after Moses's death or for the apostles after the Lord's ascension. Such deep loss is a sign of real love, but the mission must continue, and courage is needed.

The Temptation of Boromir

The Fellowship then travels down the Anduin to the northern reaches of Gondor. They stop at Amon Hen to reach some final decision about who is going where. Frodo's path necessarily takes him to Mount Doom. Boromir has stated from the beginning his intention to return to Minas Tirith, although he would accompany Frodo as far as he could before turning back. In between, everyone else has their reasons for leaning one way or the other. Gandalf's fall in Moria further changed their reckoning, although to

---

[27] Rutledge, *Battle*, 139.

this point it was not clear how exactly that reckoning would be changed for each individual.

But now Boromir will attempt to sway Frodo and thus the course of the entire Fellowship. At the Council he showed clearly where his mind was, that he sought to use the Ring as a weapon against Sauron. That is the way he knows best, and he is a fine warrior, but those with more wisdom prevailed at the Council without necessarily persuading him. He may have even accepted the wisdom of the Council up to a point, but as he continued on the Quest in proximity to the Ring, such thoughts unsurprisingly reemerged, even if he tried to obscure them while speaking his mind to others.

Boromir follows Frodo when the latter attempts to go off by himself and attempts to persuade him. Frodo says his course would seem like wisdom but for the warning of his heart "Against delay. Against the way that seems easier. Against refusal of the burden that is laid on me. Against – well, if it must be said, against trust in the strength and truth of Men" (II/10). Frodo has indeed absorbed the wisdom of Gandalf, thereby recognizing the way of necessity, and following the higher wisdom that looks like folly to the world. He also knows the tempting power of the Ring and how overwhelming it can become. He has seen how those greater than Boromir have refused it because they feared its power over them. In the end, he cannot trust to worldly power or military might, no matter how great, but he must submit in *estel* to the only goal that has a chance of bringing an end to the living evil of Sauron (even if not an end to evil itself per se).

Yet Boromir is, for now, overcome by the tempting power of the Ring. As Sméagol thought of the Ring as his present when he first killed Déagol to get it, Boromir sees the Ring as a gift to himself and the other foes of Mordor. He has accepted its lies of providing the power to fulfill his will for the salvation of his people and his kingdom. For long years he has fought the forces of Mordor with no end in sight, and no apparent hope of victory within Gondor as the Enemy grows stronger and his kingdom dwindles as it has for many years heretofore. With the threats being so immediate and without his cultivation of wisdom outside of war, he has lost his sense of *estel*. He looks rather for *amdir*, some more immediate hope that can be firmly established on what he already knows. Hence, he rejects the counsel of destroying the Ring because he does not think "reason could show any hope of doing so" (II/10). The Ring has instead taken his limited way of thinking based on what he knows best to convince him, "The fearless, the ruthless, these alone will achieve victory" (II/10).

When it becomes clear that Frodo will not be persuaded, he attempts to manipulate him physically into some kind of trap where he would take the Ring. Frodo recoils from his hand, and Boromir begins to unravel. He says Frodo has no claim on the Ring, but his people do, and "It is not yours save by unhappy chance. It might have been mine. It should be mine" (II/10). In the context of the larger story, especially Gandalf's remarks about how Frodo was meant to have the Ring, this is ultimately a rejection of the providential will of Eru Ilúvatar. Boromir thus thinks he is correcting a deficiency in Providence. But none of his talk is now geared to persuasion. It is simply him venting the deceptions the Ring has put in his heart and mind. He is now set on taking the Ring by force. In the process, Frodo notices how his face has become disfigured or "hideously changed" by the power of the Ring over him (II/10), as it had done to Bilbo.

Frodo ultimately puts on the Ring to evade Boromir, which causes the latter to curse the Ring-bearer and all the Halflings, since he thinks that Frodo will betray him and all the Free Peoples to their deaths. He then catches his foot on a stone and has the sense suddenly knocked back into him by the fall. Even as Boromir under the madness of the Ring exploiting his fears had rejected the will of Providence, it is because of Providence that his personal failure will be taken up so as to make the Quest succeed in the end and bring about many other events as a result of the breaking of the Fellowship. Furthermore, the seemingly random event of him catching his foot on the rock makes him come to his senses in time for him to serve his part in the story. The end of his story will be better than this dark middle, and the Author will work so that even what he intended for evil will be for the good (cf. Gen 50:20; Isa 46:8–11; Rom 8:28).

Frodo's Resolve

As Frodo runs away wearing the Ring, he sees a vision, which again provides some foreshadowing of where the story is going. But once again, as with the vision in the Mirror, he faces the Lidless Eye and feels it searching for him and the Ring. The reaction is fascinating: "He heard himself crying out: *Never, never!* Or was it: *Verily I come, I come to you?* He could not tell" (II/10). Nor are we told for sure who this voice belongs to. In addition to the confusion of what is actually being said, there is confusion as to who is saying what. Is Frodo saying both? If so, does that signify that the sinfulness in Frodo is being awakened in this visionary experience? Or is Frodo making the first statement and the Ring is distorting it with its own voice in the second statement? Either is possible and both reflect Primary World experiences in the struggle with one's own sinfulness or in the struggle with the demonic.

Another layer to this conflict is that another voice intervenes and tells him to take off the Ring. This voice then struggles with the Eye, and Frodo feels the struggle within himself to the point of torment. He then takes the Ring off his finger when he recalls that though he was neither the Voice telling him to take off the Ring nor the Eye, he was free to choose what to do. And he needed to do it right soon. The trials he has gone through have strengthened his will to this point, but he also might have succumbed if not for this other power. The Voice is not identified until the next book, and so we will leave further comment on that point until the next chapter.

It is clear to Frodo now that he cannot continue on with the rest of the Fellowship. The Ring poses too great a threat to everyone else. Gandalf has already sacrificed himself to protect him, and Boromir has already been overwhelmed by the Ring's temptation. He himself has succumbed to putting on the Ring despite knowing better, although in the most recent case it was an act of desperation. Who knows who else might die to protect him or be overwhelmed by its power to betray him? He cannot risk finding a more definite answer.

Providence in the Breaking of the Fellowship

As the Fellowship is discussing what to do next and what they expect Frodo will do next, Sam rightly reckons what Frodo plans to do. Aragorn acknowledges his perceptiveness, and though some among them like Pippin might wish to stop Frodo, he says, "I do not think that it is our part to drive him one way or the other. Nor do I think that we should succeed, if we tried. There are other powers at work far stronger" (II/10). We already know that the Ring is one such power at work, and Aragorn may also be referring to Sauron's influence from afar, but there is more. In this is also his acknowledgment of the providential guidance of the One to this point. He has seen the One's provision and orchestration multiple times in his journey with Frodo, he acknowledges the wisdom of Gandalf and Galadriel that the One is at work here, and he has the virtue of *estel* more generally, as we have seen.

I have noted briefly that Providence is at work even in the breaking of the Fellowship. It will take the unfolding of the rest of the story to see how this is so. But one aspect of this action that is more readily apparent is Sam being able to join Frodo. The timing of Boromir's return to the Fellowship, combined with them splitting up to search for Frodo, and combined with Frodo's attempt to slip away turns out to be the right timing for Sam to turn back and catch Mr. Frodo before he leaves. He nearly drowns in the process, and Frodo still tries to leave without him, but it is eventually clear to Frodo that Sam is keeping to his promise that he will not leave him. Frodo also says, "It is plain that we were meant to go together" (II/10). This echoes Gandalf's earlier statement that Bilbo and Frodo were meant to have the Ring. Frodo is likewise recognizing the will of Providence in Sam being his companion. Much has prepared both of them for journeying together to this point, and it is clear that there is yet more laid in front of them to do.

CHAPTER SIX

Commentary on Book III

Boromir's Heroic End

Despite Boromir's succumbing to the power of the Ring and accepting its lies in the previous book, this book opens with him heroically laying down his life in his attempt to protect Merry and Pippin. It is ultimately a battle he cannot win due to the sheer number of Uruk-hai, but that does not deter him, and he dies doing what is right. Aragorn finds him pierced with many arrows and at least a score of Uruk-hai lying dead around him. He lives long enough to tell Aragorn that they have taken the Halflings instead of killing them, and to confess his fault in trying to take the Ring. He then bids Aragorn farewell and asks him to go to Minas Tirith in his stead because he has failed. Aragorn comforts him, "You have conquered. Few have gained such a victory. Be at peace! Minas Tirith shall not fall" (III/1). Boromir then dies with a smile on his face.

And thus Boromir's story ends redemptively.[1] Until recently, he was a worthy companion, having helped the Fellowship out of the pass of Caradhras by his strength, having helped them survive in Moria (even attempting to join the fight with the Balrog when he would have been overmatched), and ensuring that everyone else made it out alive when Gandalf fell. He kept his word through it all, but the Ring did take advantage of his weaknesses and his limited thinking. But in what he was good at, few in the world could match him. His actions that led to the breaking of the Fellowship are at first tragic, but they are taken up by Providence to produce more good than would have been possible had they followed through with the plans the Fellowship tried to make (and

---

[1] An earlier draft involving Aragorn/Trotter telling Legolas and Gimli that Boromir tried to take the Ring by force further accentuated this idea when he responded to their horrified reactions by saying, "Think not ill of him … He paid manfully and confessed." Tolkien, *Treason of Isengard*, 385.

certainly more good than would have been possible if Boromir had his way). Merry and Pippin will find themselves awakening an ancient force for the reckoning of Saruman and Isengard. Aragorn, Legolas, and Gimli will contribute to the salvation of Rohan and Gondor all because they had to track Merry and Pippin. Frodo had his path clarified, and he overcame his fear and doubt about that path because of what happened with Boromir (III/1). Frodo and Sam will continue the main Quest, and it is best that this minimal pair should go on for all that would happen, for otherwise Gollum also may not have served his proper end in the Quest. Boromir's own actions in killing so many Uruk-hai will make the task less difficult on the Rohirrim who will destroy the rest of the company. And as a direct result of his protecting Merry and Pippin, Pippin will feel obligated to serve his father, which will result in the salvation of Boromir's brother and others (like Beregond) as a result. Even Boromir's temporary failure of will ultimately serves as a warning to his brother about the peril of the Ring when he encounters Frodo and Sam, which will also help to preserve the Quest.

By Boromir's glimpse of final victory by self-sacrifice as a redemption for his failure with the Ring, we see the hand of Providence in these multitudinous ways. That he should obtain his victory by self-sacrifice comports with the theologically informed ethical framework of the whole story (Letter #148a), and it thus provides a glimpse of the one through whom final victory will come. He accomplished what he accomplished because of his courage, which is itself a gift from the One for the tasks he appointed for him in the defense of his realm and the furtherance of the Quest.

Hoping Against Hope

The rest of the opening concerns Aragorn, Legolas, and Gimli taking it upon themselves to pursue the Uruk-hai who took Merry and Pippin, rather than Frodo, who clearly did not want them to follow him. Before they lay Boromir to rest and set out, they search the site of Boromir's last stand. Aragorn finds the knives Merry and Pippin dropped, which they had brought with them from the Barrow-downs and declares, "I will take these things, hoping against hope, to give them back" (III/1).

The key phrase here highlights how different notions of "hope" have been used across the story. Of course, there is a similar issue with the way people use "hope" in everyday contexts. In sentences like this one, someone might even use the same word in different senses in such proximity. In an attempt to give readers a handle on this matter, I have thus far attached the terms *amdir* and *estel* to two different concepts. In the case of this highlighted sentence, the first "hope" is *estel*, the trust in the providence of the One, while the second "hope" is *amdir*, the expectation of a good outcome that has some foundation in what is known. Aragorn has demonstrated the former as a virtue, but he acknowledges that he holds to it in the absence of an immediately clear reason for the latter.

Before Aragorn makes his final decision following the funeral for Boromir, he says, "And now may I make a right choice, and change the evil fate of this unhappy day" (III/1). As with "hope," "fate" has been used in multiple senses. Often, it is divine providence by another name. But one of the other senses it has is as a reference to an end or outcome, which is the case here. Aragorn is not so much trying to change the power of fate (or Fate) by his choices, as he acknowledges his fate is otherwise. But a right choice can change an evil outcome. However, there are always elements beyond the power of one's choices. And so it will prove here, as it is not ultimately in Aragorn's power to rescue the Hobbits. That will be the work of others.

Even so, he says, "With hope or without hope we will follow the trail of our enemies" (III/1).[2] This is reminiscent of his statement earlier upon leaving Moria. And as there, he is referring to *amdir*, as he acknowledges that there is no clear probability that he, Legolas, and Gimli will achieve their goal. As with the main Quest, that changes nothing in the calculation of what must be done. If they do otherwise, there is certainly no chance of reuniting with Merry and Pippin. Even without *amdir*, they can have *estel*, for the designs of Providence will indeed supply rescue for Merry and Pippin and involve them in a drama beyond the reckoning of the Three Hunters or the two Hobbits.

Aragorn's Humility

Aragorn also exemplifies a necessary companion of *estel*: humility. We have seen earlier that Aragorn acknowledges that he is part of a design larger than his own and has submitted himself to that design. Frodo similarly humbly submitted himself to the will of the One who meant for him to have the Ring.

We see this again here in the pursuit of Merry and Pippin by the Three Hunters. At one point, the Hunters face a difficult choice in the night. They either must wait for the light of day to read the signs on what path the Orc company have taken, which would

---

[2] Similarly, note this dialogue between Gimli and Aragorn:

"Gimli ground his teeth. 'This is a bitter end to our hope and to all our toil!' he said.

'To hope, maybe, but not to toil,' said Aragorn." (III/2)

mean losing ground and allowing such a large gap that they may well never catch them, or continue on in the general direction they think is right and thus gain ground but potentially lose the way if it proved that the Orcs took a different turn. Since they do not have sufficient moonlight to track by night, Aragorn decides that they will rest and wait for daylight. Gimli laments that Galadriel did not give them a light like she gave to Frodo. But Aragorn, one whose goals include becoming the king of Gondor and Arnor, reminds Gimli that Frodo will need it more, "With him lies the true Quest. Ours is but a small matter in the great deeds of this time. A vain pursuit from its beginning maybe, which no choice of mine can mar or mend. Well, I have chosen. So let us use the time as best we may" (III/2). This is an expression of his trust/*estel* in the designs of Providence. So much is beyond his control that he must entrust to the One and only take responsibility for what the One has given him responsibility for. He is also humble enough to acknowledge that his mission is not the most important one in the designs of Eru Ilúvatar.

Aragorn's Transfiguration

When the Three Hunters cross into Rohan and meet the Rohirrim, the meeting reminds us of how Aragorn is set apart from other Men. This is first made apparent by his declaration in contrast to Éomer that he serves no man as his king, but he pursues the servants of Sauron wherever he can (III/2). Then he declares the identity that sets him apart from others as the heir of Isildur and bearer of the Sword that was Broken, which portends that he comes to restore what has been broken. He thus puts the question to Éomer if he will help or hinder him. In that moment, he is transfigured in the eyes of Gimli and Legolas:

> Gimli and Legolas looked at their companion in amazement, for they had not seen him in this mood before. He seemed to have grown in stature while Éomer had shrunk; and in his living face they caught a brief vision of the power and majesty of the kings of stone. For a moment it seemed to the eyes of Legolas that a white flame flickered on the brows of Aragorn like a shining crown. (III/2)

This is now the third time Aragorn has been transfigured in the sight of others. Each time has been progressively more revelatory than the last. And as with Jesus's Transfiguration, such events both reveal something of his true glory and foreshadow what is to come in the climactic events of the story.

Right and Wrong in Strange Times

Seeing what was previously only the subject of legend come to life before him is but one of the matters in this conversation that makes Éomer think he lives in utterly strange times. There is also the fact that an Elf and a Dwarf are in his land, and this trio that includes the Heir of Isildur had journeyed in the land of Lórien, having met the Lady of the Golden Wood, the Dwarf has spoken in her defense as "that which is fair beyond the reach of your thought" (III/2) after he accuses them of being net-weavers and sorcerers in league with her, and he learns that the Halflings spoken of in children's tales are real. The marvels of the day make him question so much that he thought sure, and he asks: "How shall a man judge what to do in such times" (III/2)? Aragorn responds sagaciously, "As he has ever judged ... Good and ill have not changed since yesteryear; nor are they one thing among Elves and Dwarves and another among Men. It is a man's part to discern them, as much in the Golden Wood as in his own house" (III/2).

Wisdom before strange times does not become irrelevant in strange times. If wisdom is only "wisdom" in easy times, then it is of no real use. However perception may be in various places, what is truly wisdom in one place is wisdom everywhere. That is precisely why wisdom literature in the ancient world had so much cross-fertilization and had such cross-cultural appeal (notice, for example, how Proverbs includes the words of Agur and Lemuel in chs. 30 and 31). One can, of course, find new applications of wisdom, and strange settings like this can open up a broader vision of wisdom or be an opportunity for the revelation of higher wisdom, as with the Quest or the gospel, wherein divine wisdom can appear as foolishness to the world. Right and wrong remain the same, but our ability to discern them changes with growth in wisdom, as that virtue includes the capacity to judge rightly in practical matters, and practical issues can take on surprising forms.

As we have seen, one important expression of wisdom represented in this story is the recognition of necessity and acting accordingly. This is something Aragorn reminds Gimli of when Gimli says that Gandalf's foresight failed him both in the matter of his own death and in his insistence that Merry and Pippin join the Quest. He says, "The counsel of Gandalf was not founded on foreknowledge of safety, for himself or for others ... There are some things that it is better to begin than to refuse, even though the end may be dark" (III/2). And as we have seen previously in such declarations about necessity, this is wisdom that works by *estel*, trusting the One to take up whatever is done for such necessity and to work it to the completion of his designs.

Providence in the Story of Merry and Pippin

Providence is also at work in the story of Merry and Pippin, since they have a larger part to play than they could have imagined. The very fact that the company that captured them is destroyed by the Rohirrim in proximity to Fangorn Forest is why everything else that happens in their story is possible. Furthermore, their escape itself is described as if it is an act of Providence. Grishnákh had attempted to run off with them, but as he sought in desperation to kill them when the situation had changed, the sword he bore glinted in the light of a nearby fire, which was enough to make him a target in the dark. The narrator then says, "An arrow came whistling out of the gloom: it was aimed with skill, or guided by fate, and it pierced his right hand" (III/3). The fact that it is ambiguous is suggestive enough, as this is the sort of thing that happens in the hands of Providence, and it ultimately achieved divine purposes. Likewise, although a random Aramean soldier shot an arrow at Ahab without knowing him to be the king of Israel (since he was in disguise; 1 Kgs 22:29–36), it fulfilled the prophecy of Ahab's doom (1 Kgs 22:17–28).

Because Merry and Pippin are in such a position, they are able to avoid detection while escaping into Fangorn Forest. As they wander about in that forest, they meet Fangorn/Treebeard, who knew nothing of Hobbits. Neither he nor they could have planned such a meeting. And yet from this seemingly chance meeting arranged by a will other than theirs the fall of Isengard will come.

Eschatology of the Ents

As Merry and Pippin talk with Treebeard and learn more about him and the Ents, there is a point when the subject of the Entwives is broached. Then Ents lost the Entwives long ago, and it is uncertain whatever happened to them, as Tolkien has left it a mystery. Treebeard gives us insight into Ent eschatology, as he thinks the current crisis might be drawing their expected time near: "We believe that we may meet again in a time to come, and perhaps we shall find somewhere a land where we can live together and both be content. But it is foreboded that that will only be when we have both lost all that we now have" (III/4). As resurrection comes only on the other side of death, so the Ents present their hope as coming only on the side of total loss. This is a clear example of hope that is *estel* rather than *amdir*, for such an idea as they have simply cannot be founded on *amdir*.

It is also expressed in a song of the Ents and the Entwives composed by the Elves, which Treebeard sings for the Hobbits. The song proceeds through the seasons of spring, summer, and winter like it is an annual cycle, but it also signifies the larger history of this race through the markers of time they know best. Through the seasons, the Ent calls for the Entwife to come back to his land because his land is best, but the Entwife chooses to linger in her own land because her land is best. That is, until winter comes:

> *Ent*: When Winter comes, the winter wild that hill and wood shall slay;
> When trees shall fall and starless night devour the sunless day;
> When wind is in the deadly East, then in bitter rain
> I'll look for thee, and call to thee; I'll come to thee again!
> *Entwife*: When Winter comes, and singing ends; when darkness falls at last;
> When broken is the barren bough, and light and labour past;
> I'll look for thee, and wait for thee, until we meet again:
> Together we will take the road beneath the bitter rain!
> *Both*: Together we will take the road that leads into the West,
> And far away will find a land where both our hearts may rest. (III/4)

In the conception of Elves (or at least the High Elves, who know more about the Uttermost West), going into the West is their ultimate hope within the circles of creation. Thus, this is how they signify the Ents and Entwives realizing their ultimate hope. Or perhaps this is a way of signifying the rising again of the lands of Beleriand in the West, where Ents once dwelt together, above the waves they now lie under, and so this could be an indirect reference to the new creation. In a way, such expressions are fitting for the Ents and Entwives, being spirits who are bound to the created world as Shepherds of the Trees (cf. also Letter #247). We will not address here in full the origin story of the Ents, but that is essentially their function. And indeed, there will be a land where both will find their rest, although it is beyond their sight and beyond creation as they currently know it, for there will be an everlasting new creation to come and a Second Music in which they will be included.

Making in Counterfeit

Eventually, Treebeard convenes the Entmoot. He was already aware of the problems of Orcs cutting down the forest, and he suspected Saruman was behind it, but his meeting with Merry and Pippin and the news they brought (especially of Saruman) convinced him that something needed to be done soon, which led to his decision to call the meeting of the Ents. After a deliberation that was long by Hobbit standards but short by Ent standards, the Ents decide to march to war and rain doom upon Isengard. Merry asks if they are strong enough to do so. Treebeard replies, "You do not know perhaps, how strong we are. Maybe you have heard of Trolls? They are mighty strong. But Trolls are only counterfeits, made by the Enemy in the Great Darkness, in mockery of Ents, as Orcs were of Elves. We are stronger than Trolls" (III/4).

Peter Hastings took issue with this remark and the notion of creation by evil. Tolkien responded in Letter #153 that he did not accept that evil could genuinely create either, nor does anyone in his story say so. As he said in a footnote, "Creation, the act of Will of Eru the One that gives Reality to conceptions, is distinguished from Making, which is permissive." As in the Bible and traditional Judeo-Christian theology (which Tolkien's theology of sub-creation exemplifies), only God can truly create. Humans, his image-bearers, can make many things, but that action is only derivative and imitative of his creative action. Hence, humans are capable of sub-creation but not true creation. Likewise, nothing evil can truly create either, but evil beings can make things. And that is what Treebeard says, not that the Enemy "created" Trolls or Orcs. But in any case, as Tolkien says, this is only a statement that is possibly true, and it is actually *not* true of the Orcs. They were creatures corrupted from already existing rational creatures and bred into what they are at the present. Indeed, Tolkien says that Treebeard is a character and not a representation of him so that his thoughts are necessarily Tolkien's thoughts. As far as Trolls are concerned, he does think there is something to what Treebeard says of them being "counterfeits," but he is not entirely sure of their origin either. These statements connect with and exemplify Tolkien's larger theology of sub-creation at many points, as we have observed in Chapter Two.

Courage of the Ents

The Ents are indeed mighty, but they have the same weaknesses as trees. Treebeard thus thinks that this march to Isengard is likely enough a march to their own doom, "But if we stayed at home and did nothing, doom would find us anyway, sooner or later. That thought has long been growing in our hearts; and that is why we are marching now" (III/4). This is like Galdor's statement to the Hobbits that they could fence themselves in from the world, but they could not keep the world out forever (I/3). The Ents would have been content to leave the world around them alone, but Saruman made clear that the world was not going to leave them alone. Their choice is thus either to be cowed by the more assertive power or to take action and defend themselves as well as the trees that could not defend themselves. After all, this is what they were made to do as the Shepherds of the Trees. They take the path of courage in doing what must be done, and so they become willing instruments of Providence in fulfilling what they were made to do. And in the work of Providence, it will turn out that they are not so doomed as they thought. For Saruman will empty his realm of his massive army of fighting Uruk-hai, since he did not seriously consider the possibility that the Ents would attack Isengard, and so he never prepared for this contingency. Their choice to do what was right was made with the worst-case scenario in mind, but Providence took up their choice—as well as Saruman's oversight—and guided it to a better end by guiding events outside of their control and achieving the same end of the doom of Saruman's Isengard. As we will see, this is divine judgment being executed on Saruman, who flouted his mission to Middle-earth, identified himself by allegiance with the Dark Lord, sought to become like him instead of his Creator, and will reap the end of this path.

The White Rider

In the other storyline of this book, the Three Hunters track Merry and Pippin into Fangorn Forest. Because of the events that transpired in Merry and Pippin's storyline, Aragorn loses their trail. But like Merry and Pippin, the Three Hunters are not alone. There is an old man dressed in white in the forest with them. The Hunters are leery, thinking he could be Saruman, but they converse with him. At one point, they even try to fight with him, but they prove unable to best him. Afterwards, he reveals himself to be Gandalf. He is no longer Gandalf the Grey but Gandalf the White.

He has been raised from the dead and has returned transformed. This is one of the (if not *the*) primary points of reference for the argument that Gandalf is a christological type who provides christological echoes in this story. He gave his life for his mission, though unlike Jesus he was not aware ahead of time that he would need to do so (Matt 12:38–40; Mark 9:30–31; Luke 9:22; John 2:18–22). Perhaps more coincidentally, his death involved conflict with a demon, echoing Jesus's victory over demons through his cross (Col 2:15). His sacrifice was vindicated by his being raised from the dead and sent back. As Jesus was not initially recognized by his friends after his resurrection, so too Gandalf is not initially recognized by his friends, although both are eventually shown as recognizable. The resurrection bodies of both are transformations of the bodies that died and show something of the greater glory of Gandalf (as an angelic being) and Jesus (as God the Son). Moreover, here is the description of Gandalf after he is recognized by the Hunters:

His hair was white as snow in the sunshine; and gleaming white was his robe; the eyes under his deep brows were bright, piercing as the rays of the sun; power was in his hand. (III/5)

And here is how the resurrected Jesus is described in Rev 1:13–16 (NASB):

[A]nd in the middle of the lampstands *I saw* one like a son of man, clothed in a robe reaching to the feet, and wrapped around the chest with a golden sash. 14 His head and His hair were white like white wool, like snow; and His eyes were like a flame of fire. 15 His feet were like burnished bronze when it has been heated to a glow in a furnace, and His voice was like the sound of many waters. 16 In his right hand He held seven stars, and out of his mouth came a sharp, two-edged sword; and His face was like the sun shining in its strength.

Obviously, there is much more in the latter description, but where there are similarities, it is striking how close some of the points of contact are. It is also fitting that the echo and type should be less glorious and elaborate in his description than the source and fulfilling anti-type. Furthermore, as we have noted, Gandalf is not simply a stand-in for Christ in this story, but he is one of the more prominent examples of how analogies to and representations of Christ are diffused across the story.

Gandalf Provides Perspective

As Gandalf catches up with the Three Hunters in the recapitulation of what has already happened, he provides an illumined perspective on a number of points that should be noted. First, as hinted in the previous chapter, he reveals that he was the one who was the Voice in Frodo's struggle with the Ring at Amon Hen (III/5). He had power to strive with the Dark Tower well enough to ensure Frodo's escape, but he was wearied afterwards.

Second, after he hears of Boromir's end and perceives that Aragorn has not said all that he knows or guesses, he confirms how Boromir's end has been framed to this point: "Poor Boromir! I could not see what happened to him. It was a sore trial for such a man: a warrior, and a lord of men. Galadriel told me that he was in peril. But he escaped in the end. I am glad" (III/5). Galadriel had tested Boromir by mental interaction, presenting him the opportunity to have what he wants, and so she saw that he was weakened to the temptation of the Ring (II/7). But he "escaped" in the sense that he had not finally fallen, for he triumphed in the end.

Third, he provides perspective on the roles of Merry and Pippin: "It was not in vain that the young hobbits came with us, if only for Boromir's sake. But that is not the only part they have to play. They were brought to Fangorn and their coming was like the falling of small stones that starts an avalanche in the mountains" (III/5). Their coming had a part in the providential redemption of Boromir by his heroic end in defending them. But it also still (from the setting of this dialogue) has a part to play in the rousing of the Ents, which will ultimately bring about the downfall of Saruman's Isengard, along with the help provided by these other four members of the Fellowship who were brought here by the pursuit of Merry and Pippin. Elrond was not unwise to be uneasy at allowing them to join the Fellowship, but he obviously did not see all. Neither he, nor they, nor even Gandalf could have foreseen that they would be so significant for Boromir, for the Ents in Fangorn (where there no plans for anyone in the Fellowship to go), and for the reckoning of Isengard. The events concerning each of these parts of their stories could easily have gone otherwise, and likely for the worse, but for the *estel* of Gandalf and others by extension in allowing them to join the Quest.

Fourth, as Gandalf summarizes the current state of affairs, he reminds the Hunters of how this whole Quest is cloaked by a wisdom that Sauron cannot comprehend, for it appears as folly to him. As he says,

> He supposes that we were all going to Minas Tirith; for that is what he would himself have done in our place. And according to his wisdom it would have been a heavy stroke against his power. Indeed he is in great fear, not knowing what mighty one may suddenly appear, wielding the Ring, and assailing him with war, seeking to cast him down and take his place. That we should wish to cast him down and have *no* one in his place is not a thought that occurs to his mind. That we should try to destroy the Ring itself has not yet entered into his darkest dream. In which no doubt you will see our good fortune and our hope. (III/5; emphasis original)

This is another way that the Hobbits, specifically in the main Quest, trouble the counsels of the Wise and Great. For Sauron is certainly wise in his own fashion and the mightiest of the inhabitants of Middle-earth. But he could not imagine that the creatures he had overlooked until so recently should actually seek to carry the Ring into his very realm for the purpose of destroying it. He might have taken more active steps to thwart this plan, but he could not understand the refusal of such power, and therein had been his hope for keeping his own power in Middle-earth for as long as the Ring lasted.

Of course, Sauron does have defenses that Gandalf does not reckon with here. Beyond his fortresses, there is a guardian in his realm that is not his servant but who would seemingly be more reliable than any of his actual servants should someone actually dare the pass of Cirith Ungol. And the ultimate defense is at the Sammath Naur itself, for that is where the Ring's influence will be at its strongest. It proves to be something of a failsafe. But Sauron could not have imagined that anyone would actually seek to bring the Ring there so as to put it in danger of being destroyed, at which point Providence will take over. But we will get to that later.

Fifth, as Gandalf reflects on the uneasy alliance between Sauron and Saruman, as well as the treachery of the latter, he observes how Saruman's treachery has ultimately worked for his own demise and his enemies' benefit. Saruman could have been an unremitting threat by drawing off and potentially even overthrowing Rohan while Sauron pressed against Minas Tirith and Gondor as a whole. That was the plan, after all. But treason is as treason does, and Saruman sought to claim the Ring for himself. Thus, his design for bringing the Hobbits to Isengard will ultimately lead to his own doom: "So between them our enemies have contrived only to bring Merry and Pippin with marvelous speed, and in the nick of time, to Fangorn, where otherwise they would never have come at all" (III/5). As I mentioned before, there was no plan on anyone's part for Merry and Pippin to come anywhere in the vicinity of Fangorn Forest, that is, save for the plan of Eru. And he has taken up the plans of others and directed them to his own ends that no one else could have foreseen. As is typical, divine providence is best seen in hindsight.

Knowing One's Peril

As Gandalf outlines the situation with their enemies, the matter comes up that Saruman could not wait for the Ring and sought to come and spy on his Uruk-hai. And so, apparently, he had come within sight of the Three Hunters the night before. Gimli is comforted by this, as he had hoped he had not mistaken Gandalf the White for Saruman then as he did earlier when he tried to strike him with his axe. Gandalf reassures him that he does not blame Gimli for how he greeted him. He did not know any better, and Gandalf further says, "How could I do so, who have so often counseled my friends to suspect even their own hand when dealing with the Enemy" (III/5). This is a reminder that none of them are so pure as to be immune to the corrupting and deceptive work of the Enemy. None of them are without weakness that could be exploited, whether it is a weak point to sin or a strength that can be turned against oneself, as Gandalf recognized the Ring could use his pity against him. And as Elrond had said earlier, nothing is evil in the beginning, even Sauron was not so. One can be a peril to oneself, for the line between good and evil runs through each one of us. Frodo's own voice showed this the last time he wore the Ring, and so it is with us whose own hearts can be deceitful without a magic Ring tempting us (Jer 17:5–12).

Conversely, Gandalf also affirms the perilous nature of good, as we had seen in the last chapter. Gimli wonders at how Gandalf speaks of Fangorn/Treebeard as if he is a friend, but he thought Fangorn was dangerous. Gandalf affirms he is, in fact, dangerous:

> And so am I, very dangerous: more dangerous than anything you will ever meet, unless you are brought alive fore the seat of the Dark Lord. And Aragorn is dangerous, and Legolas is dangerous. You are beset with dangers, Gimli son of Glóin; for you are dangerous yourself, in your own fashion. Certainly the forest of Fangorn is perilous – not least to those that are too ready with their axes; and Fangorn himself, he is perilous too; yet he is wise and kindly nonetheless. (III/5)

A Providential Meeting

Gandalf informs the Hunters that they will ultimately not go to meet Merry and Pippin today. After all, he has spoken words of hope, but "Hope is not victory" (III/5). After all, hope that is seen is not hope (Rom 8:24). There is still work to do. This may be a disappointing conclusion to the Hunters' side-quest, but Gandalf reassures Aragorn, "Do not regret your choice in the valley of the Emyn Muil, nor call it a vain pursuit. You chose amid doubts the path that seemed right: the choice was just, and it has been rewarded. For so we have met in time, who otherwise might have met too late" (III/5).

To say the meeting is the reward for Aragorn's just choice is to speak of divine providence at work. Thus it often is with such uses of the passive voice in such contexts. As Merry and Pippin's own coming to Fangorn was providential, so too is this meeting providential, as shown in the timing of the meeting. For this reason also, he reassures Legolas, who fears that they will not see the Hobbits ever again, "I did not say so … Who knows? Have patience. Go where you must go, and hope" (III/5). This is the hope of *estel*, for it is trust in the One who has been orchestrating the events Gandalf has been outlining thus far. As Aragorn made a just choice and it was taken up and providentially rewarded, so too must his companions make another just choice in doing what must be done, and Providence will take up that choice and lead it to ends that Legolas cannot foresee. As elsewhere in the story, courage and wisdom—particularly in recognizing necessity and doing what needs to be done—are tied to hope and seeing the fulfillment of the same.

The Theological Framing of Gandalf's Mission

Before the company leaves the forest, there is one other lacuna of information they request that Gandalf fill. They know not what happened with the Balrog that Gandalf should now return. Gandalf thus recounts the grueling battle with the Balrog from the lowest pit to the heights of the peak above Khazad-dûm. After Gandalf threw down the Balrog, darkness took him, "and I strayed out of thought and time, and I wandered far on roads that I will not tell. Naked I was sent back—for a brief time, until my task is done" (III/5). Once again, we see a suggestive use of the passive voice here that raises the question, "sent back by whom?"[3]

Tolkien addressed this matter and others at more length in Letter #156, which was written in response to criticism by Robert Murray about the return of Gandalf and how it seemed like cheating. Tolkien argued that it is coherent with the established rules of his story and the nature of Gandalf and his mission. Thus, something must be said about the theological framework of the same. He had not provided much elaboration in the story here because of the urgency of the narrative to cover what is within its immediate scope, and he said he "severely cut G's account of himself." Indeed, this is part of his larger project of having "purposely kept all allusions to the highest matters down to mere hints, perceptible only by the most attentive, or kept them under unexplained symbolic forms."

Gandalf really died and came back. This fact and the fact that his resurrection has made him all the more empowered come about, in part, as a function of his being practically an incarnate angel, as noted elsewhere. As we have observed previously, his mission, along with that of the other Wizards, was to help by instruction and counsel (as well as training, where necessary) the enemies of Sauron, so that they could operate by the strength the One had given them, rather than simply being reliant on the more powerful Wizards to do what needed to be done. The incarnate nature of the Wizards was to hinder exhibitions of power, but it also presented plenty of temptations to fail in the mission, as we have seen with Saruman. According to Tolkien,

---

[3] This suggestive element is another case of Tolkien consciously revising the text so as to make it more theologically evocative, as an earlier draft simply had him say, "Naked I returned, and naked I lay upon the mountain-top." Tolkien, *Treason of Isengard*, 431. While that, of course, would raise questions of how Gandalf could return, it is not as evocative as suggested agency without an explicit subject.

> Gandalf alone fully passes the tests, on a moral plane anyway (he makes mistakes of judgement). For in his condition it was for him a *sacrifice* to perish on the Bridge in defence of his companions, less perhaps than for a mortal Man or Hobbit, since he had a far greater inner power than they; but also more, since it was a humbling and abnegation of himself in conformity to 'the Rules': for all he could know at that moment he was the *only* person who could direct the resistance to Sauron successfully, and all *his* mission was vain. He was handing over to the Authority that ordained the Rules, and giving up personal hope of success. (Letter #156)

The expression in the last sentence goes right to the heart of what constitutes *estel*. Gandalf had no idea what could happen as a result of his death as it pertained to his mission. But it turns out that this seeming failure of the mission was incorporated by Providence to redress the true failure of Saruman in his utter rejection of his mission. This is why Gandalf can say, "Indeed I *am* Saruman, one might almost say, Saruman as he should have been" (III/5; emphasis original), as he returns as Gandalf the White to replace Saruman the White. As Tolkien further explained in Letter #156, Gandalf's self-sacrifice was in accordance with the will of the One:

> The 'wizards', as such, had failed; or if you like: the crisis had become too grave and needed an enhancement of power. So Gandalf sacrificed himself, was accepted, and enhanced, and returned…. Of course he remains similar in personality and idiosyncrasy, but both his wisdom and power are much greater. When he speaks he commands attention; the old Gandalf could not have dealt so with Théoden, nor with Saruman. He is still under the obligation of concealing his power and of teaching rather than forcing or dominating wills, but where the physical powers of the Enemy are too great for the good will of the opposers to be effective he can act in emergency as an 'angel' – no more violently than the release of St Peter from prison [Acts 12:1–17].

Likewise, Tolkien made clear that though it was the Valar who originally sent Gandalf and the other Wizards with the stated mission, it was Eru Ilúvatar (who he calls "Authority" here) who "had taken up this plan and enlarged it, at the moment of its failure." He thereby supplies the answer to our query—"sent back by whom?"—for the Valar could not have done it, since in his death he passed beyond their scope, beyond time to the Timeless Halls whence he came as an Ainur before the world began. He was also careful to note that while Gandalf is insightful, he is still not omniscient, as no one in the scope of creation is: "He has no more (if no less) certitudes, or freedoms, than say a living theologian."

Healing Théoden

After this reunion, Gandalf, Aragorn, Legolas, and Gimli ride to Edoras, as Gandalf has business with the king of Rohan, Théoden. As had been indicated in the earlier meeting with Éomer, when they arrive, they find the king and his guards to be less hospitable than they wished. This is highlighted by a tense exchange about the company disarming before they enter the king's hall of Meduseld. Before the situation turns lethal, Gandalf deescalates with the reminder, "We are all friends here. Or should be; for the laughter of Mordor will be our only reward, if we quarrel" (III/6). This is akin to what we have seen previously in Haldir's line about how Sauron has worked through dissension sown among those who should be allies against him. Gandalf is focused on the larger issue at stake, as opposed to the unreasonable demands of the present, and he knows that the Enemy does not need such help as internal strife supplies.

Of course, that is not the only trial that Gandalf must endure. He must also face Gríma Wormtongue, Théoden's advisor. He has a way with words and has been whispering poison in Théoden's ear, thereby weakening Rohan from within by weakening its king. First, his words come forth from Théoden's lips as he calls Gandalf a herald of woe and "Stormcrow," and he wonders why he should welcome such a guest. Gríma then speaks up as his puppet slowly sits down. He recounts the recent bad news Rohan has had and the critical situation for them and their allies in Gondor, and so he says, "Such is the hour in which this wanderer chooses to return. Why indeed should we welcome you, Master Stormcrow? *Láthspell* I name you, Ill-news; and ill news is an ill guest they say" (III/6).

Such a description of Gandalf is reminiscent of how certain Hebrew prophets, especially in the later days of Israel and Judah, were regarded. When Ahab and Jehoshaphat thought to ally in war against Aram and the latter wished to consult a prophet of YHWH, Ahab brought forth hundreds of false prophets rather than Micaiah. He hated Micaiah because he never prophesied anything good concerning him, but only prophesied bad things (1 Kgs 22:8). And thus, when Micaiah delivers one last piece of bad news concerning Ahab's fate, he ignores him and even imprisons him for his apparent insolence (22:26–28). Jeremiah was regarded similarly when he regularly prophesied the coming doom of the kingdom of Judah. Of course, in their case, the bad news revolved around the retribution for the evil of Israel and Judah, while Gandalf's bad news is a result of living in dark times and calling for resistance to such times rather than capitulation to them.

The name Gríma gives Gandalf should also be marked for its significance. In his attempt to poison the counsels of the king and turn him ever more resolutely against Gandalf (as Gríma is working on behalf of Saruman), he calls Gandalf *Láthspell*. This is, in fact, an Old English term (the language of Rohan is rendered through Old English and modernizations of the same).[4] It is the antonym of *godspell/godspel* (having the sense of "good news," or perhaps more literally, "good story"), from which we get the English word "gospel." By Gríma's reckoning, Gandalf would be best described as either the exact opposite of a christological type or, perhaps more accurately, that he is *láthspell* precisely for that reason. He is ill news to those Gríma supports. The times are evil because of *his* allies and not because of Gandalf, who is there to assist in their overthrow. The help he comes to bring is truly ill news for Gríma, as the rest of the story will bear out. The good news brings deliverance, and this involves judgment on the powers that would resist such deliverance. Gandalf will bring what hope he can as an agent of *estel* because he is an agent of the One, and so he will point forward to the one who will likewise be sent by God (John 5:23–24; 12:44–45; 1 John 4:9–10), and whose person and story will be the subject of the true gospel.

Eventually, Gandalf tires of Gríma's snaky speech and shows forth his power and authority to remind Gríma that he is not to be trifled with, just as he showed his power to warn Bilbo against threatening him. Afterwards, he attends to the healing of Théoden, bringing him into the light of day and drawing out the poison of "twisted tales and crooked promptings" (III/6). In the process, it is as if demons are banished from oppressing Théoden, and he is transformed. He begins as a weak old man requiring help from his niece to step down from his dais and walk to his door, then he walks on his staff, then he stands tall and straight, then light returns to his eyes, and then firmness and strength return to his arm. He can now see clearly how dark his dreams have been, "but I feel as one new-awakened" (III/6). Gandalf guides him towards courses that make him more sound in mind and body. These include putting trust in the trustworthy like Éomer, "To cast aside regret and fear. To do the deed at hand" (III/6). That is, he needed his heart and mind renewed by the reassertion of courage, to do what must be done without yielding to fear.

---

[4] Appendix F.II: "The language of Rohan I have accordingly made to resemble ancient English, since it was related both (more distantly) to the Common Speech, and (very closely) to the former tongue of the northern Hobbits, and was in comparison with Westron archaic." See also Tolkien, *Treason of Isengard*, 424, 442–43, 449.

Faithless Gríma

With Théoden's healing also comes the reckoning for Gríma. He is not immediately condemned, though. Rather, he is given a chance to be of service rather than hindrance to his king. He calls himself faithful and so Théoden, showing him pity, tells him he can come to war and thereby "prove your faith" (III/6).

This interaction is notable for our purposes for two reasons. First, Théoden specifically says that Gríma has his pity. This is despite how he is well aware of Gríma's poisoning of his mind. But now that he is at least presenting himself as a willing servant asking for mercy, he restrains himself from doing something seemingly advantageous (Letter #153) in dealing with Gríma in some final fashion. As such, he shows this divine virtue that Tolkien has described as "an absolute requirement in moral judgment (since it is present in the Divine nature)" (Letter #246). Indeed, it is born out of love, for in this exercise of pity he seeks the good of Gríma (Letter #246). He is allowing him a chance to concretely show his repentance, as well as to free himself from his own failings and show himself to be faithful.

Second, it is notable how "faith" is used here. It is common in Christian circles to speak of "faith" primarily in terms of belief. Belief is an aspect, to be sure, but Tolkien is closer to reflecting the aforementioned broader range of both Hebrew and Greek "faith" terminology in the Bible here.[5]

Théoden calls upon Gríma to prove his "faith," by which he means his faithfulness/loyalty, his fidelity, his allegiance, and thus his trustworthiness (given how faith is linked to trust). There is a similar range in the presentation of "faith" in the Bible.

Unfortunately, Gríma is not willing to go to war with Théoden. He tries to talk Théoden into letting him stay behind to manage affairs as authority over Edoras, but this request and the subsequent exchange leads Éomer to threaten killing Gríma. Gandalf stays his blade, and he suggests that Gríma return to his true master, the treacherous Saruman. The two appear to be made for each other. Gandalf thus leaves the verdict to Théoden, "See, Théoden, he is a snake! With safety you cannot take it with you, nor can you leave it behind. To slay it would be just. But it was not always as it now is. Once it was a man, and did you service in its fashion. Give him a horse and let him go at once, wherever he chooses. By his choice you shall judge him" (III/6). In this way, Gandalf still promotes Théoden's exercise of the virtue of pity, for he has already established that we cannot presume such a person is too far gone. As with Gollum, he

---

[5] See also II/6: "Yet so little faith and trust do we find now in the world beyond Lothlórien, unless maybe in Rivendell, that we dare not by our own trust endanger our land."

notes that Gríma was not always evil (nor indeed was his true master), and it is possible that he may not be so again. But he will need to make the choice to accept guidance out of the trap he is currently in. Thus, Théoden ultimately heeds Gandalf's counsel and allows Gríma the choice to ride where he will. As Jesus said, no servant can serve two masters (Matt 6:24 // Luke 16:13), and so Gríma must choose which of the two opponents he wants to devote his service and allegiance to. By Gríma's choice, he ultimately proves himself faithless, for he rides to Saruman in Isengard, thinking him to be the stronger master who will triumph in the end. Sadly, this fateful choice will make repentance even harder for him to come by when it is offered again.

The Battle of the Hornburg

Thereafter, Théoden marches out with his army from Edoras accompanied by Gandalf, Aragorn, Legolas, and Gimli. He aims to confront the forces of Isengard, but he is later warned by Gandalf to withdraw to Helm's Deep, for Saruman's forces are too great to meet in the open. He tells Théoden and the others to wait for him there and that he will come with help when he can. The battle that follows is thus a test of their perseverance, as they do not have the forces to vanquish the army of Uruk-hai marching against them. That will come from sources unlooked for who Gandalf will bring with him.

The battle Is thus also a test of faith and hope. Does the army trust that Gandalf will return? Do the Rohirrim trust that if they only do what they can with what they have that this work will be taken up by Providence and directed to ultimate victory? Whether or not each individual has personal hope that he will survive the night against such an overwhelming force (or even trust in the One as such), each one nevertheless summons the courage and does what is needful for each one to do.

While our struggles in faith and hope will not tend to take the form of a physical battle with armies thus drawn up, it is important to recognize that waiting is a fundamental expression of faith and hope. Throughout Scripture there are stories and instructions about waiting upon the Lord. It is a common thread through the stories of the patriarchs and matriarchs in Genesis, Israel's time in Egypt (including Moses's three eras of waiting at forty years each time; Acts 7:23, 30, 36), followed by their time in the wilderness, the cycle of Judges (which includes multiple times when Israelites spend years being oppressed by their enemies), David's life (wherein he only became king many years after he was anointed by Samuel), Elijah's ministry, the exile in Babylon, and so on. In the NT the theme is predominant in the framing of Luke's Christmas story for those like Zechariah, Elizabeth, Anna, and the Jewish people as a whole. And then Jesus himself had to wait around thirty years before his public ministry began. Typically, the time of waiting is on the scale of years, but the principle remains the same regardless of the time scale involved, and it is clear at many points in Scripture that waiting is a crucial exercise of faith according to the Bible (Ps 25; Isa 40:27–31). In each case, as with the Battle of the Hornburg, it is not a passive waiting. Those who wait upon the Lord must be active in remaining faithful until the time comes, and they must stay engaged with doing what they must do in obedience while they wait (Deut 4:1–23; 6:4–12).

The parallel is highlighted by a line from Aragorn in his conversation with Éomer during the defense:

> 'Nonetheless day will bring hope to me,' said Aragorn. 'Is it not said that no foe has ever taken the Hornburg, if men defended it?'
> 'So the minstrels say,' said Éomer.
> 'Then let us defend it, and hope!' said Aragorn. (III/7)

Aragorn once again exemplifies the virtue of *estel*. He does not know how Gandalf's promise of aid will be able to be fulfilled in time and with sufficient force. But he saw him come back from the dead by the will of Eru Ilúvatar. He can trust the same One to deliver them by the direction of his providential action if they simply hold fast to what they have until the time comes. That is why he can speak so bravely and confidently to the Uruk-hai outside: "No enemy has yet taken the Hornburg. Depart, or not one of you will be spared. Not one will be left alive to take back tidings to the North. You do not know your peril" (III/7).

And so indeed the timing works so that when Théoden resolves to make a final, desperate charge into the Uruk-hai who have overwhelmed Helm's Deep, they are met on the other side by the reinforcements Gandalf brought with Erkenbrand in the lead. Also present at the right time is a forest that has seemingly come out of nowhere. However many Uruks fled into the forest, none of them ever came out, for this was a forest of Huorns sent by Treebeard at Gandalf's request. No one else on the battlefield expected them to be there. No one could have planned for it. But the timing of these three forces converging to win the day is ultimately the orchestration of Providence.

Mercy for the Survivors

The Uruk-hai were not the only ones who attacked Helm's Deep. Many hillmen of Dunland had joined them in the assault. Those who survived the battle surrendered and cried for mercy. They expected to receive none. But that is what they get from Erkenbrand as he puts them to work:

> 'Help now to repair the evil in which you have joined,' said Erkenbrand; 'and afterwards you shall take an oath never again to pass the Fords of Isen in arms, nor to march with the enemies of Men; and then you shall go free back to your land. For you have been deluded by Saruman. Many of you have got death as the reward of your trust in him; but had you conquered, little better would your wages have been.'

> The men of Dunland were amazed; for Saruman had told them that the men of Rohan were cruel and burned their captives alive. (III/8)

Thus, Erkenbrand exemplifies the best of the Rohirrim, as Aragorn described them earlier as being, among other things, "generous in thought and deed" (III/2). They are a warrior people, but we have seen from this example and from Théoden that they are by no means bloodthirsty. They can even show some degree of mercy to their enemies. They have thus cultivated in some measure the seed of the divine in this virtue, as they have also cultivated the grace of courage given to them.

Grace for the Dwarf

Amid this battle, there was another small example of providence in how Gimli found himself in the Caves of Aglarond behind Helm's Deep during the defense. Again, there was no plan for him to go there, but it was where he wound up with Éomer in the course of the battle. As he declares, "Happy was the chance that drove me there! It makes me weep to leave them" (III/8). It took a Dwarf's particular aesthetic sensibilities to realize the beauty hidden behind a fortress of Men. And so even as Gimli has forged bonds with the Elves through Galadriel and Legolas, as well as with the future king of Gondor and Arnor in Aragorn, he is hereby forging a bond with the kingdom of Rohan as well so that he will have leave to set up a Dwarf colony in the Caves and cultivate their beauty for others to appreciate after the War of the Ring is over.

In such ways, we see the One's special grace for Gimli at work. By these strange paths he is taking, he is forging relationships that will shape him for the rest of his life, and in turn his gifts are being and will be brought to bear for the benefit of others. He even makes a pact with Legolas in the hope that when this war is over that he will bring Legolas to the caves and Legolas will bring him to walk in Fangorn Forest (even though the latter is not much to Gimli's liking). Some of these relationships, particularly with Galadriel and the people of Rohan through his love for the Caves of Aglarond, are forged by means of Gimli's aesthetic appreciation, a grace given to him to appreciate the work of the Creator to see, albeit imperfectly, the beauty of his creation and to contribute to it as a sub-creator. Tolkien himself noted how the perception of beauty or sanctity is itself a gift from God in response to those who saw some sort of sanctity in his work: "If sanctity inhabits his work or as a pervading light illumines it then it does not come from him but through him. And neither of you would perceive it in these terms unless it was with you also" (Letter #328).

Evil Persists, and so Must We

After the battle, Gandalf leads a company to Isengard for them to see what has happened there (and to reunite what remains of the Fellowship this side of the Anduin). As they go along, they encounter Ents, much to Théoden's wonder as he thought such creatures were only the subject of children's stories and songs. Gandalf reminds him that to the Ents, who have lived for thousands of years, the entire span of the kingdom of Rohan is but a passing tale. Yet they also show how Théoden has allies in his fight against evil who are beyond his reckoning, and so he should be glad. Théoden responds that it also makes him sad, "For however the fortune of war shall go, may it not so end that much that was fair shall pass forever out of Middle-earth?" (III/8). Gandalf responds, "It may … The evil of Sauron cannot be wholly cured, nor made as if it had not been.[7] But to such days we are doomed. Let us now go on with the journey we have begun" (III/8).

Gandalf is speaking in strictly historical terms rather than eschatological terms. There is hope for the time in which all evil will be undone. But for those who are actors only within the limits of the historical plane, they cannot themselves find the cure for evil. Even should Sauron be vanquished, some fruits of his evil will persist, as was true even of his master Melkor. Evil will persist until the eschaton. But Gandalf reiterates what he had told Frodo early in the story. It is not up to us when and where in history we should be born; what is up to us is the decision of what to do with the time we are given. We can still be faithful with what has been entrusted to us. Today has enough concerns of its own without our worrying about tomorrow (Matt 6:25–34 // Luke 12:22–32). Only by focusing on the task in front of us and being faithful to do the work given to us can we see glimpses of the final victory that is part of the content of *estel*.

---

[7] An earlier draft ended the equivalent line here. Tolkien, *War of the Ring*, 45. The addition fits with wisdom Gandalf has already spoken, and it properly ends the remark on a note of exhortation to still do what must be done where and when Providence has placed one to act.

Saruman's Destructive Reform

When the company arrives at Isengard, the narrator describes the setting for us and speaks of the past glorious appearance of Isengard. But when Saruman took it over, the narrator tells us::

> Saruman had slowly shaped it to his shifting purposes, and made it better, as he though, being deceived – for all those arts and subtle devices, for which he forsook his former wisdom, and which fondly he imagined were his own, came but from Mordor; so that what he made was naught, only a little copy, a child's model or a slave's flattery, of that vast fortress, armoury, prison, furnace of great power, Barad-dûr, the Dark Tower, which suffered no rival, and laughed at flattery, biding its time, secure in its pride and its immeasurable strength. (III/8)

On the one hand, Saruman here is analogous to modernity and its impulse to industry that Tolkien so disliked for its defacing of God's creation. He had seen this in his own English country, but he also noted the even worse effect it had in America (Letter #328). He had also perceived the overwhelming influence of machines in WW2, as he said in Letter #96 to Christopher that he thought only the Machines triumphed in this war, leaving millions dead in their wake, others grieving, and others in servitude.. The machinery of the modern age links with one of the fundamental concerns of Tolkien's stories, as we can see Letter #131, which we return to. We have already quoted the larger context concerning how Tolkien's story is concerned with Fall, Mortality, and Machine, in our exposition on magic, and so we will focus on the last part here:

> Both of these [Fall and Mortality] (alone or together) will lead to the desire for Power, for making the will more quickly effective, - and so the Machine (or Magic). By the last I intend all use of external plans or devices (apparatus) instead of developments of the inherent inner powers or talents – or even the use of these talents with the corrupted motive of dominating: bulldozing the real world, or coercing other wills.

That is indeed what Saruman had fallen into with his mind for metal and machinery. This was not of his own invention, though, as it was but a manifestation of Sauron's will. Thus, on the other hand, Saruman has become in some ways like Marlowe's Faust, possessing great knowledge and wanting ever more, making an alliance with an agent of the devil (instead of a pact in blood), by which he falls, and ends up accomplishing nothing of significance with the great powers he thought to gain by this alliance. What he thought was his own wisdom that was greater than Eru Ilúvatar's was instead

Sauron's way of thinking and doing. Like Sauron, he sought to order according to his will, and instead he became a tool for ordering things according to Sauron's will as both sought "to make their own wills effective by any means" (Letter #181). As a result of his fall, he took what was once a beautiful land in Isengard and made it into an impish parody of Barad-dûr and the realm of Mordor. After all, Saruman operated by the same principles as Sauron in seeking above all else to become master of others, meaning for those with wills he could not dominate, he would seek to kill, and whatever was of use to him he would exploit as fuel for his machines (as he did with many trees). Moreover, what was not of use would simply be destroyed (so that he would have Orcs cut down some trees and leave them to rot). As with the trees in his own land and beyond, the Men on the border of his realm were to be destroyed or enslaved to his will. His will was supreme and whatever was not of use to it was as nothing to him.

But that forest that he sought to bulldoze for the use of his own ("supreme") will had turned against him with a vengeance. An ancient force of divine provision for the protection of the forest that he had arrogantly overlooked had now—both at the Battle of the Hornburg and at Isengard itself—brought his demise. He had despised his divine mission, and this was his reward.

Likewise, the treasonous Gríma shared in this judgment of treason. He rode to Isengard to join Saruman, but by the time he arrived it had already been overthrown and inundated. Treebeard catches him and gives him a choice either to wait with him to be dealt with by Gandalf and the others or to wade through the water to Orthanc. Gríma chooses the latter, and so misses yet another opportunity to own what he has done and show repentance. And so Aragorn declares, "Fate has not been kinder to him than he deserves. The sight of the ruin of all that he thought so strong and magnificent must have been almost punishment enough. But I fear that worse awaits him" (III/9). Aragorn here is acknowledging divine providence at work in this judgment by reference to "fate." However, Gríma's choices when given the chance to repent will only mean there will be worse to come for him as he makes it more and more difficult for himself to escape the sad end of the road he is travelling. That is what hardening one's heart does.

Saruman Rebuked

After the Hobbits are reunited with their companions of the Fellowship and catch them (and us) up to the present of the story, they accompany Gandalf to Orthanc, where they will confront Saruman. Saruman has been divested of his prominence in the order of the Wizards, his armies have been vanquished, and his domain is in ruin. But he still has a subtle power by which he can corrupt the faculty of reason. He has a way of speaking by which his voice is enchanting, "all that it said seemed wise and reasonable, and desire awoke in them by swift agreement to seem wise themselves. When others spoke they seemed harsh and uncouth by contrast; and if they gainsaid the voice, anger was kindled in the hearts of those under the spell" (III/10). Saruman has such expertise in manipulation precisely because of his store of knowledge and even wisdom. Some who stand by while Saruman speaks with various individuals in the company find themselves being carried along by his fair-seeming speech promising peace and salvation for those who would seek his counsel.

It Is crucial for the breaking of such a spell to give no ground In declaring the truth as the remedy for such powers of deception. The first to rebuke Saruman in this fashion is Gimli, who reminds this company, "The words of this wizard stand on their heads … In the language of Orthanc help means ruin, and saving means slaying, that is plain" (III/10). Saruman briefly breaks his façade in responding to Gimli. Then when he offers Théoden peace and reminds him that his own house has gone to war often, Théoden rebukes him for his unjust reason for the war, which was merely Saruman's will to power and rule for his own end. Saruman again breaks so as to insult Théoden and his royal house. He then conducts himself to speak with Gandalf, acting as if he is the only one truly worthy of treating with and of receiving his counsel. Gandalf is the final one to rebuff and rebuke him, first with a laugh, which delivers all others from any shred of fantasy that Saruman meant well, and then he speaks as one with authority so that Saruman's voice changes so as to seem shrill and cold. Then when Gandalf himself offers to Saruman the chance to go free, provided that he leaves the Key of Orthanc and his staff to be returned to him later if he merits them, Saruman himself laughs, but this is no laugh of relief. It is the laugh of scorn, contempt, and utter rejection of grace. His refusal to humble himself instead leads to his humiliation when Gandalf forces him back out from his room by the power of his voice and breaks his staff to signify his banishment from the order.

Strange Turns of Fortune

Saruman's humiliation leads to another consequence that will turn out to be providential provision. Gríma throws out the *palantír*, the Seeing Stone of Orthanc. It was not to help the enemies of Saruman, but it will prove important. Even as Gandalf grieves at Saruman's lack of humility and repentance, he remarks, "Still for us things have not gone badly. Strange are the turns of fortune! Often does hatred hurt itself" (III/10).[8] This is an example of how evil will can ultimately serve a good end in spite of itself by the orchestration of Providence. There was no good intent on Gríma's part, nor is he in any way acting out of character, but his action will be taken up and lead to ends that will ultimately prove beneficial to others (but not himself, since he remains unrepentant).

Another case of such a strange turn comes with the next chapter. As the Hobbits travel with the company, Pippin finds himself strangely and inexplicably drawn to the *palantír* when the company camps for the night. He had been enamored with the sight of it when he first picked it up in Isengard, but Gandalf had taken it into his own possession. He is so drawn that he dares to take it from Gandalf while he sleeps. He tries to talk himself out of taking it away, but then he talks himself into looking into it because he cannot put it back without disturbing Gandalf anyway. In this way, Pippin illustrates the slippery slope of temptation. Allowing oneself a slight step over the line makes it easier to take the next step and the next until one is deeper in trouble than one anticipated. For Pippin finds that looking into the *palantír* brings him into direct contact with Sauron. He had a *palantír* of his own that he was using to communicate with Saruman, whereby he enthralled Saruman to his will and constrained him to report to him by a similar draw that ensnared Pippin. Sauron thus thinks that this is the Hobbit who has his Ring and that he is at Orthanc. He sends a Nazgûl to retrieve it, which will cause Gandalf to take Pippin and ride with all speed to Minas Tirith, the most secure city of the Free Peoples and an inevitable point of attack for Sauron's forces.

Despite the peril brought by Pippin looking into the *palantír*, even this act proves to be a strange turn of fortune. First, Gandalf tells Pippin that he and his friends have been saved from worse peril than may have been, "mainly by good fortune, as it is called. You cannot count on it a second time" (III/11). Once again, we see some curious phrasing referring to good fortune "as it is called." And once again, it is an indication of referring to divine providence by another name. At the same time, Gandalf warns him about being reckless with it. Precisely because a mysterious will beyond any of them is at work, it is prudent not to tempt "good fortune" by acting foolishly as if that One will safeguard any action of one so seemingly favored. God's providence guides through so many trials and tribulations, but that is not a license for carelessness,

---

[8] An earlier draft of this scene was significantly different, but one such notable difference is that, while there was reference to how Gríma had been helpful despite his intent, there was no reference to "fortune" as such. Tolkien, *War of the Ring*, 66.

recklessness, and foolishness. On the one hand, this is consonant with what Tolkien says about the miraculous grace that brings about the good ending of a fairy-stories in his essay "On Fairy-Stories," as we observed earlier. From the standpoint of people within the story, precisely because miraculous grace brings a eucatastrophe about, it is atypical divine action, and not repeatable, except by divine volition, and it cannot be counted on to recur simply because it is so irregular.[9] On the other hand, we are similarly reminded in Scripture not to put the Lord God to the test by disobedience or making irresponsible decisions simply to put God to the test, as Jesus refused to do so when he was tempted (Exod 17:2, 7; Num 14:22; Deut 6:16; Pss 78:18, 41, 56; 95:9; 106:14; Mal 3:15; Matt 4:7 // Luke 4:12).

Second, this act thus reveals just what kind of object Gandalf had and now Aragorn has in his possession. After all, Gandalf passes it on to Aragorn as the only one with rightful claim to inheritance of it as the future king of Gondor and Arnor. His ancestors brought these stones from Númenor, as they had received them from the Elves of the Undying Lands. Thus is the true extent of Gríma's folly shown that he threw this out of the tower. As Théoden says, quoting a proverb, "oft evil will shall evil mar" (III/11). Evil is ultimately self-destructive, being parasitic of the good and leading to destruction and death. And so it happens often in the course of history that evil betrays evil and undermines itself. This is one way that acts of an evil will can be taken up and directed to a good end it never intended.

Third, Gandalf himself repeats, now with more insight, that he and his fellows have been "strangely fortunate" (III/11).[10] Indeed, he thinks Pippin has saved him from probing the stone himself. He would then have been revealed to Sauron and they would not have been bought precious time by the Nazgûl flying to Isengard by mistake. Gandalf knows he is not ready for such a trial as this kind of encounter with Sauron would be, and he does not know if he will ever be so ready. Thus, Pippin unintentionally saved him and the rest of the company from what could have been a debilitating error. Yet again, Providence has taken up another intention and directed it to a different end.

Fourth, this error by Pippin is crucial for his own formation. More immediately, as Gandalf says, "the burned hand teaches best. After that advice about fire goes to the heart" (III/11). He would not have been talked out of looking into the stone beforehand, but now that he has looked into it, he knows better to keep his distance. More long-

---

[9] Tolkien, "On Fairy-Stories," 153.

[10] See also Tolkien, *War of the Ring*, 74: "Things may have been meant to go much as they have gone – except that you looked in, not me! Hm! Well. They have gone so, and not otherwise; and it is so that we have to deal with."

term, this event will require him to go to Minas Tirith with Gandalf ahead of the others, where he will have uniquely formative experience serving as a guard of Minas Tirith, which will also prove to be historically significant within the broader world of the story.

Fifth, as mentioned before, this event has motivated Gandalf to put the stone in Aragorn's keeping. This is not only a symbolic pledge of his greater inheritance to come. For by this means, Aragorn will force Sauron's hand before his designs are fully wrought, the timing of which will prove crucial for both the war and the Quest. But we will need to return to this in Book V.

CHAPTER SEVEN

Commentary on Book IV

Book IV shifts the story back to the main Quest of Frodo and Sam. They are currently beyond their ken and without a guide. This is particularly problematic for them in the Emyn Muil, a labyrinthine formation of hills where the Fellowship had broken. Frodo acknowledges that it is part of a higher purpose than his own to make it to Mordor, "It's my doom, I think, to go to that Shadow yonder, so that a way will be found. But will good or evil show it to me?" (IV/1). The reconciliation between the ultimate goal of his Quest and the current disorientation is not something he can figure out on his own, and so he says something/someone else will need to show it to him and that "a way will be found" rather than that he "will find a way." He wonders if good or evil will show him the way, and in the mystery of Providence, it will thus be that the answer is a mix of both.

Gollum and the Pity of Frodo

The unwitting instrument of Providence here is Gollum, once known as Sméagol. He had trailed the Fellowship in Moria and followed them to, but not far into, Lothlórien. He picked up their trail again as they went down the Anduin, and he had followed Frodo and Sam as they crossed the River and came into the Emyn Muil. Obsession and enslavement of his will to the Ring had driven him since he had lost the Ring almost seventy-eight years ago. Unbeknownst to him, he was only able to live so long and indirectly contribute to multiple aspects of the present Quest—from informing Sauron of the Ring being related to the Shire and the name Baggins, to the consequent pursuit by the Nazgûl, to Gandalf's learning of his story, to Gandalf's advice to Frodo about pity, to Gollum's escape from the Elves of the Woodland Realm, to Frodo's arrival in

Rivendell in such time as he did, to the timing of the Quest, to his current pursuit of the Ring-bearer—because of Bilbo's pity that he had never known of. And while he intended reclaiming his Precious, his obsession with it will be directed to a different purpose when he meets the renewal of that pity, this time from Frodo.

For at this time, Gollum overtakes Frodo and Sam. After a struggle, Frodo subdues him, and Gollum begs not to be hurt. Frodo then hears in his mind part of his conversation with Gandalf from before his Quest began (I/2). Then, he could not imagine feeling any pity for Gollum, thinking him deserving of death. Now, after seeing Gollum and replaying the words of Gandalf about how he should not be too eager to deal out death and judgment, not knowing all ends to which such decisions will go, he declares, "For now that I see him, I do pity him" (IV/1). Frodo has had the Ring in his possession for less than eighteen years at this point and has borne it (and even used it) for a few months. But such experience as he has had has helped change his perspective on one who had the Ring for centuries and has thereby been reduced from a Hobbit like himself to what he is now, complete with a permanently split and enslaved will. It would have been advantageous to Frodo in some ways to kill Gollum, as it would have removed another potential obstacle in his Quest, one who was himself pursuing the Ring, and it would have saved him some treachery from one who was not particularly trustworthy. But Frodo restrains himself and wills the good for Gollum as he wills the good for himself. As Bilbo's pity would rule the fate of many—as Gandalf thought—so too will Frodo's pity rule the fate of many through bringing about the turning point of the Quest.[1]

This divine virtue of pity envelops the story of Gollum at its key points from his encounter with Bilbo to his end. It is, in fact, what makes his end possible. But we will need to return to that later, at which point we will also lay out Tolkien's own theological-ethical framing of the story.

Hope and Courage

With Gollum as their guide, Frodo and Sam are finally able to leave the Emyn Muil and make their way through the Dead Marshes. Gollum appears in turns to be attempting to earn the trust of the Hobbits, since he is able to sit by for hours or go off for hours

---

[1] I noted earlier that this was one of two places at which Gandalf's dialogue with Frodo about pity is evoked. This was so even from the initial draft of this text, as Tolkien made sure that this throughline was present even then, and it made him go back and revise the earlier dialogue and the dialogue here, in turn. See Tolkien, *War of the Ring*, 96–97.

and come back without harming them while they sleep. At the same time, he appears to be scheming against them, as Sam learns while furtively lying awake as Gollum talks to himself. Frodo wanted him to take them to the Black Gate of Mordor, but it appears that Gollum is devising for them to go another way.

But besides this issue, Sam takes thought of whether or not they have enough *lembas* to last the rest of the way to Mount Doom and perhaps some way back. He never really thought about what comes after the Ring is destroyed, and neither has Frodo. Frodo is convinced that there is no use in concerning themselves with that part. For him, "To *do the job* as you put it – what hope is there that we ever shall? And if we do, who knows what will come of that?" (IV/2). This is the hope that is equivalent to *amdir*, for there is no discernible reason, based on what the Hobbits know, that they can succeed in this Quest. If there is any hope, it is the hope of *estel*, the hope that lies beyond their knowledge. Without the latter, there could be nothing for the capacity of hope to cling to. The former, however, is not strictly necessary. In its absence, one can still operate by courage to do what must be done, regardless of the obstacles of fear and doubt. That is ultimately what the Norse did in the absence of their hope for a final victory, which did not come to them until the gospel did. And so it is for Frodo and Sam, although their Quest will provide a glimpse or echo of final victory.

Likewise, once Frodo, Sam, and Gollum arrive at the Black Gate, Frodo resolves that, despite how impassable the gate may be, he will go where he is commanded to go, "If there is only one way, then I must take it. What comes after must come" (IV/3). Sam knows it is no good to gainsay Frodo here, for neither of them know any better at the moment, "And after all he never had any real hope in the affair from the beginning; but being a cheerful hobbit he had not needed hope, as long as despair could be postponed" (IV/3). Sam thus also resolves that, no matter how unlikely the success in this adventure is, he will stick to his master. His is the indomitable courage of the servant, and he is the Wiglaf to Frodo's Beowulf. We will have more to say about that later.

Providence Foreshadowed

But Gollum stops what would have been a fruitless effort. He tells them of another way into Mordor. All ways are guarded, but this one is the most secretive, even if Gollum is not being forthright about the watch on that path. While there is reason to distrust him and this plan he suggests, Frodo calls him by his better name, Sméagol, and tells him that he will trust him once more, "Indeed it seems that I must do so, and that it is my fate to receive help from you, where I least looked for it, and your fate to help me whom you long pursued with evil purpose" (IV/3). The notion that such are their "fates" is similar to Gandalf saying that Frodo was "meant" to have the Ring and to Frodo saying that he and Sam were "meant" to go together. The same One who meant both has ordained that these two are to work together for the (not *their*) common goal, at least for a time, despite previously being enemies. It will even prove true that Gollum will not only be the one who provides help where Frodo least looked for it, but he will also be the one who provides help when and how *both of them* least looked for it.

Still, Frodo warns Sméagol that he is in danger in continuing to guide him. He is not referring to the Quest itself, but to the Ring:

> You swore a promise by what you call the Precious. Remember that! It will hold you to it; but it will seek a way to twist it to your own undoing. Already you are being twisted. You revealed yourself to me just now foolishly. *Give it back to Sméagol* you said. Do not say that again! Do not let that thought grow in you! You will never get it back. But the desire of it may betray you to a bitter end. You will never get it back. In the last need, Sméagol, I should put on the Precious; and the Precious mastered you long ago. If I, wearing it, were to command you, you would obey, even if it were to leap from a precipice or to cast yourself into the fire. And such would be my command. So have a care Sméagol! (IV/3)

In the larger context of the story, Frodo is, of course, speaking insightfully, knowing the power of the Ring from personal experience and from what he has learned of its lore. But he is also speaking beyond what he knows. He is indirectly foreshadowing what will become of Sméagol should he continue to be utterly submissive to his desire for the Ring. The Ring itself is evil and will only lead to an evil end of corruption, destruction, self-consumption, and death if it persists. Such are the consequences of the false hope it offers of exceeding creaturely limitations in defiance of the Creator. Thus it is with the death that sin ultimately leads to, which is beyond the simple end of mortal existence. But even this desire will be taken up by the Creator and turned to other purposes.

Limits of Choice

Frodo had initially gone this way to the Black Gate because he thought there was no other choice. He is now presented with a choice, but it is not remarkably better. Both ways are guarded, although he might have a marginally better chance of going in by a less obvious entrance to Sauron's realm than the front gate. He would have liked advice from his companions who knew better. But they are not here. It was up to him to find a way where neither Gandalf, nor Aragorn, nor any of the Wise and Great had found one before. He thinks, "This was an evil choice. Which way should he choose? And if both led to terror and death, what good lay in choice?" (IV/3).

This is the type of quote that gets Tolkien brought up in the typical Calvinism/Arminianism debate where he does not squarely fit either set of beliefs.[2] It is hardly unique in this regard. But it is fair to say that this thought from Frodo recognizes the limits of his choices. Tolkien was of the view that free will is derivative and limited by circumstances, but he also thought that God in some sense guarantees it: "sc. [namely,] when it is 'against His Will', as we say, at any rate as it appears on a finite view. He does not stop or make 'unreal' sinful acts and their consequences" (Letter #153). He likewise described the unlimited God as "the one wholly free Will and Agent" (Letter #156).

It is also significant for what it illustrates about what we noted in the commentary on Book II. Frodo is concerned with the consequences of his choices, and for all he knows, both options will lead the same way. But neither he nor we ultimately have complete control over the consequences of our decisions or the realization of our ends. He does not know it, but one of these choices is better than the other for reasons beyond his reckoning. The time it will take him to travel this other, longer way will allow him to encounter Faramir, who will provide critical intelligence to Gandalf as a result, and it will allow him to reach his destination at a time when an army (including Gandalf as a leader) can provide a suitable distraction for Sauron's forces. He could not have known any of this beforehand, but based on what he knows, he still makes a just choice and the One will reward his trust through that which is beyond his ken.

Frodo's Transfiguration

Frodo, Sam, and Gollum thus take the road south. At one point, Sam is keeping watch while Frodo sleeps. As Sam looks at him, there is something of a transfiguration here, as he is reminded of how Frodo looked while he was in the house of Elrond (where Gandalf himself had observed signs of Frodo's sanctification). As the narrator tells us, "Sam had noticed that at times a light seemed to be shining faintly within; but now the light was even clearer and stronger. Frodo's face was peaceful, the marks of fear and care had left it; but it looked old, old and beautiful, as if the chiselling of the shaping

---

[2] For as much as I recommend Rutledge's volume *The Battle for Middle-earth*, this is my most significant problem with her work. For more on this, see my review here: https://krharriman.substack.com/p/review-of-the-battle-for-middle-earth.

years was now revealed in many fine lines that had before been hidden, though the identity of the face was not changed" (IV/4).

As with the similar vision of Gandalf in II/1, this vision from Sam signifies Frodo's sanctification and that he is one of those "with eyes to see" it. That is, Sam is also undergoing a sanctification process of a kind that echoes the proper sanctification process interwoven with the gospel in order for him to perceive this at all (cf. Letter #328). Frodo himself is not a Christ-figure, but he is a christological type in how he bears the Ring and suffers sacrificially for it.

Holding Fast

In this journey south, the Hobbits (minus Gollum, who had gone off looking for food) encounter the Ithilien Rangers, the remnant of the forces of Gondor that operate east of the Anduin in the lands the kingdom once held. They have no chance in open war against the enemies that march through that land, but they have skill in guerrilla warfare. It is all they can do just to resist.

An exchange between two of the Rangers, Damrod and Mablung, well exemplifies their situation and their resolve. They are discussing the Southrons/Haradrim who travel through these lands on their way to Mordor to reinforce Sauron's armies. It is clear from the numbers who march north that Gondor is hard put to it to offer any kind of meaningful resistance. The kingdom has continued to dwindle since their last king died nearly 1,000 years ago. They have been without a clear sign that another king shall come ever since, but they have seen clear signs that Sauron's military might is increasing, most likely beyond their capacity to handle. Reflecting on this, Damrod says forthrightly, "I doubt not that the days of Gondor are numbered and the walls of Minas Tirith are doomed, so great is His strength and malice" (IV/4). But Mablung says in response, "But still we will not sit idle and let Him do all as He would" (IV/4). For all that the strength of Gondor is diminished, there is still strength to resist. For all that that kingdom has dwindled, there is still courageous resolve to do what must be done, regardless of the obstacles and odds faced. Even if the signs of the fulfillment of their greater hopes are not clear, there are still signs of divine providence at work in their midst, as Mablung says of their captain Faramir, "He leads now in all perilous ventures. But his life is charmed, or fate spares him for some other end" (IV/4).

In such ways, the Ithilien Rangers are like their kinsmen to the north in the former realm of Arnor led by Aragorn. These southern Rangers share in the common struggle, whether or not they know it, with the similarly diminished Elves who remain in Middle-earth and yet still offer resistance to the forces of Sauron, whether in Rivendell, Loth-lórien, or the Woodland Realm. The Dwarves in realms far to the north and east offer resistance as they have for thousands of years. Men of other realms these men have never visited do the same, some of which we have met already, and some of which are still to be met (and others of which are never in focus in the story). Even creatures beyond their comprehension like the Ents have joined in the struggle. Gandalf has spent thousands of years going throughout Middle-earth supporting the resistance against Sauron. Most importantly, these Hobbits the Rangers have found are, unbeknownst to them, the most important contributors to this resistance as the ones who have a chance of ending Sauron's manifest presence in Middle-earth for good.

Such courageous struggle against the odds can certainly seem like lonely work for those in the midst of it. Both the seemingly lonely struggle in this story and the narrative context reminding us that this is not the case are continuous with the biblical story and the history of the Church. These aspects of Tolkien's story do not *represent* these parts of the Primary World per se, but they do *exemplify* common themes from these sources that shaped Tolkien.

Elijah once thought of himself as being alone in resisting the worship of Baal in Israel as they turned against the God of their ancestors. Elijah was responsible for keeping the faith when others would not, thereby being a faithful prophetic messenger of God, and all that was his responsibility was to continue to do so for as long as he lived, whatever tides may come. But the Lord informed him, particularly at a time when Elijah felt alone in the struggle that he would have a successor, that the Lord had other instruments, and there were yet 7,000 in Israel who were faithful to the Lord (1 Kgs 19:13–18). This includes the hundred prophets Obadiah hid, which he informed Elijah about, but whom Elijah had apparently disregarded in his anxiety (1 Kgs 18:1–16).

Similarly, this part of the story is reminiscent of the suffering churches referenced in Rev 2–3. The responsibility they are given is to persevere in faithfulness and love or to return to the same. Particularly noteworthy are the faithful among the church in Thyatira, who are told simply, "only hold fast what you have until I come" (Rev 2:25, ESV). Likewise, the faithful church in Philadelphia is described as having little power but as still holding to Jesus's word and not denying his name (Rev 3:8), and they are instructed simply, "hold firmly to what you have, so that no one will take your crown" (Rev 3:11, NASB). Then, as now, it is simply good for persecuted and suffering Christians to hold fast to the faith, to be faithful in what little they have responsibility for, and to persevere in resisting the temptation to assimilate to the world that would have them abandon their faith, love, and hope. And the fact that the letters to these churches are included in one document that all seven of the assemblies were to read was not only to provide an extra layer of accountability for each assembly; it also reminded the suffering faithful that they were not alone in their struggle, no matter how much the enemy powers sought to make such an impression of isolation on them. Furthermore, these churches were engaged in a struggle that we see is pervasive across the NT, as is the call to the perseverance of the suffering faithful.[3]

As we have noted elsewhere, Tolkien knew plenty about the history of the persecuted faithful. Martyrs are often celebrated in the calendar he followed as a Catholic. His own mother was for him an example of one who suffered for her faith, and while she was isolated from her family, she was not alone in her struggle, as she could rely on Father Francis Morgan for support (and so he could be entrusted as the guardian of Tolkien and his brother Hilary when their mother died young). When Tolkien was much older, he joined a group of officials of the Newman Association to write on behalf of Cardinal József Mindszenty of Hungary, who had been arrested for his opposition of communism. He signed the letter of protest as one of the nine honorary vice-presidents in support of a priest in a land where the powers sought to isolate and pressure Christians into abandoning their faith as part of a larger effort across the eastern bloc of Europe where the Soviets had influence. The letter was published in the 28 January, 1949 edition of *The Times*.[4]

And so it is with the Men of Gondor that their responsibility is to keep the faith. Tolkien himself said in Letter #156, "But if you imagine people in such a mythical state, in which Evil is largely incarnate, and in which physical resistance to it is a major act of loyalty to God, I think you would you have 'good people' in just such a state: concentrated on the negative: resistance to the false, while 'truth' remained more historical and philosophical than religious." Such a description of "keeping the faith" is also apropos beyond remaining faithful in the resistance against the evil one. The content of that faith is obviously not as developed as it would be in Israel with the special revelation of God in the old covenant, much less in the Church with the special revelation of God in the new covenant. But they retain traces of an old religion of the Faithful of Númenor. They even invoke the Valar in battle when they face a charging Mûmak,

---

[3] We cannot properly explore the extent of this matter here, but I have a series on texts related to the perseverance of the suffering faithful in the NT beginning here: https://krharriman.substack.com/p/the-perseverance-of-the-suffering.

[4] A digital copy is available at https://tolkienandfantasy.blogspot.com/2011/11/tolkien-and-newman-association.html. Ordway's biography (*Tolkien's Faith*) highlights many other links between Tolkien and John Henry Newman, from which this organization derived its name.

saying, "May the Valar turn him aside" (IV/4). We will address another more significant example later.

War

Even in light of all that has been said to this point, it must be acknowledged that the actual form such resistance takes in this story has an ugly side to it. Such war as the Rangers of Ithilien are engaged in is necessary, if for no other reason than to disrupt the operations of the Enemy, even though final victory cannot be achieved this way. But it tragically entails killing other Men who themselves are not monstrous but who have, for whatever reason (whether compelled or not), committed themselves to die in allegiance with the greatest monster in this world. Sam has been involved in fights to this point, but he had not yet seen an actual battle of Men against Men. He even gets a look up close of a Southron man dying from the wounds sustained in this battle. The narrator tells us, "It was Sam's first view of a battle of Men against Men, and he did not like it much. He was glad that he could not see the dead face. He wondered what the man's name was and where he came from; and if he was really evil of heart, or what lies or threats had led him on the long march from his home; and if he would not really rather have stayed there in peace" (IV/4).

One can easily imagine the young Tolkien thinking such thoughts in WW1 when he was part of the Battle of the Somme. And among many other issues WW1 illustrated, it is perhaps the starkest example of the absurdity of war, not least because it needlessly became a world war due to multiple layers of entangling alliances, leading to conflict far away from where the war started and involving nations who had nothing to do with the war's incitement. The virtue of courage is needed for war, of course, but if it is not balanced by other virtues, it leads to the alloyed and tarnished heroism that Tolkien observes in old heroes like Beowulf and Beorhtnoth. They may have undeniable valor, but unremitting pride in war or combat also leads to folly. If war can ultimately not be avoided, courage needs to be balanced with virtues like truthfulness, humility, wisdom, and a genuine love for peace if it is to avoid valor becoming vanity. As one will see in Tolkien's story, these are virtues that Faramir embodies.

An example of the first virtue Is well encapsulated and exemplified In the exchange Faramir has with Frodo and Sam as he says, "I would not snare even an orc with a falsehood" (IV/5). His humility is exemplified not only by his service to his people, but also by what will be his later acknowledgment of the truth of this declaration by Frodo of a higher will that has ordained his Quest: "Go back, Faramir, valiant Captain of

Gondor, and defend your city while you may, and let me go where my doom takes me" (IV/5). Faramir is humble enough to acknowledge that his will is not superior in this matter and that he is not so great that he could make the same attempt as his brother and yet avoid the same trap should he do so. His is only a part of the larger struggle against the Enemy, and he is humble enough to acknowledge that it is so.[5] His wisdom is shown in much of his speech, including in his insight regarding Gandalf/Mithrandir as being more than the lore-master he knew him to be, for he perceived he was "a great mover of deeds that are done in our time" (IV/5). But most significantly, his wisdom shows forth in his insight regarding Isildur's Bane and what happened to his brother in relation to Frodo. And as with Gandalf and Aragorn, he could discern that he died well in triumph, for he could perceive, "His face was more beautiful even than in life" (IV/5). As for his love of peace, that is apparent when he explains why he goes to war:

> For myself ... I would see the White Tree in flower again in the courts of the kings, and the Silver Crown return, and Minas Tirith in peace: Minas Anor again as of old, full of light, high, and fair, beautiful as a queen among other queens: not a mistress of many slaves, nay, not even a kind mistress of willing slaves. War must be, while we defend our lives against a destroyer who would devour all; but I do not love the bright sword for its sharpness, nor the arrow for its swiftness, nor the warrior for his glory. I love only that which they defend: the city of the Men of Númenor; and I would have her loved for her memory, her ancientry, her beauty, and her present wisdom. Not feared, save as men may fear the dignity of a man, old and wise. (IV/5)

Wood says of this statement that Faramir is effectively articulating a "pre-Christian version of ... the 'just war' vindication of combat," since Faramir only supports using it "for defensive, non-retaliatory purposes, and in behalf of the freedom and civility that war may sometimes secure ... No such speech could ever be found in a book from the heroic cultures that Tolkien so greatly admired."[6]

There is something to be said for this comment, especially the last part, in line with what we have seen thus far, but it also exemplifies a common presumption. For as much as Tolkien has shown influence from the traditions most popularly articulated by Augustine and Aquinas elsewhere, I am not convinced that Tolkien was formally a just

---

[5] Thus, Faramir also acknowledges the wisdom in what Sam says in his attempt to lecture him: "But it's a pity that folk as talk about fighting the Enemy can't let others do their bit in their own way without interfering. He'd be mighty pleased, if he could see you now. Think he'd got a new friend, he would" (IV/5). This resembles statements like we have seen from Haldir in Book II and Gandalf in Book III.

[6] Wood, *Gospel*, 95.

war theorist, nor do I think this is what Faramir is articulating. Faramir most likely does reflect Tolkien's views of war most directly. Tolkien said in a footnote to Letter #180, "As far as any character is 'like me' it is Faramir – except that I lack what all my characters possess (let the psychoanalysts note!) *Courage*."

Tolkien himself never defined how Faramir is the most similar character to him. Most obviously, it is in how Faramir shares his dream of the Great Wave that drowned Númenor, which came from Tolkien's own dreams (VI/5; Letter #163). But I suggest it also holds true in what he says about war. He noted Faramir's comments on the matter of martial glory and true glory with approval in Letter #66. He tells his son Christopher how he is not in agreement with the parade that is scheduled in June of 1945 because "the War is not over (and the one that is, or the part of it, has largely been lost). But it is of course wrong to fall into such a mood, for Wars are always lost, and The War always goes on; and it is no good growing faint" (Letter #101). In his long letter to Milton Waldman (Letter #131) he would say of the conclusion to his story, "Finally and cogently, it is the function of the longish *coda* to show the *cost* of victory, (as always), and to show that no victory, even on a world-shaking scale, is final. The war will go on, taking other modes" (emphases original). We have already seen from his comments on Tom Bombadil in Letter #144 that he saw him as exemplifying the type of pacifist person and way of life that is ultimately dependent on the victory of the Free Peoples (but by whom it could not be achieved). In Letter #195 he did not identify Frodo's views with his own, but his comments make clear that neither he nor Frodo were pacifists, and his subsequent comments uphold the conclusion that Frodo had come to, "that physical fighting is actually less ultimately effective than most (good) men think it!" There is not a ready-made name for Tolkien's view. But he makes clear throughout these letters that his is a Christian perspective shaped by a Christian philosophy of history and a Christian eschatology.

Grace at Dinner

After the battle and the aforementioned conversation between Faramir and the Hobbits, the Rangers take Frodo and Sam to one of their refuges on this side of the Anduin, Henneth Annûn. Faramir will continue the conversation with them there, but before that, there is a notable ritual that and the other rangers observe:

> Before they ate, Faramir and all his men turned and faced west in a moment of silence. Faramir signed to Frodo and Sam that they should do likewise.

'So we always do,' he said as they sat down: 'we look towards Númenor that was, and beyond to Elvenhome that is, and to that which is beyond Elvenhome and will ever be.' (IV/5)

This is the occasion to raise the matter of religious praxis in Middle-earth. We have already noted Tolkien's extensive comment from a footnote Letter #153 in Chapter Three that there are no temples, churches, or fanes in this era among the Free Peoples. This is supposed to be fitting for the imaginary historical era they occupy, which is why Tolkien thought it would have been damaging to the sense of historicity for any explicit forms of Catholicism appropriate to the present of the Primary World to have appeared there. Due to the nefarious and corrupting work of Melkor and Sauron, what signs of religious expression there had been often were linked with their own cults, which thereby presented another obstacle to the Free Peoples showing explicit religious praxis. As far as Tolkien was aware, the Hobbits had no established form of worship or prayer, unless they had adopted such from the Elves, which would apply to only a few who had such "exceptional contact." The Númenóreans (as well as their descendants) and others like the Rohirrim were monotheists, but they did not have temples dedicated to the One. The closest analogue to this that Tolkien had conceived at the time was the place on the mountain Meneltarma in Númenor, where the One was both privately and (more occasionally) publicly "invoked, praised, and adored: an imitation of the Valar and the Mountain of Aman." For the Númenórean exiles in Middle-earth after its destruction, there are still only traces of divine worship. We will see one of those that Tolkien did not mention in Letter #153 later. The one glimpse of such practices he did mention is what appears in this chapter in "Faramir's remark on 'grace at meat'" (Letter #153).

More succinctly, he noted in Letter #211, "Almost the only vestige of 'religion' is seen on II pp. 284-5 in the 'Grace before Meat'. This is indeed mainly as it were a commemoration of the Departed, and theology is reduced to 'that which is beyond Elvenhome and ever will be',sc. [namely,] is beyond the mortal lands, beyond the memory of unfallen Bliss, beyond the physical world."[7] Likewise, in Letter #156, he noted this scene as one of the instances in which reference to "the highest matters" peeps through, along with the example we noted earlier of Gandalf speaking of another will being at work in Bilbo finding the Ring. In that same letter, he explained more

---

[7] See also Tolkien, *Sauron Defeated*, 404: "the world of eternity and the spirit, in the region of Ilúvatar."

about the background for why some of the typical marks of religion are not manifest among the descendants of the Númenóreans:

> Men have 'fallen' – any legends put in the form of supposed ancient history of this actual world of ours must accept that – but the peoples of the West, the good side are Re-formed. That is they are the descendants of Men that tried to repent and fled Westward from the domination of the Prime Dark Lord, and his false worship, and by contrast with the Elves renewed (and enlarged) their knowledge of the truth and the nature of the World. They thus escaped from 'religion' in a pagan sense, into a pure monotheist world, in which all things and beings and powers that might seem worshipful were not to be worshipped, not even the gods (the Valar), being only creatures of the One. And He was immensely remote. (Letter #156)

That last comment speaks more to the perception of the Númenóreans of the transcendent One and how they felt about trying to approach him than of the One's actual involvement in the world (or supposed lack thereof), as we have seen many times to this point. Thus, he said in Letter #297, "We are in a time when the One God, Eru, is known to exist by the wise, but is not approachable save by or through the *Valar*, though He is still remembered in (unspoken) prayer by those of Númenórean descent" (emphasis original). For such reasons, and for reasons we noted in the first three chapters, he rejects a criticism that he said annoyed him about how his story "contained no religion" (Letter #165). He said in response, reiterating what he noted in Letter #153:

> It is a monotheistic world of 'natural theology'. The odd fact that there are no churches, temples, or religious rites and ceremonies, is simply part of the historical climate depicted. It will be sufficiently explained, if (as now seems likely) the Silmarillion and other legends of the First and Second Ages are published. I am in any case myself a Christian; but the 'Third Age' was not a Christian world.

This scene appears to be quite an important one to Tolkien that he would make it a reference point for questions about religion in Middle-earth in four separate letters (the first and last of which were written thirteen years apart). It also serves as a reminder of two crucial points. One, there is indeed faith in the One among the descendants of the Faithful who devoted themselves to the same All-Father, and this has carried on in spite of the persecution of the Faithful in Númenor and all the intervening times of trial in the last 3,000 years. Two, the world of this story is set in an imaginary time before Israel, and so it is appropriate that ritualistic expressions of faith would not simply be traditional Christianity transplanted out of place and time (which is, again, consistent with what has been observed in the first three chapters).

A Proud Kingdom Subject to Decay and Death

As Faramir continues his conversation with Frodo and Sam, Frodo asks Faramir about Gondor and what hope they have in the war. This causes Faramir to launch into a grand soliloquy. It is framed by his initial response, "It is long since we had any hope. The sword of Elendil, if it returns indeed, may rekindle it, but I do not think that it will do more than put off the evil day, unless other help unlooked-for also comes, from Elves or Men. For the Enemy increases and we decrease. We are a failing people, a springless autumn" (IV/5). This is the hope of *amdir*, for based on what Faramir can tell, there is no reason to think Minas Tirith and Gondor with it will survive the war. He perceives that final victory is not possible by conventional war. Yet there will be unlooked-for help in the actual war, part of which will come from the sword of Elendil's return, and part of which will come from people he has disregarded (which we will address in Book V). But most importantly, he does not yet realize that the un-looked-for help is in his very midst with these two Hobbits and their companion. Nor does he yet realize that a higher will guides their Quest to lasting victory over and liberation from Sauron (though not from evil itself as yet).

The last comment in the above statement serves as the impetus for reflection on how Gondor has dwindled to this point. He notes how the Men of Númenor became enamored with the Darkness and the black arts while others had other failings. Gondor apparently never promoted or allowed the dark arts to be practiced, and Sauron was never honored there, much less worshiped. But there are other paths to falling. Indeed, for Gondor it came not so much with becoming enamored with the Enemy as it came from lack of vigilance against the Enemy, thinking him to be of no account for far too long, and thus turning in on themselves and making their own mortality a problem they became obsessed with. In later years, it would even mean that warriors who fight in defiance of death, protect others from it, and inflict it on others would become more esteemed than those of other crafts. As we have seen previously, the issues of mortality and immortality are central to Tolkien's stories as a whole, and this is another manifestation of the same.

As Faramir says, in the Gondorians' hunger for endless and unchanging life, "Kings made tombs more splendid than houses of the living, and counted old names in the rolls of their descent dearer than the names of sons. Childless lords sat in aged halls musing on heraldry; in secret chambers withered men compounded strong elixirs, or in high cold towers asked questions of the stars. And the last king of the line of Anárion had no heir" (IV/5). In this obsession with death, they forgot how to live, including in their interest more in those who died before them than those who would take their place after their own deaths, perhaps out of jealousy that their descendants' lives would continue after theirs ended. They had lost *estel* in seeking some sort of way past creaturely limitations set by the Creator. They had lost trust that death was not the end for them, even if it was the end of their time within the circles of the world. If they saw death as a punishment that was difficult to bear, they forgot a lesson that Tolkien articulated in Letter #212:

> A divine 'punishment' is also a divine 'gift', if accepted, since its object is ultimate blessing, and the supreme inventiveness of the Creator will make 'punishments' (that is changes of design) produce a good not otherwise to be attained: a 'mortal' Man has probably (an Elf would say) a higher if unrevealed destiny than a longeval one. To attempt by device or 'magic' to recover longevity is thus a supreme folly and wickedness of 'mortals'. Longevity or counterfeit 'immortality' (true immortality is beyond Eä) is the chief bait of Sauron – it leads the small to a Gollum, and the great to a Ringwraith.

On the one hand, one can see throughout Scripture that such acceptance of divine punishment can turn to acceptance of divine gift. This is essential to the dynamic of sin-repentance-salvation, which is itself interwoven with rebellious humans coming to accept the creature/Creator distinction. Adam and Eve's punishment for trying to be as gods on their own terms in Gen 3 rather than to be like God on God's terms (as he is the One who made them in his image and likeness to begin with) could have been an occasion for the acceptance of the same to turn into a gift as they could realize the grace given to them even in this time. The similar exile of Israelites from their land presented similar opportunity for reflection, repentance, and the greater revelation of the glory of God in salvation from the same. We see this in texts like Isa 40; Jer 29 (particularly with the note about seeking the peace of the city where one has been exiled); 31; Dan 9; Hos 2; 11; Mic 7; Zech 8; and many others,[8] most dramatically in Ezek 37 where the death of the people is turned to resurrection.[9]

Likewise, Tolkien said of the Eucharist in Letter #43:

---

[8] On this theme, see my posts here: https://krharriman.substack.com/p/israel-and-the-exile-part-2; https://krharriman.substack.com/p/israel-and-the-exile-part-3.

[9] For more on this particular text, see here: https://krharriman.substack.com/p/resurrection-in-the-ot-part-8.

> There you will find romance, glory, honour, fidelity, and the true way of all
> your loves upon earth, and more than that: Death: by the divine paradox, that
> which ends life, and demands the surrender of all, and yet by the taste (or fore-
> taste) of which alone can what you seek in your earthly relationships (love,
> faithfulness, joy) be maintained, or take on that complexion of reality, of eternal
> endurance, which every man's heart desires.

In a similar vein we can see the application in Letter #212 of Rom 8:28 and other texts (such as teachings on discipline in Heb 12:2–13, joy in suffering in Jas 1:2–4, and suffering for doing right in texts such as 1 Pet 3:14–22) that suffering which one might see as divine punishment instead is reframed as divine gift for more good than could be imagined at the time.[10] On the other hand, Letter #212 and the framework it provides on Tolkien's story and its central themes pertaining to mortality and immortality as a whole supplies a clearer reconciliation on par with the fictional work found in *Morgoth's Ring* between his story and the biblical presentation of death in the larger sweep of the canon. But I would suggest there were all along elements of his accounts that were closer to what can be found in the Bible than he initially saw.

We see in Letter #156 that mortality in Tolkien's Secondary World is not a punishment for Men, but a Gift, one that even the Valar, bound as they are to the current created order for as long as it exists, could come to envy. In a marred world well short of the new creation that will be created by the Second Music, perpetual life can become a source of constant sorrow, rather than constant joy. For many of the Elves who lived through the travails of the First Age, then the diminishing of the Elves in the Second Age, followed by their ultimate dwindling while watching the darkness wax in the Third Age, it is easy to see how such weariness can accumulate to a burden of unimaginable weight (cf. Letter #245). There is to come a time of new creation in which even this mortality is voided, but mortality is not in essence a punishment. It becomes that way due to rebellion against the will of the One, which tends to manifest in Arda in terms of fear, reluctance, and contempt for mortality. In a similar way, death as simply the end of a transient existence is not, in and of itself, a punishment. But it becomes an affliction on the world when it is combined with sin. Adam and Eve were not immortal by nature (hence the tree of life), but they could become immortal. Then with sin causing the rupture in the relationship with God, they were exiled from the garden, forbidden from ever partaking of the tree of life. This was both a punishment in that Adam

---

[10] As Tolkien also said in Letter #113 to C. S. Lewis, "It is one of the mysteries of pain that it is, for the sufferer, an opportunity for good, a path of ascent however hard. But it remains an 'evil,' and it must dismay any conscience to have caused it carelessly, or in excess, let alone wilfully."

and Eve were not allowed to partake of both the tree of the knowledge of good and evil and then the tree of life afterwards, as well as a hidden grace in that such a sinful and broken existence was not allowed to perpetuate forever. Thus, death became intertwined with this exile caused by sin to become the ultimate end of sin, the ultimate end of Godforsaken existence. Death does not have this same sense for those who are in union with the risen Christ and thus the God who raises the dead, since death becomes like a temporary state of sleep for them, after which they will awaken to the resurrection of everlasting life.

Tolkien again noted in Letter #186 how the Elves, with the weariness of time in a broken world, come to envy the mortality that is Eru Ilúvatar's Gift to Men, while many Men, faced with the cloud of uncertainty beyond death, envy the Elves' immortality and wish, in their shortsightedness, that they too could continue in perpetuity in the circles of the world. Such is the nature of humans in a Christian anthropology that they are part of creation, being creatures in many ways similar to animals, but in that they are image-bearers of God, they also transcend the rest of creation in a way. In this in-between status, they ideally represent creation to God in worship and they represent God to creation in stewardly rule.

In both the Primary World and the Secondary World, the attachment to creation combined with the reality of death ultimately points to something more for humans. In Tolkien's Secondary World it is noted from the outset of *The Silmarillion* that there will be a Second Music, in which the Children of Ilúvatar will join with the Ainur, from which a new creation will come. And in what comes from this Second Music immortality will attain its fullness and the desires of both Elves and Men will be fulfilled in the promises of Eru. In the Primary World, the "something more" will come about through the eschatological resurrection to and transformation for everlasting life and the new creation.

What would seem to be most conflicting in Tolkien's letters is his statement in Letter #208, "But certainly Death is not an Enemy!" Of course, as we see in 1 Cor 15:20–26 and 53–57, being the most vivid and not the only such declarations, that is exactly how death, as a power, is regarded biblically speaking. Tolkien would be more careful in Letter #212 about reconciling such a statement with Christian theology, but it is important to note that when Tolkien referred to death in this context, he was not referring to the allying force of sin as such, which is Paul's referent in 1 Cor 15. Rather, this is a reference to death as the simple end of transient existence, the end for mortality. In the biblical case, the reference to death is informed by Eden and the whole sweep of the biblical narrative (such as texts cited here), particularly in terms of the connection of sin and death. In Tolkien's case, this is simply referring to mortality vs. immortality in the context of the world as it presently is.

While Tolkien noted that there is an overall Elvish framework in regard to describing death as gift in his mythology, he provided the crucial point in Letter #212 of how, regardless of how death came to be, it can be accepted as divine gift. Such a teaching of how apparent or actual divine punishment can be a divine gift if accepted is informed by his own experience of loss and hardship since his youth, through which he was sustained by the Catholic faith his mother inculcated in him. Ultimately, this notion is animated by the fact that we follow the God who raised Jesus from the dead and so through his death on the cross, especially in how it functions as propitiation, God brought about a good that could not be attained otherwise and made Jesus the foundation of his grand salvific edifice. In the process, what God will bring about in the eschaton is not merely some return to Eden (cf. Letter #96), but it will be a bestowal of everlasting life that utterly conquers every trace of death, being the result of union with God that comes only by the work of God in Christ, as well as a residence with God forever in the new Jerusalem/new creation, which is Eden fulfilled rather than simply Eden redux.[11]

One point to return to in this description is his focus on the idea of "acceptance" of death as such. For Men in Tolkien's story, this is what ultimately separates those who describe death as the Gift of Men and those who describe death as the Doom of Men. In this story's theoretical framework, a good Man would die voluntarily when the time came "by surrender with trust *before being compelled*" (Letter #212; emphasis original). Although compulsion would not have been an issue for unfallen humans, Tolkien thought this same attitude would have characterized the unfallen, for whom death would have signified only the end of transient, mortal existence and not that condition of Godforsakenness under the power of death united with sin.

And here Tolkien showed the distinct influence of his Catholic theology in how he linked this idea with Catholic Mariology. On the one hand, the Immaculate Conception in Catholic theology entails that Mary was an unfallen human (as Tolkien said in this same letter), particularly in the sense that she was exempt from the stain of original sin. On the other hand, the assumption of Mary is considered to be the appropriate end-of-life complement to her conception, whereby she voluntarily gave up continuing her earthly existence and was taken up into heaven. But lest there be any confusion about

---

[11] Similarly, as Finrod says, "For that Arda Healed shall not be Arda Unmarred, but a third thing and a greater, and yet the same." Tolkien, *Morgoth's Ring*, 318.

Mary's status or any sense of how she was in any way not dependent on Christ (for Mary is exalted by her relation to Christ and participation in the Incarnation), Tolkien clarifies, "The Assumption was in any case as distinct from the Ascension as the raising of Lazarus from the (self) Resurrection."[12]

Faramir Shows His Quality

After Faramir's soliloquy on Gondor, the conversation continues with a focus on Elves, as Sam was getting a good impression of Faramir and wanted to know how he thought of Elves. This naturally leads into dialogue about the Fellowship's time in Lothlórien, where it was clear to Sam that Boromir had a strengthened desire for the Ring. He was supposed to keep the Ring secret from Faramir, but he thus inadvertently compromised the Quest. Faramir now knows all that he needs to know, and he has all the advantage if he wants to take the Ring, so he says, "A pretty stroke of fortune! A chance for Faramir, Captain of Gondor, to show his quality" (IV/5).

When Providence thus presents him with a test, especially now knowing what happened to Boromir, he passes with a relieving laugh, as Galadriel did. In this case, Faramir is helped not only by the negative example of Boromir's action with the Ring, but also by his value of his own integrity and truthfulness. Earlier, he had said to Frodo that if ever he found Isildur's Bane, he would not take it, given how dangerous it was in its corrupting power, *"Not if I found it on the highway would I take it* I said. Even if I were such a man as to desire this thing, and even though I knew not clearly what this thing was when I spoke, still I should take those words as a vow, and be held by them" (IV/5). While Faramir made no vow, he exemplifies what it means to make one's word one's bond and so to show the meaning of Jesus's teaching against taking oaths so that one's "yes" can simply be "yes" and one's "no" can simply be "no" (Matt 5:34–37; Jas 5:12).

He also says that he is wise enough "to know that there are some perils from which a man must flee" (IV/5). This fits with biblical instruction to flee sexual immorality (1 Cor 6:18; 2 Tim 2:22), idolatry (1 Cor 10:14), and the love of money and other temptations that feed into it (1 Tim 6:3–11). Each temptation presents powerful and insidious pressure to assimilate to the world and its ways rather than stand out from it in

---

[12] Ordway similarly speaks of Mary being the perfect disciples in being "always focused on leading others to Jesus," and she further clarifies, "In Catholic terminology, *latria* is the Latin word for the form of adoration or worship that may properly be given to God alone. The saints may receive only respect or veneration (*dulia*), and the Blessed Virgin Mary, as the archetypal disciples, may receive special veneration (*hyperdulia*)." Ordway, *Tolkien's Faith*, 144.

allegiance to God, and there is no sense in being foolhardy in facing them. Like with the One Ring, it is best to flee from such sources of temptation.

In the end, Faramir assures Sam that he has not, in fact, erred in revealing the secret of the Ring to him, "If you seem to have stumbled, think that it was fated to be so. Your heart is shrewd as well as faithful, and saw clearer than your eyes. For strange though it may seem, it was safe to declare this to me. It may even help the master that you love. It shall turn to his good, if it is in my power" (IV/5). And thus, this seemingly chance meeting between Faramir and the Hobbits will turn out not only to help them avoid detection by their enemies, but it will also provide key intelligence for Gandalf later in the story, which will in turn affect the course the war takes. Faramir becomes a willing participant in this providential work, and he acknowledges that a higher will guides them both their separate ways: "In the morning we must each go swiftly on the way appointed to us" (IV/5).

Another Instrument of Providence

While Faramir can acknowledge that Frodo has a higher purpose with the Ring that he should not hinder, he does not so readily accept that Gollum is also himself an instrument of the One who guides the Hobbits to this higher purpose. When he comes to the Forbidden Pool below Henneth Annûn, which bears the penalty of death to protect the secrecy of the place, Faramir does indeed think to carry out the sentence. But Frodo asks for his mercy because Gollum is "in some way bound up with my errand" (IV/6). Frodo is thus reiterating what he said earlier about being fated to receive help from Gollum and Gollum being fated to help him. They are both instruments of Providence, though Frodo is more intentionally submissive to the same.

Faramir will spend much of the rest of the chapter seeking to learn about Gollum's intentions and to dissuade Frodo from following the path he is taking. In this exchange, Frodo interrogates Faramir about what he would have him do, and Faramir does not have a satisfactory answer. Frodo's journey is certainly not ideal. Most likely, he is not taking the path that Gandalf would have chosen, but that will never be known now (at least within the scope of the story). It is his responsibility to do what he can and try to do so in as timely a fashion as he can manage. As Gandalf said at the Council, Frodo thus shows wisdom by recognizing necessity and courage to do what he must, even knowing the perils that lie ahead and that only partially.

He will also show Gandalf's virtues of pity and hope in saying that, though Faramir thinks Gollum is wicked, Frodo says he is "not altogether wicked" (IV/6). On the one hand, this is a recognition that nothing is essentially evil from its origin, something both Gandalf and Elrond have taught him. On the other hand, this signifies that he has not written off Gollum's fate, assuming him to be consigned to wickedness. He hopes for his redemption, no matter how unlikely it is.

Parting with Faramir

Frodo thus convinces Faramir to allow all three of them to leave Ithilien, for which he will escort them. As Faramir had recognized the hand of Providence at work, so now Frodo acknowledges Providence at work in their meeting, "It was said to me by Elrond Halfelven that I should find friendship upon the way, secret and unlooked for. Certainly I looked for no such friendship as you have shown. To have found it turns evil to great good" (IV/7). Not only has this meeting been so arranged as to fulfill the words of Elrond, but it has turned his evil circumstances to great good, which we have seen often is a way God's providence works.

Of course, as with the last time he found secret friendship among the Elves of Ló-rien, a requirement is made of blindfolding one of his companions. In this case, Faramir wants to blindfold Gollum, since he does not trust him not to come seeking these lands again, and perhaps with more treacherous intentions. But Frodo has learned the lesson from Aragorn earlier about humble leadership and compassion. Like Aragorn, he asks that all of them be blindfolded so as to share a common burden.

A Glimpse of Hope

Once the three companions have taken their leave of Faramir, they journey to the Cross-roads, which will lead them to Minas Morgul (formerly Minas Ithil) and the secret path near there. This was once part of the dominion of the kingdom of Gondor, and the east-west road linked what was Minas Ithil to the former capital of Osgiliath and Minas Anor (now Minas Tirith) beyond that. The first of those cities has long since fallen into enemy hands and been distorted into a dark perversion of its once moonlit beauty. The second is no longer the capital as it is dilapidated and deserted, save for soldiers defending the Anduin. The third still stands strong, though not as strong or as glorious as it once was, for it also has decayed as its White Tree has decayed.

The Cross-roads itself encapsulates the current state of these lands. It features an ancient statue of a king of Gondor. But that statue has since been maimed by cruel hands. Besides drawing the scrawls upon it, those hands have decapitated the statue, thrown its head to the ground, and replaced it atop the statue with a rough stone crudely drawn upon with the symbol of Sauron. And given where the statue is set, it no longer represents the sovereignty of the greatest kingdom of the Free Peoples, but is instead a veritable entry sign for the Lands of Shadow. The light of day will grow ever dimmer as they move eastward. And the three companions have reached it at the time of day when the sun is sinking in the west. And yet, as they turn to take the road east, Frodo notices how the last beam of daylight catches a hopeful sight:

> Frodo saw the old king's head: it was lying rolled away by the roadside …
>
> The eyes were hollow and the carven beard was broken, but about the high stern forehead there was a coronal of silver and gold. A trailing plant with low- ers like small white stars had bound itself across the brows as if in reverence for the fallen king, and in the crevices of his stony hair yellow stonecrop gleamed. (IV/7)

Just before the black night falls, Frodo exclaims to Sam, "Look! The king has got a crown again … They cannot conquer for ever" (IV/7). This is one of the last scarce and brief glimpses of hope the Hobbits will find from here on. Even as night falls and they are about to walk into deeper darkness, they are reminded that even where all seems dark, they may yet find a glimpse of light; where all seems dead, they may yet find signs of life continuing in spite of it; where all seems ugly, they may yet find beauty that the Enemy has not extinguished. This spectacle appears to have been prov- identially arranged by the One as a sign of comfort to the Hobbits. The power and presence of evil may seem overwhelming, particularly in places like this to spite what was once good, but its apparent victory is not final. Indeed, it cannot be. As Tolkien himself said, in a letter quoted earlier, "All we do know, and that to a large extent by direct experience, is that evil labours with vast power and perpetual success – in vain: preparing only the soil for unexpected good to sprout in. So it is in general, and so it is in our lives" (Letter #64). This scene is a visual representation *in nuce* of that same philosophy of history, shaped as it is by Christian eschatology. The characters involved here obviously do not share that developed Christian framing—given the setting and Tolkien's dedication to its integrity—but they do present echoes of it.

The Trials of Minas Morgul

The three companions eventually arrive in the vicinity of Minas Morgul and find the secret path that Gollum told the Hobbits of. This arrival also means the first of three tests of Frodo's will, the first two of which are nonmoral. The first comes when Frodo looks upon Minas Morgul and finds himself strangely drawn to it. He cannot explain why, and his will cannot by itself override the footsteps he makes "as if some force were at work other than his own will" (IV/8). Gollum and Sam ultimately must save him from walking to the enemy's front door, as he was not prepared for this unanticipated trial.

The second comes after the army of Minas Morgul deploys. The Lord of the Nazgûl who commands these forces has declared the beginning of their march to Minas Tirith and an army beyond Frodo's reckoning issues forth. He and his companions had managed to find a hiding place near the upward path just in time to avoid detection. But something disturbs the Nazgûl. He senses what he thinks to be another power in his valley, where none had challenged him for nearly 1,000 years. Time elongates as the army halts, all is still and silent, and the Wraith-lord turns this way and that trying to determine what he is feeling. At the same time, Frodo feels the command to put on the Ring. Unlike the last trial, this was one Frodo was prepared for by past experience when the Wraith-lord himself stared him down and pressured him to put on the Ring in response to its call on his will. Here, they are not directly facing each other down, Frodo knows better, and he is clearly aware that the Ring would only reveal his hiding place. As such, "There was no longer any answer to that command in his own will, dismayed by terror though it was, and he felt only the beating upon him of a great power from outside" (IV/8). While he might not have had any such inclination to yield, still the narrator tells us that this other will, the will of the Ring, "took his hand, and as Frodo watched with his mind, not willing it but in suspense (as if he looked on some old story far away), it moved his hand inch by inch towards the chain upon his neck. Then his own will stirred; slowly it forced the hand back and set it to find another thing, a thing lying hidden near his breast" (IV/8).

I say this is a nonmoral trial for his will because it is again about the sheer power being exerted against him. His willpower is not being tested for his virtue. He is better able to resist because he has been in a similar situation before and so his will is now further hardened so that it does not cooperate with the other will. And this trial foreshadows the climax of the plot for this whole story. But since this is a lesser trial, Frodo is just able to do enough by the stirring of his will to resist the other will, and that by the empowerment of divine grace given to resist the temptation at a critical time (Letter #246). He is also helped by the fact that he keeps the Phial of Galadriel fairly close to the Ring, which distracts his attention and gives him something concrete to latch onto so that he can resist the other will just long enough for the Nazgûl to leave. And although he has not used that Phial to this point, it will prove essential for the journey ahead.

The third trial is a moral one because it concerns what he must do now. Frodo has seen the Lord of the Nazgûl fly out to war at the head of a massive army heading for Gondor. Now it seems that he is too late. So much, if not all, of everything behind him that he sought to save will surely be destroyed, even if his Quest succeeds. After he is overcome with weakness and sleeps in his hiding place, he faces a choice. He can give into despair and go wherever because despair would counsel him that nothing matters anymore. Or he can resolve by the strength of his heart to persevere and do what must be done, even if his best wishes now seem beyond fulfillment. Despite the complete loss of the *amdir* kind of hope, and thus being afflicted with despair in that sense, "He even smiled grimly feeling now as clearly as a moment before he had felt the opposite, that what he had to do, he had to do, if he could and that whether Faramir or Aragorn or Elrond or Galadriel or Gandalf or anyone else ever knew about it was beside the purpose" (IV/8).

Arguably, no decision that Frodo makes for the rest of his Quest is more courageous than this one to overcome his own despair and to have the courage to do what he must, whether or not anyone would know what he did. There is much that he does not know about what is going on beyond his Quest. He does not know that Aragorn instigated Sauron to make this move, which will prove hasty. He does not know that Gandalf has been resurrected and is organizing the resistance against Sauron to include creatures and realms beyond his knowledge. He does not know that his fellow Hobbits will play critical roles in saving his newest friend and vanquishing the enemy he just saw leave with seemingly insurmountable might. He does not know that Aragorn will play a decisive role in defeating this army he sees marching out. He does not know that all the living members of his Fellowship are out there doing their part in helping his Quest from afar.

Such knowledge would have made his choice easier and would have shown despair as more clearly the truly foolish way of thinking that it was, but the fact that he makes this decision in the face of despair and in spite of having such limited knowledge shows Frodo's undeniable courage in doing what is right. Providence will take up this just and courageous choice and guide it to a good end, in part by all these other events beyond Frodo's knowledge, in part by Frodo and Sam's efforts, and in part by an unexpected source thanks to Frodo's earlier choices.

Like in the Old Tales That Really Mattered

With Frodo thus resolved, the three companions make slow, dreary trip up the stairs of Cirith Ungol. They must ration their water during this climb, and they do not know when they will find drinkable water again. Everything about the land seems cursed, but as Frodo says, "so our path is laid." The dialogue that follows this is one of the parts that Tolkien regarded as most moving to him (Letter #96), and I will quote it in full before providing commentary:

> 'Yes, that's so,' said Sam. 'And we shouldn't be here at all, if we'd known more about it before we started. But I suppose it's often that way. The brave things in the old tales and songs, Mr. Frodo: adventures, as I used to call them. I used to think that they were things the wonderful folk of the stories went out and looked for, because they wanted them, because they were exciting and life was a bit dull, a kind of a sport, as you might say. But that's not the way of it with the tales that really mattered, or the ones that stay in the mind. Folk seem to have been just landed in them, usually—their paths were laid that way, as you put it. But I expect they had lots of chances, like us, of turning back, only they didn't. And if they had, we shouldn't know, because they'd have been for-gotten. We hear about those as just went on—and not all to a good end, mind you; at least not to what folk inside a story and not outside it call a good end. You know, coming home, and finding things all right, though not quite the same—like old Mr. Bilbo. But those aren't always the best tales to hear, though they may be the best tales to get landed in! I wonder what sort of tale we've fallen into?'
>
> 'I wonder,' said Frodo. 'But I don't know. And that's the way of a real tale. Take any one that you're fond of. You may know, or guess, what kind of a tale it is, happy-ending or sad-ending, but the people in it don't know. And you don't want them to.'
>
> 'No, sir, of course not. Beren now, he never thought he was going to get that Silmaril from the Iron Crown in Thangorodrim, and yet he did, and that was a worse place and a blacker danger than ours. But that's a long tale, of course, and goes on past the happiness and into grief and beyond it—and the Silmaril went on and came to Eärendil. And why, sir, I never thought of that before! We've got—you've got some of the light of it in that star-glass that the Lady gave you! Why, to think of it, we're in the same tale still! It's going on. Don't the great tales never end?' (IV/8)

This exchange embodies not only Tolkien's own thoughts about storytelling and how it functions in subcreation, for which the fairy-story is the best expression, but also facts of how humans think. Sam, in particular, shows here how stories shape our thinking because our minds are constructed for receiving stories, perceiving through stories, constructing stories, analyzing stories, applying stories, and so on. Indeed, narrative is foundational to human neurology and the sense of the self. Kay Young and Jeffrey L. Saver note that, "While we can be trained to think in geometrical shapes, patterns of sounds, poetry, movement, syllogisms, what predominates or fundamentally constitutes our consciousness is the understanding of self and world in story."[13] The so-called "default mode network" or "default state network" of the brain—which is activated in daydreaming, thinking of others, thinking of oneself, remembering the past, and planning for the future—operates in the construction and comprehension of narrative.[14] Neuroscientists have devoted extensive research into how the brain functions in understanding and producing story, and the theory of embodied cognition suggests that even more features of the person are involved in such processes.[15] Young and Saver posit:

> Narrative framing of the past allows predictions of the future; generating imaginary narratives allows the individual to safely (through internal fictions) explore the varied consequences of multitudinous response options. The potent adaptive value of narrative accounts for its primacy in organizing human understanding (as opposed to pictorial, musical, kinesthetic, syllogistic, or multiple other forms). Consciousness needs a narrative structure to create a sense of self based on the features of storytelling, like coherence, consequence, consecution.[16]

One can also see negative demonstration of this idea in neurological and psychological disorders manifesting in some form of narrative impairment.[17]

Shaun Gallagher argues that one of the foundations of hermeneutics is the storied self: "The self interprets itself (and gets interpreted by others) in narrative form; the meaning of a narrative or the narration of a meaningful event are subject to interpretation; actions may interpret narrative (and not only in theatrical performance), and are

---

[13] Kay Young and Jeffrey L. Saver, "The Neurology of Narrative," *SubStance* 30.94/95 (2001): 73.

[14] Lewis Mehl-Madrona and Barbara Mainguy, *Remapping Your Mind: The Neuroscience of Self-Transformation Through Story* (Rochester, VT; Toronto: Bear & Company, 2015), 2, 65–67.

[15] Mark E. Koltko-Rivera, "A Psychology of Worldviews," *Review of General Psychology* 8 (2004): 38–40; Mehl-Madrona and Mainguy, *Remapping*, 235–56; Tamer M. Soliman, Kathryn A. Johnson, and Hyunjin Song, "It's Not 'All in Your Head': Understanding Religion from an Embodied Cognition Perspective," *Perspectives on Psychological Science* 10 (2015): 852–64; Young and Saver, "Neurology," 72–84.

[16] Young and Saver, "Neurology," 78–79.

[17] Ibid., 76–78.

interpreted in narrative; and narrative often contributes to the interpretation of others, and vice versa."[18] Narrative also enables the narrator to relate himself/herself to their sense of time by means of a narrative's internal temporality—the order of events in the "plot" of the narrative—and external temporality—the narrator's temporal relation to the events in question.[19] Such a connection of events to the narrator allows the person to identify their relation to these events in terms of the events' meaning or significance (which may or may not include the causality of events).[20] Likewise, narrative enables the narrator to establish relations to others who function as characters in the narrative.

Beyond the self, narrative is also a key aspect of community formation in how it inherently objectivizes. Even in autobiography, the person's reference to "I" points to both the person telling the story and the person narrated within the context of the story (i.e., as an objective entity with whom the narrator identifies).[21] Worldview narratives in particular are crucial for the formation of a symbolic universe to which they orient people, through which they guide people, and in which they enable people to develop identity and a sense of ethics. These narratives have what David K. Naugle calls, "a kind of finality as the ultimate interpretation of reality," which in turn serve powerfully to integrate the community both as a community and in relation to the world.[22]

We have discussed Tolkien's theology of sub-creation elsewhere, and his most extensive exploration in "On Fairy-Stories" is particularly apt here. It is not for nothing that he observed how apropos it was for God to redeem his creatures through a story, the good story. And it is shown to be the good story by the enactment of the eucatastrophe on the historical plane, whereby the Creator gives Primary Reality to what is represented with Secondary Reality in a proper fairy-story. Likewise the gospel story is the central and orienting story for theology and ethics in the NT, as our lives should be characterized by making the gospel story our story. It is the story we are all part of in some way. Even as it is rooted in larger stories of God and creation, God and humans, God and Israel, and so on (particularly as articulated in the OT), this story being their

---

[18] Shaun Gallagher, "Self and Narrative," in *The Routledge Companion to Hermeneutics*, ed. Jeff Malpas and Hans-Helmuth Gander (Abingdon, U.K.: Routledge: 2014), 404. See also Mehl-Madrona, *Remapping*, 67–72.

[19] Gallagher, "Self," 404. See also Peter L. Berger and Thomas Luckmann, *The Social Construction of Reality: A Treatise in the Sociology of Knowledge* (Garden City, NY: Doubleday, 1966), 103.

[20] Gallagher, "Self," 405.

[21] Ibid., 409.

[22] David K. Naugle, *Worldview: The History of a Concept* (Grand Rapids: Eerdmans, 2002), 303. See also James W. Sire, *Naming the Elephant: Worldview as a Concept*, 2nd ed. (Downers Grove, IL: InterVarsity Press, 2015), 119–25.

culmination allows us also to perceive where we are in relation to the larger stories we are involved in, and to get a sense of what kind of tale we are in. As with others in the stories that mattered, we simply find ourselves part of one that is already going, and we have choices to make as to what kind of part we will play.

It is also noteworthy in this conversation how Sam locates them as part of a larger story. The story of *LOTR* was, of course, designed to be part of a larger story that would be provided by *The Silmarillion* that Tolkien never finished to his satisfaction. The story that Sam references to frame their own is part of *The Silmarillion* and it is, in fact, ongoing, even after Beren and Lúthien have left the stage. It was because of that story, albeit by more twists and turns, that Eärendil came to possess one of the Silmarils and found salvation for Middle-earth in the First Age. And that same light of the Silmaril is what Frodo has a reflection of in the water contained in the Phial of Galadriel. And without that light, they could never pass through what is coming and into Mordor. Thus has the Author written them into a story much larger than themselves and guided it so that events so far in the past should have such beneficial effects for those appointed for this Quest now.

The reference to this particular story is notable not only as a key piece of the larger story of *The Silmarillion*, but also because, as Sam hints, of how it resonates with the story they are in. As Tolkien explained in Letter #131 to show how his grand story is woven together:

> Here [in the story of Beren and Lúthien] we meet, among other things, the first example of the motive (to become dominant in Hobbits) that the great policies of world history, 'the wheels of the world', are often turned not by the Lords and Governors, even gods, but by the seemingly unknown and weak – owing to the secret life in creation, and the part unknowable to all wisdom but One, that resides in the intrusions of the Children of God into the Drama.

We have already noted the biblical and theological consonances of this theme previously, and this note shows just how deeply ingrained the theme is in Tolkien's story. In addition to the language that is clearly meant to be reminiscent of statements we have noted in earlier books of *LOTR* to frame the Quest of these Hobbits, the story of Beren and Lúthien has many more links with *LOTR*, including the line of the kings of Númenor from which Aragorn comes, the love of Aragorn and Arwen reiterating the love of Beren and Lúthien, the fact that Elrond exists and is part of a family that can choose whether they want to partake of the fates of mortals or immortals, and so on we could go. What is of particular relevance to this story, as Sam indicates, is that it involves an outlaw mortal and an Elf maiden—as well as Huan, the goodest of good boys—succeeding where entire armies led by the greatest Elf heroes had failed and would continue to fail. They themselves reclaimed a Silmaril from the Iron Crown of Melkor himself in the midst of his impregnable fortress. And now two Hobbits will need to find a way into the realm of the Enemy—where the Wise, the Great, and all the forces at their command could not go—to complete a seemingly impossible mission.

Response of Creation

Frodo and Sam continue discussing what they expect of their story and how others will tell it. This dialogue does not require further comment beyond what we have already noted. But the narration provides an interesting detail that is noteworthy. In response to what Sam has been saying about how others will tell the story of Frodo, he laughs, "a long clear laugh from his heart. Such a sound had not been heard in those places since Sauron came to Middle-earth. To Sam suddenly it seemed as if all the stones were listening and the tall rocks leaning over them" (IV/8).

This shows a glimpse of the delivering joy that good stories can bring, in that they reflect (in however fragmentary and refracted a fashion) *the* good story. This is another aspect of eucatastrophe as the crowning aspect of the fairy-story that Tolkien especially emphasizes. It is in this regard that such stories represent *evangelium*. Frodo is in a most depressed and depressing landscape, but through story and the presentation of his own life and mission as part of a good story, he can transcend that context, if only for a little while. The motif we have observed to this point of relief and deliverance being expressed in laughter thus continues here.

Moreover, the response of creation is remarkable. The landscape is almost personified in response to the laughter that had not been heard there in thousands of years, which makes it a most curious and attractive sound. It reminds us that in this era of imaginary history, as in the present age, that creation is enslaved to decay/corruption and is eagerly awaiting the freedom of the glory of the children of God, which will be the redemption of their bodies, for creation will share in this redemption when it also will be renewed (Rom 8:19–23). This fits with a larger biblical motif of how creation responds when God acts in judgment and salvation (besides the story of the exodus and the judgments of Revelation, see Lev 18:25–28; Pss 96:11–13; 97:1–6; 98:7–9; 107:25–29; 114; 148; Isa 44:23; 55:12–13; Jer 4:23–26). Here, it is more of a reaction at simple joy that this land has been devoid of hearing for far too long.

Redemption so Near and Now so Far

After this conversation between Frodo and Sam ends, and Gollum is nowhere to be seen, they decide to sleep while they can. Gollum returns to find them still asleep. The scene that follows is another that Tolkien listed as among the most moving passages in his story (Letters #96 and #165; cf. Letter #246),[23] but for a different reason than the other one noted previously. Again, I shall quote it in full:

> Gollum looked at them. A strange expression passed over his lean hungry face. The gleam faded from his eyes, and they went dim and grey, old and tired. A spasm of pain seemed to twist him, and he turned away, peering back up towards the pass, shaking his head, as if engaged in some interior debate. Then he came back, and slowly putting out a trembling hand, very cautiously he touched Frodo's knee—but almost the touch was a caress. For a fleeting moment, could one of the sleepers have seen him, they would have thought that they beheld an old weary hobbit, shrunken by the years that had carried him far beyond his time, beyond friends and kin, and the fields and streams of youth, an old starved pitiable thing.
>
> But at that touch Frodo stirred and cried out softly in his sleep, and immediately Sam was wide awake. The first thing he saw was Gollum—'pawing at master,' as he thought.
> 'Hey you!' he said roughly. 'What are you up to?'
> 'Nothing, nothing,' said Gollum softly. 'Nice Master!'
> 'I daresay,' said Sam. 'But where have you been to—sneaking off and sneaking back, you old villain?'
> Gollum withdrew himself, and a green glint flickered under his heavy lids. Almost spider-like he looked now, crouched back on his bent limbs, with his protruding eyes. The fleeting moment had passed, beyond recall. (IV/8)

Gollum is only here because of the pity of Frodo, and this moment represents what could have been the culmination of that pity. Gollum is internally conflicted, hence the part of him that still desires friendship, kindness, love, and to be the simple Hobbit he used to be once more could be called to the forefront at times, even if only for a moment. This happened when he encountered Bilbo, it had happened again when he swore to serve Frodo, and it is happening again here in spite of his contrary designs to this point. The book later indicates that Gollum had gone off to talk with Shelob to get her agreement to his scheme. And so this scene is Sméagol, on the verge of having his plan

---

[23] Also see the unpublished letter to Baronne A. Baeyens referenced earlier: https://www.manhattan-rarebooks.com/pages/books/2144/j-r-r-tolkien/autograph-letter-signed-als-typed-letter-signed-tls.

come to fruition, possibly reneging and doing right by the one he calls "Master." But this possible eucatastrophe in Sméagol's story of redemption is thwarted at the key moment by Sam's typically rough words for him. His appearance shifts again from being, "an old weary hobbit, shrunken by the years that had carried him far beyond his time, beyond friends and kin, and the fields and streams of youth, an old starved pitiable thing," to a spider-like creature, "crouched back on his bent limbs, with his protruding eyes." Most hauntingly of all, Tolkien says, "The fleeting moment had passed, beyond recall." This is the point at which Sméagol comes the closest he has ever been to redemption, and Sam has practically ensured that he will never go beyond that point again. While the eucatastrophe of the whole story will show how Providence turns this event to a good end, the audience is left to wonder what could have happened if Sam had not been so rough toward Sméagol, if his typical treatment of him did not come at the worst possible time (Tolkien himself thought through such a scenario in Letter #246).[24] Sam may be the chief hero of this story, but in this action he has pushed another further away from redemption, despite that one's desperate need for it. The one time after this that Sam tries to be more merciful toward Sméagol proves to be too late because he did not recognize the time when it was right (of course, we will address that later in Book VI).

Unfortunately, this is all too in-character for Sam, as Tolkien explained well in Letter #246:

> Sam was cocksure, and deep down a little conceited; but his conceit had been transformed by his devotion to Frodo. He did not think of himself as heroic or even brave, or in any way admirable – except in his service and loyalty to his master. That had an ingredient (probably inevitable) of pride and possessiveness: it is difficult to exclude it from the devotion of those who perform such service. In any case it prevented him from fully understanding the master that he loved, and from following him in his gradual education to the nobility of service to the unlovable and of perception of damaged good in the corrupt. He plainly did not fully understand Frodo's motives or his distress in the incident of the Forbidden Pool. If he had understood better what was going on between Frodo and Gollum, things might have turned out differently in the end.... His repentance is blighted and all Frodo's pity is (in a sense) wasted. Shelob's lair became inevitable.

Indeed, Sam's protectiveness of Frodo, which has always been his chief concern in the Quest, has at times been overweening and gotten one or both of them into trouble.

---

[24] See also Tolkien, *Sauron Defeated*, 5.

It was so when he almost drowned himself in the Anduin. And it was so when he inadvertently revealed the fact that Frodo has the One Ring to Faramir. Now it has again proven dangerous for them as well as excessively damaging to Sméagol, thereby quelling any second thoughts he had about his murderous intentions for the sake of his Precious.

This story resonates with many stories—fictional and non-fictional—of redemption and failed redemption, of teetering on the edge of salvation or destruction until one action or one remark pushes the person over that edge, one way or the other. Tolkien himself said that Gollum's failure to repent when interrupted by Sam, "seems to me really like the *real* world in which the instruments of just retribution are seldom themselves just or holy; and the good are often stumbling blocks" (Letter #165; emphasis original). This quote is reminiscent of the prominent emphasis on verisimilitude and the inner consistency of reality in Tolkien's theology of sub-creation. The scene is true to the character dynamics involved in the story itself and it is true to stories from the Primary World (as should be clear from Tolkien's comments on scandals in the Church in Letter #250).

Who is to say how many opportunities for redemption have been thwarted because the righteous have been stumbling blocks along the path? How many times has someone pronounced a bad name on someone else and that person has responded by sinking to the occasion when they could have been ready to rise to a different one? When we consider the fact that the story will ultimately end with Gollum saving Middle-earth in spite of himself, it calls to mind other stories when what we intend for ill has nevertheless resulted in good (as we have noted elsewhere). And this scene is especially effective at raising the perpetual inquiry of "What if?" While Sam, like others in similar situations, is not primarily responsible for another person's failure to repent, it certainly does not help when one is a stumbling block in the way of repentance through conduct that one thinks is righteous (in Sam's case, righteous indignation and protectiveness). Such events make one ask questions like, "What if I had responded differently?" "What if I had been more charitable?" Likewise, the scene reminds us that, even for a character who could be despicable like Gollum, there is a person underneath the evil, a person who still has a chance for redemption, potentially for as long as he draws breath. When mercy meets the repentance of the evil one, a powerful act of deliverance can take place.

Instead, the tragedy of the tale will continue. After some bickering following Gollum's indignation at Sam's accusation after all he has done for him and Frodo, Gollum leads the two Hobbits up to the entrance of a cave. At this point, Frodo thinks to release

Sméagol from his service to go wherever he wishes and do what he wishes, thereby keeping his word. But he does not realize what transpired while he slept and that this was not the liberation that Sméagol needed, nor is it one that he wants, as he insists that he must continue to guide them through the dark caves ahead. And he will indeed guide them, albeit to a peril that they could not fathom.

A Light in the Darkness

The cave they enter leads them to a darkness unlike any they have experienced before. It blocked out even the memory of light and colors. So thick was the dark vapor that sound fell dead. And in the midst of this darkness, the only one who could possibly guide the Hobbits has left them. They are trapped in the lair of Shelob, the last of Ungoliant's children in Middle-earth. Ungoliant herself took a massive spider form and was once an ally of Melkor, Sauron's lord, and assisted him by consuming the light of the Two Trees of Valinor and poisoning them so that they could not be renewed (save by their light captured in the Silmarils). The power she received from Melkor combined with the power she received from draining the light and belching forth her "unlight" made her dangerous even for him, and she threatened to eat him when he withheld the Silmarils from her all-consuming maw. She was prevented from doing so when Melkor's piercing screams called forth the Balrogs who drove her off. After she had mated with the spiders of Middle-earth to produce offspring like Shelob and the spiders Beren had to fight off in Nan Dungortheb before he ever met Lúthien, it is said that she ultimately consumed herself in her unremitting hunger.

Like her mother, Shelob is no servant of the Dark Lord, but she is not even an intentional ally to Sauron. Yet their purposes tend to align in that neither of them want anyone to come through her lair and out the other side. She desires to dwell in deep darkness, and Sauron keeps his realm dark even outside of her lair. She may not obey his will, but Sauron could not have asked for a better guard on this obscure entrance into his realm. Unaided, even great heroes would most likely become her next meal that she would greatly desire to replace the Orcs she eats more regularly. None had ever escaped her webs, and the Hobbits surely would have been her next victims, if not for the unexpected implements they carried.

In a moment of inspiration, Galadriel appears like a Marian figure in Sam's mind to remind him of the light Frodo has:

> Then, as he stood, darkness about him and a blackness of despair and anger
> in his heart, it seemed to him that he saw a light: a light in his mind, almost

unbearably bright at first, as a sun-ray to the eyes of one long hidden in a win-
dowless pit. Then the light became colour: green, gold, silver, white. Far off, as
in a little picture drawn by elven-finders, he saw the Lady Galadriel standing
on the grass in Lórien, and gift were in her hands. *And you, Ring-bearer*, he
heard her say, remote but clear, *for you I have prepared this.* (IV/9)

Thus, he is reminded of the Phial of Galadriel he had mentioned in their earlier
conversation. It was a reflection of the brightest star in the sky, being the light of a
Silmaril. And by the guidance of Providence, it is brought here as the light that can
overcome this impenetrable darkness. When Frodo pulls out the Phial, he also has a
moment of inspiration as he says words he does not understand to declare the power of
this relic, "*Aiya Eärendil Elenion Ancalima!* he cried, and knew not what he had spoken; for it seemed that another voice spoke through his, clear, untroubled by the foul
air of the pit" (IV/9). This other voice is guiding him by inspiration to grow in courage.
As the eyes he sees in the distance attempt to creep closer, he invokes the name of
Galadriel and gathers his courage to lift the Phial and to use his Elvish dagger Sting,
which unlike most swords can cleave through her webs with relative ease. He even
dares to press towards the eyes with the Phial in one hand and Sting in the other. Shelob
had never been confronted with such light in her lair, and she was dismayed, beating
her retreat in an attempt to outmaneuver this courageous prey that would not go easily.

By Shelob's cunning work of tunneling over the long years, she is able to outmaneuver them while Sam holds the Phial and Frodo holds Sting. Frodo is able to get
ahead of Sam as the one cleaving the path for them, but she is able to jab Frodo with a
sting to the neck above his invulnerable mithril shirt while Gollum restrains Sam. He
had planned to let Shelob eat Frodo while he killed Sam, and he would attempt to reclaim the Ring when she spat it out. But Sam would not be so easily subdued. Between
fury at Gollum's treachery and his desperation to save Frodo, he proved much stronger
than Gollum expected. Sam eventually escapes, causes Gollum to flee, and makes a
desperate charge at the most formidable foe he will ever encounter.

The Courage of Samwise Gamgee

Sam has shown his stout heart many times over the course of this story in his service
to Frodo. But no instance better demonstrates that courage and provided the purest example of the northern spirit of courage that so interested Tolkien (Letter #45) than his
charge against Shelob:

> Sam did not wait to wonder what was to be done, or whether he was brave, or loyal, or filled with rage. He sprang forward with a yell, and seized his master's sword in his left hand. Then he charged. No onslaught more fierce was ever seen in the savage world of beasts, where some desperate small creature armed with little teeth, alone, will spring upon a tower of horn and hide that stands above its fallen mate. (IV/10)

His unyielding and unhesitating will pushing him forward to do what he must, no matter the odds or the cost, vividly exemplifies what one can find of the courage of servants in Old English classics. We have already noted that Sam is akin to Wiglaf serving the hero Beowulf. But he is also like the retinue of Beorhtnoth in *The Battle of Maldon*. They were put in an impossible situation by their master's approach to battle as sport and his desire for a greater share of glory and honor. After he died and much of his army had fled, the remaining courageous ones rallied to die inevitable but heroic deaths on the battlefield. The most notable lines come from Beorhtwold/Byrhtwold, who had long served Beorhtnoth, as he admonished those who remained on the field, "Each mind shall be the sterner, heart the bolder, each our spirit greater as our strength lessens!"[25] Tolkien thought that the quote is older than even the event referenced: "Byrhtwold probably spoke these exact words because they were either proverbial or a familiar quotation."[26]

Tolkien provided his own commentary on these lines in his essay "Ofermod":

> The words of Beorhtwold have been held to be the finest expression of the northern heroic spirit, Norse or English; the clearest statement of the doctrine of uttermost endurance in the service of indomitable will. The poem as a whole has been called 'the only purely heroic poem extant in Old English'. Yet the doctrine appears in this clarity, and (approximate) purity, precisely because it is put in the mouth of a subordinate, a man for whom the object of his will was decided by another, who had no responsibility downwards, only loyalty upwards. Personal pride was therefore in him at its lowest, and love and loyalty at their highest.
>
> For this 'northern heroic spirit' is never quite pure; it is of gold and an alloy. Unalloyed it would direct a man to endure even death unflinching, when necessary: that is when death may help the achievement of some object of will, or when life can only be purchased by denial of what one stands for. But since such conduct is held admirable, the alloy of personal good name was never

---

[25] Tolkien, *Battle of Maldon*, 67 (ll. 309–313). Compare to this description from later in the story of Sam: "His weariness was growing but his will hardened all the more" (IV/10).

[26] Tolkien, *Battle of Maldon.*, 81.

wholly absent. Thus Leofsunu in *The Battle of Maldon* holds himself to his loyalty by the fear of reproach if he returns home alive. This motive may, of course, hardly go beyond 'conscience': self-judgement in the light of the opinion of his peers, to which the 'hero' himself wholly assents; he would act the same, if there were no witnesses. Yet this element of pride, in the form of the desire for honour and glory, in life and after death, tends to grow, to become a chief motive, driving a man beyond the bleak heroic necessity to excess—to chivalry. 'Excess' certainly, even if it be approved by contemporary opinion, when it not only goes beyond need and duty, but interferes with it.[27]

For the servants like Wiglaf in *Beowulf* and the retinue here, they best embody what in Greek was described in terms of πίστις or πιστός—that is, they embody courage in the forms of fidelity, allegiance, and steadfast loyalty. In Tolkien's words, "It is the heroism of obedience and love not of pride or wilfulness that is the most heroic and the most moving,"[28] which is what these servants, including Samwise Gamgee, exemplify. They, even more than the more well-known heroes, thus showed how this virtue was preparation for the gospel and the perseverance called for among the faithful to embody the gospel story. The Christian framework thus provides the fulfillment that brings this virtue to fruition, including in supplying the final victory—via participation in Christ's victory—that was not possible in the old worldview narrative.

Without the special implements Frodo had received for his Quest by the various orchestrations of Providence, Sam could not have triumphed in this battle with a foe beyond his worst nightmares. But without his courage in service to another, he would have never been able to use them either. His indomitable will to withstand her attack ultimately led to her extending herself to bring about her own demise. While her hide had grown so tough that not even the strongest arms with the best weapons forged in Middle-earth might have pierced her, her own strength used in dropping her entire weight to crush Sam was enough to impale herself on the dagger. None had ever wounded her so severely, and in spite she thought to spring one last time to tear him limb from limb.

But once more inspiration comes to Sam, "as if some remote voice had spoken" (IV/10), and thus he brings forth the Phial of Galadriel. He invokes the name of Galadriel as Frodo had done, but he adds to it the invocation of Elbereth that he had heard from the Elves. At this point, he begins to speak in a tongue he does not know:

> *A Elbereth Gilthoniel*

---

[27] Ibid., 28–29.

[28] Tolkien, *Battle of Maldon*, 32.

> *o menel palan-diriel,*
> *le nallon si di'nguruthos!*
> *A tiro nin, Fanuilos!*[29] (IV/10)

In response to this invocation, and perhaps spurred on by the fire of Sam's enkindled courage, the star-glass burns brighter than ever, and so Shelob is cowed, defeated, and pressed into withdrawal. Thus, Sam has triumphed in this battle by grace. That is, there is here a combination of the common grace of the seed of courage given to the Hobbits that has been cultivated by this Quest, the special grace of extra courage given to Sam for the purpose of his work on this Quest, the gift of Sting to Frodo from Bilbo (which itself was a gift to him), the gift of the Phial of Galadriel to Frodo (itself a still potent fruit of divine providence from long ago), and even the gift of being able to speak in a tongue he did not know (thereby anticipating the gift of speaking in tongues). Sam's "indomitable spirit" (IV/10), which is of course part of the gift of his very life, put such gifts to work, as he, the instrument of Providence that he is, brought such grace to bear for the protection of Frodo and the salvation of the Quest.

The Choices of Master Samwise

Sam attempts to stir Frodo, but Frodo is so unresponsive that Sam believes Shelob's sting was fatal. He now faces a decision of what to do next with Frodo seemingly dead. He does not believe he's the proper person to carry the Ring, but he remembers that Frodo and Bilbo also were seemingly not right and proper for such a task, "They didn't choose themselves" (IV/10). He tries to convince himself that someone needs to carry the Ring to Mount Doom, and he is the only one who can do so now. He takes the Ring and says goodbye to the master he thinks dead, but "what he was doing was altogether against the grain of his nature" (IV/10). Here, then, we see why Sam would not make a good Ring-bearer. His courage was what it was because it was in service of another. He was so bent to do all that he had done for someone else that he could not lead on such a Quest, much less do it all on his own. He is not immune to the power of the Ring, as we see him rather unintentionally find himself putting on the Ring when Orcs approach. The first chapter of Book VI will also show that the Ring can still do its work

---

[29] According to Letter #211, this can be translated as,
"O Elbereth Starkindler
from heaven gazing afar,
to thee I cry now in the shadow of (the fear of) death!
O look towards me, Everwhite!"

on his mind, even if his deeply ingrained humility helps him in the struggle. But his real weakness as a Ring-bearer is that he cannot let go of Frodo. Like Beorhtnoth's retinue, he would rather die with him, "He flung the Quest and all his decisions away, and fear and doubt with them. He knew now where his place was and had been: at his master's side, though what he could do there was not clear. Back he ran down the steps, down the path towards Frodo" (IV/10).

Sam again embodies what we have seen elsewhere, that "Greater love has no one than this, that a person will lay down his life for his friends" (John 15:13, NASB). And so Sam is willing to do even after his master has died, just to keep the Orcs from desecrating his body, if nothing else. But while he wears the Ring, he is able to overhear the conversation between the Orcs, whereby he learns that Frodo is not actually dead. He is not even mostly dead. He has simply been paralyzed by Shelob's sting for what would have been a fresh and pliant meal.

Sam thus chides himself, "You fool, he isn't dead, and your heart knew it. Don't trust your head, Samwise, it is not the best part of you. The trouble with you is that you never really had any hope" (IV/10). Sam is scolding himself for what is a deficiency of *estel*, hope in what cannot be pieced together by the senses, but which transcends the empirical. In the absence of it, he tried to move on by his own thinking and by his own strength, only to find that it was not enough. In the end, he was right that he could not leave Frodo, as he never meant to do from the beginning. But even the decision he made when it seemed like there really was no hope of Frodo's recovery will be taken up by Providence and turned to a good end, as he can ensure that the Enemy will not take the Ring for as long as he bears it.

Unfortunately, his initial act of leaving Frodo will mean that Frodo will be taken by the Orcs to the Tower of Cirith Ungol and held prisoner there. Sam is not in a position to save him and fails in his attempt at the end of the book. Frodo was alive but taken by the Enemy.

CHAPTER EIGHT

Commentary on Book V

Arrival in Gondor

With the next book, we are returned to the storylines of the rest of the Fellowship, beginning with Gandalf and Pippin as they arrive at Minas Tirith. The greatest city of the Free Peoples is preparing for war, including by sending out calls for aid to the rest of Gondor and to Rohan. The soldiers are also attempting to bolster the recently built fortification of the Rammas Echor, the extensive perimeter wall encompassing the Pelennor Fields set out miles from the city. This is where Gandalf and Pippin encounter Ingold, a leader of the guards. He says Gandalf is, of course, allowed to pass through, as he is known and knows all the passwords, but he is hesitant to let Pippin go with him as they are generally not allowing strangers in, "unless they be mighty men of arms in whose faith and help we can trust" (V/1). We see again the use of "faith" that is in line with the broader biblical range of use for the Hebrew and Greek equivalents, here referring to fidelity and trustworthiness. Gandalf insists that he can vouch for Pippin. Although Ingold may doubt Pippin's valor, Gandalf reminds him that this cannot be measured by stature and that he has gone through more and worse perils than Ingold himself has. He even calls him a very valiant man.

Pippin stirs to protest Gandalf's characterization, "I am a hobbit and no more valiant than I am a man, save perhaps now and again by necessity. Do not let Gandalf deceive you" (V/1). Ingold replies, "Many a doer of great deeds might say no more" (V/1). This combines insights we have seen elsewhere in the story that it is wisdom that recognizes necessity and courage that acts in recognition of it to do what must be done. Such are the trials by which divine providence cultivates the seeds of both of these virtues God has sown in his creations.

Ingold then lets both of them pass and hopes that Gandalf will bring good counsel to Denethor, but he has a similar concern as voiced by Théoden and Gríma that "you come with tidings of grief and danger, as is your wont, they say" (V/1). He does not take this accusation as far as Gríma in naming him *Láthspell*, but it is clearly something that people of multiple realms have noted. As in Rohan, Gandalf says this is not because of him but because of the times, for he rarely comes when his help is not needed. Although I think the correlation of Gandalf with either prophets or the prophetic office of Christ is overstated or overaccentuated, this is one respect in which it holds true. Micaiah and Jeremiah are only the most vivid examples of true prophets seemingly being doomsayers, when it is more the case that they come and speak when they are needed most. We have little record of their oracles or other speeches from times of peace and plenty, either because those messages were not as important for posterity, or because they did not speak prophetically as often, or maybe some measure of both. It is when the people of God face some kind of crisis that they most need to be heard from. And so people like Ahab and Zedekiah came to think that it was their wont to come with tidings of grief and danger, that something was wrong with them, when in fact it was because of the times they lived, times made bad and ever worse by people like Ahab and Zedekiah, that they spoke the message of God that was as dire as it was.

And as with the prophets, Gandalf's counsel is not one of some simple doom and gloom, for he also speaks encouragement and calls to the way out. In this case, he tells Ingold that the repairs to the Rammas Echor are too late, "Courage will now be your best defence against the storm that is at hand—that and such hope as I bring" (V/1). Courage, as we have already noted, is a common grace of the One, and it is one that is cultivated by response to situations where it is required to do what must be done in the face of obstacles of fear and doubt. But courage cannot assure triumph here. Hope is also needed, hope that comes from beyond the realm of Gondor. That is what Gandalf seeks to enkindle by his presence and his counsel. In this way, he is like Aragorn, the one known as Estel, the kindler of hope. And it is to Aragorn that he will point as the instrument of Providence to bring to fulfillment the long-held hope of Gondor. Yet, there is an even more significant hope beyond him, as the ultimate hope of victory in this war depends on two Hobbits that come from far beyond Gondor—and far beyond their reckoning—who are on a Quest into the heart of Mordor.

We have commented elsewhere on the relation of hope and courage. To summarize, they meet in perseverance while working from different directions. Courage can be said to motivate perseverance by pushing it forward in required action. Hope can be said to motivate perseverance by pulling it forward to its goal.

Apparent Power and Wisdom vs. Higher Power and Wisdom

After Gandalf and Pippin pass through the seven levels of Minas Tirith, they come to the hall of Denethor, the steward of Gondor, father of Boromir and Faramir. Denethor is, in fact, a wise man and had been a great leader that few of the stewards in Gondor's history could rival. He not only has insight concerning the history of his kingdom and in preparing operations pertaining to the protection of that kingdom, but he also has insight into people, as Gandalf says, "He can perceive, if he bends his will thither, much of what is passing in the minds of men, even of those that dwell far off. It is difficult to deceive him, and dangerous to try" (V/1). I have not partially titled this section "Apparent Power and Wisdom" to imply that the wisdom of Denethor or the power he projects are only a false appearance, but to indicate that his power and wisdom are more visible, more immediately impactful than his foil. But for reasons we will review later, he has become akin to Saruman. He has not betrayed the Free Peoples by making any secret alliance with Sauron, but he has given himself over to counsels of despair.

This has become more severely the case since he learned of Boromir's death. Boromir was his favorite son, and that was obvious to all. Such was his affection for his dead son that he tells Gandalf, "But though all the signs forebode that the doom of Gondor is drawing nigh, less now to me is that darkness than my own darkness" (V/1). This is a common effect of despair in amplifying one's own troubles and making them seem as if they are the worst that has happened to anyone simply because they are the ones most immediately felt by oneself. Even a wise man like Denethor can lose all sense of perspective. But in this case, despair had simply greased the slope for Denethor's descent. He had already come to have a myopic view of Gondor so as to despise "lesser men" and to see his lot as "Gondor against the rest" (Letter #183).

Between such myopia, now fueled by despair, and the store of his own wisdom and his clear projection of power, he is a foil for Gandalf. That should be apparent from all that we have noted about Gandalf to this point, but it is also made clear by their first conversation in this chapter. On the one hand, Pippin perceives in the course of this conversation that there is something higher about Gandalf, despite the impression Denethor makes, "Denethor looked indeed much more like a great wizard than Gandalf did, more kingly, beautiful, and powerful; and older. Yet by a sense other than sight Pippin perceived that Gandalf had the greater power and the deeper wisdom, and a majesty that was veiled" (V/1). Gandalf embodies that higher wisdom by his incarnate limitations that were supposed to remind him of the nature of his mission not to compel others by his superior power, by his faithfulness to that mission, and by his declaration of higher wisdom throughout this story that has the appearance of foolishness to the world (as the gospel itself will appear as foolishness to the world).

On the other hand, one particular piece of the conversation highlights how Gandalf shows a higher wisdom than Denethor's because he is concerned not only for Gondor, but also for other realms of the Free Peoples as well. As he says:

> But I will say this: the rule of no realm is mine, neither of Gondor nor any other, great or small. But all worthy things that are in peril, as the world now stands, those are my care. And for my part, I shall not wholly fail of my task, though Gondor should perish, if anything passes through this night that can still grow fair or bear fruit and flower again in days to come. For I also am a steward. Did you not know? (V/1)

Gandalf's mission is as an itinerant minister—or steward, in his words—across Middle-earth, in service to a higher Authority. He was sent for the help of this continent in general, and so he cannot be faithful to his mission and myopic at the same time. He also knows better than to think that victory in battle for Gondor will mean victory for all. First, he knows the war has a broader scope and that others have their own troubles. Second, more importantly, he knows that ultimate victory will not be achieved by strength of arms, even if that factor is not irrelevant in holding out until victory can be achieved by other means, as we have highlighted previously in the relationship between hope, courage, and ultimate or final victory.

Gandalf's Joy

Pippin also notes something else about Gandalf after this conversation is finished. After Gandalf laughs with him, the narrator tells us, "Yet in the wizard's face he saw at first only lines of care and sorrow; though as he looked more intently he perceived that under all there was a great joy: a fountain of mirth enough to set a kingdom laughing, were it to gush forth" (V/1). Gandalf has such joy because his source of joy is transcendent. He can, of course, enjoy the world around him, and circumstances affect how he feels, the same as anyone, but the joy remains through it all because its source is beyond this world. And if ever that transcendent joy from "beyond the walls of the world" (as Tolkien phrases it in "On Fairy-Stories") were to come forth, it would be as a great fountain of mirth abundant enough to refresh a kingdom, as will indeed come true later in this story.

We thus see reflected here how joy is an internal disposition that is not always expressed outwardly in obvious ways like mirth. Nor is it restricted to a feeling responding to good circumstances. As there can be joy in the midst of suffering (e.g., Jas 1:2–4), Gandalf has joy even as his face might convey otherwise. Joy is a characteristic he has that is inherently connected with *estel*, since both transcend present circumstances and have their source and object in the same One who is beyond the walls of the world (cf. Rom 15:13; Gal 5:22). Gandalf brings or will bring both because he is a minister of the same.

Pippin's Hope

In the midst of this opening conversation, Pippin swears fealty to Denethor, offering his services to the steward of Gondor in honor of how Boromir gave his life to protect him. He is thus made a guard of Minas Tirith and is linked with Beregond, with whom he becomes fast friends. After Beregond shows Pippin around, they discuss the prospects of the war before the reinforcements from elsewhere in Gondor arrive. Beregond even asks Pippin if he sees any hope that they will withstand the great blow that is coming from Sauron. Pippin thinks of his journey thus far, and he even blanches for a moment after faintly perceiving the flight of a Nazgûl somewhere far off. But when Pippin realizes this was only momentary, he states confidently, "No, my heart will not yet despair. Gandalf fell and has returned and is with us. We may stand, if only on one leg, or at least be left still upon our knees" (V/1).

Pippin's hope is linked to something visible, but its source is ultimately invisible. That is, he has seen Gandalf come back from the dead. If the same One who resurrected him from the dead and empowered him further is still at work in guiding his mission, then surely there is reason to hope beyond what one can see. That is only the most dramatic example of divine providence, wherein even death could not stop the purpose of the One, but it is hardly the only one Pippin has seen in his journey. There were the several instances he saw when he was part of the Quest. He has also seen it in how he and Merry were conveyed in the nick of time to Fangorn, where they had no plan of going, and that arrival in turn set off the fall of Isengard by providential orchestration, in which Gandalf's return from death itself was crucial. And even when things have seemingly gone wrong, as in his decision to look into the *palantír*, that has mysteriously been taken up and turned to the good. The armies that arrive to reinforce the defense of Minas Tirith may be disappointing in their size, but this will yet be beneficial for reasons beyond what Pippin or anyone else can perceive at the time. There may be no guarantee of how well preserved the Free Peoples will be in the struggle that is coming, but there is reason to trust that, somehow, they will still be standing if the One is still at work. The next day, there will be no dawn, and the days will be dark for some time, yet hope will still come beyond sight. Until such a time, courage and perseverance will be needed to see it come to pass.

Paths Appointed

The story then shifts to the rest of the former Fellowship back in Rohan. They are discussing the path ahead. Aragorn does not necessarily plan to ride with Théoden, but he does plan to go to Minas Tirith, although he does not yet see how he will go there. He simply knows that he must because "An hour long prepared approaches" (V/2). He may not know the way, but he trusts that it will be shown to him because he trusts in the larger plan that he has been incorporated into. This has been clear about his character since Book I. Estel is not only one of his names; it is a central characteristic, as is signified through statements like this and the action he has taken in light of that trust.

Another evidence of providence is in the timing of the solution thus provided to Aragorn's uncertainty. Rangers from the North, accompanied by Elladan and Elrohir, Elrond's sons, have come to find Aragorn in answer to a summons, and they have found him in the nick of time. But Aragorn says that he did not summon them, "save only in wish" (V/2). Unlike the earlier example of the Council of Elrond, where no such summons went out, there was a summons for the Rangers. It is said later in the chapter that Galadriel was the one who summoned them (she was the one who spoke through Gandalf to Aragorn about the coming of the Grey Company; III/5). The summons itself was not so much providential, as it was in the Council of Elrond, but the timing of it and their arrival were, considering the separation of weeks between when Gandalf got the message, as well as when it would have needed to be sent north, and when the Grey Company arrived. In fact, Elrohir brings a message from Elrond that declares the answer to where Aragorn must go, as Elrond tells him, "If thou art in haste, remember the Paths of the Dead" (V/2).

Aragorn goes silent after this for the rest of the journey. When the company arrives in Helm's Deep, he goes into the tower there at night with the *palantír* and confronts Sauron. He is able to wrench the Stone to his will, barely having the willpower to do so. But that indomitable will combined with Aragorn appearing "in other guise" (V/2) are enough to leave Sauron shaken. Although Sauron may be the most powerful resident of Middle-earth, he still knows fear, and he certainly fears the Heir of Isildur, the descendant of the one who cut the Ring from his very hand. He sought to exterminate the Dúnedain, and he had managed to leave those in the North scattered and without a kingdom while he left those in the South a diminished realm without a king. This echoes—although not with precise parallel, of course—the attempt to destroy the Son of David. Herod the Great attempted to kill Jesus by slaughtering the infants of Bethlehem (Matt 2). But as with Sauron working through other powers, Rev 12 shows that Satan was at work through Herod in this attempt on Jesus's life.[1] In the end, the powers cannot stop the King's arrival, and they cannot thwart his purpose.

But now that Sauron knows for certain that the Heir of Isildur lives and that, as far as he is aware, he could be in possession of his Ring thanks to the Halfling, he fears the prospect of losing everything to the one he hates the most. And so he decides to launch his massive assault ahead of when he planned it in order to hinder any attempt for Aragorn to unite the Free Peoples as his ancestor Elendil did. This will prove costly to Sauron because his haste will mean he sends out less force than he might have, his opponents will be less weakened prior to the attack, and, most importantly, his realm will be less guarded against the Hobbits on a secret Quest. But even Sauron's hasty stroke can be deadly. Thus it might have been, if not for other orchestrations of Providence, including Aragorn's own path to Minas Tirith.

As Elrond advised him, Aragorn knows that he must take the Paths of the Dead. Théoden and Éomer, undeniably brave men, blanch at the mere mention of this road. But Théoden nevertheless declares, "It is your doom, maybe, to tread strange paths that others dare not" (V/2). And so he says more than he knows, for Aragorn's road is thus appointed. It was the subject of prophecy by Malbeth the Seer in the reign of the last king of the Northern Kingdom:

> Over the land there lies a long shadow,
> westward reaching wings of darkness.
> The Tower trembles; to the tombs of kings
> doom approaches. The Dead awaken;
> for the hour is come for the oathbreakers:
> at the Stone of Erech they shall stand again
> and hear there the horn in the hills ringing.
> Whose shall the horn be? Who shall call them

---

[1] Tolkien had written a poem in September of 1916 while he was in the trenches in WW1 titled *Consolatrix Afflictorum* or *Stella Vespertina*, in which he referred to Mary as "throned amid the stars," the imagery of which is derived from Rev 12. See Christina Scull and Wayne G. Hammond, *The J. R. R. Tolkien Companion and Guide*, rev. and exp. ed., vol. 1: Chronology (London: HarperCollins, 2017), 97.

> from the grey twilight, the forgotten people?
> The heir of him to whom the oath they swore.
> From the North shall he come, need shall drive him:
> he shall pass the Door to the Paths of the Dead. (V/2)[2]

Again, this was prophesied over a thousand years before the events of the story, and Aragorn carried the words with him for so long. Only now can he see that he must fulfill these words. By no other means can he do what he must. He even appropriates the words of the prophecy in saying to his fellows, "But I do not go gladly; only need drives me" (V/2). And by taking this road rather than traveling with the Rohirrim, he will come with help unlooked for where no one else could have managed such a victory. And so, in echo of Jesus and as a type of the same, he aligns himself with the words of prophecy and thereby fulfills God's purpose for him.

Also like Jesus, he warns his fellows of the cost of following him on his path, "only of your free will would I have you come, for you will find both toil and great fear, and maybe worse" (V/2). Jesus warned his disciples about counting the cost of following him and of the trouble they would have. This was true not only after his first passion prediction, but it was also a frequent theme in his teaching (as I have noted elsewhere concerning the perseverance of the suffering faithful in the NT). But such is the demonstration of faith, of *estel*, and that is the quality that Aragorn's companions show in following him on this path.

When Aragorn later meets Éowyn as he tries to pass through the entrance to the Paths at Dunharrow, she tries to dissuade him from taking this way. But with her also he reaffirms what he has said previously that "I go on a path appointed.... But I shall take the Paths of the Dead, alone, if needs be" (V/2). Likewise, he says he goes on this road because he must, "Only so can I see any hope of doing my part in the war against Sauron. I do not choose paths of peril, Éowyn" (V/2).

---

[2] Originally, this was a rhyme of Gondor, rather than a prophecy by a seer of Arnor, and it was more "on the nose" in being correlated with the narrative (Tolkien, *War of the Ring*, 300):

> *Out of the mountain shall they come their tryst keeping;*
> *at the Stone of Erech their horn shall blow,*
> *when hope is dead and the kings are sleeping*
> *and darkness lies on the world below:*
> *Three lords shall come from the three kindreds*
> *from the North at need by the paths of the dead*
> *elflord, dwarflord, and lord forwandréd,*
> *and one shall wear a crown on head.* (See also Tolkien, *War of the Ring*, 305, 307).

A Time for Unheralded Valor

Éowyn thus tries to change tactic to ask Aragorn if she can ride forth with him. But Aragorn does not presume authority to permit this, as her duty is with her people. Éowyn is bitter at such talk of "duty" as she has heard throughout her life for what it means for her as a woman. She has the spirit of a warrior, and she wonders why she should not be able to go forth and win renown with the other warriors instead of wasting her life with womanly responsibilities. Aragorn warns her that there may come a time, and that right soon, when she will be needed in a last defense of her realm because the men have not returned, "Then there will be need of valour without renown, for none shall remember the deeds that are done in the last defence of your homes. Yet the deeds will not be less valiant because they are unpraised" (V/2).

This statement is similar to the ethos of the Christian author of *The Battle of Maldon*. In fact, he held the valor of the retinue in higher regard than that of Beorhtnoth. Their heroism might have gone without renown across the generations, if the poet had not taken it upon himself to give it to them. But their deeds would not have been unvaliant simply because they were unheralded. They had still cultivated the seeds of courage planted within them by the Creator, and they did so in faithful service when others fled in cowardice. Of course, Éowyn takes this as hollow comfort, and she will still eventually find her way to the battle she seeks to join.

The Paths of the Dead

As for Aragorn, he pushes forward to the Paths of the Dead. The passage proves to be a test of bravery for the company. Halbarad of the Rangers even anticipates that his death lies on the other side of the path, but he commits himself to going through. Still, he does suggest leaving the horses, since it is clear that they are spooked by their setting. Aragorn countermands him in saying that the horses will be needed if they make it through. And thus, Aragorn leads the way, "and such was the strength of his will in that hour that all the Dúnedain and their horses followed him" (V/2). As we have seen, courage, like hope, can be contagious, just as their opposites can be.

At this point, I have seen multiple authors attempt to link Aragorn taking the Paths of the Dead and coming out the other side accompanied by the army of the dead with the tradition of Jesus's Harrowing of Hell. While I have written in support of various christological echoes in Aragorn's character and story, this is a case where I think people are reaching too far because it relies too much on superficialities. The Paths of the Dead is a peculiar place in Tolkien's mythology that is more comparable to a haunted location than to the realm of the dead, whether in Old English, Norse, Greek, Christian, or other conceptions. In such a case, Aragorn or someone else would need to be bringing spirits out of the Halls of Mandos. The dead men still reside here not because they are dead, but because they are cursed as Oathbreakers. After all, they dwelt here before they were cursed. Their being led forth by Aragorn is not simply some salvific liberation that he performs for their benefit; it is the means for them to finally fulfill their oath and thus break the curse placed on them by Isildur. They broke their oath because they worshiped Sauron, and that allegiance undermined their eventual allegiance to Isildur when they swore to be his allies.[3] In these ways, the story is not comparable with the Christian tradition, much less with Jesus's resurrection, in any fashion but the most superficial ones of involving the dead and a person traveling through a place they occupy.

In line with the theme of help unlooked for and the contributions of those the powers have overlooked, this is yet another example. The Dead Men of Dunharrow had either been disregarded and feared as being only haunters of the White Mountains, or they had been forgotten. Since it is unclear how well Malbeth's prophecy was known outside of the Dúnedain and Rivendell, it is likely that anyone outside of those circles would have thought it impossible that they could ever be allies to the Free Peoples. Yet, by the work of the man who will be king, they will have an essential role in the coming victory. And all of this was orchestrated by Providence through the declaration of the prophecy long ago—whereby the One revealed his intention to take up their evil deed of oath-breaking and turn it to good purpose beyond anyone's reckoning thousands of years after the fact—and the fulfillment of the same, as well as all that has transpired to bring the various participants in the action to this point at this time for such purpose.

---

[3] An early draft of Book V had also described Dunharrow as once being the location of a dark temple during Sauron's reign. Tolkien, *War of the Ring*, 238, 257. Tolkien had also said the name itself was "A modernization of Rohan *Dūnhaerg* 'the heathen fane on the hillside', so-called because this refuge of the Rohirrim at the head of Harrowdale was on the site of a sacred place of the old inhabitants (now the Dead Men)." Tolkien, *War of the Ring*, 267 (See also J. R. R. Tolkien, "Guide to the Names in The Lord of the Rings," in *A Tolkien Compass: Including J. R. R. Tolkien's* Guide to the Names in The Lord of the Rings, ed. Jared Lobdell [LaSalle, IL: Open Court, 1975], 183). Although this particular conception of the temple was not explicit in the published draft, it still shows that this notion of the worship of Sauron was a consistent point in Tolkien's imagination about Sauron and his lordship over the Men of Middle-earth. This shows deeply ingrained his notion of the conflict in *LOTR* that he explained to W. H. Auden was (Letter #183).

A Fool's Hope

The next two chapters concern preparations for the great battle to come. The Rohirrim muster their forces and leave the smaller portion behind to defend their lands, as they correctly discern that an attack could still come from behind them. Still, they are able to send 6,000 cavalrymen to reinforce Minas Tirith.

Meanwhile, the outer defenses of Minas Tirith are stretched thin at Osgiliath, Cair Andros, and the Rammas Echor itself. Faramir comes to report to Denethor concerning those outer defenses after being harried by the Nazgûl, from which he is saved by Gandalf. In the process of the conference he has with Denethor, Gandalf, and others, he tells Denethor and Gandalf that Pippin is not the first Halfling he has seen. Gandalf thus learns of where and when Frodo, Sam, and Gollum passed beyond Faramir's watch. Naturally, there is a dispute about why Faramir did not bring the Hobbit with the One Ring to Minas Tirith. Gandalf supports Faramir's decision and defends it from Denethor's attacks against his character. Boromir would not have done better for Denethor in this regard, and even if Denethor did have the Ring, it would overthrow his mind. Denethor is ultimately dismissive of such claims, but he acknowledges that there is no sense in continuing to talk about counterfactuals now. The Ring is out of reach and what will be will be.

After this conference, Gandalf and Pippin return to their lodging and Pippin poses a question to Gandalf:

> 'Tell me, is there any hope? For Frodo, I mean; or at least mostly for Frodo.'
> Gandalf put his hand on Pippin's head. 'There never was much hope,' he answered. 'Just a fool's hope, as I have been told.' (V/4)

This is in reference to something Denethor had said at the conference. It also indicates how Gandalf has the higher wisdom, as it appears to be folly to the world. At this point, Denethor appears to have lost *estel*. For his hope, he prefers to latch on to what is most immediately available, controllable, and usable to worldly power (a form of *amdir* hope). Gandalf eschews such, for he remains devoted to a higher source of hope.

Precisely because of that higher hope, he trusts in the ever-surprising ways of Providence. Thus, in his reflection on the timing provided by Faramir and the timing of Sauron's attack, he surmises that "Maybe even your foolishness helped, my lad" (V/4). That is, he confirms what we observed at the end of Book III of how even Pippin's act of looking into the *palantír* was turned to good purpose. After all, it led to Aragorn taking the Stone himself and revealing himself to Sauron in time for him to hasten his designs and divert his attention outside of his realm.

Also because of his *estel*, he is not so perturbed at the fact that Frodo and Sam are traveling with Gollum. He had guessed it would be so eventually in any case. His trust is not in Gollum, of course, and he suspects that they are taking their current path due to his treachery. But he assures Pippin, "Let us remember that a traitor may betray himself and do good that he does not intend" (V/4). Pippin himself has seen this himself already with Saruman and Gríma. It will yet prove true again at the climax of the plot, but we will get to that later. Gandalf trusts in the truth of this declaration because he trusts in the One who is the source of such works of providence.

We see similar displays of hope and the fruit it bears in courage through Gandalf's actions in the Siege of Gondor. Faramir returns from his doomed defense of Osgiliath, but that happens only by the skin of his teeth thanks to the intervention of Gandalf and Imrahil with his knights. For his trouble, Faramir has been pierced by a poisoned dart and he has succumbed to the Black Breath that afflicts those who are too close for too long to the Nazgûl. He appears to be on the verge of death, Denethor—whose scornful treatment of Faramir led him to his current state—has been rendered impotent by succumbing to despair in response to Faramir's condition, and thus Denethor gives up the defense of the city. The tactics of the besiegers, especially with the Nazgûl wheeling overhead just out of bowshot and terrorizing the troops, have been such effective psychological warfare that many defenders of the upper levels have simply abandoned their posts. Gandalf takes up the leadership of the defense and rides throughout the city rekindling hope and encouragement where he can. By such means, the defenses of the city are just able to hold through all that presses against them.

But it is not enough. For with the defenders busy in so many places with responding to projectiles, rebuffing the siege towers, and fighting the fires, Grond is able to roll up to the gate. The Witch-King of Angmar directs its strikes against the gate until they burst asunder. Then he alone proceeds through the gateway of Minas Tirith, being the first enemy ever to do so. And before him, all who would have defended the gate flee. Save one.

Gandalf, sitting upon his fearless companion Shadowfax, is alone against Sauron's most powerful servant and the massive host of Mordor tens of thousands strong behind him. By his *estel*-inspired courage and his increased power given to him by the One when he was sent back to complete his task, he can stare them all down and speak with confidence. It is akin to what is seen in the Bible in expressions of one putting many to flight (Lev 26:8; Josh 23:10; cf. Deut 32:30), or of the 300 led by Gideon putting to flight the 135,000 Midianites (Judg 7–8), though here it is sufficient to hold the line. The role of putting the armies of Mordor to flight will be given to others.

And so Gandalf says to the Lord of the Nazgûl, "You cannot enter here … Go back to the abyss prepared for you! Go back! Fall into the nothingness that awaits you and your Master. Go" (V/4). This is less evocative than what he said to the Balrog, but it is spoken in that same spirit with more of an emphasis on the doom of his opponent. In Tolkien's presentation of his overall mythology, Melkor has been banished to the Void until the end of days, and so this is also the expectation of what would happen should Sauron be vanquished in this world. So too it would happen to his wraith slaves with him. There is still final judgment, so this fate is more comparable to Satan being thrown into the abyss in Rev 20:1–3, but it is not a direct parallel (since, again, this is set in an imaginary time thousands of years before Christ). But it is foreshadowing of the ultimate fate of Sauron and those devoted to him and his original master, for such rebellion in the absence of repentance leads only to destruction.

Of course, the Lord of the Nazgûl is unconcerned with such declarations about his fate, since by all that he sees and knows, his victory this day should be assured. And so he prepares to clash with the most powerful of the leaders of the Free Peoples, being so assured of the power of his Dark Lord channeled through him that he can triumph even here. But Gandalf, uncowed, does not move. Instead, another force is moved onto the field by the work of Providence:

> And in that very moment, away behind in some courtyard of the City, a cock crowed. Shrill and clear he crowed, recking nothing of wizardry or war, welcoming only the morning that in the sky far above the shadows of death was coming with the dawn.
> And as if in answer there came from far away another note. Horns, horns, horns. In dark Mindolluin's sides they dimly echoed. Great horns of the North wildly blowing. Rohan had come at last. (V/4)[4]

The timing of this whole event is clearly providential, as will be shown further in the next chapter. Rohan coming as they have in full force is also due to the orchestrations of Providence. And, of course, Gandalf himself is an agent of Providence and has participated in bringing this part of his own hope to fruition. Tolkien even notes this event as an example of his increased power for his mission while also noting that his faithfulness to his mission has helped it come to pass:

> He is still under the obligation of concealing his power and of teaching rather than forcing or dominating wills, but where the physical powers of the

---

[4] Small wonder that Tolkien considered the scene of the horns of the Rohirrim at cockcrow as one of the most moving passages in his story (Letters #165 and #294).

Enemy are too great for the good will of the opposers to be effective he can act in emergency as an 'angel' – no more violently than the release of St Peter from prison. He seldom does so, operating rather through others, but in one or two cases in the War (in Vol. III) he does reveal a sudden power: he twice rescues Faramir. He alone is left to forbid the entrance of the Lord of Nazgûl to Minas Tirith, when the City has been overthrown and its Gates destroyed — and yet so powerful is the whole train of human resistance, that he himself has kindled and organized, that in fact no battle between the two occurs: it passes to other mortal hands. (Letter #156)

We now must explore how it is that the Rohirrim have come here in time to interrupt this confrontation at the gates.

The Overlooked Drúedain

When the story shifts back to focusing on Merry and the Rohirrim he rides with to explain how they have arrived on the scene, we see another case of how the wheels of the world are turned by the hands of the seemingly unknown and weak because they must do so. For on the road to Minas Tirith the Rohirrim encounter the overlooked Drúedain (who they had called the Woses or Wild Men of the Woods) at the Drúadan Forest. Like the Hobbits, they had been disregarded as significant allies in the political calculations of the world for thousands of years. They were considered simple in mind and unlovely in appearance, not far above wild beasts and even treated by some like such.[5] Yet, they had a remarkable capacity of foresight, lore of plants that was rivaled by few, and they were thus remarkably crafty in the woods they inhabited.

Their leader, Ghân-buri-Ghân, supplies crucial intelligence and help to the Rohirrim. He does not offer the aid of him or his people in open battle, where they would be much less helpful. But he informs them that a larger force of their enemies awaits them on the road to Minas Tirith should they try to take that way. He and his people can rather quickly and accurately count how many the Rohirrim are, and he assures them that the Orcs have more. The Lord of the Nazgûl or Sauron had taken account of the Rohirrim coming to the aid of Minas Tirith, but neither of them had accounted for the Drúedain, and this proved to be a critical mistake, even as Saruman made a critical mistake in not accounting for the Ents and the Huorns. For despite grievances he had with the Rohirrim in that at some time they had hunted his people like beasts, Ghân-

---

[5] For more on their history, see J. R. R. Tolkien, *Unfinished Tales*, "The Drúedain." Also see J. R. R. Tolkien, "Nomenclature of *The Lord of the Rings*," in *The Lord of the Rings: A Reader's Companion*, ed. Wayne G. Hammond and Christina Scull (London: HarperCollins, 2008), 764–5.

buri-Ghân had common cause with them in wanting to rid the land of the *gorgûn*, and he promised them safe passage through the forest secured by the Drúedain. All he asked in return was that they leave the Wild Men alone.

And so Ghân-buri-Ghân and his people become instruments of Providence, whereby Eru Ilúvatar chose those who were overlooked to play crucial roles in the War of the Ring. If the Rohirrim had gone the main way to Minas Tirith, they may have defeated the force awaiting them, but it would come at a significant cost, and they would have arrived at Minas Tirith as a diminished and fatigued force. It would have also caused delay that could have been fatal. But thanks to the overlooked Drúedain, the Rohirrim were able to bypass that force and come to Minas Tirith fresh for battle and in good timing so as to provide a two-pronged counterattack to the besiegers from their flank and from the defenders of the city being encouraged by these reinforcements. But for them, the battle would have been significantly more costly, if not lost altogether.

More Signs of Providence

The Drúedain's actions are not the only sign of the involvement of Providence in this arrangement. Éomer observes that the overconfidence of their enemy in guarding their northern flank and in the seeming advantage—psychological, if nothing else—of the gloom that had lasted for days now has led them to destroying the Rammas Echor instead of defending it, which has actually helped the Rohirrim: "Even in this gloom hope gleams again. Our Enemy's devices oft serve us in his despite. The accursed darkness itself has been a cloak to us. And now, lusting to destroy Gondor and throw it down stone from stone, his orcs have taken away my greatest fear. The out-wall could have held long against us. Now we can sweep through—if once we win so far" (V/5). This is another example of how even malintent can be taken up by the providential work of God and turned to good purposes beyond what the agent in question willed. And it reiterates a point that has been made multiple times of how self-destructive evil is and how it thus can serve good ends in its despite.

Moreover, signs in nature itself indicate the providential turn of the tides of fortune in this War. The Drúedain are especially attuned to nature, as Ghân-buri-Ghân tells Théoden that although it has been dark for days, they know it is daytime because they can feel the sun even when she cannot be seen. And so he has a particular sense for the change that is coming after he takes his leave of the Rohirrim: "But suddenly he stood up looking up like some startled woodland animal snuffling a strange air. A light came in his eyes. 'Wind is changing!' he cried, and with that, in a twinkling as it seemed, he and his fellows had vanished into the glooms, never to be seen by any Rider of Rohan again" (V/5). This is the first sign of the changing of the wind that will drive away the gloom sent by Sauron, which will have effects on multiple fronts of this conflict. It is an unusually strong wind from the south, and it is a natural force being used for providential ends. Just as the gloom that had extended from Mordor was not a merely natural phenomenon, but a work of Sauron used to aid his purposes, this wind is not a merely natural phenomenon, but a work of the One who has power over the winds to aid his purposes (Exod 15:10; Pss 135:7; 147:18; Mark 4:39–41).

The change is confirmed later by Wídfara as they approach Minas Tirith, "Already the wind is turning. There comes a breath out of the South; there is a sea-tang in it, faint though it be. The morning will bring new things. Above the reek it will be dawn when you pass the wall" (V/5). He is another who is especially sensitive to the wind and the messages it brings. But as the Rohirrim arrive on the field, Merry himself finally perceives what these others had mentioned beyond any doubt, "a change. Wind was in his face! Light was glimmering. Far, far away, in the South the clouds could be dimly seen as remote grey shapes, rolling up, drifting: morning lay beyond them" (V/5). Their arrival thus coincides with the revelation of the dawn after five days of deep gloom and with the falling of the gates of Minas Tirith. The arrival of both the Riders and the dawn beyond any apparent hope will thus come at the right time to motivate the defenders of Minas Tirith to stage their own attack with a now-strengthened hope. We will return to another effect of this providential change in the winds of fortune later.

The Battle of the Pelennor Fields

Thus, the Siege of Gondor ends and the Battle of the Pelennor Fields begins with the charge of the Rohirrim. Théoden himself is described as reminiscent of Oromë, the Huntsman and Horseman of the Valar, such is the power of his onslaught. This charge coinciding with the dawn also means that the sun gleams brightly off of him and his golden shield, bewildering the host of Mordor by being caught between the sun and its image, "For morning came, morning and a wind from the sea; and darkness was removed, and the hosts of Mordor wailed, and terror took them, and they fled, and died, and the hoofs of wrath rode over them" (V/5). At the same time, we are told, "And then all the host of Rohan burst into song, and they sang as they slew, for the joy of battle was on them, and the sound of their singing that was fair and terrible came even to the City" (V/5).

This is another passage that illustrates how people try too hard to correlate Tolkien's views to one or another paradigm about war, as they do with ideas about the will and divine sovereignty. Peter Kreeft thinks this narration shows Tolkien's view that war can be glorious if it is just.[6] Rutledge, on the other hand, is positively consternated by what she describes as the one scene of "undiluted bloodthirstiness" in the story and follows this remark with question upon question to signify her disquiet with it.[7] But there is no reason to be so disturbed or to think that this in some way reflects Tolkien's own views of war. It is simply consistent with how the Rohirrim have been portrayed to this point in their disposition towards war. And it is consistent with how, although Tolkien's entire story is indirectly inspired by his beloved Old English and Norse stories, the Rohirrim are the most direct analogues to the Anglo-Saxons, besides their love of horses (Letters #144, #190, #193, #211, #297).

In any case, for all that this initial onslaught proved difficult for the enemy armies, the narrator reminds us that it is the Lord of the Nazgûl who commands this host. And he had much at his disposal. He may have lost control, "fortune had betrayed him for the moment, and the world had turned against him; victory was slipping from his grasp even as he stretched out his hand to seize it. But his arm was long" (V/6). This notion of "fortune" betraying him further supports that these events are providential, orchestrated by the One who is behind "fortune," in turning now against the Lord of the Nazgûl after he had presumed that everything was going his way. And the One has yet more instruments to use beyond what this captain of Mordor reckons.

Indeed, this is shown in how the captain falls. In an attempt to stem the charge of the Rohirrim, he attacks Théoden and brings down his horse Snowmane upon him. Théoden is dying, but he is not dead yet. The Witch-King may have hastened his death, if not for one warrior alone withstanding him: "Dernhelm the young, faithful beyond fear" (V/6). This warrior would seemingly be no match for this abominable terror who has existed for thousands of years, conquered the Northern Kingdom, and took Minas Ithil when Gondor was much stronger. Yet this Dernhelm, revealed to be Éowyn, cares nothing for such things. What matters is her loving loyalty to the man who is not only her king, but who has been a father to her since her own parents died. Her courage alone cannot save her, but it motivates her to do what she can to hinder him. The Witch-King tells her that no living man can hinder him, evoking the prophecy of Glorfindel

---

[6] Peter Kreeft, *The Philosophy of Tolkien: The Worldview Behind The Lord of the Rings* (San Francisco: Ignatius, 2005), 168.

[7] Rutledge, *Battle*, 287 n. 60.

from over 1,000 years ago that he would not fall by the hand of man (Appendix A.I.iv). But Éowyn laughs at these words, declaring that she is a woman, and she will smite him if he touches Théoden. The Ringwraith thus responds with silence, "as if in sudden doubt" (V/6). Again, he thought fortune was in his favor, and that the prophecy meant he had nothing to fear from any Man. Yet, he realizes that Éowyn could portend a loophole in that prophecy, not unlike the prophecy to Macbeth that "none of woman born / shall harm Macbeth" (Act 4, scene 1), only for him to learn that Macduff was "from his mother's womb / untimely ripped" (Act 5, scene 8), and so he dies by his hand.

Éowyn's dauntless courage has also proved contagious on the only witness to this fight. Merry had been thrown from his horse as it panicked at the coming of the Nazgûl. He was filled with fear, having been daunted by this Ringwraith previously, but now seeing Éowyn, after first being stirred by her laughter (which again shows its often delivering quality), "Pity filled his heart and great wonder, and suddenly the slow-kindled courage of his race awoke" (V/6). By the many strange roads Merry has taken to come here, the courage that was the common grace of his people now faced a situation that would cultivate it to full growth by the special grace of the One. And so Merry himself will serve as an instrument of Providence to fulfill the words spoken through Glorfindel that the Lord of the Nazgûl's doom was indeed far off at that time and that he would not fall by the hand of a man. Instead, he would fall by the hand of a Hobbit— a people even Glorfindel could not have foreseen being involved in the Witch-King's doom—and a woman in the greatest battle of the Third Age. Providence had taken up the defiant choice of Éowyn to ride to war and turned it to good purpose by inspiring the Hobbit to action, and his action would in turn save Éowyn from the much more powerful Lord of the Nazgûl so that she would be in a position to deliver the killing blow. Merry could not have done what he did without Éowyn's help, whether in encouraging him to start by her own dauntless courage or in finishing what he started. And Éowyn could not have done what she did without Merry's help, whether in him saving her from a killing blow by her foe or in his strike with his dagger being necessary for her to land a killing blow with her mundane sword that otherwise would not have harmed him.

Speaking of that dagger, we are told later in the narration that Merry attempts to pick it up, but it withers away, as do other weapons that contact the Nazgûl. But it did its damage before passing away:

So passed the sword of the Barrow-downs, work of Westernesse. But glad would he have been to know its fate who wrought it slowly long ago in the North-kingdom when the Dúnedain were young, and chief among their foes was the dread realm of Angmar and its sorcerer king. No other blade, not though mightier hands had wielded it, would have dealt that foe a wound so bitter, cleaving the undead flesh, breaking the spell that knit his unseen sinews to his will. (V/6)

Númenóreans and their descendants once learned the lore of making great blades from the Elves, and this is but one example. The Dúnedain had used this traditional knowledge in the hopes of striking down the enemy who would destroy their Northern Kingdom. None of them were able to use such swords or daggers in such fashion. It would take over 1,000 years and someone of completely different lineage to bring it against him. The fact that it has made it here at all shows the intricate, wide-ranging, and surprising work of Providence.

The sword itself lay in the Barrow-downs for years untold. There it would have stayed but for the Hobbits coming through there, which was itself the result of Providence as Tom Bombadil saved them from Old Man Willow and sent them off, after which he would save them from the Barrow-wights and give to them blades like this one. Then Merry carried that sword with him all the way to Rivendell. If Elrond had his way, he would have been sent back, and the blade never would have come so far.[8] Instead, Merry came on the Quest, holding fast to the blade from Rivendell all the way to Amon Hen. Although his intent was to go with Frodo to Mordor, the Uruk-hai captured him and Pippin, and their daggers were left behind while they went on a most incredible journey to Fangorn to attend the fall of Isengard. Providence again guides events so that Aragorn is able to return their blades to them when they reunite at Isengard. And because Merry had this dagger when he swore his fealty to Théoden and would not be parted from him, he was able to be near the king to meet the Witch-King on the battlefield and so use it to accomplish the seemingly impossible. Neither the man who wrought it nor the men who bore it for however long could have imagined the winding path the blade would take to accomplish its purpose. But such is the route Providence took it on to accomplish his purposes of judgment against the Witch-King and the thwarting of Sauron in this battle.

---

[8] Similarly, Gandalf will later say, "He has well repaid my trust; for if Elrond had not yielded to me, neither of you would have set out; and then far more grievous would the evils of this day have been" (V/8).

While this is a mighty blow against the host of Mordor, they still vastly outnumber and outpower the combined forces of Gondor and Rohan. While the rest of the Nazgûl have fled the field at the death of their captain (as is made clearer in Book VI), the second-in-command, Gothmog, still has much at his disposal. Although the Men of Gondor had charged forth from the city, they became separated from the Rohirrim and could not clear a path for them. When the watchers from the city see the fleet of Corsair ships in the distance, it appears all hope is truly lost, as the Men of Gondor retreat to the city, and the Rohirrim are cut off. Thus, Éomer, grieved at the death of his king and father figure—as well as (he thinks) the death of his sister—has become fey and rallies to him all who could come. He thinks to make a last stand, to die as courageously as he lived, now that there is no hope for victory left. In this way, he embodies that indomitable will staring in the face of inevitable defeat that characterized the northern peoples before the gospel came.[9] He even lifts his sword in defiance as the next host arrives to join the battle. Even as the *amdir* hope dies in him, suddenly he sees something else: the coming of Estel.

Now we see what else the south wind has blown in besides the clearness of the dawn, for the Corsair ships do not bear the banner of Umbar but the banner of Gondor enhanced by recalling past glory through the symbols of Elendil. This is the banner of Aragorn made for him by Arwen. As elsewhere in the story, he comes to bring hope beyond what anyone had expected. He has been driven here from far away by the winds of Providence to arrive just as hope seemed to die for the armies of Gondor and Rohan. And with him are Legolas, Gimli, and the armies of southern Gondor that had been drawn away from the defense of Minas Tirith by the need to defend their own homes from the Corsairs. This is the last blow in the psychological warfare between the sides, and it turns the tide once and for all in favor of hope/*estel* over despair.

When all is said and done, the three leaders of the armies—Aragorn, Éomer, and Imrahil—are said to be unscathed, "for such was their fortune and their skill and might of their arms, and few indeed had dared to abide them or look on their faces in the hour of their wrath" (V/6). In this case, "fortune" refers to the preserving work of Providence. Their gifts of skill and might are special graces given to them for their purposes

---

[9] This characterization also fits the song he composes for the occasion:

> "Out of doubt, out of dark to the day's rising
>
> I came singing in the sun, sword unsheathing.
>
> To hope's end I rode and to heart's breaking:
>
> Now for wrath, now for ruin and a red nightfall!" (V/6)

as warrior leaders, and they have been cultivated with much experience from all those involved.

Many others were not so fortunate. This victory was costly for all involved, but it was certainly not a Pyrrhic victory either. The fighting is not over, but the cost of it all shows that ultimate victory in this war will certainly not be possible through strength of arms. But courage in battle is not irrelevant either, and we have multiple examples in this battle alone of how the Author takes each act of courage up and directs it to higher purposes and orchestrated designs.[10]

Denethor's Despair

We mentioned before how Denethor gave up the defense of his city, and that is related to why Gandalf's involvement in the battle after the gate is breached was not mentioned in the previous chapter. Pippin found him at the gate, and after the showdown between Gandalf and the Lord of the Nazgûl ended, he pleaded for Gandalf's help with the despairing Denethor, who has surrendered to despair and thinks to immolate himself and Faramir. Although the battle outside the gates will go worse for the lack of Gandalf's help, he is the only one who can help in this situation far above the battlefield.

Gandalf thus observes how "Even in the heart of our stronghold the Enemy has power to strike us: for his will it is that it as at work" (V/7). Similarly, when he and Pippin arrive at the Closed Door leading to the Rath Dínen, and they see the porter lying slain before the open door, he calls it the work of the Enemy, "Such deeds he loves: friend at war with friend; loyalty divided in confusion of hearts" (V/7). This is similar to other such statements we have seen from Gandalf, as well as Haldir, to the effect of treason being a weapon of the enemy, as well as the devastating effect of sown mistrust between those who should be allied against the enemy. Here, Denethor's despair and its deadly consequences have caused a divided loyalty for Beregond. He has a duty to serve the steward and his will, but that now interferes with his characteristic loyalty to Faramir, for his loyalty to Denethor would dictate that he stands by and does nothing while Faramir dies, but his loyalty to Faramir would dictate that he must defy

---

[10] As Tolkien said in an outline of this part of Book V, particularly in reference to "The Last Debate," "Gandalf does not hope to conquer Mordor or overthrow Sauron and his tower. 'Not in these latter days, nor ever again by force of arms.' Yet arms have their place; and sloth now might be ruinous." Tolkien, *War of the Ring*, 360.

Denethor's will to be burned alive with his son.[11] And so Beregond takes unprecedented steps in slaying on hallowed grounds in defense of Faramir. Beregond is not himself an agent of the enemy in this regard, but as evil corrupts what is good, the despair that Sauron has inflicted on Denethor has corrupted the loyalty of his soldiers to support his evil deeds simply because of his command. Unfortunately, the only way Beregond can check such corruption is by taking drastic measures himself, without which Faramir would have become a victim of Denethor's despair, and they all would have been complicit in his murder-suicide.

Because of the responsibilities of leaders like Denethor and the loyalty they command, they also have a powerful influence on the fidelity of the people in the Bible. Judges, the books of Samuel, and the books of Kings demonstrate this again and again. The character of Israelite faith ebbs and flows to the rhythm of the leaders. There are exceptions, of course, such as the 7,000 faithful ones in the reign of Ahab, the various prophets through the declines of Israel and Judah, or, in contrast, the high places of idolatry being present even in the reigns of good kings. But the course of faith in Israel as a whole is affected by having no leader, a bad leader, or a good leader. And so this case could be if Denethor has his way without intervention.

Gandalf arrives on the scene to defuse it as best he can. He first disarms Denethor, who might have killed Beregond, and chastises them all for the fighting that has gone on here. He then rescues Faramir from what would have been a pyre, and Denethor weepingly says not to take his son from him. While Gandalf calls upon him to take up the defense of this city that he had prepared for, Denethor thinks all battle is vain and that he ought to be able to order his death as he wishes. Gandalf's response highlights how there is indeed a crux of faith for Denethor and the kingdom of Gondor in this moment: "Authority is not given to you, Steward of Gondor, to order the hour of your death ... And only the heathen kings, under the domination of the Dark Power, did thus, slaying themselves in pride and despair, murdering their kin to ease their own death" (V/7).

The phrasing Is especially noteworthy. Denethor had used the same description earlier in his stated intention not to be buried, but to "burn like heathen kings before ever a ship sailed hither from the West" (V/4). The term "heathen" has largely fallen out of use, but it broadly has the same sense as "pagan" in referring to polytheists adhering to traditional religious practices. In other words, anyone who could not be

---

[11] See also Tolkien, *War of the Ring*, 379.

considered a Christian, a Jew, or a Muslim would be considered a "heathen."[12] It was used this way in *The Battle of Maldon*, as well as Tolkien's sequel *The Homecoming of Beorhtnoth Beorhthelm's Son*, including in reference to funerary practices, and in other such works (like *Beowulf*). And yet the term appears here in what is a story set in a decidedly pre-Christian era, as we have noted before. The monotheistic natural theology held by the Númenóreans—being enlightened by the Elves of the Undying Lands who learned from the Valar and Maiar—and other Men, like the Rohirrim (to say nothing of others like the High Elves still in Middle-earth), is a kind of precursor to the revelations declared in Judeo-Christianity. Tolkien even says the Númenóreans of Gondor are Hebraic in their theology, even though they were like Egyptians in other respects (Letter #211).

As such, the people of kingdoms like Gondor conduct (or are expected to conduct) themselves in ways that are distinct from their heathen forebears, much like how there were different expectations of kings when Christianity came to heathen lands than there were prior to that advent, as there were also different expectations of funerary practices. What Gandalf refers to corresponds with known history. Indian cultures even used the term *sati* (Anglicized as "suttee") to refer to when widows would burn themselves on their husbands' funeral pyres. Others, like the Scythians with their royalty, were known for being buried with their still-living wives (one or more of them) along with any servants they wished. This also seems to have been the case with Vikings, as well as the Anglo-Saxons to some extent, and although they widely practiced cremation, it is unclear how often they might have combined the two as with the *sati*. Beowulf, whose story is conveyed in Old English by a Christian, is emblematic of the heathen past in departing this life on a funeral pyre. Moreover, the view of suicide here is in marked contrast to cultures like the Anglo-Saxons, where this could be considered an honorable death as an exercise of will to die on one's own terms. Although the Gondorians are not Christians, since Christ has not come yet, they are still to act as people whose theology and practice sets them apart from those who engage in such rituals (and put them in greater continuity with Tolkien's Catholicism, which could not brook such suicide). Denethor does not have authority to order the time of his own death as by suicide, and he certainly does not have the authority to order such for his son.

---

[12] The notions of atheism, agnosticism, and broader non-religiosity in some form or another were not unknown in times when this term was more broadly used, but they were distinctly exceptional, and such terms as we tend to define them would not apply to entire people groups as anything but a polemical label on par with "godless."

Almost, it seems as if Gandalf's exhortation and Denethor's longing for Faramir, his last son whom he had mistreated for far too long in his favoritism of Boromir, might be enough to bring him to his senses. He is said to be in throes, like pangs of childbirth. Gandalf even calls upon him to do what must be done, for both Gandalf and Denethor are needed, and there is much yet to do.

And then Denethor laughs. This is not the delivering laughter we have seen at multiple points in this story, whether of relief or of a sign of the joy beyond the walls of the world. This is the demented laugh of arrogant resolution to despair. For now Denethor reveals that he has been looking into the *palantír* of Minas Tirith, claiming to have seen more than Gandalf knows. This, in addition to what has happened to his sons, is what has driven Denethor to final despair. He had been the only steward to consult it, for none had dared to do so since Minas Ithil was taken and thus the *palantír* of that tower passed into Sauron's hands. But Denethor felt the need for more knowledge and trusted in his own strength of will. This was not for nothing, as Denethor was indeed strong enough in will that Sauron could not dominate him without the One Ring. What he did instead was more insidious. He allowed Denethor to see far off places and events through the *palantír*, and Sauron did not have the power to create false images so as to make the *palantír* lie. But what Denethor could see in that Stone was limited, it took a toll on his mind and body to struggle with Sauron each time he looked into it, and Sauron himself had power over what he could see, which presented Sauron in a stronger light than what a freer sight might have beheld. Denethor received the extra knowledge he wanted, but always at a cost and in limited (and distortive) fashion, and it had an effect of making him ever more distrustful of those who did not serve him and ever more susceptible to myopia contracting via his growing despair at Sauron's seeming invincibility.

By his pride and despair, he had lost that crucial virtue of *estel*. He had lost the sense that he could have higher hope than what he could control. And because what he learned from the *palantír* told him that there was no hope of victory against Sauron, he thought himself certain of the outcome and so gave into despair. Even the sign of Providence in the wind from the south was something he rejected as bringing hope: "And even now the wind of they hope cheats thee and wafts up Anduin a fleet with black sails. The West has failed. It is time for all to depart who would not be slaves" (V/7). While Gandalf responds that such things as he has said against hope will make the Enemy's victory certain, Denethor has made clear that such wisdom has no effect on him, since he does not trust Gandalf either. He knows of Aragorn (in part from Aragorn's venture under the name Thorongil, as told in Appendix A), and he thinks

Gandalf plots to supplant him. Ultimately, Denethor thus rejects the charge of his office. He was not to be a king but a steward who abided until the king should come again. Now that he knows there is still an heir to the throne, he utterly scorns this hope and the claim it has on his office.

Without a hopeful vision of the future, Denethor thus no longer has a sense of eschatology, and so his desire is for the past. For him, what would be best is not what the One could yet bring forth in the future, but what has already passed him by in his life: "I would have things as they were in all the days of my life ... and in the days of my longfathers before me: to be the Lord of this City in peace, and leave my chair to a son after me, who would be his own master and no wizard's pupil. But if doom denies this to me, then I will have *naught*: neither life diminished, nor love halved, nor honour abated" (V/7; emphasis original). With such words, and after one last attempt to attack Gandalf and take Faramir, Denethor lights his own pyre, snaps his steward's staff, and lays down to be engulfed in the flames.

This last state of Denethor shows him to be an example of the type of person that in online discourse is referred to as a "doomer" or one who is "blackpilled." They waste their energy and the energy of others on their despair. They believe that whatever bad thing they expect to happen is inevitable, that there is no point in hoping, and that there is no point in resisting. And since misery loves company, their only consolation, if they are too far gone, is for others to share in their despair. Like Denethor, they have fallen for the propaganda not so much by becoming adherents to it—as Denethor did not become a servant or worshiper of Sauron—but by being demoralized by it, which is its leading purpose.

It is not for nothing that hope is a virtue in the Christian worldview (1 Cor 13:13; 1 Thess 1:3; 5:8; 1 John 3:1–3; cf. Letter #64). As we have indicated already in the description of *estel*, it is so in the Bible as well that hope and faith are inherently linked. In texts like Hebrews, especially ch. 11,[13] faith can even be characterized in terms of hope. One can see this similarly in Rom 4:18, following as it does the exposition on righteousness and faith in Rom 4:9–17. Hope is the capstone of development from tribulation in Rom 5:3–5, building as it does from tribulation to perseverance to proven character to hope (cf. Rom 15:13; 2 Cor 1:7–10; 3:12; Phil 1:18–24; 1 Thess 1:3; 1 Tim 4:6–10; Heb 6:11–20; 10:23–25). Perseverance is likewise linked to hope in Rom 8:24–25 after the content of hope has been summarized. As with this scene, we are reminded

---

[13] For more on this text, see: https://krharriman.substack.com/p/a-mini-commentary-on-hebrews-part-82f.

in 1 Thess 4:13 that hope also should set us apart from those who have no hope in terms of how we grieve. Where you set your hope shapes your character, as it orders your values, directs your virtues, and centers your vision for the future, which is why Paul says to those who are rich in the present not to set their hope on their riches but on God (1 Tim 6:17 in the context of 6:6–19; cf. 1 Pet 1:13–16). The cruciality of hope is why Peter instructs us to always be ready with an answer for the *hope* that is in us (1 Pet 3:15).

Such light of the gospel as we have received, the fuller picture of hope, would not have been available in the imaginary time in which this story is set. But people are still responsible for how they respond to what they have received. Denethor knew his charge but failed in it by pride and utterly forsook it in his despair. He had thrown away *estel* as it had been passed down all these years in Gondor, and in the end he eventually threw everything else away, including his life.

So passes Denethor, son of Ecthelion, a man who was once a great steward of Gondor more like his Númenórean forebears—in both good and bad ways—than many predecessors had been. And with his passing goes Gondor as its citizens have known it, "for good or evil they are ended" (V/7).[14] Sauron had attacked Minas Tirith from without on the battlefield and from within through slowly poisoning the mind of Denethor. But there is still a Gondor that survives, and Sauron's larger purposes have been thwarted by Providence and the agents of the same.

The Hands of the King Are the Hands of a Healer

Gandalf thereafter attends to Faramir, then Éowyn, then Merry, among others who have come up from the battlefield to the Houses of Healing. As noted earlier regarding Gandalf's mission, this is another case where he does not intervene by his own power, whatever healing powers he may possess, but he seeks to guide the people to more lasting solutions. And so he finds it when Ioreth, an old healer, says in response to Faramir's condition that she wishes now that there was a king, then she quotes an old saying, "The hands of the king are the hands of a healer. And so the rightful king could ever be known" (V/8).[15] After this, Gandalf goes down to find and fetch Aragorn, so

---

[14] Similarly, note Aragorn's statement, "Behold the Sun setting in a great fire! It is a sign of the end and fall of many things, and a change in the tides of the world" (V/8).

[15] This is an example that proves true something Celeborn had said earlier in the story, "But do not despise the lore that has come down from distant years; for oft it may chance that old wives keep in memory word of things that once were needful for the wise to know" (II/8). Beyond the correlations I

that he may come to the Houses of Healing and make himself known there. He has unfurled the banner of the king on the battlefield, and now he shall reveal himself by his healing hands.

This feature of Aragorn's character does fit in the context of the story. He is the healer and renewer of broken things. He bears the Sword that was Broken, which is now renewed to fight against the forces of Sauron once more. While the line of Isildur was never broken in the North, their kingdom was, and Aragorn aims to renew it. While the kingdom of Gondor was never broken, their line of kings through Anárion was, and Aragorn aims to renew the line of kings. He is so dedicated to this renewing role that he would not dare to present the slightest presumption or impropriety so as to potentially undermine the current leader of Gondor (as he has not received news of Denethor) that he obscures his self-identification after the battle, "But I deem the time unripe; and I have no mind for strife except with our Enemy and his servants" (V/8). The Dúnedain as a whole have been diminished, and Aragorn comes to renew them. By his journeys, he has healed the broken bonds between the Dúnedain and other realms, which will bear fruit in his reign. He has also strengthened the existing bonds between Minas Tirith and her allies by his leadership in this war, and thus his kingdom will be strengthened when he comes into his own. And so he rightly calls himself *Envinyatar* ("Renewer") at the Houses of Healing, where he comes to show his literal healing power. And this will be an example of what Tolkien has written of in Letter #155 where what Hobbits perceive as "magic" is an inherent power, in this case of the line of Lúthien that extends among the Kings of Númenor, Gondor, and Arnor. That it is a special grace is indicated by him saying of the need to heal Faramir, Éowyn, and Merry, "Here I must put forth all such power and skill as is given to me" (V/8).

But this quality of Aragorn's character also points beyond the story, as it is another way in which he is a christological type. In that Jesus is the one who inaugurates the kingdom, he is also the Renewer in that respect. In that Jesus is the one through whom God created all, he is also the Renewer in that it is through him that God will bring about the new creation. Moreover, there is an important comment that Tolkien makes in Letter #250 that points to a further significance in this connection when he reflects on how he has never left the Church or scorned the Eucharist since he was brought into it, and yet his son Michael was currently struggling in his faith. We need not quote it in its entirety here, but his prayer in particular is notable:

---

note in the rest of this section, one example of this belief about human kings can be found in Macbeth, Act 4, scene 3.

> Now I pray for you all, unceasingly, that the Healer (the *Hælend* as the Sav-
> iour was usually called in Old English) shall heal my defects, and that none of
> you shall ever cease to cry *Benedictus qui venit in nomme* [sic. *nomine*] *Domini*
> [Blessed is he who comes in the name of the Lord; as said in Communion].

As Tolkien indicates, Healer/*Hælend* was indeed a common reference to Christ in Old English literature. It is what replaces references to the name "Jesus" in Old English renderings of earlier Latin sources. One can see also this linkage with Christ and God in texts like Old English Bible translations, biblical poems, *The Dream of the Rood*, Aelfric's *Homilies*, the *Crist* poems attributed to Cynewulf, *The Blickling Homilies*, *The Heliand*, and others. Aragorn has this virtue because of his participation in being a christological type.[16]

The particular kind of healing shown here—physical healing—also resembles a prominent aspect of Jesus's ministry, as well as subsequent ministry in his name as recorded in Acts (and hinted at elsewhere in the NT). Most often, Jesus performs his exorcisms and other healings with a word (whether or not touching is also involved). Aragorn uses combinations of words, spiritual struggle, and his inherent capacity— such as his breath on the leaves that helps to counter the Black Breath—to draw out the potency of *athelas*, which for almost anyone else would be simply a sweet-smelling weed. His healing of Faramir seems most exorcism-like, as we are told,

> Now Aragorn knelt beside Faramir, and held a hand upon his brow. And
> those that watched felt that some great struggle was going on. For Aragorn's
> face grew grey with weariness; and ever and anon he called the name of Fara-
> mir, but each time more faintly to their hearing, as if Aragorn himself was re-
> moved from them, and walked afar in some dark vale, calling for one that was
> lost. (V/8)

When Faramir wakes from his affliction by weariness, grief, a wound, and the Black Breath from his extended close encounter with the Nazgûl, he says to Aragorn, "My lord, you called me. I come. What does the king command?" (V/8). No one had heard such a call but by his reference to the name Faramir, which would indicate there was more to this call that Faramir heard wherever his consciousness was. And as in Jesus's parables of the coming of the king or the master of the house, he says, "For who would

---

[16] For more on the use of this term and its background, see Damian Fleming, "Jesus, That Is *Hælend*: Hebrew Names and the Vernacular Savior in Anglo-Saxon England," *JEGP* 112 (2013): 26–47; Larry Swain, "The '*Hælend*' and Other Images of Jesus in Anglo-Saxon England," in *Illuminating Jesus in the Middle Ages*, ed. Jane Beal, Commentaria 202 (Leiden: Brill, 2019), 58–75.

lie idle when the king has returned?" (V/8), and thus he becomes the first of the residents of the city to proclaim Aragorn as king upon being healed by him.

When he comes to Éowyn, he likewise speaks of the condition of her spirit and her body. The state of the one will take healing beyond what he can now provide, but the healing of the other is in a way reminiscent of the raising of Jairus's daughter. Unlike with Faramir, where the call was only occasionally audible, here he says to her, "Éowyn Éomund's daughter, awake! For your enemy has passed away" (V/8). And so he continues to call for her to awake while a keen wind blows through, reminiscent of how the wind of the Spirit comes and breathes into the dead in Ezek 37:1–14. Her healing is not a resurrection like with Jairus's daughter, but the narrator still speaks of how "he took her right hand in his and felt it warm with life returning" (V/8). And the command to "awake" is, of course, resonant with some of the major terminology used for resurrection in Hebrew, Aramaic, Greek, and Latin.

Merry's healing is more light-hearted than the others, unsurprisingly (his first words when waking from his stupor are "I am hungry. What is the time?"). But Aragorn touching his eyelids and calling him by name is not far off from how Jesus healed the blind on a few occasions (Matt 9:29–30; Mark 8:23, 25; John 9:6).[17] And the report of Aragorn's healing spread so that he continues healing people through the night, with some help from the sons of Elrond. He is rumored to be the king, and they name him Elfstone, "because of the green stone that he wore, and so the name which it was foretold at his birth that he should bear was chosen for him by his own people" (V/8). In such a way, we see Providence at work in the fulfillment of prophecy and Aragorn acting intentionally with that fulfillment in mind, as Jesus also did (not only in his passion, but also in cases leading up to it like his riding a donkey colt into Jerusalem with Zech 9 in mind). Indeed, Elessar ("Elfstone") will be part of his royal name.

Ennoblement of the Humble

There is also in this chapter an expression of a central matter in Tolkien's story. After Aragorn heals Merry, the latter converses with Pippin. Pippin notes how

---

[17] Beyond what I have observed here, Katharyn F. Crabbe has noted that each of the three waken to impressions of what is most important to them, concluding, "What this tailoring of the sense impressions to the greatest joys of the three wounded warriors suggests is that *athelas* heals by helping people to be more fully themselves." Katharyn F. Crabbe, *J. R. R. Tolkien*, Modern Literature (New York: Ungar, 1981), 95–96. More precisely, *athelas* has such effects only insofar as its potency is unleashed by the hands of a healing king. This way of making people both sound and whole in more ways than one is another way in which Aragorn acts as the Renewer.

uncomfortable he feels in Minas Tirith, since it is so different from his home. He notes that Brandybucks and Tooks cannot live long on the heights. Merry agrees, but he also says,

> at least, Pippin, we can now see them, and honour them. It is best to love first what you are fitted to love, I suppose: you must start somewhere and have some roots, and the soil of the Shire is deep. Still there are things deeper and higher; and not a gaffer could tend his garden in what he calls peace but for them, whether he knows about them or not. I am glad that I know about them, a little. (V/8)

This contrasts with a note Tolkien made in the Prologue that for a long time the Hobbits tended to heed the outside world less and less, "until they came to think that peace and plenty were the rule in Middle-earth and the right of all sensible folk. They forgot or ignored what little they had ever known of the Guardians, and of the labours of those that made possible the long peace of the Shire. They were, in fact, sheltered, but they had ceased to remember it." This shows how Merry has grown, being one of the Hobbits specially graced for such a journey as he has taken and given an appreciation for the deeper and higher things (Letter #246; cf. Letter #328).

Along with the quote from Elrond about how small hands move the wheels of the world, Tolkien cites this quote as exemplifying one of the main points of the story in Letter #186. He articulates this two-sided point in Letter #131 as a moral of the whole, that "without the high and noble the simple and vulgar is utterly mean; without the simple and ordinary the noble and heroic is meaningless." As we have explored elsewhere, this is a biblically shaped vision of both sides of this distinction.

Outsiders' Views

In the next chapter, Legolas and Gimli once again reunite with Merry and Pippin. But before they get to that, they have a conversation as they walk through the city. In line with their own proclivities, they comment on how glorious the city must have been once and how they will improve the stonework and gardens of the city. After they later speak with Imrahil and remark how he is still a sign of Gondor's former glory, they have this interesting exchange:

> 'And doubtless the good stone-work is the older and was wrought in the first building,' said Gimli. 'It is ever so with the things that Men begin: there is a frost in Spring, or a blight in Summer, and they fail of their promise.'

'Yet seldom do they fail of their seed,' said Legolas. 'And that will lie in the dust and rot to spring up again in times and places unlooked-for. The deeds of Men will outlast us, Gimli.'

'And yet come to naught in the end but might-have-beens, I guess,' said the Dwarf.

'To that the Elves know not the answer,' said Legolas. (V/9)

From the perspectives of two outsiders, themselves members of races doomed to recede in the Dominion of Men, we have some reflections on the often-sad state of Men and their works in their fallenness. And yet there is a trace of enduring glory that perhaps reflects that they are the image- and likeness-bearers of God, albeit distorted in their fallenness. Legolas's own expression foreshadows an interesting parallel that will be drawn in a later chapter. It may also be a way of articulating the providential guidance of Men and their descendants as a whole to some higher purpose. As Tolkien says in Letter #64, "All things and deeds have a value in themselves, apart from their 'causes' and 'effects'. No man can estimate what is really happening at the present *sub specie aeternitaris*. All we do know, and that to a large extent by direct experience, is that evil labours with vast power and perpetual success – in vain: preparing always only the soil for unexpected good to sprout in. So it is in general, and so it is in our own lives." Without such work by God to allow for some deeds to have more lasting effect, so that they can be compared to foundations of gold, silver, and precious stones (1 Cor 3:10–15), they would not resonate across the generations at all, much less into the new creation. But that is a matter that goes beyond the scope of this story into eternity future, so that characters within the story (whether of the Secondary World or the Primary World) might say no more than Gimli or Legolas, save by *estel*.

This is also a passage that reminds us that Tolkien's characters are not meant to be reflections of him. They can be in fragmentary ways, but neither Legolas nor Gimli is meant to stand in for Tolkien here. It is rather reminiscent of one of my favorite scenes of *Star Trek: Deep Space Nine* in the wonderful Season 4 opener "The Way of the Warrior." It is a scene involving Quark and Garak, two outsiders to the United Federation of Planets, reflecting on their current situation and how they feel about the fact that their safety depends on the Federation. Their views are their own as outsiders and not necessarily representative of the authors. But in their own ways, they convey something truthful about those to whom they are outsiders.

Providence in the Journey North

After this, Gimli and Legolas relate to the Hobbits, and thus to the audience, how it was that they came out of the south to the battle in time to turn the tide. For such to have been possible, it was first necessary for them to hasten the journey through the Paths of the Dead and to Pelargir. That they accomplished after being hardened by the resolve of Aragorn.

Second, they needed to defeat the great Corsair fleet without the southern Gondorians suffering too many casualties. This they accomplished thanks to the Dead Men being invulnerable to the Corsairs and causing them to flee in fear, even to their own deaths. Thus, Gimli observes, "Strange and wonderful I thought it that the designs of Mordor should be overthrown by such wraiths of fear and darkness. With its own weapons was it worsted" (V/9). As we have seen already, the Dead Men have become instruments of divine providence in spite of their initial intentions and in spite of their being overlooked as contributors to the war with Sauron. After this, in fidelity to his word, Aragorn dismisses them to their rest, as they have finally fulfilled their oath over 3,000 years later.

Third, they needed to be able to travel quickly across the forty-two leagues of the Anduin that separated Pelargir from the Harlond port near Minas Tirith. This they could not have accomplished in as timely a fashion as they would have wished, for no matter the effort exerted by the rowers, the ships were slow going against the stream without wind. And that is when Legolas laughed at sensing the changing of wind that we have noted before, as he typifies *estel* in declaring, "Oft hope is born, when all is forlorn" (V/9). For a powerful wind came out of the south great enough to push the fleet upstream faster than they could have expected, and it did so without damaging the ships. By this stroke of divine providence that accomplished other purposes as well, the ships were able to arrive before Gondor and Rohan could be routed.

The Last Debate

After this recap is finished, the story shifts in focus to the discussion among the leaders of the Free Peoples as are gathered here of what to do next. Gandalf observes how they have survived, albeit with much loss, the first great assault, but the battle has shown that there is no hope for victory by arms in this war.[18] Sauron's forces are too

---

[18] See also Tolkien, *War of the Ring*, 385: "We fought as best we could, because we had to; and it is so appointed in this world that resistance must be made to evil without final hope."

great. Prudence might dictate that the best chance for the Free Peoples is to retreat into what strongholds they have and resist as best they can. But Gandalf does not counsel prudence, for, "I still hope for victory, but not by arms" (V/9). He then reminds them of what is at stake in Frodo and Sam's Quest with the One Ring. If Sauron regains the Ring, no defensive strategy will save them. If the Ring is destroyed, so too will Sauron and his kingdom crumble so as never to rise again. This is not the end of evil as such. As Gandalf says, "Other evils there are that may come; for Sauron is himself but a servant or emissary. Yet it is not our part to master all the tides of the world, but to do what is in us for the succor of those years wherein we are set, uprooting the evil in the fields that we know, so that those who live after may have clean earth to till. What weather they shall have is not ours to rule" (V/9). This reiterates the wisdom that Gandalf spoke to Frodo all the way back in Book I that it is not for us to decide what times we are in, but it is for us to decide what to do with the time that is given to us and what to do for the times that we are given to.

Gandalf's comment also highlights that the victory they can possibly achieve is not eschatological. That final victory is beyond any of their power, and no one knows when it will come. Sauron was not evil in the beginning, and he is not the end of evil. There may not be others quite like him as incarnate demons, but until the eschaton, the possibility for evil powers arising and even dominating will ever be with us. But we are not ultimately responsible for finding a final victory that is unachievable for any but the Creator. Our responsibility concerns what faces us in the present, and thus what we leave to those after us, not the unforeseen events they will face.

In this case, the responsibility is to do what can be done to help the Quest from afar. Sauron's Lidless Eye has been drawn to them by how surprisingly "the winds of fortune" turned in his enemies' favor and how much he has lost in this defeat (V/9). Thus, he advises to attack Mordor itself:

> We must walk open-eyed into that trap, with courage, but small hope for ourselves. For, my lords, it may well prove that we ourselves shall perish utterly in a black battle far from the living lands; so that even if Barad-dûr be thrown down, we shall not live to see a new age. But this, I deem, is our duty. And better so than to perish nonetheless—as we surely shall, if we sit here and know as we die that no new age shall be. (V/9)

As Frodo himself has journeyed sacrificially, and as Gandalf has sacrificed his own life and so been vindicated for it, the Free Peoples led by those in this council must also go forth in self-sacrifice for the sake of the Ring-bearer. As with the suffering faithful throughout Scripture, they may well face their own deaths for all that they know. But if that is what is required, that is what is required. The faithful one must have courage to do what must be done. They themselves have seen multiple times over how Providence has honored courage by taking it up into the divine purposes and directing it to surprising ends. And so they must show courageous *estel* again, whether or not they will live to see their hopes fulfilled. This will be all the more remarkable for those who follow the lead of this council, for they know little or nothing of their chances or what exactly they are marching to achieve. Yet they march anyway, putting their trust in those who command them, and in the One to use this strategy to whatever good end.

Aragorn is the first to assent to Gandalf's plan. He has come to see his mission through to the end and to help Gandalf achieve his purpose, and so he says, "We come now to the very brink, where hope and despair are akin. To waver is to fall" (V/9). This is the *amdir* hope that he is referring to. As Gandalf has already said, there is not necessarily hope that they will come out of this trial alive, and so the expectation may be as likely (if not more) for an evil outcome than a good one (i.e., the despair that is the opposite of *amdir* rather than the despair that is the opposite of *estel*). In such a situation, one must stand firm with courage and *estel* to resolve to do what must be done. There is no room for vacillation or "limping between options" (1 Kgs 18:21).

Éomer follows him in this. All he needs to know that this is the right way is his commitment to fidelity (or πίστις) in friendship: "I have little knowledge of these deep matters; but I need it not. This I know, and it is enough, that as my friend Aragorn succoured me and my people, so I will aid him when he calls. I will go" (V/9).

Imrahil then follows. He has known Aragorn for the shortest time, but he is satisfied with his claims to kingship. Thus, he too commits in fidelity to follow the same path as Aragorn, "As for me … the Lord Aragorn I hold to be my liege-lord, whether he claim it or no. His wish is to me a command. I will go also" (V/9). He then raises the matter of where prudence is needed, which is the defense of Minas Tirith and the lands behind them. Thus, much of the rest of the chapter concerns preparations for what army can best be assembled in two days. Their army of 7,000 that sets out is again a pale reflection of the great armies of Gondor's past, but it is enough for their purposes: to challenge the Dark Lord and to draw his attention, especially since this army includes some of his most hated enemies.

The March to the Black Gate

The last chapter of Book V concerns the long march to the Morannon, the Black Gate of Mordor. Various stops are made along the way, including a skirmish at the Cross-roads that was only a feint from the forces of Mordor. But between the Free Peoples' long march in the shadow of Mordor, the felt presence of the Nazgûl wheeling overhead out of bowshot, and the arrival to the desolate lands leading to Mordor's entrance, some of the soldiers became unmanned. They were young men from Rohan and Gondor for whom Mordor always seemed like a distant tale of evil, one without immediate impact on their lives. And now here they were marching to the place of nightmares. For them, the fear became too enormous to keep moving.

Aragorn shows here a wisdom shaped by the divine virtue of pity. He does not scold or chide them. He does not tell them to keep marching because he told them so. But he also cannot allow this damage to their morale to spread through this army that will need every bit of courage to walk into a battle for which there is no expectation that they will return from (cf. Deut 20:8). Thus, he gives them a choice to go and take Cair Andros, which is still held by the enemy. Some were shamed by such a show of mercy, so that they responded with renewed resolve to march to Mordor, while the others "took new hope, hearing of a manful deed within their measure that they could turn to, and they departed" (V/10). Both groups are able to act manfully thanks to Aragorn's leading with a healing and encouraging hand rather than an iron fist. Both groups found purpose and thus the motivation for courage that filled up what was lacking for them.[19]

And so they finally march to Mordor with less than 6,000 (as some were left to guard various passes and others left for Cair Andros). The representatives of the Free Peoples go forth to parley with the embassy of Sauron, led by the Mouth of Sauron. He bears tokens to them that appear to spell the end of all hope: Sam's Arnorian blade, one of their cloaks from Lothlórien, and Frodo's mithril coat. Gandalf, speaking on behalf of all, asks for Sauron's terms, and it is even expected now that he will accept them. But once the terms are stated, Gandalf takes the tokens and rejects utterly the terms of the treacherous and faithless one. Here and in the battle that follows the spirit of courage exemplified in the indomitable will is shown in its most manifest kind of form. There is now no apparent hope, for by all signs, Frodo appears to be captured, which would mean, as far as they know, that the Ring is also taken. But still, like the northern

---

[19] Initially, Tolkien had written the speech in question to be Gandalf's. Tolkien, *War of the Ring*, 430. It would not be out of character for him, of course, but it makes more sense that the line should come from the one who will be king and who is already treated as such.

warriors who had no final hope, Gandalf and the others will not be cowed; they will not fail in their commitments that have led them here. They thus face their seemingly inevitable demise by fighting to the end, thereby doing what is right because it is right, even in the absence of the *amdir* kind of hope.

The story is told from Pippin's perspective, and before he loses consciousness after saving Beregond, he hears a report of the Eagles coming. These agents of Providence have made a rare appearance, even if it seems to be for naught. Thus it would be, if there was not hope from another quarter and the arrival of the Eagles did not prove timely, as has been the way of Providence in this story.

CHAPTER NINE

Commentary on Book VI

The Courage of Samwise the Servant

With Book VI, we return to the storyline of the main Quest. Frodo has been captured and taken to the Tower of Cirith Ungol. Sam has been left behind without any apparent means of reclaiming Frodo. The Quest is now in his hands. We saw before that Sam would not make a good Ring-bearer precisely because of his devotion to Frodo. But that is also what made him a good and faithful servant and what inspired his heroic courage. Unlike his persistent doubt about taking the Ring and going on with the Quest, we are told here, "He no longer had any doubt about his duty: he must rescue his master or perish in the attempt" (VI/1).

He has no apparent hope of accomplishing the former. He has no idea how many Orcs occupy the fortress, nor does he have any idea of how to get in with minimal risk. In fact, he can only think to go in through the front door. And he is not lacking for fear, but he approaches the fortress nonetheless. Because of such a courageous decision, he finds hope, at first only hearing a faint echo of it in the distance. For reasons beyond his control, the treacherous character of the Orcs had broken their fragile homeostasis, and the entire fortress was consumed with infighting that had begun between the leaders. The timing was providential, as was the fact that the divine gift of courage had brought him to the possible realization of his hope to rescue Frodo. His faithfulness (both in terms of his fidelity to Frodo and his exercise of *estel* here) is thus rewarded, and he has a chance to rescue his master.

The Problem of the Ring

Even so, Sam must take a leap of faith here. He does not know how the fighting goes within. He does not know if any eyes from the tower are still watching so as to detect him. One might think he could use the Ring for stealth. He had done so recently, after all. But for as briefly as he had borne the Ring, he noticed a change as he drew closer to the Tower and was able to survey the Land of Mordor, including Mount Doom in the distance. As the narrator tells us, "As it drew near the great furnaces where, in the deeps of time, it had been shaped and forged, the Ring's power grew, and it became more fell, untameable save by some mighty will" (VI/1).

This foreshadows the problem that the Ring will pose as the plot reaches its climax. And the way it expresses its power now is through ever-stronger temptation to the point of delusion. For as simple a Hobbit as Samwise Gamgee is, and as simple as his wishes for his life are, the Ring can play upon his will so as to give him delusions of grandeur if he would but use the Ring. It gives him grand visions of how he could be the savior Middle-earth needs, even exploiting his love of story, as his vision now goes beyond that of what Frodo had said of Samwise the Brave, as he now envisions "Samwise the Strong, Hero of the Age" (VI/1). He could overthrow Sauron and his forces with this power, and then he could use it to make even this desolate land of Mordor into a garden paradise.

Ultimately, Sam is able to resist this temptation because:

> In that hour of trial it was the love of his master that helped most to hold him firm; but also deep down in him lived still unconquered his plain hobbit-sense: he knew in the core of his heart that he was not large enough to bear such a burden, even if such visions were not a mere cheat to betray him. The one small garden of a free gardener was all his need and due, not a garden swollen to a realm; his own hands to use, not the hands of others to command. (VI/1)

We have seen before how this devotion upwards is part and parcel of how Sam provides the purest manifestation of that northern spirit of courage seen otherwise in characters like Wiglaf and the retinue of Beorhtnoth. That devotion simplifies his will and the scope thereof so as to help him see clearly through the deception of the Ring. If he thought his role to be otherwise in the story he finds himself in, the Ring could well have exploited that to lead him to ruin, but he was content to be the good and faithful servant who acts courageously for the sake of his master, and not for his own sake.

In this way, Sam anticipates the type of servant that Jesus will praise in his teachings about vigilance in conduct. The good and faithful servant is not one who "watches for signs" of the master's coming, but one who faithfully discharges the master's will in the time of waiting (Matt 24:42–51; Mark 13:33–37; Luke 12:35–48; 21:34–36). This is shown even more clearly in the parables of the talents and the minas in Matt 25:14–30 and Luke 19:11–30. Sam and these exemplary servants simplify their lives by attending to the will and purposes of their master, rather than seeking after their own ambitions (or, worse, the will of other masters).

Moreover, Sam is like what I observed from Bilbo in my study of *The Hobbit* in that he embodies the virtue of simplicity.[1] In this he echoes several statements from Ecclesiastes. The author, known as Qoheleth, speaks of how it is good to be joyful, do good, eat, drink, and take pleasure in toil in the days God has given one (3:12–13; 5:18–20; 8:15; 9:7–9), which are fundamentally related to "remembering your Creator" (12:1). This is part and parcel of what it means to be faithful against the temptation of the Ring in this pre-Christian age. The Ring tempts one to exceed creaturely limitations, while accepting creaturely limitations is an expression of *estel* in the Creator who set those limitations.

Likewise, Jesus teaches against both storing up treasure on earth as opposed to in heaven and worrying about clothing, food, and drink, for the Father knows what those who listen to him need, and he will provide, but their focus is to remain on pursuing the kingdom (Matt 6:19–33). As Paul was one who followed this teaching faithfully, he could speak of being content with whatever he had, for he had known both need and plenty (Phil 4:11–13). Thus, he also speaks of the gain that comes when one combines godliness and contentment with what God has given (1 Tim 6:6–10).

By such virtues, Sam can overcome the temptation of the Ring. But one should remember that he does not overcome it in such a way that the Ring has no power over him. He still realizes that the temptation is dangerous. He is not like the mysterious Tom Bombadil who can put on the Ring without it overcoming him. He simply has the insight to see that he cannot use the Ring anymore. To do so would invite disaster.

Journey's End?

Sam then enters the fortress after a fierce strain on his will from the ghastly Watchers at the gate, but inside he finds little resistance, as the Orcs have effectively

---

[1] Harriman, *God Has Chosen the Little Ones*, 103.

neutralized each other. But based on what he hears, there is still reason for fear for his master's safety and for himself. We even see in this process a minor demonstration of the power of the Ring, for despite Sam knowing better than to use the Ring, at one point his hand still clutches the Ring, as his will was too weak and slow to resist it. Only the sudden sight of an Orc and his fleeing from him in surprise was enough to jolt him out of this near-incidental fall.

But then he ultimately reaches what appears to be a dead end. His way to Frodo is blocked by locked doors, and he has no apparent way of getting through otherwise. With no recourse, and for reasons Sam could not discern, he finds that he begins to sing. At first, he simply recalls tunes from the Shire, now being a reminder of his far-off home. But eventually "new strength rose in him" and "words of his own came un-bidden" to fit one of these simple tunes (VI/1). The second part of this short song is most pertinent for our purposes:

> Though here at journey's end I lie
> in darkness buried deep,
> beyond all towers strong and high,
> beyond all mountains steep,
> above all shadows rides the Sun
> and Stars for ever dwell:
> I will not say the Day is done,
> nor bid the Stars farewell. (VI/1)

Again, this song does not appear to be sung for any particular purpose but defiance, as far as Sam is concerned. But it nevertheless serves as self-encouragement from un-bidden words and a declaration of his resolve. The song is thus a providential gift. Indeed, Sam says more than he knows here, as a later scene will show him coming to a realization that is in line with these words that he has not yet internalized. And it is also a declaration of *estel*. As with his earlier decision, he perseveres in hope, despite the lack of a way forward. And that perseverance will be rewarded by Snaga the Orc unintentionally helping him by opening a door to punish Frodo for the singing. That gives Sam his chance to finally rescue his master and resume the Quest from there. This is one of the many surprising ways we have seen in this story of what happens when courage and *estel* meet the providential guidance of events.

On the Nature of Orcs

As Sam prepares to leave the fortress with Frodo, he takes stock of what they have and realizes the severity of their situation with food and drink. He then wonders what Orcs do for food and drink, or if they even eat and drink. Frodo responds, "No, they eat and drink, Sam. The Shadow that bred them can only mock, it cannot make: not real new things of its own. I don't think it gave life to the orcs, it only ruined them and twisted them; and if they are to live at all, they have to live like other living creatures" (VI/1).

Tolkien himself quotes these words in Letter #153 as a counter to what Treebeard had said of the Orcs. Peter Hastings had objected to the notion of the Orcs being products of creation by evil. Tolkien notes that Treebeard himself did not say this; he simply parallels them to Trolls as those he said were "made" in counterfeit. But he did not actually know this. Tolkien quotes Frodo as nearer the mark as a result of having more insight on the matter. Tolkien never fully settled on what the origin of the Orcs was, although in this letter he references what came to be featured in *The Silmarillion* that the Orcs came from some of the earliest Elves that Melkor subjugated and corrupted. For now, we need not go through the various explanations he considered over the years since what is consistent in each case is that Melkor and then Sauron (as well as Saruman derivatively) corrupted what was already created. The Orcs, as living creatures, could not be made immune to the creaturely limitations of their origins. And as Tolkien says elsewhere, this is a point that is *consonant* with orthodox Christian ontology (Letter #269), as we have noted in some detail previously.

He later closes Letter #153 with pertinent reflections on free will in relation to the divine will and the corresponding relation of sub-creation to divine creation. One of the ways Tolkien has used the term "sub-creation," is, "in a special way to make visible and physical the effects of Sin or misused Free Will by men." He has already referred in this letter to sub-creational counterfeits, but it could also refer to how Saruman and Sauron—in their own ways—have used Magic and Machine to corrupt and destroy the earth and living creatures around them, including in how they imitated Melkor in breeding Orcs. Like sub-creation—good or bad—volition is derivative and limited by circumstance. But for it to exist, Tolkien insists, "it is necessary that the Author should guarantee it, whatever betides: sc. [namely,] when it is 'against His Will', as we say, at any rate as it appears on a finite view. He does not stop or make 'unreal' sinful acts and their consequences."

In other words, for volition to be real and effective, it must have real consequences, whether the choices or consequences are good or evil. In the Primary World, the capacities designed to aid humans in the vocation of image-bearing are not removed even when humans use them for sin (even for grievous sin on massive scales). In the Secondary World, even Morgoth does not have his ability to make removed, despite the most perverted use to which he puts it in corrupting creation to make Orcs his fearful slaves who acknowledge him as lord and creator. Eru Ilúvatar allows such things into existence as an extreme upholding of volition, even though Morgoth's corruptions must be naturally—though not irredeemably—bad. Tolkien makes this important qualification because, "by accepting or tolerating their making – necessary to their actual existence – even Orcs would become part of the World, which is God's and ultimately good." (Thus, again, we see the impact of orthodox Christian ontology with which Tolkien sought to be consonant.) Still, volition is limited and cannot make what is impossible possible. There are many powers that God in the Secondary World—like God in the Primary World—has not delegated, such as making spirits, which are required for rational creatures like the Orcs. Hence, Orcs are corrupted pre-existing creatures, rather than actual creations by Morgoth.

Signs of Hope

After this conversation, Frodo and Sam escape the Tower of Cirith Ungol, narrowly and painfully managing to avoid detection by a Nazgûl who has flown there. They then proceed on the trek north and then east to Mount Doom. They have cladded themselves in Orc gear, but Frodo now finds this to be a wearisome weight after the Ring has become heavier upon him. And both he and Sam are parched from this desolate land's lack of fresh water anywhere nearby. Given how Galadriel's gifts have helped these Hobbits thus far in their Quest, Sam now thinks if she could see and hear them, he would ask her for some light—as in plain daylight, rather than the star-glass—and some clean water. Not much later in this very day, Sam will get what he wished for.

The wish and its fulfillment prove to be providential in timing, as not much later in the narration we are told:

> Light was growing behind them. Slowly it crept towards the North. There
> was battle far above in the high spaces of the air. The billowing clouds of
> Mordor were being driven back, their edges tattering as a wind out of the living
> world came up and swept the fumes and smokes towards the dark land of their

home. Under the lifting skirts of their dreary canopy dim light leaked into Mordor like pale morning through the grimed window of a prison. (VI/2)

The timing is providential because this is the same wind from the south that drove away the darkness over Minas Tirith at the coming of the Rohirrim and pushed Aragorn and his forces to the battlefield in a timely fashion. This same wind with the light it reveals now provides a sign of hope for Frodo and Sam, in part because it is a positively answered prayer for Sam. Sam even exclaims, "He's not having it all his own way. His darkness is breaking up out in the world there" (VI/2). Sadly, Frodo does not take this sign to heart, as the light and the sound of the Ringwraiths flying in dismay back over the mountains signal events happening far away, but for him the Ring is more immediate and more pressing, as he now sees it in his mind at all times as a wheel of fire.

But then later that day they find another sign of hope: the unmistakable sound of water trickling. And so Sam exclaims, "If ever I see the Lady again, I will tell her!... Light and now water" (VI/2). And Frodo now takes some comfort in this more immediate aid, as he eschews Sam's caution at allowing him to test the water first by saying, "I think we'll trust our luck together, Sam; or our blessing" (VI/2). The description of "blessing" is, of course, theologically evocative, and so it is here when paired with a use of "luck" that is another name for the work of Providence in their favor.

The timely provision of water in particular is reminiscent of God's provision of water in stories of the OT. The two that are most like this one—in that they involve individuals and not many people, as with the provisions for Israel—involve Hagar and Samson. Hagar and her son Ishmael had been sent away by Abraham. As they wandered in the wilderness of Beersheba, their skin of water eventually ran out. As Ishmael cried out, an angel of the Lord came and opened Hagar's eyes to a well of water to provide for them (Gen 21:14–19). In Samson's case, after he had slaughtered his Philistine captors with the jawbone of a donkey, he cried out to the Lord wondering why he would give him this victory and allow him to die of thirst where they had taken him. Then God provided a spring for Samson to revive with (Judg 15:17–19).

To clarify, the framing of this part of the story is not to say that Galadriel herself answered such a request as if she could answer prayers. But the divinely providential quality of the response to such an invocation once again presents her in a Marian light, as we have seen before. Tolkien himself said that though Galadriel was herself a penitent, "it is true that I owe much of this character to Christian and Catholic teaching and imagination about Mary" (Letter #320). This whole situation could thus rightly be considered analogous to how Catholics pray for Mary and the exalted saints to pray for them, which does not mean that they answer prayers instead of God. In this conception, God answers prayers through their invocation, as the ones invoked pray to God on behalf of those who invoked them.

Light Beyond the Reach of the Shadow

At the end of that day's journey, Frodo falls fast asleep from the exhaustion of the day. Sam crawls out from their bramble-covered shelter to take a look around in order to keep himself awake. While he is out, he looks to the west in what is now a somewhat clearer night sky. The wind had driven away the lower cloud cover, but Mount Doom spewed ever more fumes even higher into the air, and so night here was still a deep dark. But Sam then has a vision that might possibly be reflective of something that happened to Tolkien himself in WW1:

> There, peeping among the cloud-wrack above a dark tor high up in the mountains, Sam saw a white star twinkle for a while. The beauty of it smote his heart, as he looked up out of the forsaken land, and hope returned to him. For like a shaft, clear and cold, the thought pierced him that in the end the Shadow was only a small and passing thing: there was light and high beauty for ever beyond its reach. His song in the Tower had been defiance rather than hope; for then he was thinking of himself. Now, for a moment, his own fate, and even his master's, ceased to trouble him. He crawled back into the bramble and laid himself by Frodo's side, and putting away all fear he cast himself into a deep untroubled sleep. (VI/2)

This is the ultimate sign of transcendent hope for Sam. It is by this sight that he internalizes what he had earlier put to song. The transcendent light and beauty points beyond itself to the One who is transcendent, the source of light, beauty, and the fulfillment of hope. The trust that Sam shows here to cast himself into a deep untroubled sleep that is not simply the product of exhaustion is precisely the characteristic of *estel*.[2] The One who is the source of these things, the One from whom came the stars and their light forever beyond the reach of the Shadow, is the same One who has their well-being in his hands. There have been many such reminders of this throughout the Quest for those with eyes to see. But this has been the most dramatic reminder of all because of its high contrast of a small shaft of unconquerable light far above the vast canopy of the darkest realm in Middle-earth. The Shadow, though it is more immediately

---

[2] Whether or not this is the star of Eärendil, as has sometimes been speculated, it should be remembered that, if it is the same star, Eärendil's star was called "Gil-Estel" (Star of High Hope) by the Elves.

pressing, is shown to be small by its lack of reach in space, and, by implication, it is also shown to be passing by its lack of reach in time. The Quest the Hobbits are on aims to limit the present Shadow's reach even sooner. And it is being guided by the One who is light far beyond the Shadow's reach (John 1:3–9; 8:12).

This reflection of Sam's is also of a piece with the orthodox Christian ontology that undergirds this story. Nothing is evil in origin, as evil is parasitic. God is the only eternal one and all that he has made was originally good. Evil is thus inherently limited in a way that good is not. Unlike other worldviews as represented by Manichaeism (which Augustine and others of his day combatted), there is no everlasting dualism at work here. Nor is there the expectation, as in Norse eschatology, that eventually the forces of chaos will triumph even over the gods, that even their final defeat is inevitable. Instead, in anticipation of the revelation of final victory and the ultimate Victor, there is light that shines in the darkness and hope with substance that transcends the despair impressed upon the world by the dark powers.

Luck in an Unlucky Land

As the continuing journey to Mount Doom shows us, this *estel* hope is an essential resource because there is no apparent sign of *amdir* hope to be found in the Land of Shadow. One way this becomes apparent is when they face the massive forces in between them and the mountain. Frodo says he never hoped to get across the open country with the vast host before them, and indeed he says, "I can't see any hope of it now. But I've still got to do the best I can" (VI/2). This is a determination born out of courage and the fact that Frodo has seen time and again how Providence has taken up courageous acts and directed them to a good end. They cannot afford to wait for a sign of *amdir*; they simply must have the will to do without it.

This is reaffirmed when seemingly their only path to where they need to go is to cross by the forts of Carach Angren. Sam simply says "We must take it and chance our luck, if there is any luck in Mordor" (VI/2). He also says he must leave Frodo and "trust to luck" in hopes of finding water for the journey (VI/2). Sam finds what he needs, and they take to the road again. But during that march, their fears of discovery are realized. They see Orcs marching towards them, and they have no means of escape. In his despair Frodo says, "We've trusted to luck, and it has failed us" (VI/2). Sam then acknowledges that there is nothing for it but to wait and see. They are still in their Orc gear and can disguise themselves well enough for rushed and inattentive eyes to force them to march along without being immediately unmasked. Despite Frodo's initial despair at what appeared to be the failure of his Quest, they end up being lucky enough to be able escape through the confusion of Orc companies merging and scuffling.

Through this part of their Quest, we see how Frodo and Sam are reliant on what they call "luck." They must be smart about how they proceed, but there is only so much they can do where they simply have no ideal path to their goal. Thus, they must trust that events that are beyond their control can, potentially, work in their favor if "luck" is in their favor. When that which is beyond their control seems to take a disastrous turn to put the entire Quest at risk of failure, Frodo speaks of luck failing them. This is akin to that sense of Godforsakenness seen in the lament psalms, such as the opening of Ps 22 or the darkest of the psalms in Ps 88.[3] It is as if in this moment that Frodo fears that he has been forsaken by the One who brought him so far. But he learns before too long that it was not so. Certainly, the ever-growing weight of his burden and how it presses upon his mind, body, and spirit have combined to make him think the worst in this moment. And yet, there was still hope unlooked for by the uneasy alliance of their enemies—which they have seen work in their favor multiple times to this point—that provided them a way out. What they call "luck" has, in fact, not failed them, because the One who is guiding these events beyond their control has not failed them.

As they continue on their journey, now free of the Orcs busied in forming up for war, Sam comes to a haunting realization that he had tried to stave off for as long as he could, but which Frodo had long since come to terms with: whatever happens, they will not have enough provisions to last after they reach their goal. There is no hope (as in *amdir*) of a way out. For all that they can tell, their goal is now their end. Sam stubbornly resolves in his lack of *amdir* that if his job is to help Frodo to the end and die with him, then that is what he must do. But then the narrator tells us, "But even as hope died in Sam, or seemed to die, it was turned to a new strength. Sam's plain hobbit-face grew stern, almost grim, as the will hardened in him, and felt through all his limbs a thrill, as if he was turning into some creature of stone and steel that neither despair nor weariness nor endless barren miles could subdue" (VI/3). Sam is once again as pure an example as one can find in this story of the embodiment of that northern spirit of courage in the indomitable will. He is not the strongest, the smartest, the most cunning, the swiftest, the most skilled, the most valiant, and he is nowhere near the most powerful. But he is undeniably steadfast and stouthearted. He has been specially graced with such characteristics and the extent of these that he has, which have been further cultivated

---

[3] On this text, see here: https://krharriman.substack.com/p/psalm-88.

by the trials that he has faced, and they are all he needs for the task that has been given to him.

Even so, though he focuses on what he can do and what efforts he and Frodo can make, since those facts are all that they can control, he acknowledges that there are forces and events beyond their control. This means, once again, that they must "trust to luck." He says, "It nearly failed us last time, but it didn't quite" (VI/3). They are all too aware of the necessity of their trusting to luck in their situation, but Sam reminds Frodo that while they thought it would fail them earlier, it did not, in fact, fail them. They may not know the One by name, but Eru Ilúvatar has not forsaken them nor betrayed their trust. Indeed, he will take up events and characters beyond their control, as well as their own decisions, to bring about the great eucatastrophe of this story in a way that they could not imagine.

Sauron himself appears to have perceived something of the work of a higher power. For the narrator tells us the movements of his forces, which ultimately benefited Frodo and Sam after initially appearing to doom them, were because "even in the fastness of his own realm he sought the secrecy of night, fearing the winds of the world that had turned against him, tearing aside his veils, and troubled with tidings of bold spies that had passed through his fences" (VI/3).

Foreshadowing the Ultimate Trial

But even as the obstacle of the Orcs and their allies has been removed from before the Hobbits, their journey is no less wearisome. The Ring grows heavier as they come ever closer to Mount Doom. And Frodo's mind is tormented so that with his left hand he would try to shield himself from the gaze of the Eye he feels to be searching him, probing for weakness to overwhelm. At the same time, "sometimes his right hand would creep to his breast, clutching, and then slowly, as the will recovered mastery, it would be withdrawn" (VI/3). While Frodo has engaged in physical struggles with flesh and blood at times in this Quest, his chief battle has been a spiritual one. It is mostly unseen, but inevitably, as in any intense spiritual conflict, it manifests outwardly, as with this struggle we see here. He has been specially graced with incredible willpower, as Tolkien himself has declared in remarks that we will get to later. He has borne this weight sacrificially for so long because of it. As we have discussed before, he has been sanctified for this task, and he has grown in that sanctification as he has gone through his journey. But that has not meant his struggles got easier. While enough practice can make resisting temptation become habitual, temptations also become stronger the more they are resisted. And beyond temptations there are other trials that test our limitations beyond our moral ones.

This struggle is foreshadowing his ultimate trial not because he will have one last chance to prove if his willpower is strong enough. That last trial will not be about whether he is a good enough person to have a strong enough will to survive anything that is thrown his way. His willpower will not save him. His hand grasping the Ring is not his will almost giving in. It is simply what happens when his will is not alert. When his will is alert, he can just fight off involuntarily putting on the Ring. There is simply another power at work. But there is yet another will at work, the Author, the One who was at work when the Ring abandoned Gollum to ensure that it was picked up by Bilbo. And so that One will be at work yet again in spite of the Ring's efforts.

The Grace of Lembas

In this last leg of the journey, we have focused on grace in the form of what the Hobbits call "luck," as well as in the characteristics they have as internal means of providence. But there is an external grace they have borne with them since Lórien. The last food they have left to eat is the *lembas* the Elves gave them. It gave them the strength they had left. For as the narrator tells us:

> The *lembas* had a virtue without which they would long ago have lain down to die. It did not satisfy desire, and at times Sam's mind was filled with the memories of food, and the longing for simple bread and meats. And yet this waybread of the Elves had a potency that increased as travelers relied on it alone and did not mingle it with other foods. It fed the will, and it gave strength to endure, and to master sinew and limb beyond the measure of mortal kind. (VI/3)

This is consistent with how the waybread was described in its introduction (after Gimli had scarfed down a cake of it) as being strengthening beyond the food made by Men, even when one ate only a little at a time (II/8). It had served the Three Hunters well in strengthening them even as they ran (III/2). When Merry and Pippin ate of it, "The taste brought back to them the memory of fair faces, and laughter, and wholesome food in quiet days now far away" (III/3), and Merry remarked, "*Lembas* does put heart into you! A more wholesome sort of feeling, too, than the heat of that orc-draught" (III/3). But it is particularly in this chapter that this strengthening aspect has a larger significance that Tolkien says, "one might hesitatingly call a 'religious' kind" (Letter #210).

Holly Ordway observes how Tolkien fundamentally changed the way the term "waybread" was used through his fiction and his letters:

> Before Tolkien's writing of *The Lord of the Rings*, "waybread" had only one meaning: it was the medieval common name for plantain, a wide-leaved plant growing beside the "way" (i.e., the road). The suffix "-bread" had nothing to do with food but rather comes from the Old English word for "broad" (referring to the leaves). Tolkien's repurposing of "waybread" to mean "food for a journey" converts it into an English equivalent of the Latin *viaticum*, which comes from *via* ("way") and, as the *Oxford English Dictionary* notes, means literally "provision for a journey."[4]

Tolkien further confirms this connection with his religious beliefs when he notes with approval the comments of a reader linking the *lembas* with *viaticum*, "and the reference to its feeding the *will* ... and being more potent when fasting, a derivation from the Eucharist" (Letter #213; emphasis original). The sense of the Latin term noted in the quote above makes it all the more apt a comparison with *lembas*'s function in the story, although it should be noted that this term is particularly applied to the Eucharist when given in Last Rites as preparation for death. That would make it an apropos analogy for the *lembas* as Frodo and Sam make the final approach to Mount Doom, expecting their deaths at the end.

This is not to say that the *lembas* simply *is* the Eucharist. It is not. Nor, per what we observed in Chapter One, is it an allegory of the same. It is merely the Secondary World's anticipation of it, being the nearest analogy in the "order of nature" of what will come to be in the "order of grace." The Eucharist derives its effect from the work of Christ. Tolkien would not imagine that there could be a true Eucharist, as such, before Christ's incarnation, even if there might be an anticipatory one (like the manna from heaven). But the description of *lembas* is partially derived from the Eucharist's secondary effects, which, one could reason, might be anticipated in the order of nature, as its primary effects are the direct result of the redemptive work of Christ. The knowledge for making it was given to the Elves long ago, but its greatest fruit is borne only now as a grace given to the heroes of this story to bring them to that eucatastrophic resolution that will provide a christological echo with the one who is a type of Christ the High Priest.

Likewise, Wood has paralleled Frodo and Sam's experience with the *noche oscura del alma*, the dark night of the soul St. John of the Cross describes in the poem of the

---

[4] Ordway, *Tolkien's Faith*, 114.

same name.[5] This experience is one of walking in darkness and emptiness and thereby finding the light of life after all else has been stripped away. It is a particularly memorable version of what Paul described as power being made complete in weakness, finding that God's grace is sufficient (2 Cor 12:7–10). And so it is for Frodo and Sam here when they find peculiar strength from the *lembas* when everything else has been stripped away in this realm of darkness.

Frodo Cannot Lay Down His Burden

Indeed, we see how this dark night manifests for Frodo as they approach Mount Doom. Each step only brings more weariness as the burden grows with them. The only sign of invigoration he gives is when Sam offers to carry the Ring for a bit, to which he suddenly responds with a wild light in his eyes, "'Stand away! Don't touch me!' he cried. 'It is mine, I say. Be off!' His hand strayed to his sword-hilt" (VI/3). Frodo is again having a moment like Bilbo had in Rivendell (or like Bilbo had in Bag End with Gandalf), a moment where he seems like Gollum. But the moment passes, and Frodo more calmly explains that no one else can bear this burden anymore but him. He says he could not give it up, not fully realizing the significance of what he is saying in light of the task still set before him. The Ring has become an all-consuming object for him. He sees it all the time, and even his pleasant memories cannot be seen anymore, "No taste of food, no feel of water, no sound of wind, no memory of tree or grass or flower, no image of moon or star are left to me. I am naked in the dark, Sam, and there is no veil between me and the wheel of fire" (VI/3).

This further demonstrates how Frodo in particular is going through a sort of dark night of the soul. This is the closest equivalent in his story to a Gethsemane moment. The nature of his burden and the nature of his character differentiate his story from the Gospel accounts of Jesus in the garden of Gethsemane, but in function they are similar. No one else can take on his burden, but because Frodo is only a type of Christ and not a Christ-figure himself, he cannot get where he needs to go without Sam, who has his own crisis to face.

Hope, Despair, and the Empowerment of the One

We have not gone into all the details here, but this entire book, being told from Sam's perspective thus far, has shown the swings of Sam's mind and emotions. He has

---

[5] Wood, *Gospel*, 110–11.

been a hopeful character not because he is endlessly positive, but because he clearly can be otherwise. We see him clearly do without the hope of *amdir*, and he even teeters on the edge of the kind of despair that is the lack of *estel*. But each time he has overcome it through finding some surprising external sign (or a striking one like the star) and in all cases, even in the absence of the signs, through an act of will. For hope, like faith and love, is a repeated act of will (Rom 4:18; 5:4–5; 1 Thess 1:3; 5:8; Heb 6:18; 1 Pet 1:13). This is the primary manifestation of his courage and his stoutheartedness in this book, that he uses his indomitable resolve to keep hope alive.

And this he must do again when he has one last debate with himself as they approach the mountain. He was surprised to find Frodo walking with renewed strength, but that too petered out. He tried to reassure himself that they had gotten farther in a march than he expected, but another thought using his own voice questioned how far they could get, what they could even do once they reached their goal, and what the point of it all is anyway. Thus, he is once again tempted to despair. But Sam states his resolve to get Frodo where he needs to go if it kills him, and so he tells the voice in his head to shut up.

Thus, they continue on, but Sam finds now that he is not so fatigued as he expected. And this is because his head is clear, "No more debates disturbed his mind. He knew all the arguments of despair and would not listen to them. His will was set, and only death would break it" (VI/3). His will had been forged to indomitability by this Quest; the seed of courage has been cultivated to abundant growth to carry both Sam and Frodo this far.

But even with an unquestionable strength of heart, there remains a question of if his body is strong enough to complete the Quest. Frodo also has been pushed to his limits. Sam cannot carry the Ring for him, but he can carry Frodo, and that is just what he does. With Frodo on his back, he staggers to his feet, "and then to his amazement he felt the burden light" (VI/3). The narrator tells us:

> He had feared that he would have barely strength to lift his master alone, and beyond that he had expected to share in the dreadful dragging weight of the accursed Ring. But it was not so. Whether because Frodo was so worn by his long pains, wound of knife, and venomous sting, and sorrow, fear, and homeless wandering, or because some gift of final strength was given to him, Sam lifted Frodo with no more difficulty than if he were carrying a hobbit-child pig-a-back in some romp on the lawns or hayfields of the Shire. (VI/3)

The Initial description of Sam finding the burden light Is reminiscent of Matt 11:30. But I do not know that too much should be hanged on that similarity. More significant is that both texts in their contexts draw from the well of divine refreshment and empowerment. In Tolkien's text, this is signified by describing this experience as possibly being due to "some gift of final strength." The gift implies the giver, and we have seen throughout this story how Eru Ilúvatar has been the Provider for Frodo and Sam, as well as others. He has provided for them in multitudinous ways, including special graces like such gifts of empowerment when they have been needed.

This part of the story also shows other signs of divine providence at work. First, when the Hobbits make it further up the slope and come within sight of Sauron's Road that led to the Sammath Naur (the Chambers of Fire), they take a rest, but, "Suddenly a sense of urgency which he did not understand came to Sam. It was almost as if he had been called: 'Now, now, or it will be too late!' He braced himself and got up. Frodo also seemed to have felt the call" (VI/3). Both Frodo and Sam experience this sensation as an external call, a coinciding event that surely points to an external will being the source of this impetus.

Second, as we have noted elsewhere, the fact that Sam is here at all is a long work of divine providence in bringing these two together for this Quest. Sam has not only carried Frodo up this mountain, but he helps him to resist the Ring's attempt to move Frodo's hand to it, since Frodo himself cannot stop it (VI/3). This shows again that the problem is not Frodo's willpower but another force that is at work. And for this moment, Sam is the gift of yet another power, namely, the One who has brought them here. Without him, this would have marked the time of failure, as Frodo had been stricken at the sudden glimpse of the top of the Tower of Barad-dûr, even though the Eye was turned elsewhere.

Third, while the road to the Sammath Naur is not made smooth for Frodo and Sam, we are told, "By fortune the fires that had poured forth in the great turmoils when Sam stood upon Cirith Ungol had flowed down mainly on the southern and western slopes, and the road on this side was not blocked" (VI/3). We have seen before how "fortune" is one of the ways of referring to divine providence by different names. And by the favor of the One, it turns out that their road is kept free of such natural obstructions that would cause unnecessary delay to get around. However, that is not to say there are no more obstacles, as one reemerges at this point in the story.

Sam's Pity

After a long absence, Gollum has reappeared to attempt to finish what he started. Yet, despite his surprise attack, he fails to reclaim the Ring, for Gollum has become weaker through starvation in this desolate land and Frodo has been stirred by a sudden fire within him at the attempt of someone else to claim the Ring. He is fiercer and stronger than anyone expected him to be at that point. Frodo thus stands above the defeated creature and warns him, in words that prove prophetic, that "If you touch me ever again, you shall be cast yourself into the Fire of Doom" (VI/3).

Sam then gets between Frodo and Gollum to defend the former as he makes his way to the Sammath Naur. This should be a moment of grim satisfaction for Sam as he would have the chance to deal with Gollum once and for all in mortal combat. But Gollum shows no interest in fighting. Instead, he collapses into a whimpering mess and begs for his life, short and hopeless as it may be. And so,

> Sam's hand wavered. His mind was hot with wrath and the memory of evil. It would be just to slay this treacherous, murderous creature, just and many times deserved; and also it seemed the only safe thing to do. But deep in his heart there was something that restrained him; he could not strike this thing lying in the dust, forlorn, ruinous, utterly wretched. He himself, though only for a little while, had borne the Ring, and now dimly he guessed the agony of Gollum's shriveled mind and body, enslaved to that Ring, unable to find peace or relief ever in life again. But Sam had no words to express what he felt. (VI/3)

Sam finds himself in the same position as Bilbo decades ago when he had the upper hand on Gollum. He had seen Frodo in that same position as well, and he had repeated what Bilbo did in showing the divine virtue of pity. Now, as in both of those cases, pity prevents him from doing something advantageous, and he finds that he is no longer eager to deal out death and judgment. Like Frodo, and now like Gollum, he also had some experience bearing the Ring. And that was but for an infinitesimal fraction of the time Gollum had possessed the Ring and become possessed by it. That experience gives him a source of pity for Gollum that he had never had before. Unfortunately, it was too late to give Gollum the pity that would have been most beneficial to him. Sam had missed his chance in that regard. But it will turn out that him showing pity to Gollum at all will ensure the resolution of the Quest, even though he does not know it yet. He simply wants to be rid of Gollum and tells him to be off. But with his life given back to him, Gollum will use it in the only way he knows how: for his Precious.

Is Frodo Not a Hero After All?

And so we come at last to the resolution of the Quest and the sudden turn of fortune leading to eucatastrophe by which it is accomplished. Frodo has the Ring, seemingly being ready to throw it into the fire to destroy this great darkness once and for all. But instead, he turns and declares to Sam that the Ring is his. It was not without reason that Sauron did not think anyone would have the will to destroy the Ring even if, beyond his imagination, they had dared to make it so far as Mount Doom. The Ring was at its most powerful here. And no will, save of one even more powerful than Sauron himself, could throw it away willingly here. In the end, Frodo could not give it up. And so the Quest could well have ended as a failure right there, if not for Gollum.

Gollum had returned and knocked Sam to the ground. Frodo had put the Ring on his finger. But that did not stop the avaricious Gollum from grabbing him and biting off the finger on which he had the Ring. After many decades, Gollum has finally reclaimed his Precious. His response was obviously one of unrestrained jubilation. Yet in his jubilation, he took a step too far and fell with the Ring into the fire below.

So ended the Quest to Mount Doom. It was not quite as anyone had purposed or expected.[6] Frodo is now free of the burden that tormented his body, mind, and spirit. He had a peace about him that had been gone for what seemed an interminably long time. And Sam, even amidst all the ruination wrought by the destruction of the Ring, knows only joy, that transcendent joy from beyond the walls of the world that has come with the sudden joyous turn in events just when all had seemed lost. Frodo cannot help but acknowledge that this was because of Gollum as he recalls Gandalf's words from over a year-and-a-half ago: "But do you remember Gandalf's words: *Even Gollum may have something yet to do?* But for him, Sam, I could not have destroyed the Ring. The Quest would have been in vain, even at the bitter end. So let us forgive him" (VI/3).[7]

The climax being as it is and the subsequent celebration of Frodo as a hero have proven to be controversial for some readers. After all, Frodo failed, did he not? If, like me, you are irritated by some online discourse referring to Sam as the "real hero" (as

---

[6] While the details would be ironed out later, such as Frodo speaking of forgiving Gollum (one of those examples of Tolkien being conscious of the character of his story in the revision), it is noteworthy that at least as early as 1939, Tolkien had determined that Gollum would take the Ring and fall. Tolkien, *Sauron Defeated*, 3, 41.

[7] This is similar to a statement from Frodo that appears in an earlier version of the last chapters of Book IV: "But we could not have got even so far without him. So if we ever manage our errand, then Gollum and all his wickedness will be part of the plan." Tolkien, *War of the Ring*, 195. The remark that Tolkien has now is better refined and better placed, and thus we see that even though the line itself did not make his published draft, Frodo's sense of the action of Providence remained.

opposed to Tolkien's phrasing of "the chief hero" in Letter #131) of *LOTR*, as if to deny that Frodo was a real hero, or by some of the more explicit denigrations of Frodo as a hero, just know that such notions have been around since before the Internet. Tolkien dealt with such criticism of Frodo all the way back in the 50s. And it is noteworthy that he did so through an ethical approach that was theologically informed by his Christian faith. We will examine five letters in which he demonstrated such an approach.

The first letter that demonstrates this approach Is Letter #181 to Michael Straight. He responded to a question Straight had about the climactic scene of the Quest. He said it exemplifies an aspect of the petitions in the Lord's Prayer in Matt 6:12–13: "and forgive us our debts as we also have forgiven our debtors. And do not bring us into temptation, but deliver us from the evil one" (LEB). Particularly, it exemplifies the first clause of the second verse. Frodo, as the Ring-bearer, is led deeper into temptation than others in order to accomplish a goal of delivering the world from the evil one. It is a sacrificial situation in which Frodo is essentially "doomed to failure" of one kind or another because his circumstances "demand of him suffering and endurance far beyond the normal" (Letter #181).

It is a truth of the Primary World exemplified in the Secondary World that makes Frodo's failure realistic and even inevitable. He may be a christological type in his enacting of a priestly and even suffering servant role (cf. Isa 52:13–53:12) in direct confrontation of evil and temptation, but he is clearly not Christ, the only one who could overcome this inevitability. In this sense, the story of this Secondary World is *praeparatio evangelica*, preparation for the gospel. But it is only anticipatory because the deliverance brought about by the sudden turn was in spite of Frodo and happened by the providential provision of Gollum's presence at the crucial moment, an outcome which was in turn influenced by the pity of Frodo and, on one occasion, Sam.

If the plan entirely relied on Frodo, or any other worldly agent, the sheer power of the Ring would have overwhelmed them and made them "apostatize" (to use Tolkien's term from this same letter).[8] Fortunately, Providence takes up Frodo's previous action of pity and forgiveness and turns this action of divine virtue to an end Frodo could not have imagined. Tolkien even says it was by a "grace" that Gollum's ultimate betrayal happened when it could be turned to the most benefit (Letter #181).

---

[8] Tolkien goes on to mention how he had no idea how "topical" this ending would prove after WW2 revealed techniques of torture and disruption of personality that were akin to the Ring's influence, so as to break men of good will and turn them into "apostates and traitors."

This complicated, but clear, moral, providential, and salvific picture reflects Primary Reality while having the inner consistency of its own Secondary Reality, meaning that it enables the sub-creation to fulfill one of its purposes to which Tolkien returned constantly in his letters (as well as his main essay on the subject).

In line with his Primary World beliefs, he also refuses to make any sort of ultimate judgment on Gollum. He said this would amount to investigating what the medievals would call "Goddes privitee" (the "private" divine knowledge that is not for humans to know at the present time). Still, he acknowledges that there are people "who yield to temptation, reject their chances of nobility or salvation, and appear to be 'damnable'." And it is no simple matter to say how the fact that what he intended for evil worked to ultimate good for others should weigh on his judgment. As Tolkien rightly says, "But we who are all 'in the same boat' must not usurp the Judge."

A second letter similar to this one, although dated one or two months earlier (12 December 1955), addressed a similar point from a review of *The Return of the King* by David Masson in the *Times Literary Supplement*.[9] Masson had made an issue of there being no references to the Orcs receiving quarter from the Free Peoples. While Tolkien does not explain why he never mentioned this—any more than he mentioned Orc females, although they surely existed within the world of the story—he thought the matter was beside the point. The whole story "breathes Mercy from start to finish." This was a point Tolkien made elsewhere in his letters, of which we will see more examples in this section. In the course of his story, it is a point that has appeared in various guises through reference to mercy, pity, forgiveness, and so on. As in Letter #181, he linked the climactic scene at Mount Doom to the part of the Lord's Prayer in Matt 6:12–13. He simply put a finer point on the connection here by saying that the scene in the Sammath Naur "was meant to be a 'fairy-story' exemplum" of this part of the Lord's Prayer. Letters like these show where Tolkien is most explicit about the links of his story with the Primary World, as well as the biblical and Christian terms in which he articulates those links between the Secondary World and Primary World.

The third letter that demonstrates this approach is Letter #191 addressed to Miss J. Burn. Tolkien affirmed here that it was quite impossible for Frodo to surrender the Ring at the place where it was at its maximum power, and, as we have noted at multiple points, this failure "was adumbrated from far back." That does not mean he was unworthy of honor, however, "He was honoured because he had accepted the burden voluntarily, and had then done all that was within his utmost physical and mental strength

---

to do. He (and the Cause) were saved – by Mercy: by the supreme value and efficacy of Pity and forgiveness of injury." Frodo deserved honor less for what he personally had done at the very last moment of the Quest as he did for how he began it in voluntarily receiving the burden, how he carried that burden for so long, and how his own virtue, cultivated from the grace of the One, was essential in bringing the Quest to its conclusion. He participated in the divine grace of Pity, and by his act of pity, Gollum lived and was able to save the Quest, albeit unintentionally, when Frodo was inevitably overwhelmed by the power of the Ring. Frodo may not have thrown the Ring into the fire himself, but the Quest would not have succeeded at all if he had not shown pity to Gollum, who ultimately brought the Ring to its destruction, which was quite beyond his own designs.

He also brought a couple Scriptures to bear on his commentary of the climax. First, he noted 1 Corinthians 10:12–13: "Therefore let the one who thinks he stands watch out that he does not fall. No temptation has overtaken you except something common to mankind; and God is faithful, so He will not allow you to be tempted beyond what you are able, but with the temptation will provide the way of escape also, so that you will be able to endure it" (NASB). It is unclear if Miss Burn herself referenced this text, but Tolkien noted that it may not at first sight seem to fit the situation, "unless 'bearing temptation' is taken to mean resisting it while still a free agent in normal command of the will." This is the closest text to the Christian cliché that "God will not give you more than you can handle" or something to that effect. Of course, that is not what the text says, and I would think the lament psalms, Lamentations itself, and the larger history of those who have suffered in persevering faithfulness in the Bible and post-biblical history would tell against such a notion.

Paul himself would write of being burdened beyond his and his companions' strength/ability to bear (2 Cor 1:8). Moreover, Paul knew what it was to share in the sufferings of Christ (Phil 3:10), as is made clear in Acts and 2 Cor 11, among other texts. He was imprisoned multiple times. He received the punishment of thirty-nine lashes from Jewish authorities five times over by the time he wrote 2 Corinthians. He was beaten with rods three times over by that same time. Once, a crowd tried stoning him to death. He was shipwrecked four times, including once when he was adrift in the Mediterranean for a full day. It did not matter how he traveled, where he went, or who he encountered, he knew danger as a constant companion. He knew what it was to be sleepless, hungry, thirsty, cold and naked. And on top of it all, he knew what it was to be anxious about the several congregations in his care across the Mediterranean world.

Tolkien's understanding of the text from 1 Corinthians is closer to the mark than the cliché in terms of how to understand temptation and what is bearable in the present age. The statement is made in the context of Paul's instruction to the Corinthians concerning idol feasts, partaking of meat offered to idols, and so on. The temptation they face now is hardly unbearable so as to make them commit sexual immorality associated with idol festivities or to make them commit idolatry. They have no reason to be lax and leap across the line into idolatry just to fit in better in their society.

Second, Tolkien found another Scripture even more applicable, which was the closing petitions of the Lord's Prayer in Matt 6:13: "And do not bring us into temptation, but deliver us from the evil one" (LEB). He had already referenced this scriptural prayer in the previous two letters, but here he additionally observed based on this petition that there is a possibility of, "being placed in positions beyond one's power. In which case (as I believe) salvation from ruin will depend on something apparently unconnected: the general sanctity (and humility and mercy) of the sacrificial person." Tolkien is thus implicitly connecting this petition to the earlier one about forgiveness of sins that we noted in exploring the previous letters. That is, one's own pity/mercy can redound to one's own deliverance in such situations in that forgiveness of debts/trespasses (as Tolkien's preferred translation had it) is related to one's own forgiveness of debts/trespasses against oneself (Matt 6:12, 14–15).

More directly than in the previous letters, he also noted the analogy of this story with those who have been "brainwashed" and broken so that they praised their torturers. As with such stories, one cannot judge them for not doing what the will could not do unaided. The best judgment one can form is based on "the will and intentions with which they entered the *Sammath Naur*." It is not right in the Primary World or the Secondary World to "demand impossible feats of will, which could only happen in stories unconcerned with real moral and mental probability." As we have seen, Tolkien's concern for his project of sub-creation means that he is absolutely concerned with such probability and truthfulness, including on the moral plane, which is among the most realistic aspects of his sub-creation (cf. Letter #148a).

Instead, he affirms, "Frodo 'failed'. It is possible that once the ring was destroyed he had little recollection of the last scene. But one must face the fact: the power of Evil in the world is *not* finally resistible by incarnate creatures, however 'good'; and the Writer of the Story is not one of us" (Letter #191; emphasis original). While the final scene makes sense of the internal dynamics of the characters involved, it was also directed in such a way to the larger purposes of the Author who made them so that their different desires, wills, actions, and goals were taken up and ultimately directed to divine ends beyond what the characters within the story could have imagined beforehand. Only by the direction and guidance of God can Good finally overcome Evil. He has been at work in this story well before this scene, and so it is only fitting that he should direct it to its long-planned end. And so it was that the Author brought about the resolution of this story and thereby foreshadowed the eucatastrophe to come in the Primary World.

The fourth letter that demonstrates this approach is Letter #192 addressed to Amy Ronald. This was dated the day after the previous letter, and so it has plenty of overlap with it. He reiterated the inevitability of this climactic scene, its verisimilitude of moral plausibility, and how it is possible even for the saintly "to be subjected to a power of evil which is too great for them to overcome – in themselves." He even mentioned near the end of the letter the analogy of the "brainwashed." He likewise said that the "cause" was triumphant "because by the exercise of pity, mercy, and forgiveness of injury, a situation was produced in which all was redressed and disaster averted."

What is different this time is that he adds the observation that Gandalf foresaw this situation, as he saw both that Gollum had some part to play yet and that the pity of Bilbo would rule the fate of many. But the point of him telling Frodo that was not utilitarian, "it would not then be mercy or pity, which are only truly present when contrary to prudence." Still, this story illustrates the point of Matt 6:12 (as well as the follow-up statement in 6:14–15) and the parable of Matt 18:21–35 in the connection between being forgiven and forgiving others. In Tolkien's words, "we must be ourselves extravagantly generous, if we are to hope for the extravagant generosity which the slightest easing of, or escape from, the consequences of our own follies and errors represents. And that mercy does sometimes occur in this life."

He also reiterated the claim that Frodo did, in fact, deserve honor. He did as much, if not more, than anyone else in the world in his situation could have done. He was able to bring the Ring to where it needed to go, even if he was simply not powerful enough to overcome it himself so as to actually throw the Ring away. That was where the other agent, Eru Ilúvatar, who had never been absent but who had not been explicitly named, came in: "The Other Power then took over: the Writer of the Story (by which I do not mean myself)." This repeated what Tolkien had said in the previous letter, and it also alluded to the key reference from Gandalf to "another power" in I/2.

The fifth and final letter that we reference for demonstrating this approach is Letter #246 to Eileen Elgar. As with the first letter, the climactic scene is one point among others that he addressed, and he even entertained hypotheticals of how the ending might have gone if Gollum had repented, or if Gollum had not been around at all and Frodo kept the Ring for himself. But to the fundamental point about Frodo's failure, Tolkien made much the same points as he had in previous letters on the subject. He did expand on the significance of "pity" and how simple-minded readers can forget its divine quality and necessity in moral judgment:

> In its highest exercise it belongs to God. For finite judges of imperfect knowledge it must lead to the use of two different scales of 'morality'. To ourselves we must present the absolute ideal without compromise, for we do not know our own limits of natural strength (+grace), and if we do not aim at the highest we shall certainly fall short of the utmost that we could achieve. To others, in any case of which we know enough to make a judgement, we must apply a scale tempered by 'mercy': that is, since we can with good will do this without the bias inevitable in judgements of ourselves, we must estimate the limits of another's strength and weigh this against the force of particular circumstances.[10] (Letter #246)

Importantly, he clarified in this letter that Frodo's failure was not a moral one, which he said, "can only be asserted, I think, when a man's effort or endurance falls *short* of his limits, and the blame decreases as that limit is closer approached" (emphasis original). In fact, this letter presents most succinctly the situation Frodo faces:

> At the last moment the pressure of the Ring would reach its maximum – impossible, I should have said, for any one to resist, certainly after long possession, months of increasing torment, and when starved and exhausted. Frodo had done what he could and spent himself completely (as an instrument of Providence) and had produced a situation in which the object of his quest could be achieved. His humility (with which he began) and his sufferings were justly rewarded by the highest honour; and his exercise of patience and mercy towards Gollum gained him Mercy: his failure was redressed (Letter #246).

Likewise, to paraphrase a comment he made later in the letter, Frodo is no more blameworthy for the breaking of his will by the overwhelming power of the Ring than he would have been for his body being broken by another overwhelming force (like, say, a massive weight falling on him that his body could not have borne).

Still, another factor that he noted in this letter is that, despite the misled character of the criticism, Frodo actually agrees with the perception of his failure. His trauma is characterized by, "not only nightmare memories of past horrors that afflicted him, but

---

[10] Tolkien says here in a footnote: We frequently see this double scale used by the saints in their judgements upon themselves when suffering great hardships or temptations, and upon others in like trials.

also unreasoning self-reproach: he saw himself and all that he done as a broken failure." There was even a temptation born out of pride that amplified his melancholy existence: he wanted to have returned as a "hero," "not content with being a mere instrument of good." Furthermore, although he was ashamed to admit it, he was tempted to regret the Ring's destruction because of how much he had become possessed by it. All the sacrifices that he had made, all that he had endured, and all the weight he bore with every decision had taken their toll on him, and he could not go back to how he was before; he could not return to his simple Hobbit life in the Shire that was all he wanted as he journeyed across Middle-earth. The fact that the finger on which he wore the Ring had been bitten off was an ever-present reminder of those final moments in the Quest. He could not avoid feeling disconnected from the old familiar place he would return to later in the story. He could not find healing or even "a truer understanding of his position in littleness and in greatness," except by taking the ship to the Undying Lands, a spot on which will be given to him by another act of sacrifice from Arwen (as we will see later).

Another element that Tolkien noted here in a footnote is the element of grace at work in the story through, "the enhancement of our powers as instruments of Providence." We have seen already that Frodo was identified as an instrument of Providence in this same letter. And indeed, Frodo had received grace at multiple points in the story. One example that Tolkien cited in this letter was his answering the call to take up the Quest at the end of the Council of Elrond (one which he was not specifically asked to answer). Beyond how the Quest started, grace manifested also in his recurrent resistance to the temptation to use the Ring when it would have been most dangerous to do so, as well as in his general "endurance of fear and suffering." But the grace given to him was to do what he was appointed to do, and it was sufficient for that purpose. He was not given grace so far beyond his capacity as to overcome the power of Sauron himself in personally destroying the Ring. God's providence beyond that point ensured that the ultimate point of the Quest would be fulfilled in any case.

Eucatastrophic Joy

What follows in the story embodies how Tolkien has described the joy brought by eucatastrophe. The eucatastrophe of this story has been brought about by the Ring being destroyed in a surprisingly good turn of events. It is worth quoting once again in full Tolkien's words on this matter:

> [T]he good catastrophe, the sudden joyous 'turn' (for there is no true end to
> any fairy-tale): this joy, which is one of the things which fairy-stories can pro-
> duce supremely well, is not essentially 'escapist,' nor 'fugitive.' In its fairy-
> tale—or otherworld—setting, it is a sudden and miraculous grace: never to be
> counted on to recur. It does not deny the existence of *dyscatastrophe*, of sorrow
> and failure: the possibility of these is necessary to the joy of deliverance; it
> denies (in the face of much evidence if you will) universal final defeat and in
> so far is *evangelium*, giving a fleeting glimpse of Joy, Joy beyond the walls of
> the world, poignant as grief.[11]

The first example of this eucatastrophic joy that we see after the climactic event is
Sam's joy that transcended the chaos around him. Another example also comes from
Sam in the next chapter, as he is surprised to find himself awake in a pleasant place,
after he expected that he and Frodo were laying down to die. Moreover, he awakes to
find that Gandalf is somehow alive and is asking him how he feels. Sam wonders if
everything sad will now come untrue as Gandalf's death has, but it is not the eschaton
yet.[12] Still, this is a time for joy as Gandalf confirms to Sam that a great Shadow has
now departed from the world. Then the narrator tells us:

> [A]nd then he laughed, and the sound was like music, or like water in a
> parched land; and as he listened the thought came to Sam that he had not heard
> laughter, the pure sound of merriment, for days upon days without count. It fell
> upon his ears like the echo of all the joys he had ever known. But he himself
> burst into tears. Then, as a sweet rain will pass down a wind of spring and the
> sun will shine out the clearer, his tears ceased, and his laughter welled up, and
> laughing he sprang from his bed. (VI/4)

This description recalls Pippin's perception of Gandalf's hidden mirth, the heavenly joy he could bring. And to say it was like water in a parched land is reminiscent

---

[11] Tolkien, "On Fairy-Stories," 153.

[12] While it makes sense for Sam to ask such a question, one ought not to take it as a literalistic
description applicable to the eschaton. Such an idea would go against Tolkien's description of the eucatastrophe where the joy is a product of emerging from the meeting with grief/sorrow in the catastrophe
one has been delivered from. Even Gandalf's resurrection was not so much making his death come untrue
as it was taking up what had gone wrong and directing it to a higher end in Gandalf's transformation,
increased power, and greater glory. Eschatological resurrection is not time travel so as to undo what once
went wrong, but it corrects what went wrong and incorporates the fact of death as a means by which God
produces everlasting life. Nor is that how it will work even in this wonderful ending that anticipates the
climactic eucatastrophe. As Tolkien himself said in Letter #153, even God does not utterly stop the
possibility of the misuse of free will nor make the effects thereof unreal. What he does do, as Tolkien
has exemplified many times over, is take even these acts and direct them to glorious ends beyond what
those in the world of the story can foresee.

of the last couple chapters when that sound of water was a delight to the Hobbits on the rare occasions that they found water to drink in Mordor. And as for the sound of laughter, it had indeed been nearly a month since Sam had heard such, and his perception of that time would be elongated from the exhausting trial and the long healing from it. Sam himself finds it difficult to put into words how he feels, but it is not too far off what the narrator has said, "I feel like spring after winter, and sun on the leaves; and like trumpets and harps and all the songs I have ever heard" (VI/4). And to think this is but a taste of such joy, as the greatest eucatastrophe is still to come from the perspective of this story.

The third example comes from Sam and the rest of the host gathered at Cormallen for this victory celebration. After Frodo and Sam have reunited with Aragorn and taken their places of honor next to him, a minstrel of Gondor begged leave to sing. And he sang of "Frodo of the Nine Fingers and the Ring of Doom" (VI/4). This is exactly what Sam wished to hear when he thought he was going to die earlier in this chapter:

> And when Sam heard that he laughed aloud for sheer delight, and he stood up and cried: 'O great glory and splendour! And all my dreams have come true!' And then he wept. And all the host laughed and wept, and in the midst of their merriment and tears the clear voice of the minstrel rose like silver and gold, and all men were hushed. And he sang to them, now in the Elven-tongue, now in the speech of the West, until their hearts, wounded with sweet words, overflowed, and their joy was like swords, and they passed in thought out to regions where pain and delight flow together and tears are the very wine of blessedness. (VI/4)

We need not reiterate everything we have already said concerning eucatastrophe in Chapter Two and how it applies to the case here. But it is particularly notable how this is reminiscent of both "On Fairy-Stories" and Letter #89, both of which were written years before Tolkien first drafted this chapter. This scene and the earlier one are the peak expressions of the delivering character of laughter in this story, now that it accompanies the long-held sigh of relief for Sam, Gandalf, and all the Free Peoples. It is also an outward expression of the internal joy that had previously been suppressed by sorrow. And now with the laughter mixed with tears, we see the flowing together of joy and sorrow, their reconciliation in the life of healing that will follow hereafter, at least for a time (because, again, it is not yet the eschaton). In such ways, this eucatastrophe anticipates the gospel and its eucatastrophe in the resurrection of Jesus. The minstrel's voice rising like silver and gold as he recounts the tale not only displays the surpassing beauty of the story he tells and how tells it; it also attests to its transcendent glory that comes from beyond itself. Silver and golden light are, of course, linked with the moon and sun, respectively, but in Tolkien's mythology their light is derivative, being the last vestiges of the light of the Two Trees of Telperion and Laurelin. The Silmarils, one of which is set in heaven as the star of Eärendil/Gil-Estel, have the last remnants of the intermingled golden silver light from both trees. Such light and the colors linked to it point to the transcendent source of light, beauty, and joy. This is further supported by where their thoughts pass to, which resembles Tolkien's description of joy beyond the walls of the world, which is to say, transcendent joy.

Furthermore, Tolkien's own reaction should be noted. He stated in Letter #131 that this scene of eucatastrophe that represents the hallmark of a fairy-story, being, "the resolution and justification of all that has gone before," ultimately, "brought tears to my eyes to write, and still moves me, and I cannot help believing that it is a supreme moment of its kind." There has even been a reproduction of the tear-stained page of his manuscript.[13] Tolkien's own story had its proper effect on its author, and he had realized that *telos* of the fairy-story, and thus his work could function as *evangelium* pointing to that good story by which the Author brought Legend to fruition on the plane of History in the Primary World.

Additionally, there are two more relevant features of this chapter to note before we move on in this story. One, at dinner, where Frodo and Sam reunite with the rest of the Fellowship, we are reminded once more of the practice now called "the Standing Silence" observed before dinner (VI/4).[14] This has already been established as a daily practice in Gondor, but it takes on an extra layer of significance now in acknowledgment of where this great victory came from and in silent gratitude of the graces that have brought it. Two, Gandalf repeats the declaration that "The hands of the King are hands of healing" (VI/4). He tells them now how Aragorn brought them back from the brink of death, "putting forth all his power, and sent you into the sweet forgetfulness of sleep" (VI/4). Gimli also implies that Aragorn did the same for Pippin. Since we have commented at length on the significance of this aspect of Aragorn's character elsewhere, we will not repeat it here, but it is notable that it is emphasized here, as well as in the dialogue between the Warden of the Houses of Healing and Éowyn in the next chapter (VI/5).

---

[13] *J. R. R. Tolkien: The Art of the Manuscript* (Hagerty Museum of Art, Marquette University, 2022), 94.

[14] This name was added in the second edition.

Sing, Ye People

In that next chapter, the scene switches back to Minas Tirith. It begins in a time after the Host of the West has departed, and the focus is on the Houses of Healing, where Faramir, Éowyn, and Merry are still recuperating. During this time, Faramir and Éowyn are attracted to one another, and though Éowyn regrets that she did not die a glorious death in battle alongside her uncle (and she was not in condition to accompany her brother and Aragorn to Mordor), she finds some comfort in speaking with Faramir, as Faramir also finds comfort in speaking with her. For five days they carry on, until they stand together on the wall, unwittingly clasping hands, waiting for the stroke of doom. And indeed, there are portents that would seem to point to the end of days for the Free Peoples. Yet, Faramir expresses to Éowyn that while his reason thinks that they have come to a dark end, "my heart says nay; and all my limbs are light, and a hope and joy are come to me that no reason can deny" (VI/5). Only then do other more hopeful portents come of the Shadow departing with the wind, a brighter day, and "in all the houses of the City men sang for the joy that welled up in their hearts from what source they could not tell" (VI/5). As wind from the south had been an act of Providence ten days previously, the wind from the north also acted to speed the flight of the Eagles, to drive away the great Shadow of Mordor, to remove the cloud cover of darkness, and to bring fresh air of hope to the Free Peoples. And as elsewhere in Tolkien's stories, joy is described as emerging, as if from a hidden source because of the previously pressing darkness and despair. Although the language of "welling up" is properly internal in reference, Faramir's description of it as coming to him indicates an impetus outside himself that is causing the welling up. In these and other ways, Providence is at work in Minas Tirith preparing them for the good news to come.

And so it is that a great Eagle comes sometime later, bearing good news beyond what the people could have hoped:

> *Sing now, ye people of the Tower of Anor,*
> *for the Realm of Sauron is ended for ever,*
> *and the Dark Tower is thrown down.*
>
> *Sing and rejoice, ye people of the Tower of Guard,*
> *for your watch hath not been in vain,*
> *and the Black Gate is broken,*
> *and your King hath passed through,*
> *and he is victorious.*
>
> *Sing and be glad, all ye children of the West,*

> *for your King shall come again*
> *and he shall dwell among you all the days of your life.*
>
> *And the Tree that was withered shall be renewed,*
> *and he shall plant it in the high places,*
> *and the City shall be blessed.*
>
> *Sing all ye people!* (VI/5)

Some have compared this to the *Exsultet* of the Easter liturgy of the Roman Missal.[15] In some ways, it is reminiscent of that triumph, though it remains suited to the Secondary World setting, and it is not as properly eschatological. Likewise, it is reminiscent of some scenes of Revelation, wherein one of the four living creatures around the throne of God leading in worship is described as being like an eagle (Rev 4:7–8; cf. 5:6, 8, 14; 7:11; 8:13; 14:3; 19:4). One could also compare this declaration to other calls to sing and rejoice (Deut 32:43; Zeph 3:14; Zech 9:9; Rev 19:7) and to the Psalms more generally.[16] The similarities are more in function than in any specific wording, though the texts from Zechariah and the latter parts of Isaiah are perhaps the closest overall. Again, this is not quite representative of eschatological victory, but it is the brightest anticipatory glimpse within the scope of this story, being among the occasional glimpses of final victory Tolkien has referred to.

Éowyn's Resolution

However, not everyone in Minas Tirith is jubilant after this proclamation of good news concerning the king. Éowyn is strangely and uniquely downcast. The insightful Faramir determines that this concerns her unresolved feelings for Aragorn. She admired and loved him (or, at least, the idea of him), and she desired to have love from him that he could not give. When all she did receive from him was understanding and pity, she sought rather for death in battle, but even this was taken from her, and that ironically, in part, by Aragorn's own doing. Faramir understands her love for Aragorn, for he is the greatest of Men in the world at this time. But he also tells her, "Do not scorn pity that is the gift of a gentle heart" (VI/5).

Aragorn did not mean it as condescension or disregard. When he understood her feelings for him and knew he could not reciprocate them, it hurt him more deeply than

---

[15] Rutledge, *Battle*, 348. More distantly, Freeman, *Tolkien Dogmatics*, 338.

[16] Freeman, *Tolkien Dogmatics*, 337, 453 draws more connections to new creation and the Second Coming than I am willing to make.

she could perceive. His pity was meant as an expression of love of a different kind, for still it is a virtue by which one wills the good (i.e., shows love) for another. He will even say later, "I have wished thee joy ever since first I saw thee. It heals my heart to see thee now in bliss" (VI/6). Moreover, as we have seen many times, pity is a divine virtue, and for that reason alone one ought not to scorn it.

On the other hand, Faramir declares clearly that he loves her in the way she might wish to be loved, and he would love her even if she were, like Aragorn, exalted above him. In response, her inner coldness and the last vestige of bitterness depart, and she declares, "I stand in Minas Anor, the Tower of the Sun … and behold! The Shadow has departed! I will be a shield-maiden no longer, nor vie with the great Riders, nor take joy only in the songs of slaying. I will be a healer, and love all things that grow and are not barren" (VI/5). Her time in the Houses of Healing and the influence of Aragorn himself inspire this pursuit in her to find such a purpose in time of peace. For indeed the needs of the time are different now as there will still be much healing to do, and the time for new growth has come with this new spring.

Aragorn's Coronation

The day long hoped for in Gondor finally arrives when the king returns. He has come before as a warrior and a healer, and now he must take his throne. In his coronation we once again see his humility. Even though he is obviously at the center of this ceremony, he insists, "By the labour and valour of many I have come into my inheritance. In token of this I would have the Ring-bearer bring the crown to me, and let Mithrandir set it upon my head, if he will; for he has been the mover of all that has been accomplished, and this is his victory" (VI/5). This reflects his deference to both of these figures elsewhere in the story as the one with whom was the true Quest and the one who was the true leader of the alliance of the Free Peoples (and his remark is also similar to Faramir's perception of Gandalf as "a great mover of the deeds that are done in our time" [IV/5]). Aragorn is certainly an important character, but he knows he is part of a much larger story of which he is not the Author, nor even the main character.

This is also a text that problematizes any notion of one or all of these three characters being a Christ-figure or Christ-figures per se. If one follows a simplistic equation of linking each character to one of the three offices of Christ as Prophet, Priest, and King, one cannot make sense of one office being in such deference to the others. They are each analogies and types of Christ in various respects, but they are not simply Christ in other guise like Aslan in C. S. Lewis's stories.

Gandalf then declares that these are now the days of the King. And he calls for their being blessed "while the thrones of the Valar endure" (VI/5). In this way, his reign is thus, ideally, connected to their reign, and both are to operate as agents of the King who reigns from the Timeless Halls beyond creation. For that is who Gandalf also serves, and it was as an agent of Providence that he worked as a mover of deeds. It is only appropriate that he should thus participate in the consummation of this reign that is one of the prime fruits of his millennia of labor.

Immediately after this declaration is one last transfiguration of Aragorn:

> But when Aragorn arose all that beheld him gazed in silence, for it seemed to them that he was revealed to them now for the first time. Tall as the sea-kings of old, he stood above all that were near; ancient of days he seemed and yet in the flower of manhood; and wisdom sat upon his brow, and strength and healing were in his hands, and a light was about him. (VI/5)

It is fitting that this coronation is the climactic transfiguration of Aragorn in this story. Particularly interesting is the description of him as "ancient of days." In the immediate context, it signifies how he has the gravitas of one who is ancient while also being in the prime of life. But the curious phrase also brings to mind the description of God in his divine glory in Dan 7:9, 13, 22. Similarly, Rev 1:13–15, which we have referenced previously in comparison to the resurrected Gandalf, describes the "one like a son of man" in terms reminiscent of the Ancient of Days in Dan 7 (among other OT connections). The description of healing being in his hands, while obviously connected to other parts of this story, is also reminiscent of the promise of the Sun of Righteousness/Justice arising on Israel and having healing in his wings (Mal 4:2). The imagery of this text has had widespread impact in Christian tradition, including in Christmas celebrations and texts on Christmas. Aragorn is thus described in Christ-like terms, albeit with enough distance and distinction for him to remain an echo and type of Christ.

Besides the glories of his reign thereafter described, we are also told of his initial acts as king. He receives embassies from distant lands, pardons the Easterlings who surrender, makes peace with the Haradrim, and releases the slaves of Mordor to keep the land that they have worked to be their own. Finally, he renders judgment for Beregond. He had saved Faramir from an untimely demise at the despairing hands of his father, but he did so at the cost of disobeying the charge of his lord and defiling the Hallows with blood. Thus, Aragorn determines that the proper sentence for him is to leave the Guard of the Citadel and to be appointed to the White Company who will guard Faramir, now the Prince of Ithilien. Beregond perceives in this decision both mercy and justice, balanced as they should be. Thus, we see Aragorn showing both divine virtues, and his wisdom shaped in connection to these other virtues resembles Solomon's at the beginning of his reign, albeit without the subsequent fall in his reign.

The King and the Tree

One other part of this chapter has primary relevance for our purposes.[17] While Aragorn waits for Arwen to arrive at Minas Tirith, he goes with Gandalf privately to a high hallow where the kings once went. Gandalf tells Aragorn that the time comes for the Dominion of Men and that his time in Middle-earth is coming to an end, since his task is now complete. Aragorn would still have his counsel, but Gandalf says that will not last long. Aragorn thus expresses his concern about what will happen after Gandalf and the Elder Kindred of the Elves depart. He himself will die one day, even if that is many years hence, and the symbol of his kingdom, the White Tree, is still withered, seeming now to be a portent of imminent demise, despite the king's return. He thus asks, "When shall I see a sign that it will ever be otherwise?" (VI/5). Gandalf responds, "Turn your face from the green world, and look where all seems barren and cold" (VI/5).

This is advice that Gandalf means literally, as the answer he looks for is not in the vast green lands of his realm, but it is in the snowy barrenness nearby. Yet, these words are also symbolically significant, not only for their irony, but for how they resonate with Aragorn himself. For nearly a millennium, the people of Gondor had waited for a king, and he was not to be found among them, but he was to be found in the barren and cold lands of the North. And now in what appears to be a cold and barren land he will find something else growing.

The sapling tree is none other than a scion of Nimloth from which the White Tree also came, and that old tree was a seedling of Galathilion,[18] which was a fruit of Telperion, the Eldest of Trees, being one of the Two Trees that once provided the most

---

[17] Of secondary significance is Frodo's declaration near the end when Arwen comes to the city at evening, "At last I understand why we have waited! This is the ending. Now not day only shall be beloved, but night too shall be beautiful and blessed and all its fear pass away" (VI/5). The significance of this line is not so much any particular part of Scripture, but it does well describe what the state of *shalom* ("peace" in a fuller sense than the term is often used today) is like, and it thus offers a poignant glimpse of the eschatological consummation to come.

[18] Another link in this ancestry is Celeborn, the tree of Tol Eressëa, but that was a later revision of the ancestry that Tolkien made, as it was initially Galathilion that was the tree of Tol Eressëa. See Tolkien, *Peoples of Middle-earth*, 147–49.

beautiful lights. The moon itself is said to be but the last fruit it bore of its diminished light. But this tree is odd, for it is not even seven years old, yet it has somehow been born here in the barren cold. Gandalf simply says:

> Who shall say how it comes here in the appointed hour? But this is an ancient hallow, and ere the kings failed or the Tree withered in the court, a fruit must have been set here. For it is said that, though the fruit of the Tree comes seldom to ripeness, yet the life within may then lie sleeping through many long years, and none can foretell the time in which it will awake. Remember this. For if ever a fruit ripens, it should be planted, lest the line die out of the world. Here it has lain hidden on the mountain, even as the race of Elendil lay hidden in the wastes of the North. (VI/5)

As we have noted before, both the tree and the king are in this way similar to the line of David brought to fruition in Jesus. And both also signify how *estel* can come to fruition in surprising ways, as the God in whom one has *estel* can bring life out of both apparent and actual death. And the fruit of his promises come to bear even centuries after they were first spoken.

It is not for nothing that this hallow is the place where Aragorn found this sapling. It is the nearest equivalent to the hallow of God that was on Meneltarma in Númenor, and thus it was an ancient place of worship of the One God. The planting of the sapling here was truly an expression of *estel* in Eru Ilúvatar. And it would be from here that the fuller worship of the One would return. As Tolkien said in Letter #156:

> It later appears that there had been a 'hallow' on Mindolluin, only approachable by the King, where he had anciently offered thanks and praise on behalf of his people; but it had been forgotten. It was re-entered by Aragorn, and there he found a sapling of the White Tree, and replanted it in the Court of the Fountain. It is to be presumed that with the reemergence of the lineal priest kings (of whom Lúthien the Blessed Elf-maiden was a foremother) the worship of God would be renewed, and His Name (or title) be again more often heard.

We have already seen that the descendants of the Númenóreans had maintained the vestige of thanksgiving in the Standing Silence. Their closest expressions to petitionary prayers were invocations of intermediaries of the One (particularly, the Valar). But with the return of the king, now the institution of the priest king, and all that pertained thereto, could be renewed.

The notion that the king would be a priest king is also in line with how Tolkien has described the Númenóreans and their descendants as being "Hebraic" in their theology (Letter #211). The fundamental notion that humans were created to bear the image of

God and that this meant serving as his viceregents is foundational to this conception. The ideal king in Ps 110—a text used many times in connection with Christ in the NT— is thus spoken of as one is who is priest in the order of Melchizedek, as befits one who is both priest and king as Melchizedek was in Gen 14:18–20. Aside from the ideal king, the Israelite king could also function in a priestly capacity, as seen in 2 Sam 6:14, 17– 18; 8:18; 1 Kgs 8:14, 55, and 62–64. In Tolkien's presentation, Aragorn and his ancestors are meant to exemplify such truth, to anticipate such later history, and, ultimately, to point to the Lord who will be High Priest and King.

Arwen's Gift to Frodo

After Arwen arrives in Minas Tirith and marries Aragorn, more days of rejoicing follow. The members of the Fellowship then think of returning to their own lands. Frodo informs Aragorn of his wish to return to the Shire by way of Rivendell, since he wishes to visit with Bilbo, who had not come with Arwen and the other Elves to Minas Tirith. Aragorn promises to accompany him as far as the country of Rohan, since he will go there anyway to accompany the procession of Théoden. Before they depart, though, Arwen promises a gift to Frodo. She has made the choice of her ancestor Lúthien to live a mortal life, and as a descendant of Eärendil by Elrond, she had the peculiar privilege to decide between the fate of Elves and Men. This meant that she would have no place in the Undying Lands. Thus, she offers Frodo her place on a ship to there, if he should desire it. His life will still end there, but he can yet find healing that he may not find in Middle-earth after all he has gone through (VI/6).

Tolkien stated in a footnote of Letter #246 that he did not make explicit how she could arrange this. While she had the authority to choose her fate between the immortality of Elves and the mortality of Men, she did not have the authority to permit entry to the Undying Lands. And it was not as if she could speak to the Valar about this and deliver their verdict herself. Tolkien thus clarified:

> What is meant is that it was Arwen who first thought of sending Frodo into the West, and put in a plea for him to Gandalf (direct or through Galadriel, or both), and she used her own renunciation of the right to go West as an argument. Her renunciation and suffering were related to and enmeshed with Frodo's: both were parts of a plan for the regeneration of the state of Men. Her prayer might therefore be specially effective, and her plan have a certain equity of exchange. No doubt it was Gandalf who was the authority that accepted her plea. The Appendices show clearly that he was an emissary of the Valar, and virtually their plenipotentiary in accomplishing the plan against Sauron. He was also in

special accord with Cirdan the Ship-master, who had surrendered to him his ring and so placed himself under Gandalf's command. Since Gandalf himself went on the Ship there would be so to speak no trouble either at embarking or at the landing.

Once again, we see how the Christian ethic frames this event, as both Arwen and Frodo have engaged in self-abnegation and sacrifice for the benefit of others (e.g., Phil 2:1–13). Furthermore, Tolkien says the actions of both contributed to a plan for the regeneration of the state of Men (which we have noted elsewhere in terms of sanctification). This plan was obviously that of the only One who could see so far into the future and had such a plan for Men and the time of their Dominion. That is, both of them were part of plans for God's grace to Men given in preparation for more to come in the order of grace.

The Song of Théoden

One day, the royal company then leaves Minas Tirith to accompany the members of the Fellowship and the alliance of the Host of the West, with their first brief pause coming at the Drúadan Forest. There, Aragorn makes his royal declaration that this forest is reserved for Ghân-buri-Ghân and his people in perpetuity, and no one may enter without their permission. Thus, they are justly rewarded how they would wish for how they helped in the War of the Ring.

Then the first extended stop comes at Edoras. Here, the company buries Théoden. His body had been interred in the company of kings in Gondor, but now he must return to be buried in the company of his royal ancestors in Rohan. The Riders of the King's House sing the song of Théoden, enrolling his name in the list of their kings and their great deeds, ending with these lines describing his charge on the fields of Pelennor:

> Out of doubt, out of dark, to the day's rising
> he rode singing in the sun, sword unsheathing.
> Hope he rekindled, and in hope ended;
> over death, over dread, over doom lifted
> out of loss, out of life, unto long glory. (VI/6)[19]

When this song ends, Merry bids one last tearful farewell to the king who graciously allowed him to serve as his esquire.

---

[19] For more on the funerary rites, which are clearly not conformed to Christian rites, see Hammond and Scull, *Lord of the Rings Companion*, 642–43.

Although it is somewhat out of narrative order, this song gives us occasion to reflect on the comparison and contrast of Théoden and Denethor, the respective leaders of Rohan and Gondor when this story began. Théoden was a proper king, but most would have held Denethor as occupying a higher station because his rule was over a greater realm, and many likely would have perceived him as the greater man. He was, after all, one of the closest to a pure Númenórean in the days of this story. He had much store of his own wisdom so that, while he had counselors, he was not reliant on them. Théoden, however, was reliant on his counselor, and that proved dangerous to him, for that was the means by which Saruman whispered poison in his ear. Denethor also was poisoned, albeit by his limited visions in the *palantír*.

While Saruman played on the perception of Théoden that he was a lesser son of greater sires—in contrast to Denethor, who would be considered one of the greatest of his line—no one could rightly question his quality as a father. His wife had died in childbirth, leaving him with one son. And when his beloved little sister died after giving birth to Éomer and Éowyn, he took them in as his children, and they loved him as a father. And so his manner was also with Merry. Nor did his grief at his son's death lessen his fatherly care for these others.

Denethor faced similar griefs but responded quite differently. He lost his beloved wife Finduilas a few years after Faramir was born and he had become steward. His grief at her death made him more permanently grim, leading him to sit in his tower alone in deep thought, which eventually led to his use of the *palantír*. He quite obviously favored Boromir over Faramir, and he was not the kind of man to act as a generous father to others. This was all the more remarkable because he believed his own father favored Thorongil (an alias of Aragorn) during his time in Minas Tirith over him, and yet he would reflect his perception in reality with his own children. He became even more melancholic when Boromir died. He loved Faramir in his way, but he was unable to express himself properly, which added to his despair when he convinced himself that there was no saving Faramir or himself. When Pippin entered his service, as Merry had entered Théoden's, Denethor was not particularly hospitable to him, and indeed acted toward him as a lord.

More could be said about each, but each story highlights a key difference between them. Théoden had moved from one afflicted by despair to one who was enkindled by hope and so enkindled it in others. This was, in turn, related to his generosity of heart, which he had shown even to Gríma after his treachery was exposed. And so, with rekindled *estel*, he rode in hope and ended in hope, dying for his fidelity to his friends in the hope of contributing to victory, as he did. And thus, he is glorified after his death and rose from being a lesser son of greater sires to among the greatest of the kings of Rohan. But Denethor was a man who loved and trusted a precious few, and this was, in turn, related to his inclination to despair. Denethor had lost his *estel* and turned ever more inward upon himself, thereby magnifying his griefs until they became all-consuming despair, and he took his own life by burning himself like a heathen king of old, scorning his charge as a steward of the kings of the descendants of the Númenóreans who had worshiped the One.

Again, it is not for nothing that hope is a virtue in the Christian theological-ethical framework. And we see yet again how it is linked with other virtues like faith/fidelity, love, and expressions in qualities like generosity. Hope is a pivotal difference between these characters in how they responded to grief and trials.

Whispers of Hope in a Fading World

Eventually, the company takes their leave of the Rohirrim and their new king. They then head to Isengard to meet with Treebeard. He tells them of the battles that had happened behind where the story had focused. He also informs Gandalf that he let Saruman go, for he hates the caging of living things, although he did not release him without having him surrender the keys to Orthanc.

Treebeard then converses with the others, eventually coming to Celeborn and Galadriel. He conveys his regrets of how long it has been since they met and that they should meet now only at the time of their fading, for he can sense the world changing. For how long it has been since they last met, he thinks they shall never meet again. After all, the Elves must pass into the Uttermost West or dwindle themselves. Treebeard knows that he must dwindle, and he has no intention of going to the Uttermost West without the Entwives, if such a path would even be open to him.

Galadriel confirms that they will not meet again in Middle-earth, "nor until the lands that lie under the wave are lifted up again. Then in the willow-meads of Tasarinan we may meet in Spring" (VI/6). This is a land of Beleriand where Treebeard mentioned that he once went (III/4). As such, Galadriel is hinting at her hope for the new creation, where all of them shall be restored and reunited, wherein also the Ents hoped to be reunited with the Entwives.

Last of all, Treebeard bids farewell to Merry and Pippin after sharing one last draught with them. He reminds them to pass on any news they hear of the Entwives to him. And then they part for seemingly the last time.

The Stubbornness of Evil

After the company takes their leave of Aragorn, Arwen, Legolas, and Gimli, they encounter Saruman on their road. Although he has now been reduced to a vagabond, he scorns every word spoken to him, for he thinks they have all come to gloat over him. Such is his mind now that he assumes malice from everyone. They did not desire further punishment of him, and everyone in that company was willing to offer him help, but he was too stubborn to humble himself to seek help. Galadriel even says that Saruman should have seen this encounter as him being overtaken by good fortune "for now you have a last chance" (VI/6). Saruman scorns this grace too, as he says, "If it be truly the last, I am glad … for I shall be spared the trouble of refusing it again. All my hopes are ruined, but I would not share yours. If you have any" (VI/6). Truly, misery loves company, and he only comforts himself by the thought that the powerful Elf lords will share his misery of dwindling. He likewise twists their self-sacrifice into a portrait of them having "pulled down your own house when you destroyed mine" (VI/6). He even speaks scornfully of what pipe-weed Merry offers him, though he at least takes that.

We also see how he continues to mistreat Gríma, who still follows him about. He clearly says that he hates him and wishes to leave him. Gandalf simply tells him that he should leave him then. But Gríma is apparently too terrified to put action to his words.

Both characters in their own ways well exemplify the tragic stubbornness of evil. The state of both characters was already a pitiful one. Turning back would not have brought them any lower. All that was needed was the humility to acknowledge that they had gone wrong and the willingness to repent by turning around. But habitual evil presents a downward spiral in the way that habitual good presents an upward spiral. And one can find it easier to keep going the way one has been going than to make a change, even if the benefits of the change may be obvious. That is the trap that sin lays. When one steps over the line, it can seem easier to continue in that direction than to turn back and admit wrongdoing. And eventually, one has taken so many steps that they can no longer see the line to cross back over, and repentance seems both unfeasible and undesirable. Thus it is with them, and the rest of the story will show that they find a way to dig a bigger hole for themselves.

Full-Grown Hobbits

After the company takes their leave of Celeborn and Galadriel, takes their leave from Rivendell after an extended visit with Bilbo, and finally makes a visit to Barliman

Butterbur in Bree, Gandalf has gathered that something smells rotten in the Shire. Even so, he informs the Hobbits that he is going to visit Tom Bombadil, rather than returning to the Shire with them. Clearly, they would have wished to have his help in whatever problems he thinks are occurring there. But he tells them:

> You must settle its affairs yourselves; that is what you have been trained for. Do you not yet understand? My time is over: it is no longer my task to set things to rights, nor to help folk to do so. And as for you, my dear friends, you will need no help. You are grown up now. Grown indeed very high; among the great you are, and I have no longer any fear at all for any of you. (VI/7)

We have seen elsewhere how Tolkien speaks of the ennoblement of the Hobbits (particularly Frodo) as their sanctification. As with parent-child relationships, thus it is with discipleship that there comes a time when one who has matured must stand on his/her own, apply the lessons learned, and replicate what they have been taught for the benefit of others. This is that moment for the ennobled/sanctified Hobbits. For indeed, in the next chapter, they will be responsible for delivering the Shire from the brutish, oppressive rule it had fallen under.

The Scouring of the Shire

In the four Hobbits' absence, Lotho Sackville-Baggins, Frodo's cousin, has taken over the Shire with his vast wealth acquired through his pipe-weed crop in the South-farthing. He was able to enforce his authority with ruffian Men from the south. He owed such wealth, power, and connections to the fact that he traded this pipe-weed and other supplies with Saruman. He eventually came to call himself the Chief Shirriff and the ruffians were thus called the Chief's Men. But in recent months, after one called "Sharkey" came, something has changed. Lotho had not been seen in public for some time, and his own mother was imprisoned in the Lockholes along with those who had challenged him to that point.

The Hobbits' initial encounter with ruffians proves that all the Hobbits needed was some courage to make them flinch. They are cowardly bullies who rely on cowing others and being bigger than them. But they are nothing compared to what these Hobbits have seen in their travels. And so it will be up to them to cultivate that seed of courage in other Hobbits who have not yet organized a resistance.

But Frodo also reminds the other Hobbits that they must apply other virtues they have cultivated in their journey besides courage. Particularly, he shows the virtue of pity. He wishes to save Lotho, even though Pippin would rather destroy him. But Frodo sees him rather as a wicked fool who got caught up in schemes that were too big for him. Before anything else is done to him, he should first be saved from his own folly, if it is possible.

Frodo admits the necessity of fighting to clear out the Shire, although he never draws a weapon to do so. Tolkien notes that this is a personal attitude of his; he was not a pacifist, properly speaking. Rather, he was more interested in avoiding civil war between the Hobbits, and he had concluded that physical fighting is less effective than most people give it credit for being (Letter #195). This is not to say that such fighting is ineffective, as the rest of the story shows, and it will indeed prove useful for clearing out the Shire. But it is not the ultimate problem-solver, and it will not fix all the problems in the Shire. It must be tempered and complemented with other things, even as the War of the Ring would not have been won by physical fighting alone.

And so Frodo tells the others,

> But remember: there is to be no slaying of hobbits, not even if they have gone over to the other side. Really gone over, I mean; not just obeying ruffians' orders because they are frightened. No hobbit has ever killed another on purpose in the Shire, and it is not to begin now. And nobody is to be killed at all, if it can be helped. Keep your tempers and hold your hands to the last possible moment! (VI/8)

Thus, not even a right traitor like Ted Sandyman is killed by another Hobbit. Some Hobbits, sadly, inevitably die in the fighting at Bywater when facing a large enough force of the Chief's Men, but for those who must live here after the scouring, no further hurt or grudge is caused thanks to Frodo thinking of the things that make for peace and not only of the things that make for war.

But as the Hobbits make their way from Bywater to Bag End, they see how many trees have been felled. This includes the great Party Tree where the Shire had turned out for Bilbo's great birthday all those years ago. And like other trees in the Fangorn Forest, and now here in the Shire, it was cut down and then left to rot. Sam considers this all worse than Mordor because he remembers what this place was like before it was ruined. Frodo confirms that this is one of the works of Mordor, just as Saruman did the work of Mordor in Isengard, which we commented on previously.

The Petty Evil of Saruman

When the Hobbits arrive at Bag End, they learn that Sharkey was none other than Saruman himself. He is behind the more destructive policies of recent weeks. Gandalf had warned them that he was still capable of "a little mischief in a mean way," to which Saruman responds:

> 'Quite capable,' said Saruman, 'and more than a little. You made me laugh, you hobbit-lordlings, riding along with all those great people, so secure and so pleased with your little selves. You thought you had done very well out of it all, and could now just amble back and have a nice quiet time in the country. Saruman's home could be all wrecked, and he could be turned out, but no one could touch yours. Oh no! Gandalf would look after your affairs.'
>
> Saruman laughed again. 'Not he! When his tools have done their task he drops them. But you must go dangling after him, dawdling and talking, and riding round twice as far as you needed. "Well," thought I, "if they're such fools, I will get ahead of them and teach them a lesson. One ill turn deserves another." It would have been a sharper lesson, if only you had given me a little more time and more Men. Still I have already done much that you will find it hard to mend or undo in your lives. And it will be pleasant to think of that and set it against my injuries.'
>
> 'Well, if that is what you find pleasure in,' said Frodo, 'I pity you. It will be a pleasure of memory only, I fear. Go at once and never return!' (VI/8)

It was not even a year ago that Saruman had ambitions of claiming the One Ring for himself and deposing the Dark Lord. Failing that, he still would have sought to conquer Rohan. And now failing that, he settles for trying to ruin the Shire out of spite. He is barely a petty tyrant, but he takes what satisfaction he can in what little evil he can sow. The only thing that now gives him joy is others sharing some measure of his misery.

Of course, his pettiness well preceded his fall. This was once manifested in more harmless fashion when he criticized Gandalf for smoking, only to surreptitiously take up the habit himself without being willing to admit any change in his mind (as recorded in *Unfinished Tales*). But when his realm had been conquered, he was too petty to allow himself either to repent or to do something like commit suicide in shame or despair, as Tolkien said in Letter #210, "to cling to life to its basest dregs is the way of the sort of person he had become." Thus, what he does to the Shire is one last petty expression of his will to power and domination, to show that his will can still change the world around him. Even this mean, little mischief (relatively speaking) was a way for him to leave his mark to show that he was there and that his will still had power and Influence on the world.

Still, Frodo will not have him slain. He has no power left, save his voice. And, "It is useless to meet revenge with revenge: it will heal nothing" (VI/8). Even when

Saruman attempts to stab him and finds the blade snapping against his mithril coat, Frodo will not permit him being killed:

> 'He was great once, of a noble kind that we should not dare to raise our hand against. He is fallen, and his cure is beyond us; but I would still spare him, in the hope that he may find it.'
>
> Saruman rose to his feet, and stared at Frodo. There was a strange look of mingled wonder and respect and hatred. 'You have grown, Halfling,' he said. 'Yes, you have grown very much. You are wise, and cruel. You have robbed my revenge of sweetness, and now I must go hence in bitterness, in debt to your mercy. I hate it and you!' (VI/8)

In this way, Saruman shows his disdain for the divine virtue of pity, and thus for Frodo's sanctification, which he cannot help but acknowledge. With a few more parting words, he departs with Gríma trailing him. Frodo extends mercy to him as well, but Saruman reveals that he was the one who killed Lotho, and he even implies that he ate him. Gríma grovels in his hopeless existence, but after one last kick from Saruman, he snaps and cuts his throat, after which he is felled by Hobbit archers.

With this, we get one last moment of Saruman that reveals his true state:

> To the dismay of those that stood by, about the body of Saruman a grey mist gathered, and rising slowly to a great height like smoke from a fire, as a pale shrouded figure it loomed over the Hill. For a moment it wavered, looking to the West; but out of the West came a cold wind, and it bent away, and with a sigh dissolved into nothing.
>
> Frodo looked down at the body with pity and horror, for as he looked it seemed that long years of death were suddenly revealed in it, and it shrank, and the shriveled face became rags of skin upon a hideous skull. Lifting up the skirt of the dirty cloak that sprawled beside it, he covered it over, and turned away. (VI/8)

Saruman was an incarnate angel, and this mist signifies his spirit departing, being no longer able to cling to the dregs of incarnate existence. His spirit looks to the West, for that is where he came from, and a cold wind blows it away in token of the judgment that is coming against him, like the other fallen angels he aligned himself with. The toll of the corruption of his spirit is now shown in the shriveling of his body, for since he had turned his back on his mission, on the Powers who gave it to him, and on the One he was to serve, he had thus committed himself to the way of sin and death, and so he was as one afflicted with years of death.

The Restoration of the Shire

With this whole affair concluded, the work begins on restoring the Shire. Saruman amused himself with the idea that it would take a long time for the Hobbits to heal the hurt he had inflicted on the land. But he was unaware of Galadriel's gift to Sam that would, in fact, repair his damage surprisingly quickly. After weeks of work, Sam remembered that he still had his box, which he finds is full of grey dust with a seed that turns out to be a *mallorn* tree of the kind they saw in Lórien.

When Sam shows this to the others, Frodo advises him, "Use all the wits and knowledge you have of your own, Sam … and then use the gift to help your work and better it." (VI/9). This highlights how this gift from Galadriel is, indeed, a special grace for Sam. The combination of wits/knowledge with the special gift is similar to what we have seen elsewhere of how grace works in *The Hobbit* and in this story. Of course, as a gardener (and like farmers), he is aware that there are plenty of tools, skills, and techniques he can bring to bear on plants, but he cannot ultimately make them grow. He is reliant on forces outside of his control, and this gift further highlights that, as it will bring growth and beauty beyond what he could imagine.

For the narrator tells us that the spring "surpassed his wildest hopes. His trees began to sprout and grow, as if time was in a hurry and wished to make one year do for twenty" (VI/9). All of this came from planting saplings along with a single grain of the dust with each plant. And the *mallorn* tree quickly replaced the Party Tree, now being the only one of its kind between the Misty Mountains and the western Sea.

As much as Saruman sought to leave his desecrating marks on the world through destruction of nature, in the end, his marks did not last long. Whether in the vicinity of his former realm or in the Shire, his destruction ultimately cleared the way for new growth, so that good which he never intended still emerged from his malintent. Thus, the Forest of Fangorn, Isengard, and the Shire came back more glorious than they had been before his acts of destruction. And in the Shire's case, by special grace, it took but a season to surpass what Saruman had destroyed. This exemplifies what Eru Ilúvatar said to Melkor in the opening of *The Silmarillion* before the world was made: "And thou, Melkor, shalt see that no theme may be played that hath not its uttermost source in me, nor can any alter the music in my despite. For he that attempteth shall prove but mine instrument in the devising of things more wonderful, which he himself hath not imagined."[20] By the strange ways of Providence, whereby Sam was not only able to

---

[20] Tolkien, "Ainulindalë" in *Silmarillion*.

receive this gift but also keep it through all his wild travels, the work of one who made himself an agent of Melkor's servant has been taken up and turned to a better end for the glorification of the Shire.

Sacrifice and Healing

In the year-plus that follows, Frodo finds that he truly cannot go home again. He is back in the Shire, it has been saved and returned to peace, and it is now more beautiful and prosperous than it has ever been. But the trauma of his Quest remains, and he can find no lasting rest there. His friends have reestablished their places in the Shire (for example, Sam had married Rosie Cotton and started a family with her), but he has not found his place there. This exemplifies what Tolkien says in Letter #181, "Yes: I think that 'victors' never can enjoy 'victory' – not in the terms that they envisaged; and in so far as they fought for something *to be enjoyed by themselves* (whether acquisition or mere preservation) the less satisfactory will 'victory' seem" (emphasis original).

Eventually, he resolves to take Arwen's offer of a place on the ship going into the Uttermost West, although he does not yet tell anyone this. At first, he asks Sam to see if Rose can spare him for about a fortnight to see him on his way with Bilbo. Sam admits that he is torn between wanting to go with him and not wanting to be anywhere else but home. Frodo assures him, "It will feel like that, I am afraid … But you will be healed. You were meant to be solid and whole, and you will be" (VI/9). This is a testament to Frodo's *estel* that he should be speaking in a fashion reminiscent of Gandalf that Sam was "meant" to be whole. As with those noted similar expressions, this raises the question of "meant by who?" He was meant to be this way by his Creator who made the world to be good and whole. And from what Frodo has seen and learned over the years, especially on his Quest, he trusts not only that this is what the One means for Sam, but also that the One will see him to that end. As for Frodo himself, he knows he will need to find his wholeness elsewhere.

And so Frodo and Sam meet with Bilbo and those who had borne the Three Rings, and they travel to the Grey Havens. When Frodo finally tells Sam his intention of sailing away from the Grey Havens, he explains that he has been too deeply hurt by his sacrifice to enjoy the victory in the Shire: "I tried to save the Shire, and it has been saved, but not for me. It must often be so, Sam, when things are in danger: some one has to give them up, lose them, so that others may keep them" (VI/9). Tolkien centered this line in Letter #148a addressed to Katharine Farrer, the wife of the biblical scholar Austin Farrer:

> In fact I was delighted that you stressed the 'morality'. I think actually it is that which gives the story its 'realness' and coherence – which my critics seem to feel – rather than any pictorial vividness. It was not 'planned', of course, but arose naturally in the attempt to treat the matter seriously; but it is now the foundation. For me the 'kernel' is in Frodo's last words to Sam: 'I have been too deeply hurt. I tried to save the Shire, and it has been saved, but not for me. It must often be so, Sam, when things are in danger: someone has to give them up, lose them, so that others may keep them … all that I had or might have had, I leave to you.' Bernadette refused to go to Lourdes for her own healing.

We have seen before how the moral framework and its truthfulness were crucial to Tolkien's project of sub-creation and the verisimilitude of his storytelling. And here he shows how it is exemplified in the resolution of his story. Frodo has brought a victory to all that he loved by his sacrificial participation in the work of Providence, but his very sacrifice meant that he was not able to enjoy it. He had indeed committed to self-abnegation (Matt 16:24 // Mark 8:34 // Luke 9:23), laid down his life for his friends (John 15:13), and sacrificed himself for others (e.g., Phil 2:1–13), but he could not take his life back up again. Although he lived in an imaginary pre-Christian setting, Frodo thus provided a form of *praeparatio evangelica* in anticipating the NT moral framework that would be formed around the gospel story of Jesus. But only in that story could the eucatastrophe come true in the Primary World through Jesus laying down his life, taking it up again in his resurrection, and ascending to take his place at the right hand of God the Father.

What further underscores the Christian character of this moral framework is the analogy he drew in this letter to "Bernadette." This is St. Bernadette Soubirous or Bernadette of Lourdes. Tolkien was quite enamored with her story, as he conveyed in commenting on the movie he saw of her life titled *The Song of Bernadette* in Letters #94a–c. We need not get into all the details of this story, though I encourage the reader to look it up. The specific aspect of it that he points to is how she denied herself the possibility to go to Lourdes again for her healing from tuberculosis after she was associated with the miracle of healing through water at Lourdes. She denied herself this in order that she would more effectively and sacrificially serve as a witness by conforming herself to Christ.

Frodo Sails to the Undying Lands

Before our commentary of the main story ends, something should be clarified about Frodo's end. Once he says goodbye to Sam, as well as Merry and Pippin, who have come at Gandalf's bidding, and he embarks in the ship, the narrator gives us the following description:

> And the ship went out into the High Sea and passed on into the West, until at last on a night of rain Frodo smelled a sweet fragrance on the air and heard the sound of singing that came over the water. And then it seemed to him that as in his dream in the house of Bombadil [I/7],[21] the grey rain-curtain turned all to silver glass and was rolled back, and he beheld white shores and beyond them a far green country under a swift sunrise. (VI/9)

Frodo is heading to the nearest resemblance of Arda Unmarred in the Undying Lands. This is not, in fact, meant to be a portrayal of heaven or any form of afterlife, properly speaking. Frodo and Bilbo will die in the Undying Lands, though their lives will be sublimely peaceful until then. And since they are an offshoot of the race of Men, their spirits will go beyond the bounds of creation when they die. Still, their ultimate fate waits for the eschaton when they will be resurrected to take part in the Second Music and the new creation. For now, they can have a glimpse and a taste of paradise before they arrive in the even greater everlasting one.

---

[21] Tolkien had anticipated making this link as far back as near the end of 1944 (Letter #91).

CHAPTER TEN

Commentary on Appendices

The Fall of Númenor

In this final chapter, we will examine the biblical and theological consonances of the appendices. This commentary will be weighted heavily to Appendix A because it has more story to it. It begins with an incredibly brief outline of the stories contained in *The Silmarillion*, as there are dozens of entities from those stories referenced here. While this is the most concentrated group of references, I have explored elsewhere how there are literally hundreds of links between *LOTR* and *The Silmarillion*. It would not be strictly accurate to analogize *LOTR* to the NT and *The Silmarillion* to the OT, since both are set in pre-Christian times. But it is fair to say that there are similar intertextual relationships between the stories as one can identify between the NT and the OT. A fuller understanding of the story of *LOTR* is available only to one who knows *The Silmarillion* as a fuller understanding of the NT is available only to one who knows the OT. In both cases, the former is deliberately written in relation to the latter. Appendix A simply makes this fact more explicit.

This appendix first focuses on what brings us to the story of the Second Age kingdom of Númenor, which is perhaps the most pervasive link between the story of *LOTR* and the story of *The Silmarillion*. We are told of how the Eldar of the Undying Lands came to the Edain of Númenor "and enriched them with knowledge and many gifts" (Appendix A.I.i). This resembles a statement Tolkien wrote much earlier when he sometimes referred to the Elves as "fairies" that "the fairies came to teach men song and holiness."[1] I think Freeman is on the mark when he says, "Recalling that Elves symbolize artistry, creativity, and a delight in the world, we might say that Tolkien sees

---

[1] Tolkien, "Qenya Lexicon," 35.

a re-infusion of these traits as important to the sanctification process, which is not merely a painful endurance of suffering but a growth toward receptivity to the joy and holiness of God, which shines through all of creation."[2] In Tolkien's larger mythology, not all of which made it into the published *Silmarillion*, this clearly included the knowledge that helped them develop their theology of Eru Ilúvatar and what marks of religion they associated with their faith in him.

Only one command was given to them, which was "the Ban of the Valar": "they were forbidden to sail west out of sight of their own shores or to attempt to set foot on the Undying Lands. For though a long span of life had been granted to them, in the beginning thrice that of lesser Men, they must remain mortal, since the Valar were not permitted to take from them the Gift of Men (or the Doom of Men, as it was afterwards called)" (Appendix A.I.i). This is, of course, simplified from a quite long dialogue that is featured in *The Silmarillion*. The Númenóreans setting foot on the Undying Lands would change nothing about their nature. The Undying Lands are not undying because they grant immortality. It is simply that the undying live there. The Númenóreans attempting to travel to (much less reside) there would cause discontent with their creaturely limitations, here signified by their Gift or, as others would later call it, their Doom. This is something we have gone over elsewhere in Chapters Seven and Eight, as well as other areas where we have discussed the characterization of death in Tolkien's story.

What is also notable in this particular text is how it resembles the Edenic story of Gen 2–3. Only one command places any restriction on the Númenóreans' freedom. They are free to sail as far as they want in any other direction but westward. And they do become great mariners exploring these other directions over the centuries. But eventually they chafe against this one restriction and desire that which is forbidden, as with Adam and Eve when tempted by the serpent. This is not to say that what happens to Númenor is the one-to-one correspondent with Eden in Tolkien's story. The Fall of Man has already happened at this point in the story, but another fall is coming, and it is unsurprising that it resembles what happened in Eden.

And so we are told that shadows were forming around halfway through the Second Age in the reign of Tar-Minastir. He was of great help to the Elves in the War of the Elves and Sauron. They would have lost the war to Sauron if not for his help. Truly, he loved the Elves, but he also envied them. He reflected how at this time the Númenóreans loved their lives for how good, full, and joyful they were. But with such

---

[2] Freeman, *Tolkien Dogmatics*, 299.

loving attachment came, for many, the fear of losing what they loved and the wish for the contrary: that such lovely life would go on forever. They did not know what was on the other side of death for them, and the unknown made them afraid and reluctant to give up what they loved. Their lives were so blissful that they had forgotten that they lived in a fallen world, and so they became disdainful of the creaturely limitation of their lives that the Elves and even the Valar and Maiar would eventually envy, for their gift meant that they were not bound to the fallen world like these immortals were. But more and more Númenóreans would fail to see their lot in life this way. They wanted everlasting life on their terms and not on the terms Eru Ilúvatar, who had given them this gift, had established.[3]

Then Tar-Atanmir, the thirteenth king, would dare to speak openly against the Ban of the Valar, "and declared that the life of the Eldar was his by right" (Appendix A.I.i). With this, there became a clearer and growing dividing line among the Númenóreans that was centered on how they regarded death and, by extension, the Eldar and the Valar and what they received from them. On one side were "the King's Men," who were fearful of death (the "Doom" of Men) and thus became estranged from those who they thought were withholding immortality from them. And on the other side were the "Faithful," who maintained their *estel* in Eru Ilúvatar, accepted his Gift, and maintained friendship with those of the Uttermost West. As Tolkien said in a footnote of Letter #156, "A good Númenórean died of free will when he felt it to be time to do so."

Of course, not all kings after the shadow fell on Númenor followed this trend, even as not all the kings of Judah followed the general trend of their kingdom. Most notably, Tar-Palantir was practically the Josiah of his kingdom, as he sought to reform the Númenóreans and restore their ancient traditions maintained by the Faithful. But generally speaking, this divide remained, and the Númenóreans were on a downward slope of spiritual decline. The narrator tells us, "The power and wealth of the Númenóreans nonetheless continued to increase; but their years lessened as their fear of death grew, and their joy departed" (Appendix A.I.i). In this way, they are comparable to the kingdom of Israel, both united and divided. Their time of greatest prosperity under Solomon also witnessed a great spiritual decline. Likewise, economically speaking, the Northern Kingdom of Israel reached its peak in the Omride dynasty, particularly the time of Omri and Ahab. But this was also the time that portended the destruction of the kingdom as it was a time of great spiritual decline in idolatry.

---

[3] See also Tolkien, *Sauron Defeated*, 346.

Finally, when Númenor was peaking in its military might, the last king, Ar-Pharazôn, challenged Sauron. So overwhelming were the Númenóreans that Sauron's forces fled before them, and Sauron was taken captive back to Númenor. Then Sauron took down the kingdom from within by becoming an advisor to Ar-Pharazôn. He talked him into severing all ties with the Undying Lands, including by ceasing to worship Eru Ilúvatar and worshiping Melkor instead, which led to a cult that involved human sacrifices in Melkor's temple with the Faithful as their victims. Ultimately, he convinced Ar-Pharazôn to act on the belief that many Númenóreans had already convinced themselves of, "that everlasting life would be his who possessed the Undying Lands, and that the Ban was imposed only to prevent the Kings of Men from surpassing the Valar. 'But great Kings take what is their right,' he said" (Appendix A.I.i).

Ar-Pharazôn then assembles an armada of 1,000 ships to sail on the Undying Lands, while the Faithful depart the island kingdom with nine ships to Middle-earth, taking with them "the knowledge of the True God" (Letter #156), the *palantíri*, a sapling of Nimloth, and other artifacts of their kingdom. And so a faithful remnant was spared in the cataclysmic judgment that follows (as in the Noah story, which Tolkien noted as a comparison in Letter #156). For when Ar-Pharazôn landed on the shores of the Undying Lands, "the Valar laid down their Guardianship and called upon the One, and the world was changed. Númenor was thrown down and swallowed in the Sea, and the Undying Lands were removed for ever from the circles of the world. So ended the glory of Númenor" (Appendix A.I.i).[4]

And so also ended the current incarnation of Sauron, as he was destroyed in the wreck of Númenor that served as the initial judgment of God against him. This judgment thus constitutes an example of what Tolkien would describe as a "miracle," since Eru "reserves the right to intrude the finger of God into the story: that is to produce realities which could not be deduced even from a complete knowledge of the previous past, but which being real become part of the effective past for all subsequent time (a possible definition of a 'miracle')" (Letter #181). With this notion of "miracle" in mind, he said that Sauron was here "defeated by a 'miracle': a direct action of God the Creator, changing the fashion of the world" (Letter #211). The fact that Sauron survives this initial judgment is something he sees as reflecting reality and his Christian beliefs concerning it: "the problem of evil, and its apparent toleration, is a permanent one for all who concern themselves with our world. The indestructibility of *spirits* with free wills,

---

[4] The changing of the fashion of the world was an aspect of Tolkien's mythology that he went back and forth about over the years, as one can see in *Sauron Defeated* and *Morgoth's Ring*.

even by the Creator of them, is also an inevitable feature, if one either believes in their existence, or feigns it in a story" (Letter #211; emphasis original). The problem of evil is thus something this story must incorporate, as we have seen that it does at many levels. After all, there is no expectation that evil will be ultimately defeated and eradicated within the normal scope of history. There is no solution to the problem of evil without eschatology, the expression of which is influenced by Tolkien's Christian eschatology.

This was also the first time Sauron's incarnate form was destroyed, and it had such an effect on him that he could never assume a fair form again but only a hideous one. Previously, like Satan, he could masquerade as one like an angel of light (cf. 2 Cor 11:14), as he deceived the Elves into the forging of the Rings of Power while he was in the disguise of Annatar, Lord of Gifts. But now, he aims to work primarily through terror and despair.

Decline and Waiting

What follows in the rest of this portion of the Appendix concerns the Faithful remnant of the Númenóreans allying with the Elves (and others) in the Last Alliance to defeat Sauron upon his attack against the Númenórean exiles when he returned to Middle-earth, the fallout from this war at the end of the Second Age, and the histories of the kingdoms of Arnor and Gondor. Much of it is not directly pertinent to our purposes. But it is notable how certain aspects "rhyme" with biblical and theological themes. For example, we are told of how the Hobbits chose a Thain to rule in place of the King of Arnor when Arnor had collapsed, even though they still hoped for the king's return, yet eventually, "that hope was forgotten, and remained only in the saying *When the King comes back*, used for some good that could not be achieved, or of some evil that could not be amended" (Appendix A.I.iii). This reflects how some would come to speak of the Second Coming or of the eschatological state summarized as "kingdom come." Of course, within the scope of this story, the type of this hope was fulfilled, which points to the author's expectation that the anti-type will be fulfilled.

Another example comes from how, despite the various wars Gondor went through, the greatest damage to them was done internally. This included their neglected vigilance on Mordor, the civil war of the Kin-Strife fought over their intermingling with the Northmen, and the more general reemergence of the existential problems that plagued Númenor. The kingdom thereby negatively illustrates the importance of vigilance and perseverance in faith.

At the same time, we see Providence at work in how the line of the Northern Kingdom is sustained and the realm of the Southern Kingdom is sustained. This includes by surprising victories, the providential work among the Northmen, and the provision of help from the Eorlingas who rode to the salvation of the steward of Gondor at the Battle of the Field of Celebrant (which was described as "help beyond hope" [Appendix A.I.iv]). We also see the subtle work of Providence in the help Thorongil brings, as well as in his acknowledgment that he will come back to Gondor, "if that be my fate" (Appendix A.I.iv).

The Tale of Aragorn and Arwen

One particularly pertinent section for our purposes is the tale of Aragorn and Arwen. I noted earlier that Tolkien said in an unpublished letter to Rayner Unwin that this particular tale was "an allegory of naked hope."[5] This seems to be a sense of allegory as "exemplary representation" of the spiritual theme in question. Indeed, this whole story is suffused with hope of the *estel* kind, exemplifying how it motivates both of the titular characters, and demonstrating the trials that come with *estel*.

First, we are told of how Aragorn's parents were wed. Arathorn sought to marry Gilraen, but her father Dírhael opposed it, thinking that his daughter was too young relative to when most of the Dúnedain women married (she was twenty-two while Arathorn was fifty-six), and he foresaw that Arathorn would be short-lived (again, especially for a Dúnadan, whose lifespans were still double or triple that of other Men). But her mother Ivorwen, who also had her own share of foresight, said, "The days are darkening before the storm, and great things are to come. If these two wed now, hope may be born for our people; but if they delay, it will not come while this age lasts" (Appendix A.I.v). Both of them saw rightly, as Arathorn died when Aragorn was only two, and Aragorn was indeed the one who brought their hope to fruition. In token of this, when he was taken to Rivendell, his identity was hidden until he was twenty, but he bore the name Estel.

Naturally, we have referred to *estel* many times over the course of this commentary. Aragorn would be raised to know the meaning (and not simply the translation) of his name. As we are told in *Morgoth's Ring*, Elvish tradition held that Ilúvatar demanded two things from all his Children: "belief in Him, and proceeding from that, hope or trust in Him (called by the Eldar *estel*)."[6] Aragorn was named Estel, was raised to grow

---

[5] Available online at: https://tolkiengateway.net/wiki/Letter_to_Rayner_Unwin_(12_May_1955).

[6] Tolkien, *Morgoth's Ring*, 338.

in *estel*, maintained *estel* through all his hard years, and would himself be the One's agent in fulfilling the content of *estel* for his people and many others.

He first met Arwen when he was twenty, and he had thought he either had a dream or "he had received the gift of the Elf-minstrels, who can make the things of which they sing appear before the eyes of those that listen" (Appendix A.1.v). This shows what we have already seen in Book II of how Elves can be sub-creators extraordinaire, and Aragorn was singing a song of Beren and Lúthien. He thought she was Lúthien, and like Beren, he was smitten. But for long years, after speaking with Elrond and out of respect for him, he did not pursue her, as much as it pained him.

He did not see Arwen again until he was nearly fifty, and it chanced that he came to Lothlórien while Arwen was staying there. Galadriel refreshed his appearance and offered him a time of rest after so many years of long labor, and Arwen beheld him as one transfigured, "and as he came walking towards her under the trees of Caras Galadhon laden with flowers of gold, her choice was made and her doom appointed" (Appendix A.I.v). We have seen similar statements, particularly in Book II, of how choice and doom/fate are interlinked, but it should be noted that terms like "doom" and "fate" have multiple senses across such statements. In this case, her "doom" refers to the outcome of the choice she must make in terms of whether she will meet the end of the Elves in terms of forever being bound to the world of creation, or she will meet the end of Men in having a mortal life that takes her spirit beyond the circles of the world. The implied agent behind the action of appointment is, of course, Eru Ilúvatar, as the choice of fates for the house of Eärendil are a special grace granted by him, which, as we have noted earlier, contributes to the regeneration of Men.

A similar passive use of "appointed" with divine implications appears in Elrond's response when he hears of Arwen's choice to be bound with Aragorn in matrimony. He is grieved to hear it, as he knows this will mean much pain for Arwen and a divergence of their fates for time untold, yet he says, "Maybe, it has been appointed so, that by my loss the kingship of Men may be restored" (Appendix A.I.v). But he says that for them to be wed, Aragorn must fulfill his fate in becoming the King of Arnor and Gondor; otherwise, her choice would be cheapened. But he still recognizes in this choice the work of Providence, and he shows *estel* in believing that Providence will bring about the "bride-price" he sets for Arwen wedding Aragorn.

Less than thirty years later, Gilraen meets with her son one last time when he returned to the area after his adventures in far-off lands. She again calls him "Estel" (as Arwen had in the previous episode of this story), and she wishes him farewell, as she says she has been aged prematurely by her years of care. She says that she cannot face the darkness of their time. Aragorn attempts to comfort her that there may be a light beyond the darkness, and he would have her see it. Sadly, her last words to Aragorn are of resignation, *"Onen i-Estel Edain, ú-chebin estel anim"* (Appendix A.I.v). This is translated, "I gave Hope to the Dúnedain, I have kept no hope for myself." Hers was less a condition of utter despair, since she did not go the route of Denethor, as it was a condition of long-held anxiety, made worse by the early death of her husband and her regular loneliness. Still, she died believing that she had given *estel* to her people, as was signified with often calling him "Estel," as it would be through him that the content of their *estel* would be fulfilled, even though it would not be shown for years thereafter how Sauron would be overthrown, and how "hope beyond hope was fulfilled" (Appendix A.I.v). Such are the strange ways of divine providence.

Thus, as was told in the main story, Arwen came to wed Aragorn. And after they lived together for 120 years, Aragorn declares that his time had come. That is, he is giving up his life voluntarily before he must give it up perforce. We have already noted from Letter #156 that Tolkien said a good Númenórean would die of free will when he felt it was the time, and he likewise said in a footnote for Letter #212 that this was an Elvish expectation of good Men as well, further positing, "This may have been the nature of *unfallen* Man; though *compulsion* would not threaten him: he would desire and ask to be allowed to 'go on' to a higher state" (emphases original). He then makes the comparison to Mary when the time came for her assumption. But it is in this moment that Arwen tasted the bitterness of mortality, for this was happening before she was weary of her days, and she wished for him to stay with her yet longer.

Before they part, Aragorn reminds her that this was the fate they both chose long ago. He also reminds her that this is fitting for him to do as a proper descendant of Númenor, instead of clinging to life until all its dignity is gone, as the later kings of Númenor had done. Rather, he acknowledges that he has been given the blessing of a span thrice that of many other Men, "but also the grace to go at my will, and give back the gift" (Appendix A.I.v). This is, of course, his statement of *estel* in acknowledging that his life is a gift from Ilúvatar and that the time has come to give it back. When he describes death as "sleep," I think this is also a statement of *estel*, as he trusts that there will come a time when he will awaken (i.e., be resurrected). After all, reference to death as sleep was much less frequent outside of the Judeo-Christian context than within it (Isa 26:19; Dan 12:2; 1 Thess 4:13–15),[7] and thus it is appropriate that this story, which

---

[7] For more, see Marbury B. Ogle, "The Sleep of Death," *MAAR* 11 (1933): 81–117.

anticipates the order of grace to be revealed later, should have such an indirect expression of the hope that is to come.

Aragorn says she has a final choice to depart into the Uttermost West or to endure the Doom of Men, but she reaffirms that this choice was made long ago. Yet, she admits that she had not understood his people and their relationship with death until now. For she says, "As wicked fools I scorned them, but I pity them at last. For if this is indeed, as the Eldar say, the gift of the One to Men, it is bitter to receive" (Appendix A.I.v). The efforts of humans to avoid this fate or to wish to put it off as long as possible, even to the point of attempting to transgress creaturely limitations, now make sense to her, even if she should maintain that they cannot be condoned.

Aragorn can offer her no comfort that comes from within the world, or what may be called the hope of *amdir*. But he does remind her of the hope of *estel*, as he exhorts her, "But let us not be overthrown at the final test, who of old renounced the Shadow and the Ring. In sorrow we must go, but not in despair. Behold! we are not bound for ever to the circles of the world, and beyond them is more than memory" (Appendix A.I.v). And so it is that Arwen calls him for the last time the name she knew him by in his youth: Estel. He was born to enkindle hope, and now he dies pointing to hope beyond the world. The One who acted in him will yet bring hope beyond what they can rightly imagine, and thus he trusts in this One again while calling others, such as his wife, to do the same.

Even as Aragorn dies, it is said that he undergoes one last revelatory transfiguration: "Then a great beauty was revealed in him, so that all who after came there looked on him in wonder; for they saw that the grace of his youth, and the valour of his manhood, and the wisdom and majesty of his age were blended together. And long there he lay, an image of the splendor of the Kings of Men in glory undimmed before the breaking of the world" (Appendix A.1.v). The reference to the "breaking of the world" points to eschatology with what precedes the new creation. Likewise, when Arwen lays herself down to die on the mound where she and Aragorn plighted their troth (as he gave her the Ring of Barahir), it is said that "there is her green grave, until the world is changed, and all the days of her life are utterly forgotten by men that come after, and elanor and niphredil bloom no more east of the Sea" (Appendix A.1.v). There remains an eschatological framework for this story, one in which, as yet, there is only a vague hope of what lies beyond the next change of the world, though it seems to involve some reunion in resurrection. In the end, all of Ilúvatar's Children must abide in *estel*, trusting that he wills for their good in that far-off time.

A Meeting by "Chance"

The rest of Appendix A features some scattered points of interest for our analysis. For example, we are told in the section on the House of Eorl how Éomer rode often with Aragorn in fulfillment of the Oath of Eorl, "For though Sauron had passed, the hatreds and evils that he bred had not died, and the King of the West had many enemies to subdue before the White Tree could grow in peace" (Appendix A.II). This comports with other statements about evil and its persistence across this story. Sauron was neither the be all nor the end all of evil. And it is unsurprising that his effects resonate after he is gone.

We also see a brief note that reinforces the ethical framework of this story when the Dwarves say at the end of the War of the Dwarves and Orcs, "We fought this war for vengeance, and vengeance we have taken. But it is not sweet. If this is victory, then our hands are too small to hold it" (Appendix A.III). The war was incredibly costly to them, and the motivation of vengeance was not enough to vindicate all that had happened. This is not to say that the war was of no benefit, as many things in the North might have been worse if the Orcs had not been so diminished as they were by this war. But this is more of a case of good results coming from ill motives, as this tragic victory was taken up and directed to better purposes. But the origin of the war did matter, and its seed being one of vengeance made it all the more bitter for the Dwarves after the fact. However, besides the general benefit that came from a diminished force of Orcs in that part of the world, there was another good fruit that surprisingly came from all of this. And this is a point that will occupy us for the rest of this section.

Thorin Oakenshield had gone with his father to Dunland and afterward to the Ered Luin north of the Shire. There he forged in anger at still being dispossessed of his home in Erebor and at the loss of his father, who had gone off to try to return to Erebor. But one day, while he and Gandalf were going about in that region, "there came about by chance a meeting between Gandalf and Thorin that changed all the fortunes of the House of Durin, and led to other and greater ends beside" (Appendix A.III). They both happened to stay in Bree on the same night in 2941 (the same year of the Quest for Erebor). Thorin was returning from somewhere eastward, and Gandalf was on his way to the Shire for the first time in twenty years.

They each learn that the other had thought often of them, though neither had the meeting that night in their designs. Thorin described Gandalf coming into his thoughts, "as if I were bidden to seek you" (Appendix A.III). For Gandalf's part, he had thought of Erebor because he knew that Sauron was plotting war, and the North was not well poised to resist. Erebor was occupied by a dragon who Sauron might put to terrible use. Dale was diminished to the residents of Esgaroth. The Woodland Realm was doing all it could to resist the evil that had taken over Mirkwood with the occupancy of Dol Guldur. The Dúnedain of the North had persisted, but they were not of great numbers. The High Elves were leaving Middle-earth, but if Sauron attacked Rivendell, the nearest aid was weeks of travel away in either direction. The Dwarves still had strength left, but they were scattered or concentrated in areas that were too far flung between the Ered Luin in the West and the Iron Hills in the East. They needed to reclaim Erebor to bring the exiled Dwarves back under one banner, which would, in turn, strengthen their allies as well. And so began the story that has been told in *The Hobbit*.

Because of those events, Sauron fled from Dol Guldur to Mordor, and his focus turned southward. But one of the great forces he unleashed before his designs were fully wrought attacked the reinvigorated kingdoms of Dale and Erebor in the North. Sadly, both realms lost their kings in the initial Battle of Dale, but their successors and their alliance were saved by retreating into Erebor, whence they emerged when the news of decisive defeat in the South threw their enemies into disarray.

In reflecting on these events, Gandalf had said to Frodo and Gimli during their time in Minas Tirith:

> Yet things might have gone far otherwise and far worse. When you think of the great Battle of the Pelennor, do not forget the battles in Dale and the valour of Durin's Folk. Think of what might have been. Dragon-fire and savage swords in Eriador, night in Rivendell. There might be no Queen in Gondor. We might now hope to return from the victory here only to ruin and ash. But that has been averted—because I met Thorin Oakenshield one evening on the edge of spring in Bree. A chance-meeting, as we say in Middle-earth. (Appendix A.III)

The suggestive phrasing is akin to other statements we have seen from Gandalf, as well as others like Tom Bombadil and Elrond. This could be seen as something that happened "by chance," but "chance" is another name for the work of divine providence here.

In the same way, Joseph meeting the unnamed man in Shechem looking for his brothers is but a small event in Gen 37:14–17, easily missed for its significance as the reader progresses through the story. But without it, the rest of the story does not happen. For then Joseph would not have found his brothers in a timely enough fashion that they would have been able to catch him, have the debate about what to do to him, and then find the caravan passing at just the right time to have the idea occur to them to sell him into slavery. Without selling him into slavery, he does not go to Egypt. Without him going to Egypt, he does not end up in Potiphar's house. Without ending up in Potiphar's house, and in an honored position at that, he does not go to prison when he does after being falsely accused by Potiphar's wife to encounter the baker and cupbearer of the pharaoh. Without that encounter, he does not ultimately (after a long delay) get out and into the pharaoh's favor. Without getting into the pharaoh's favor such that he can be second in power over the kingdom, he cannot enact his plan for the famine to come. Without enacting his plan for the famine to come, many, many more would have suffered much worse, including his family. And thus, without him being where he was, his family would not have had reason to move to Egypt, and the events of the story of Exodus would not have happened as they did. And all of this was set in motion by an unnamed man being in the right place at the right time (which someone in the time of the story could have easily described as a "chance" encounter) to tell Joseph what he needed to know, which seems to be coincidence, but we are reminded in Gen 50:20 that God intended what had happened for good, including his brothers' evil intentions.

Thus are the strange ways of Providence that a supposedly chance meeting had such wide-ranging ramifications. But so it is that the Author takes such events up and directs them to greater purposes than anyone involved in the story might have imagined at first. Even one who is an intentional agent of Providence like Gandalf marvels at it in hindsight when the great web of the story can be seen more fully. One can only imagine how it will be when the whole mega-narrative of history is laid out for review.

Gimli's Fate

One last point of interest in Appendix A concerns what happens to Gimli. I have commented elsewhere on the hope of the Dwarves in this book and in the commentary on *The Hobbit*.[8] Naturally, Tolkien has tried to maintain some ambiguity in keeping with how his fictional works are supposed to be depending on sources that operate from certain perspectives. The ancient stories particularly tend to represent Elvish views, although they do not ignore what the Dwarves say for themselves.

In any case, it is noteworthy that there is a regular allowance for the possibility that the Dwarves will still be as Ilúvatar's adopted children in taking part with his other Children in the new creation, and thus that their fate will be an embodied one (i.e., a resurrected one). The fact that Gimli's end features him being united with the Elves is a further hint in this direction. For it is said that he left Middle-earth with Legolas and

---

[8] Harriman, *God Has Chosen the Little Ones*, 99–102.

went into the Uttermost West to see Galadriel before he died, "and it may be that she, being mighty among the Eldar, obtained this grace for him" (Appendix A.III). It would, indeed, be surpassingly strange for Gimli to be allowed to spend his last days in the Undying Lands if his ultimate fate with the rest of his Dwarven brethren is to be sundered from the other Children of Ilúvatar.

The Angelic Istari

The other appendices can be treated more briefly for our purposes simply because there is not as much pertinent material in them. One point that is reemphasized in Appendix B is the theological framing of the Istari that we have already noted in the main story through reference to Tolkien's letters. Here, it is said when referring to their coming to Middle-earth in the Third Age, "It was afterwards said that they came out of the Far West and were messengers sent to contest the power of Sauron, and to unite all those who had the will to resist him; but they were forbidden to match his power with power, or to seek to dominate Elves or Men by force and fear" (Appendix B). They are thus presented as "angels" in the most basic sense of the Greek term ("messenger"), although they are also "angels" in the more metaphysically loaded sense as members of the race of the Ainur.

December 25 and March 25

One element that Appendix B makes the reader aware of is that the Fellowship set out from Rivendell on December 25 and that the Quest was completed on March 25.[9] One cannot make Christian correlations with all the dates Tolkien gives, despite how much he knew of the calendar of the feast days.[10] But these two narratively significant days being on these dates are not merely coincidental, even if Tolkien did not set out

---

[9] Tolkien once had the Fellowship leaving Rivendell on November 24, but he thought it made more sense for the Fellowship to stay longer in Rivendell, and so said that Frodo should not start until December 24, which eventually changed to December 25. Tolkien, *Treason of Isengard*, 422–23.

[10] In addition to the major seasons of Advent, Christmas, Lent, Easter, and All Saints, there are references to other commemorations and feasts in his letters, including Rogation Days (Letter #69), St. Stephen's Day (Letter #94), Septuagesima (Letter #113), Santa Chiara's feast (Letter #167), and Corpus Christi (Letter #324a). Also, in his short story "Farmer Giles of Ham," he makes many references to Christian feasts, including: the feast of St. Michael, St. Nicholas' Day, Christmas (as well as Christmas Eve), St. John's Day, Twelfthnight, Epiphany, the feast of St. Hilarius and St. Felix, the feast of Candlemas, and St. Matthias' Day.

to place them there from the beginning.[11] This is arguably a case where he was more conscious of the religious and Catholic character of his story in the revision. Given his liturgical formation, it is clear that he would appreciate the providential significance of these coinciding dates and that the correspondence should occur apart from his deliberate design at the start. This was a point that Shippey made, though his analysis was not focused on what we have been attending to.[12]

On one level, the significance of December 25 is obvious to Tolkien's readers today. On another level that will be less obvious to most, December 25 was once the day of the winter solstice on the Roman Julian calendar. One ancient homily—succinctly and accurately titled *On the Solstices and Equinoxes of the Conception and Birth of our Lord Jesus Christ and John the Baptist*—correlated the conception and birth of Jesus with the vernal equinox (March 25) and the winter solstice (December 25), respectively, while also correlating the conception of John the Baptist with the autumnal equinox (September 24) and his birth with the summer solstice (June 24). This was part of a larger theological framework in which creation events/creation history and salvation history were correlated, as I have noted in my series on why Christmas is on December 25th.[13] In a different way, Tolkien is in continuity with that tradition by making his imaginary period in history correlate with and anticipate the gospel story to come. This date in the pre-Christian world did not yet have the significance it would acquire in the Christian era, but it points forward to the same.

Thus it is also with the date of March 25. Its significance is less obvious today. As noted above, it was once the date of the vernal equinox on the Roman Julian calendar, but it also corresponded to two other significant dates according to many: it was considered the date of the world's creation, and it was considered the date of Jesus's crucifixion or resurrection (at least in Western tradition). The anonymous *On Computing the Paschal Feast* (*De Pascha Computus*) from the mid-third century indicated that his predecessors (at least the Latin ones), likely including Hippolytus of Rome, had considered March 25 as the day of creation and the day of Jesus's crucifixion (4). Julius Africanus in his *Chronographiae* also considered March 25 the day of creation, but he may have linked that day to Jesus's resurrection rather than his crucifixion. In any case, it was the day he reckoned as the day of the new year for the purposes of his chronology.

---

[11] Indeed, this assignment was part of Tolkien's extensive work in revising his chronology, as an early draft of the Fellowship's departure had it taking place in November (Tolkien, *Return of the Shadow*, 416, 432, 434–36).

[12] Shippey, *J. R. R. Tolkien*, 208–9.

[13] On this, see here: https://krharriman.substack.com/p/why-is-christmas-on-december-25-part.

Others who linked this date to one or both of the events of creation and crucifixion include Tertullian (*Against the Jews* 8.17–18), the Quartodecimans (according to Epiphanius, *Panarion* 50.1.7–8; 51.26.1–4), Augustine (*Trinity* 4.5), Pseudo-Cyril (in *Preface* 3 to Cyril's paschal computus), and the paschal cycle of Victorius of Aquitaine. For some years, it was the earliest possible date for celebrating Pascha/Easter in the Roman reckoning (as opposed to the Alexandrian one).

Furthermore, these authors and many others also linked the date of March 25 with the date of Jesus's Annunciation/Incarnation (as is apparent from the author of *On the Solstices and Equinoxes*). Among those who made such correlations was Dionysius Exiguus, developer of the BC/AD system. Old English tradition would also follow Latin tradition in such correlations, although the English also eventually came in line with more prevailing views of when to celebrate Easter (which I have addressed, among many other issues, in my series on Easter).[14] For several centuries, it was also the date that marked the beginning of the new year in the British Isles to coincide with the Feast of Annunciation/Lady Day. Likewise, Aragorn instituted the New Reckoning in TA 3019, in which the new year began on March 25 to commemorate the downfall of Sauron (VI/4; Appendix D). In both of these respects, Tolkien corresponds his calendar with significant dates on the Christian calendar, which in turn celebrate significant dates in the gospel story.

Language Matters

The last appendix concerns language. The section on translation (Appendix F.II), in particular, is one of those sections that especially reinforces the notion we have observed elsewhere that this is set in an imaginary time in the past and that his story serves as a translation of an ancient source. It is notable that he refers to the language of Quenya, the High-elven tongue of Eldamar, as becoming practically an "Elven-latin" among the High Elves of Middle-earth, as it was used "for ceremony, and for high matters of lore and song" (Appendix F.I).[15] This corresponds with how Latin was, before the Second Vatican Council at least, traditionally used for liturgy and ecclesial ceremonies, as opposed to the vernacular of whatever country a particular church operated in. In an unpublished letter to Patricia Kirke (28 March 1956), Tolkien expressed his abstract acknowledgment of the reform at the time of the liturgy linked to the Easter

---

[14] Available at: https://krharriman.substack.com/p/why-do-we-celebrate-easter-when-we.

[15] In an earlier draft, Gildor had remarked how Frodo knew the "elf-latin." Tolkien, *Return of the Shadow*, 60.

season, but, "one feels a little dislocated and even a little sad at my age to know that the ceremonies and modes so long familiar and deeply associated with the season will never be heard again!"[16] As such, it has often been noted that Tolkien more actively objected to the change in the liturgy of the Mass introduced by the Second Vatican Council (cf. Letters #289d and #294a), because of which the Mass could be—and typically would be—conducted in varying (and increasing) extents in the vernacular rather than in Latin. Simon Tolkien, his grandson, has remarked that Tolkien would attend Mass and loudly give the responses in Latin while everyone else was doing them in English.[17] His granddaughter Joanna and Fr. Gerard Hanlon also confirmed that he did this.[18] Such was Tolkien's commitment to the tradition in which he had been raised.[19]

In line with what Frodo said about how the Shadow that bred the Orcs can only mock and not make, it is said that the Orcs "had no language of their own, but took what they could of other tongues and perverted it to their own liking; yet they made only brutal jargon, scarcely sufficient even for their own needs, unless it were for curses and abuse" (Appendix F.I). Even by the Third Age, Orcs mostly used a corruption of Westron/Common Speech. But it is noteworthy that Sauron devised the Black Speech for his servants to use, yet it was never completely implemented. For those besides the Nazgûl and the captains of Mordor, it mainly survived in certain terms that we see the Orcs utter in *LOTR*. Likewise, inasmuch as the Trolls of Mordor (specifically, the Olog-Hai) spoke, they used the Black Speech. As for representing Orc language, Tolkien says that it was more degraded and filthy than he has indicated, "I do not suppose that any will wish for a closer rendering, though models are easy to find. Much the same sort of talk can still be heard among the orc-minded; dreary and repetitive with hatred and contempt, too long removed from good to retain even verbal vigour, save in the ears of those to whom only the squalid sounds strong" (Appendix F.II). We have seen before how Tolkien's faith related to his philological work in diverse ways, and this is yet another example in terms of how it attuned him to evil's corruption of that which he devoted his life to studying.

---

[16] Scull and Hammond, *J. R. R. Tolkien Companion*, 1:514.

[17] Simon Tolkien, "My Grandfather – J. R. R. Tolkien," https://www.simontolkien.com/my-grandfather-jrr-tolkien-2.

[18] Daniel Helen and Morgan Thomsen, "A Recollection of Tolkien: Canon Gerard Hanlon," *Mallorn* 54 (Spring 2013): 41; Joanna Tolkien, "Joanna Tolkien Speaks at the Tolkien Society Annual Dinner, Shrewsbury, April 16, 1994," in *Digging Potatoes, Growing Trees*, vol. 2, ed. Helen Armstrong (Telford: Tolkien Society, 1998), 35.

[19] In Hanlon's case, he recalls that Tolkien insisted on engaging in the liturgy in Latin because, "I like to pray to God in Latin." Helen and Thomsen, "Recollection," 41.

Indeed, Tolkien's theological-ethical framework shaped much of his language in this story. It shaped the general character of his story, as we observed in Chapter One. It also shaped the foundational structure of his sub-creation in that it shaped his ideas whence his sub-creation emerged, as we observed in Chapter Two. It shaped the story in ways that he considered fitting for an earlier (albeit imaginary) era of our own world operating with the order of nature prior to the order of grace, as we observed in Chapter Three. And we have observed throughout this commentary that it shaped many themes and details of his work, so that he regularly expressed Primary World truths in appropriate Secondary World forms. The work of God that he described in multitudinous ways throughout was simply the fictionalized equivalent of how he perceived God working in the Primary World in the order of nature and the order of grace. After all, the One God of his fiction is supposed to be none other than the One God he knew: the Lord of Heaven and Middle-earth.

INDEX OF TOLKIEN'S LETTERS

INDEX OF SCRIPTURE

Old Testament

Author Index

Subject Index